**"I heard shots and I came downstairs.
Evan's gone and there's a dead man looking up at me."**

Now that I had turned to Curtis for help, my strength began to leak out like sticky sap and gunk up my faculties.

"Okay, I'm on my way. Are you safe now?"

"I think so. I was going to check the house—"

"Don't," he said sharply. "Are you armed?"

"Yes. I've got Evan's gun."

"All right, I'm dispatching a squad car to you right now. Do what I told you and *nothing else!*"

Remembering the times I had done anything but what Evan and Curtis had told me to do, I decided that this time, it was excellent advice. I hung up the phone and tried not to look at the body on the floor.

The Man She Thought She Knew
The sultry new Cally Wilde thriller by Shari Shattuck

**Turn the page to read rave reviews for Shari Shattuck
and her entrancing Cally Wilde novels. . . .**

While shopping in L.A.'s Little Japan district, Cally encounters a crime-in-progress—and embarks on an exotic adventure inside a lethal world of drugs, murder, and the sensual secrets of the geisha. . . .

LETHAL

"A sequel to the successful *Loaded, Lethal* continues to trace Cally and Evan's steamy relationship while unraveling an adventure worthy of more experienced writers. Brimming with crackling dialogue and well-nuanced characters, this book is engrossing. Shattuck weaves a complex plot peopled by complex characters."

—*RT Bookclub*

"Whirlwind entertainment for those who like the feel of the wind in their hair."

—*Publishers Weekly*

"Cally is a fully formed, strong, and engaging character throughout this fast-paced and suspenseful mystery."

—*Booklist*

"A stellar follow-up to *Loaded*. . . . *Lethal* should be on everyone's beach-read list!"

—BookReporter.com

She's got beauty, brains, and more money than God—but who would want to kill Callaway Wilde? The truth will shake her to the core, and Cally must rely on her wits—and one sexy LAPD detective—to survive.

LOADED

Named One of the Best Novels of 2003 by Publishers Weekly

"Exploding like a string of firecrackers let loose beneath one's feet, Shattuck's debut novel keeps the reader deliciously on edge. Raw action collides with secrets and family conflicts as one of the most vivid heroines to hit the shelves recently tries to discover who wants her dead. . . . Cally's voice spins a siren's call that, combined with Shattuck's electric pacing, will keep readers glued to this novel."

—*Publishers Weekly*

"*Loaded* is just that—loaded with emotion, sexual tension, greed, familial rivalry, and jealousy that all add up to a suspenseful, sexy tale."

—TheBestReviews.com

"I didn't want to stop reading and it kept me guessing. . . . There's enough sexual tension to heat Cally's expansive home, with some wattage left over to take care of the swimming pool."

—MysteryReader.com

"Crackling with repressed sexual desire, so much so that one should use pot holders while reading this book. There are so many suspects with viable motives that readers will go crazy trying to figure out who the perpetrator is. . . . [This] has the making of a great series."

—AllReaders.com

The
Man She
Thought
She Knew

- - - - - - - - - -

Shari Shattuck

POCKET BOOKS

New York London Toronto Sydney

POCKET BOOKS, a division of Simon & Schuster, Inc.
1230 Avenue of the Americas, New York, NY 10020

Library of Congress Cataloging-in-Publication Data is available.

ISBN-13: 978-1-4165-1668-2
ISBN-10:   1-4165-1668-9

This Pocket Books trade paperback edition August 2006

10 9 8 7 6 5 4 3 2 1

For information regarding special discounts for bulk purchases, please contact Simon & Schuster Special Sales at 1-800-456-6798 or business@simonandschuster.com.

For Creason,
who read it first.
My daughter, my teacher, my friend.

Acknowledgments

First, I'd like to thank Amy Pierpont, without whose hand at the helm this ship would have been navigated without a compass, and Megan McKeever, for detangling the ropes. Thanks, Paul— as always, your enthusiasm is the wind in the sails. Many thanks to Kyle O'Brian and Dr. Robert Huzanga for their computer and medical expertise, respectively. I could have done it without you, but it would have been wrong.

Last, but far from least, thanks to my Joseph for your most masculine perspective, and your love and support. You are my port in any storm, and my destination in fair weather.

The
Man She
Thought
She Knew

Chapter

1

His weight was crushing my body. Deep inside me a guttural scream was building, desperate for release, but each time he thrust, the breath was forced out of me. His fingers gripped my wrists so tightly that I feared the skin would break. His eyes burned into mine as his breathing quickened to short, hard bursts. I struggled to break away, to move, to shift his weight off mine and get control again. But as his movements quickened, his weight and his strength held me down. I strained for dominance, lost the battle, and succumbed to the inevitable. He lowered his face to mine and covered my mouth with his.

Panting and shaking, I met his kiss and returned it. Laughing lightly, I said, "Okay, you win." Smiling, and without breaking the full contact of our bodies, we both rolled onto our sides, and I nestled my head into his shoulder.

Running a finger down his chest, I admired the strength and shape of my man, especially pleasant after enjoying what that strength and shape could do to me.

I'd only known him a year; we'd met as suspect and detective, moved quickly to tentative lovers, to my accepting his proposal. It had been quite a ride.

"Evan?" I asked, looking up into his deep-water-blue eyes and sinking a hand into his thick, black hair to pull his head back.

"Yes?" he answered lazily, pulling his gaze with pleasing reluctance away from scanning the length of my legs.

"Do you want a big wedding?"

The edges of his mouth twitched just enough for me to see the joke coming. "Well, you know," he began, and I started to laugh, "that all little boys dream of a big wedding and wearing a fancy white dress. Queen for a day, that's me," he finished in a fake lisp; it didn't come off on my ultimate man's man.

I smacked him on his firm butt and he grabbed my arms, pinning me down again. "I'm serious, honey," I pleaded. "I've got to get started planning this." I was exaggerating a little. I had already hired the most expensive event team in town, given them a budget that would have bought a three-bedroom house in Beverly Hills, and all I would have to do was tell them what kind of cake I wanted. They'd pretty much take it from there.

"Yes," Evan said after considering seriously for a moment. "I want a big wedding," he said, then started kissing my neck, mumbling the next words as he moved down. "I want a gigantic wedding. I want everyone to know that little ol' Detective Evan Paley is marrying the most beautiful woman in the world, Callaway Francine Wilde." He came up for air, then said, "And I don't care if they *can* see the ring through my nose," before diving back onto the skin where my neck curved into my shoulder.

The roughness of his morning beard touched off a skirmish in that ticklish spot, and the heat of his mouth was turning my after-sex glow into a flashing green light. If he went on this way, we'd never get out of bed.

I fought for control. "If you want everybody to know, then are we going to be able to announce the engagement?" I asked. "I think, uh," I moaned, distracted. "Stop that. You usually let other people know you're getting married *before* you send out the invitations."

"Soon. I don't think it'll be real helpful to the undercover drug bust I'm working on right now to have my picture published in the social section of the *L.A. Times*." His words were muffled as he nuzzled my neck, biting softly.

"You think the crack dealers *read* the social section of the *L.A. Times?*" I asked.

"Read? No, but they can look at the pictures."

"Let me go," I said, struggling to release my arms.

"If you promise to be good," he told me with the low, throaty vibrato that worked on two of my most sensitive areas—only one of which was my inner ear—and kissed me long and hard.

Looking up at him mischievously, I said, "Oh, I'll be very good."

He let go, and I smacked him on the butt again. Then, laughing, I rolled out of his reach onto the floor, and he came after me, trying his best to land a retaliatory smack on my backside. Laughing, I slipped away and he chased me across the bedroom, but I made it to his walk-in closet and slammed the door behind me, turning the lock just as his fingers reached the knob on the other side.

"Fine," he called through the door. "You can just stay in there."

"I'm not coming out until you call a caterer!" I yelled back.

"Leave it to me!" came the muffled response. "I'm sure our guests will love having Tito's tacos at the reception. Don't worry about a thing. I can picture it now. The grand ballroom of the Ritz-Carlton on Maui, the tables decked with nothing but the finest in purple plasticware, our classy guests expressing their gastronomic delight as they sip Cook's champagne and enjoy their taquitos and menudo."

His voice was growing fainter, as though he were leaving the bedroom, or at least pretending to.

I spoke loudly so that my voice would carry through the thick door. "This is exactly why straight men aren't allowed to plan their own weddings!"

"You're only saying that because you think I'll forget to order the piñata."

Stifling a laugh, I put my ear to the cherrywood door and listened intently. We were at Evan's house, and his master bedroom was a spacious affair. There was a good twenty feet of sisal flooring between the bed and the closet, and I could just picture him sneaking across it. I closed my eyes to try to pick up a soft footfall or a crackle in the matting, but all I got was eerie silence.

Most likely he was watching the door from the other side.

I could play the waiting game. I sat down on the thick wool carpet.

Through the door I heard the muffled ringing of a phone. I hoped he'd answer it and give himself away, but it rang a couple more times and then stopped. Still no activity, and I bore easily.

"Honey?" I called out, cracking the door open an inch or two.

The bed was empty; so was the room. I came out cautiously in case he was waiting to ambush me. But the room was absolutely still. I walked to the foot of the bed and looked out through the floor-to-ceiling windows at the back garden and the pool. "Evan?" I tried again, softly, so as not to seem a fool if he was right there somewhere.

No answer.

Then I heard a slight murmuring coming from the bathroom. I tiptoed to the door and got ready to spring on him when he came out. He was whispering, but the marble room magnified the sound, bouncing it out at me.

"I can't come right now. I told you, you need to stay calm and it'll be all right." He was quiet for a moment, and then he said, "That's not fair. You know I care about you, and you should know by now what I'll do for you."

I leaned my head around the doorjamb until I was at an angle where I could see Evan's reflection in the long mirror. He had the phone up to one ear, and as he listened he backed up a step and looked out the half-opened door to check the closet.

Glancing back, I realized I'd left the door open, and I heard him say quickly, "I'll have to call you back."

With a chill in my heart I moved to face the open door. He appeared in it and saw me standing there looking at him.

It seemed as if my inner ear had given up on my sense of equilibrium. The room was rocking, and Evan's face looked guilty and pained.

Trying to keep my voice from freezing up, I asked, "Who was that?"

He sighed and dropped his head, caught. I suppose I should have been grateful that he didn't just lie to me. On the other hand, I was so afraid that I was ready to buy even a weak excuse.

"It's . . . something I can't talk about." Not surprisingly, he wouldn't meet my eye.

"Why not?" I asked, feeling the closeness between us fall away, as though he were being reeled backward away from me at incredible speed, growing more and more distant, until he was nothing more than an unrecognizable speck.

"Cally, listen." He reached out for me, but I backed away, so he let his hands drop and said, "We've talked about this. There are things it's better you don't know about."

I wasn't going to be put off by that. "Who was on the phone?"

Now his arms came up across his chest; the defensive stance served to alienate me even further by arousing my anger. "You need to let this go," he said in a voice that was half beseeching and half radioactive.

I knew that Evan was such a good detective that he would recognize even the slightest signs of fear or panic. So, I turned my back on him and walked to the bed. When I felt that my indignant anger was shielding the rest of my physical responses, I sat down and faced him. "Listen," I began, "we're engaged. We're picking a date for our wedding. I'm supposed to be the woman you love and trust. How can we ever expect to share each other's lives if there's a huge part of you that's off limits to me?"

Having a tense conflict with someone you're vulnerable to when you are both stark naked is like double exposure. I knew he was affected when he reached for a robe and put it on before he came into the room. "Callaway, this isn't something new."

"Yes," I corrected him, "it is. Because from what I just heard, that wasn't police work, that was something personal." I watched his face carefully and saw a struggle pass across it: an urge to soften and open up versus a trained response to harden and hide.

The training won. "I can't tell you about it, you have to trust me." He moved to the bed and sat down next to me. He touched my leg, then put his hand on my face, turning it gently to look at his. "Please, trust me."

Never in my life had I wanted anything so much; it was right there, trust it, let it go, let him have his life, let him have mine, and know that I was safe anyway. But nothing in my past had taught me how to do that. Starting with a mother I couldn't trust, I'd moved on to a stepbrother who hated me, a father who died when he was the only one I had, and men who loved me for my money.

Trust wasn't something I could bank on.

I looked at Evan, handsome, strong, smart, everything I always wanted, and said, "I'd really like to trust you. I really would." And then I got up and walked toward the bathroom. When my feet touched the cool marble of the bathroom floor I turned back, feeling like something more should be said. "Trust goes both ways, Evan. I know I haven't had much practical experience with that in my life, so who am I to spout off about it? Then again, maybe that's exactly why I'm so clear on the theory."

He was angry now. I knew I'd crossed the line. "Damn it,

Callaway, I've *told* you that you're much safer not knowing some things about my work."

"And I said I could handle that," I finished for him. "And I thought I could, but now . . ." I paused as I recognized the numbness in my heart that came from being pushed out, and I knew, consciously for the first time in my life, what my reaction to that would be: a revengeful secretive life of my own. "Now I know myself much better. I wouldn't want to pull away, but I would."

"That's a choice," he insisted.

But I shook my head sadly. "It's self-defense," I told him.

He leaned forward and said earnestly, "You don't have to defend yourself from me."

That might be true, but right now I didn't feel certain of that. I felt cold and numb. "Listen, I'm going to take a shower," I said. "I'll be out in a little while. Can you"—I could feel myself slipping into tears—"can you just give me a few minutes? Please?"

He looked as though he wanted to say more, to stop me, but he held back and nodded his head. Rising, he said softly, hopefully, "I'll be downstairs. Take your time."

As I turned away he spoke again. "Cally?" I turned back. "I love you," he said, "more than anything. I adore you."

I regarded him, and his pain. It looked real, but I couldn't find the words to form a response. Instead, I nodded and closed the door.

Turning the water on so hot that it stung my skin served to punish the first chill out of me, yet I couldn't help going over the phone call in my head. Didn't I have a right to know to whom he was saying "I care about you?" Wasn't he culpable too? I might need to learn to be more trusting, but not from someone who wasn't trustworthy, and I sure didn't need to learn to be a victim. Better to be the suspicious one than the fool.

But even with this diatribe raging in the steam of the shower and my brain, I could hear the sane voice of my best friend,

Ginny, saying something sage like, *If you trust someone and they cheat on you, it doesn't mean you're a fool, it means that they are an asshole.*

I stayed in the shower until my skin was stinging and so many thoughts had come into my head that it felt as crowded in the spacious shower as Santa Monica Pier on Cinco de Mayo, with all the pathetic litter to boot.

Turning off the water, I opened the solid glass door and grabbed a towel. The mirror was steamed up, and I could only make out a shadowy suggestion of myself as I dried off and began to brush out my hair. Being thick and wavy, my blond hair was much longer wet than it was dry, and even then it fell to the center of my back. When I had wrestled my impetuous tresses into long, neatly combed rows, the ends of which dripped now lukewarm droplets of water onto my rounded bottom, I reached forward and smeared my palm back and forth across the mirror, revealing a streaky image of a pensive me.

My usually bright blue-green eyes looked as though I had drawn a curtain over them from the inside. And though my body was reflected as shapely and taut as ever, my mouth was set and thinner than usual, making me look older than my thirty-five years. I put down the brush and tried to catch my own eye and make it smile, but I didn't respond.

And then I heard the shots.

They sounded like the sharp popping of fireworks from the rooms downstairs, two quick and then one deeper, louder retort. Catching up the towel and wrapping it around me with both hands, I yanked open the door and ran through the bedroom to the hallway, where I paused and listened, trying to hear over the resounding booming of the blood pulsing in my ears.

Very faintly, I heard angry male voices and then two more piercing rounds of gunshot.

Stepping back into the bedroom and trying to keep my breath from coming too quick and shallow, I spotted Evan's holster over the armchair in the corner. His badge glinted at me mockingly, and then I focused on the gun. As quietly as I could manage, I crossed to it and tried to pull the gun from its nest with one hand, but it was strapped in and I needed both hands to free it. Without a thought, I dropped the towel, pushed the snap open, and slid out the heavy nine-millimeter. It was a man's gun, meant for Evan's large, strong hands and arms. I pushed the safety off and struggled to land a round in the chamber. The action was hard and required almost more strength than I had in my fingers. I caught a piece of skin between my thumb and forefinger when it snapped back, and I saw rather than felt the indentation and the blood that seeped from it.

Moving to the bedroom door again, I leaned my back against the wall, listening. Nothing. Holding the heavy, awkward weapon in both hands to steady it, I peered cautiously down the hall and over the banister to the front door. From my vantage point I could see only the top of it, and not much of the floor of the entrance hall.

Why doesn't Evan call out to me, tell me that everything is all right?

But nothing came. That meant that either someone was still in the house or . . . I didn't want to think about it. Instinct silenced me, sharpening my hearing.

Hugging the wall with my naked back, I moved with slow sidesteps toward the head of the stairway. Still, I heard nothing.

I started down, and three stairs from the ground level I heard a door creak.

Is it Evan?

Someone, I was sure, had tried to open the office door very quietly and it had betrayed them. I waited. Somewhere, in the back of my brain, as though I were observing the fact from a distance rather than as a sensation, I became vaguely aware that I was not only naked, but cold. It was so still that I could hear the wine refrigerator in the bar humming quietly, and it was two rooms away.

Forcing my breath through a small O-shaped mouth to try to control both my panic and the noise of my breathing, I leaned all my weight onto my downstairs foot and very slowly lifted the other one to bring it to meet it. Then, painfully slowly, I began the next creeping move down one more eight-inch stair. As I tentatively placed the toes of my bare foot on the lower step and began to shift my weight, the step creaked. Too late to pull back. I planted myself as firmly as I could and brought the gun straight up in front of me just as I saw a man spin out from the hallway and drop to one knee, pointing his weapon at me.

His gun, a big-ass forty-five, had a gaping void for a muzzle that looked to me like a long dark tunnel of death with no light at the other end. I forced myself to look past the gun and aim at the face beyond it, adjusting my hands with a minuscule motion to get the face down my sights. As I aimed, I could feel that the trigger was too big for my hand, I didn't have a firm grip on it, and it was tight, hard to squeeze steadily, which made it very hard to keep my aim. I forced all my focus into the gun and my target, willing them to meet, expecting to see the flash of his explosion before mine. But it didn't come.

He had had time to finish me, but he hadn't done it. The nasty weapon was still extended toward me, exhibiting all its lethal potential, and Evan's gun in my hand was every bit as eager to launch a bullet. But we both held.

He wasn't a young man. His hair was wavy and graying. I noticed a few flecks of dandruff on the shoulders of his dark houndstooth jacket. The thought flashed through my mind that he was somewhat overdressed for an armed assault. The irises of his eyes were wide with adrenaline, and they watched my face hard for signs of firing.

But I held. Locking in on his eyes, I watched his lids to see if they started to close to protect themselves from his own gun's blast. But his eyes stayed open, looking at mine.

Two seconds lasted a year, and then his eyes flickered, but not protectively. They slid down my naked body and then back up. With a sudden movement that made my spinal cord jolt six inches backward, he yanked his gun back, and then, with a last strangely respectful look at me, he spun away and disappeared down the hall.

Exhaling hard, I sank onto the stairs, shaking. But I could only allow myself three quick inhalations to inflate myself before I moved again. I had to find Evan. *What the fuck is going on?*

I moved on down the hallway, keeping the gun extended in front of me, though the weight of it was making my arms shake. They were vibrating, and everything around me was following their example, moving, pulsing. As I took each cautious step I jerked the gun from side to side to follow movements caught in the corner of my eye. It took my shake-and-baked brain half a minute to realize it was my own heartbeat that was making the material world around me pulse.

I choked back the cry for Evan that was rising in my throat. Someone else might answer my call. Someone who was the antithesis of help. So I clenched my jaw and crept quietly forward. *Is he hurt?*

The office door was opened halfway. Following an example set by Evan in a similar situation that I did not want to think about right now, I went up against the wall next to it, then pushed the door open a little with my foot. The door swung open a few more inches, but nothing else happened. Namely, it didn't acquire any new holes.

Wishing to hell that I had Evan to do this for me, I spun into the doorway, dropped onto one knee, and scanned the room fast from one side to the other, lining up the gun with my point of view.

It was completely devoid of human life.

But there *was* a human. A body on the floor.

Chapter

2

It wasn't Evan. This man was smaller, with sandy blond hair and a face pitted with scars. And though I went to him and checked for a pulse, I'd seen enough bodies in the last couple of years to know when one had been recently vacated.

I could taste bile in my throat as the terror rose up inside me. *Where is Evan?*

The French door that led from the office into the side yard was open, and I approached it faster than caution should have dictated. My eyes swept the yard outside: nothing. Evan's house was big. Not as big as mine, of course, but it was unlikely that any neighbors would have noticed the gunshots and thought it was anything more than a backfiring lawn mower.

Turning back into the office, I grabbed the phone off its base and scanned the directory that was typed out on it. I found what I wanted in the third row. It read, "Curtis, cell phone." Punching the button, I waited. As the phone speed-dialed the number, my eyes fell on a postcard propped up against Evan's computer. It was a picture of Humphrey Bogart dressed as Sam Spade. Flipping it over, I read the words *Only my girlfriend's money can save me now.* It was not signed. I was so distracted that I barely heard the gravelly voice of Evan's partner, Curtis, coming through the phone lines.

"What's up, Paley?"

"Curtis," I said, and was surprised that I had a voice and it didn't sound serrated. "It's Callaway. Something has happened, I don't know what. But I'm at Evan's house, and I heard shots and I came down. Evan's gone and there's a dead man looking up at me." Now that I had turned to someone else, my strength began to leak out like sticky sap and gunk up my faculties.

"Whoa, hold on." Curtis's calm, slow manner of speaking sped up, but he maintained that practiced police deliberation that saved lives when others panicked. "Okay, I'm on my way. Are you safe now?"

"I have no idea, I was going to check the house—"

"Don't," he said sharply. "Are you in a room with doors that lock?"

"Yes," I told him, glancing at the office door.

"Good, then stay where you are. Lock any doors that you can get to without exposing yourself. Are you armed?"

"Yes. I've got Evan's gun."

"Where is Evan?" Although his voice was still measured and deliberate, I could hear the alarm in it.

"I don't know. I think . . ." I trailed off, not wanting to say or think it. I flipped the postcard back and forth in my hand, reading it again. "I think that someone took him."

"*Who* took him?"

"I don't know." The frustration overwhelmed me, and my thought processes started to dissolve. "I don't know, Curtis. I just know I heard shots when I got out of the shower and I came downstairs with Evan's gun and there was a man here who could have shot me but he didn't and then I found this, this *postcard*, and . . ." My voice broke with the effort of repeating it.

"All right, you'll tell me when I get there. I'm dispatching a squad car to you right now. Do what I told you and *nothing else!*"

Remembering the times I had done anything *but* what Evan and Curtis had told me to do, I decided that this time, it was excellent advice. I hung up the phone, locked the door to the yard, and tried not to look at the body on the floor.

Though outside it was a hot midsummer day, inside the air-conditioning made the office chilly. The sensation made me remember, with a faint air of not caring, that I was naked. Going to the closet just outside the office in the hallway, I took out one of Evan's light coats and put it on. The smell of him on it almost made me swoon.

In spite of what Curtis had told me, I couldn't go back into the office with the body. The small hallway felt safer, more contained, and I could see the front door from there. I slumped down on the floor and rested Evan's gun on my lap.

And then I felt the emptiness, the horrible pending possibility of my life without Evan in it. A terrifying panic took me; I couldn't breathe, I couldn't cry, I couldn't think.

It was in that harried state that the first officers on the scene found me. Moments later, Curtis came through the door with a purposefulness that calmed the dragon in me considerably. Just the competence of the man reassured me, gave me something to pin my hope on.

I shifted myself into his arms, and though they were comforting, there was the awkwardness of unfamiliarity and of treading on ground that shouldn't be disturbed. Evan's partner had always had an attraction for me, we both knew it, and more than that, he was now dating my best friend.

So after a moment, I pulled myself away and together. After searching the house and finding nothing to help him, he sat me in the living room with a small glass of brandy, and I told him everything I could remember, from the gunshots to the cryptic postcard, which I pulled from the pocket of Evan's coat and handed over. He took it carefully, by the edges, and I realized I'd been a fool to handle it. I gave him as thorough a description as possible of the man I had seen, although I could recall more about the gun and the houndstooth jacket than his face.

By now, the house was crawling with police and the forensics team. The front door stood open, and a constant flow of traffic came through it. I sensed an urgency in their work that was unlike the everyday attitude I'd experienced before. This was one of their own who had gone missing; this was personal.

A commotion in the entrance hall drew our attention. The officers at the door were trying to detain someone, and it only took one sentence from the person they were restraining for Curtis and me to identify her.

"Back off and let me through or shoot me. 'Cause I'm going in," my best friend Ginny was saying, making her usual loud-voiced entrance. "I don't mean any disrespect, but I will not stand out here while my friend is in trouble in there, and you might *think* you can stop me, but it's not gonna happen."

"It's all right," Curtis called out. "Let her in."

The officer looked annoyed, but he stood to one side and interested himself in something else.

"What the fuck is going on now?" Ginny asked as she put her arms around me and pulled me up against her. "Thanks for calling," she added to Curtis.

He smiled at her sincerely, but the expression was within a distracted glance. "I thought you might want someone to take you home," he told me.

I nodded and added tearfully, "Thanks for coming," to Ginny. Just the sight of her beautiful dark-skinned face and the feel of her thousand tiny braids against my cheek gave me permission to let go of the sobs that had been compressed into a small, burning square inside me.

Curtis rose and found something else to do for a few minutes. Ginny's arms were long and feminine but strong as steel wire, and they constricted around me in an embrace I could not have broken even if I'd wanted to.

"It's gonna be okay," she said firmly. "Evan is as smart and as tough as they come, he'll get himself out of this."

"Out of what?" I asked her, accepting a tissue she'd offered. "What the fuck is going on?"

"That's what I need to know," Curtis said as he approached us, then lowered his voice. "Listen, I don't know what it is exactly, but Evan's been up to something."

"What?" I asked, my core temperature dropping a few degrees.

He glanced over his shoulder to make sure no one was in earshot, then said, "We both know he occasionally takes a 'personal' interest in a case, possibly outside strict police policy. When that happens, I don't see, and I don't hear, and I don't ask. But now I need to know if you noticed anything. Anything at all." He nailed me with his gray eyes, and I knew it would be damn close to impossible to hide from that gaze.

"A few minutes before I heard the shots, he got a phone call. He wouldn't tell me who it was and I got mad. It sounded like he was protecting someone, someone . . ." I trailed off, not liking to admit that I was jealous or that I might have cause to be.

"Someone who what?" Curtis asked urgently.

"I don't know." The memory of Evan saying "You should know by now what I'll do for you" and the spinning supposition that that might mean betraying me stuck in my chest like a lump of rancid mud and wouldn't come up. I swallowed hard, but it wouldn't go down either.

Curtis watched me with his eyes narrowed, trying to draw the rest out of me with his will. "Listen, we need to keep this quiet. I talked to Lieutenant Bickson, and the department is eager to keep this out of the papers. The local TV networks would make a miniseries out of it by Tuesday. 'Los Angeles Detective Disappears.' " He sighed and rubbed one long-fingered hand through his salt-and-pepper hair. "And, for the reason I just stated, I agreed." He turned and glanced at his associates in the entrance hall to be sure they were out of earshot again, then went on. "If Evan *is* up to something he shouldn't be, it could cost him his job, and possibly some jail time. And if anyone finds out I've been turning a blind eye, *my* pension is dust." There was nervous fear in his eyes. "The most important thing is to get him back, and don't worry, the entire force will be jonesing to get the fuckers who did this, they'll be working twenty-four hours a day, but it will not help us to be on the evening news. Got it?"

Curtis's intensity was frightening me even more. So I only nodded, then asked, "So you think it's more than one person?"

"Absolutely," he said without hesitation. "The dead guy on the floor was most likely shot by Evan—I found Evan's spare gun under the desk. And it's a good bet ballistics will tell me it fired the bullets in the corpse. You saw a man still in the house after the shooting, after Evan must have been taken away." Curtis paused and smiled grimly. "I don't see Evan going easily, so probably there were at least two others. So that makes four, including Houndstooth."

I must have looked confused, because he explained, "You said the guy's jacket was houndstooth check." He fixed me again with his stone-gray eyes. "If you know anything else, anything he might have been up to, you need to come clean now."

Then, when I added nothing more, he said to Ginny with a note of impatience, "Take her home."

"Wait," I said, not wanting Curtis to be upset with me. "Who was the dead man?"

"Don't know yet. His card said he was an importer. Other than that, all I know is, he's got an Armenian last name. *If* his ID is real."

Ginny went with me upstairs and waited while I found some clothes and put them on with shaking hands. When we got back downstairs, forensics and the coroner were just packing up. I walked down the short hall to the office to find Curtis standing alone, looking down at the bloodstains on the carpet. He sighed and turned when we came in. "I'll have a cleanup crew get in here in a few hours. I've got to go see if we can get a positive ID on this body, or get any prints from the card or the room, any leads that might help me find Evan. I'll give you a call as soon as I know anything. But *you*"—he pierced me with a stare—"call me if you hear from them or *remember* anything else."

"Okay," I mumbled. What else could I say?

Curtis's eyes went to Ginny, and they shared a long look before he said to her, "Can I talk to you for a minute?"

She looked to me first. "You okay?"

"Sure," I said, and sat down heavily in Evan's desk chair. They left me, but I could hear the murmur of their voices in the hallway and could guess the nature of the discussion. I was not to be left alone, if possible, and—I was guessing here—she was to let him know if she got any more intimate information out of me.

Turning away from the dark red stain on the crème carpet, I stared blankly at Evan's computer screen. It was on screensaver, and photos of planets drifted past the liquid screen. Without thinking I reached out and touched the space bar.

The computer went immediately to his email.

There was an open message on the screen, and Evan had been drafting a reply, but it broke off in midsentence. What caught my eye was the reference to the phone call.

It read: **I've asked you not to call me at home, it makes things too difficult. I know this is hard for you, but you're going to have to trust me and be patient. Remember what I told you.**

At that point he must have been interrupted, because the cursor was sitting at the end of the last word, blinking at me.

Just below it were the words: **Original message, sent 12:15 p.m. on June 23.**

With a shaking hand, I scrolled down and read what followed: **Evan please, don't push me away, I need to be able to talk to you, you are the only one who matters to me now. I'm frightened. You said you would always love me, and I believe you. I need you now. B.**

My breath was running ragged through my chest. *What the hell is this?*

I heard footsteps coming back through the entrance hall and knew I only had a few seconds; I quickly forwarded the email to myself, then, my finger hovering over the delete button, I hesitated for a split second, wondering if this could be connected to Evan's disappearance and I could be hindering Curtis's attempt to find him. With shaking hands I punched the delete key and the email disappeared from the screen just as Ginny stuck her head in the doorway. Curtis hovered in the hallway behind her.

"Ready to go?" she asked softly.

"Yeah, I guess so." I got up and started toward her. Curtis noticed that the email screen was illuminated, and it was obvious I'd been looking at it; he gave me another suspicious glance. "Did you find anything?" he asked me.

"No," I lied, but I couldn't look at him. He crossed past me and sat down at the computer. I felt nauseated. I should tell him. Stopping, I turned back. "Curtis?"

He swiveled toward me and said sternly, "What?"

I stood there like a lump of Jell-O, a congealed mass of spineless indecision. Curtis was watching me, and I knew that he could see right through me. But somehow I couldn't bring myself to tell him. I didn't want to even think, much less reveal, that Evan might have a girlfriend. I needed more time to think.

"I just wanted to say thank you." I fumbled. When he watched me without waver or response, I turned to Ginny and silently begged her to get me out of there.

But when we got out to the wide circular drive and were out of earshot, I said to Ginny, "You've got to help me. I think I've made a horrible mistake."

Ginny gave me a sideways look but tried to be reassuring.

"Don't go there. Girl, you went after a homicidal kidnapper *naked*. Don't go acting like you should have done more and shit. What the hell else *could* you do?"

"Well," I said, as though I were giving it some thought, "I could have not lied to Curtis."

There was a hesitation in her step—not a stop exactly, just a hitch—which she quickly turned into an increase in pace, pulling me more forcefully along. We got to her hybrid SUV, and she pushed me to the passenger door. All she said was, "Get in."

She looked angry when she climbed in the other side and started the car.

"Let me explain," I began. "First, I didn't really tell him the whole reason we argued. And there was an email on his computer that shouldn't have been there, and I deleted it."

Ginny turned to me as she put the car into reverse and said flatly, "He's not stupid. He told me he knows you're holding."

I swallowed, but my throat had closed up. "What did you say?" I asked her.

She shook her head, and her voice revealed her sense of betrayal. "I defended you."

Ashamed, I dropped my face into my hands and tried to still the rush of hot blood. On top of everything else, I couldn't bear for my best and only true friend to be disappointed in me. If she thought I was wrong, if I *was* wrong, then I couldn't function, couldn't do anything except stand by and be a victim. I heard her put the car into drive, but we didn't move forward. After a few seconds I looked cautiously up at her.

She was staring straight at me. She sighed deeply and shook her head, resigned.

Then she punched the accelerator and said, "This had better be good."

Chapter
3

I knew it was only a matter of a couple of minutes until Ginny heaved the broken truth out of me, and I resented that; I clung desperately to a forlorn hope that I was wrong, that my relationship with Evan was perfect, or at least that I could keep it looking that way and hold on to my sanity in the midst of this hellish nightmare.

Not a chance. "So who do you think it was that called?" She watched me, her gorgeous, gold-flecked cat eyes riveted on me.

"I don't know, an informant or something."

"And what happened right after?"

Feeling ashamed at the memory of him telling me how he adored me and my inability to respond, I muttered, "We had a fight." Little wisps of possible scenarios, like shots in a horror movie, kept running through me like wooden stakes: Evan hurt and in pain, Evan bound and gagged, Evan dead, his eyes staring up sightlessly from a cold floor. The images robbed me of breath and I found myself hyperventilating, sucking in huge gulps of air.

Even the fact that he'd been kidnapped, that he was gone, was too much for my nervous system to accept. I alternated between cold fury, broken sobs, and forgiving numbness, the last sensation lasting for briefer and briefer periods.

"You had a fight because an informant called him?" Ginny was rubbing my back to try to calm the hysteria, but she wasn't buying my sketchy story outline.

"He wouldn't tell me who it was."

"Mm-hmm," she intoned accusingly. "Does he usually give you his phone bill to review? I didn't realize you were so insecure."

That pissed me off. "Oh, please! You would have done the same thing if you'd heard Curtis saying what I heard Evan say, especially if he was hiding in the bathroom whispering at the time!"

"Mm-hmm?" The intonation took on a victorious sound, and too late I realized that she'd trapped me. "What, exactly, was he whispering?"

I snorted in self-disgust and looked out the window for a few seconds, tears streaming down my flushed cheeks, before I could bring myself to answer. When I told her exactly what I'd heard, I didn't look at her, just stared straight ahead and felt the numbing disbelief of it all over again. And something else: a sense of failure.

"He said, 'You know how much I care for you, and you should know by now what I would do for you.'" I let my head fall hard against the glass, hot from the sun. "And then, when he saw that I wasn't in the closet anymore, he said he had to go and hung up quickly."

I don't know what I expected—sympathy, I suppose—so when she reacted, it snapped me back to attention.

"That's it?" she bellowed. "What the fuck is wrong with you?"

Confused, I sputtered, "He told someone that he cared about them, and that he'd do anything for them!"

"So?" She took both hands off the wheel and threw them up in the air in a gesture of surrender, using her knee to steer around a small pickup truck, narrowly missing it.

"So, obviously he's involved with someone else!" It was amazing, even to me, how fast I made the shift from denial to accusation.

"Maybe it was his mother feeling needy," she said, and raised both eyebrows at me.

"Watch the road," I snapped at her. "Evan's mother is French, lives in a villa overlooking the sea in the south of France with her second husband, an incredibly handsome Olympic gold medallist in the long ski jump who adores her. She is a celebrated beauty, socialite, and art historian. Sonet is the *least* needy woman I can think of."

"His sister?" Ginny ventured.

"Melissa, along with Evan's brother, handles the family businesses. She's president of a multimedia conglomerate that includes three magazines, five radio stations, and two cable channels."

"Damn," Ginny exclaimed. "I'm impressed." Then she smiled at me in a way I didn't like very much, and I knew what was coming. "Just because," she began, "a person is very successful, obscenely rich, and runs multiple corporations and shit doesn't mean she can't be a smidgen insecure." She waggled a finger at me. I smacked it down.

"I get your subtle comparison," I admitted reluctantly. "But you can't do what I do and *act* weak. You'd be eaten along with the bagels at your first power breakfast. And he wasn't using a 'family concern' voice. Besides, neither of the names Sonet or Melissa starts with a *B*."

She glanced at me like I was nuts, so I just said, "There's the email too. I forwarded it to myself, I'll show you." I crossed my arms and held on to myself tightly to keep from flying apart.

We were just pulling into my driveway. The view of my massive home through the huge oak trees, the marble sculptures surrounded by beautiful flowerbeds, and the sweeping lawn was perfect and unaffected. That couldn't be right. I felt chaotic, everything else should be too.

"I should warn you," Ginny said, keeping her eyes on the house, "I called Sabrina and told her what was going on."

The front door flew open, and my half sister, Sabrina, flew out, her Swedish white-blond hair streaming out behind her, her baby-blue eyes filled with tears. Almost before I was out of the car, she had enveloped me in her ample arms, pulling me up against her zaftig body. "Oh, Cally, honey! I'm so sorry. But don't you worry; we'll get him back. This is just horrible!" she drawled.

We were the odd couple of sisters. She'd been raised in the South in a small town, where people were decent and helpful and trusting. I'd been raised in a cynical, harsh, competitive place. I tried to extricate myself from her ample breast, still vaguely uncomfortable with the display of sibling affection. In a little more than a year and a half, I had gone from not knowing Sabrina existed to her living with me.

My butler, Deirdre, was standing respectfully in the doorway. Though her British reserve and the formality of her position in my household restrained her from becoming overly familiar, she expressed her anguish with an infinitely compassionate look and a soft query. "Is there anything I can get for you?" she asked as I came up the steps, trailing Sabrina on one arm.

I looked at her and thought it was funny that sometimes the people who seem so peripheral can be the ones who really know us best. Deirdre had been beside me through my father's terminal illness in this very house, and the number of times she'd offered something as simple as a warm cup of tea or a hand laid unobtrusively on my arm as I'd sat by his bed watching him waste away had somehow fortified me enough to struggle through another impossible hour.

As I came into the entrance hall, I remembered how she had gathered the staff to stand respectfully in this room as the men from the funeral home had carried my father's body out the grand front door for the last time.

The image rushed through my head and my heart in the space it took for me to smile sadly at her and reach out and take her hand. I suppose I thought of that moment now because I was feeling so desolate all over again. "Thank you, Deirdre. Just having you here makes all the difference."

She inclined her head and retreated silently to the kitchen. There was no need for her to say that she would be there if I needed anything. She always was.

We went through into the living room. A tall, handsome, young Asian man was standing respectfully near the sofa. He greeted us with a bow.

"Hello, Darrien," I said to him.

Sabrina gushed apologetically, "Darrien was already here when Ginny called to say what happened, and I was so upset he didn't want to leave me. I hope that's all right."

"Of course it is," I reassured her. "Thank you for staying with her," I said to Darrien.

Though Darrien and Sabrina had known each other for several months, his traditional Japanese values and her innocence had kept them from doing more than circle each other in mutual awed attraction. Any other time I would have encouraged her to take him upstairs and get it over with, but right now I could think of nothing but my own gnawing angst. I had to find out what was going on with Evan; I had to get him back.

That meant getting to my computer. "Excuse me, Darrien, but I have something I need to do."

"Of course. If there's any way at all I can help, please, you have only to ask." He bowed again, and I was genuinely moved by his obvious sincerity.

I thought about Korosu, his gorgeous, powerful boss, who had become the object of Evan's investigation a few months before. I hadn't seen him since. Which was probably a good thing, because even as I asked the next question, I felt my pulse quicken.

"How is Korosu-san?"

"Very well, thank you. He asks about you often."

"Really?" I asked before I could stop myself. And then, to try to make a joke out of my frazzled state and all the tension, I added, "What do you say?"

"That to the best of my knowledge, you are well. He has the greatest respect for you and Detective Paley. He will be very distressed to hear the news of Detective Paley's . . ." He faded off, unsure of whether to speak the word.

I opened my mouth to finish his thought but found I couldn't speak the word either, and anyway what was it? Kidnapping? Abduction? *Death*? The words boomed, unspoken, in my head.

"You can't tell him," I said quietly, remembering Curtis's directive. I included Sabrina in my stern look. "Neither of you can say anything now. Curtis is afraid it might make things worse. Do you understand?"

Darrien nodded immediately, but I wasn't worried about him. Sabrina, on the other hand . . .

"But why?" she asked.

"Because Curtis and his lieutenant think it's best, and they know better than *you*." I was fading fast, I didn't have any reserve strength to grapple with tangential conflicts, to take on anyone else's fear. Not even Sabrina's.

So I looked hopefully up to Darrien, who said soothingly, "I understand, I'll explain."

Finding myself spinning into a cycle of panic, I made a small bow to Darrien, muttered a choked sentence of thanks, and went quickly to my library, beckoning Ginny to join me.

Deirdre intercepted me in the entrance hall with a manila envelope. "This came for you early this morning," she told me.

Half afraid that it might be connected to Evan's disappearance, and half afraid it wasn't, I glanced at the return address. It was from Dana Scheiner, my brilliant—and very gorgeous—estate planning attorney.

I flashed on my first meeting with Dana. She'd been recommended by Evan and I'd been jealous that she and Evan might have been an item at one time. She turned out to be his estate attorney and the sharpest one I'd ever worked with. Was I overreacting now too?

"What's that?" Ginny asked.

"It must be the paperwork for adding Sabrina to my will." I opened the door and went quickly into the library, tossing the envelope onto my desk.

As I sat down and hit the mail icon on my laptop, Ginny picked up a solid oak, high-back chair and lifted it over the sofa as though it had been made of balsa wood. Ginny worked as a stuntwoman, and in her business, strength and reflexes could make the difference between being successful and being dead. She had both assets in excess, and both of us were very much alive because of it. It was she who'd insisted that I learn how to handle a gun and defend myself.

"Okay, look." I pulled up the email from B. and she scanned it. Then she sat back in the chair, exhaled loudly, and crossed her arms.

"What do you think?" I asked her. "Maybe we can trace the sender from the email address?"

"Curtis probably could," she said pointedly, but when I groaned she added, "and I understand your hesitation, but girl, this is serious. We don't know what Evan's gotten mixed up in. Curtis is his partner, and a damn fine cop. And if Evan's involved in something that will affect Curtis, he deserves to know." Her cat eyes flashed at me angrily. "And *maybe* he can save Evan's life."

"I know," I groaned, and dropped my head onto my desk,

feeling drained of any life force. "But Ginny, what if this doesn't have anything to do with Evan's . . . disappearance?"

She sat for a moment, staring at the screen, and then she put her head down on her arms so that she was on my level, facing me. "And what if you find out that he is having an affair?"

"Do you think so?" I asked, ashamed at the quiver in my voice.

"I don't know," she answered honestly, sounding like she didn't have an opinion one way or the other. "But what if he is?"

The top of Ginny's left arm was only a few inches in front of me, and I could see the scar on it where she had taken a bullet that had been meant for me. That memory brought on another memory: of Evan, lying on the hard concrete floor of a parking structure, bleeding from a bullet. I remembered how I had felt then, holding Evan's hand while he'd grimaced in pain; I'd been horrified that I might lose him. I felt the same way now.

"It doesn't matter," I told Ginny. "I just want him back."

She nodded, which wasn't easy to do while her head was perpendicular. "Just so you know," she said to me, "I don't think for one second that he has eyes for anyone but you." She reached over and put her long-fingered hand on my head. "There isn't anybody like you."

Her face went all cloudy and out of focus. "Thanks," I managed to get out, though my throat was clenched. Then, sitting up and willing the tears away, I forced myself to try to focus, grappling with my mane of thick blond hair until I'd twisted it into a knot on top of my head, work mode. "So, what can we do?"

"We can call Curtis." When I began to object, she interrupted me. "Listen to me. What's your option? To sit here until you get passed another note?"

My brain had felt as sluggish and thick as butternut squash soup since I'd found Evan was gone. But now, finally, it was beginning to warm up, to thin and move, allowing limited visibility. "I know a man," I told Ginny. "He's my computer expert, sets up all the systems at my offices and here at the house. He would know how to trace this address."

"So would Curtis."

"His name is Wayne." I ignored her and went on. "I'll call him."

"Stop it." Ginny tried to take the phone from my hand. "Wise up, Callaway. I am not going to let you keep Curtis in the dark just because your pride is wounded." She sounded bitter, reprimanding, and I realized that her loyalties had shifted, split between Curtis and me, and I'd better respect that if I wanted to keep her as my friend.

I hadn't surrendered the phone yet. We both stood with a hand on it, pulling slightly. Finally, hurt and completely unsure that I was making the right decision, I let it slide from my grasp. Ginny started to dial when, as though on cue, a sharp electronic note sounded on my computer. The YOU HAVE MAIL sign flashed.

This was my personal email, and very few people had access to the address. With an irrational rush of hope that it might be Evan, I clicked on the icon.

It was a simple note, from an address I did not recognize. It read, **If you want your partner to live, you won't tell his partner anything you hear from us.** I looked at Ginny, who had stopped dialing and was staring at the message.

"There's an attachment," she told me.

When I found I couldn't move to click on it, she did it for me, and a photo came up. But it wasn't Evan. It was Curtis, standing outside Evan's house. The photo looked as if it had been taken from the street this morning with a long lens, and someone had added an artistic touch: circular target lines with the bull's-eye centered on Curtis's heart.

Unable to breathe or comment, I looked from the pointed message up at Ginny. She had stopped breathing and her eyes had widened in fear. "No," she said softly. "No." She pressed a button that killed her outgoing call to Curtis and held the receiver out to me. The look on her face was changing from shock to determination.

When I looked at the phone blankly she prompted, "Do you know that Wayne guy's phone number by heart, or shall I look it up for you?"

Chapter 4

When Curtis came by an hour later, he told us that the corpse seemed to be at least partially who his forged ID said he was: a recent immigrant from Moscow, where, it appeared, he had a criminal record of some kind.

"And apparently this guy had done his time and moved on to richer waters, the good old U.S. of A.," Curtis said grimly. "He'd been deported once already." As I listened to Curtis, I tried to erase the mental image of a bull's-eye's concentric rings that my mind kept superimposing over him.

"Then why is he here?" Ginny asked.

"You have no idea how many people are here illegally," Curtis said, as though he could feel the weight of those tens of thousands on his shoulders personally.

I remembered Evan talking about the fact that so many Soviet bad guys had moved to L.A. that the police force was facing a whole new level of criminals. Not only were they experienced but they were also far more likely to fight than surrender.

"What could he have wanted from Evan?" I asked.

"Could be Russian Mafia looking for ransom, could be a hired hand," Curtis speculated. "God knows there's been an increase of crime since the curtain fell. Serious crime. Hell, the *average* Russian or Armenian immigrant will get aggressive and argumentative about a *jaywalking* ticket, for God's sake. I don't even want to talk about the career criminals." He put his hands in his pockets, and his face darkened.

"The CEO of my primary bank is Russian," I said defensively. "I know his family, and I've never met a more honest man with stronger values."

"I'm not talking about everybody, Callaway, you know me better than that." Curtis cut me off sharply. "My point of view is based on seeing the worst small percentage of any new wave of immigrants, the ones who commit the crimes, so it's difficult not to be a little cynical. And this latest group is the most brutal I've seen in thirty years on the force."

I must have blanched visibly, because Curtis seemed to notice and he quickly amended his assessment. "But like I said, this guy is most likely a hired hand. Somebody here has hooked up with some thugs to get a job done, and, I'm guessing, paid them in cash to do it. This guy had a wad of hundreds in his back pocket." He patted my knee. "I will tell you this, if they'd wanted Evan dead, they would have killed him. These are not people with scruples."

"And that's a good thing?" Ginny asked incredulously. I could see the concern for Curtis in her eyes.

"In this case, yes. Because if their objective was to kill Evan, he'd be dead. So I think that whoever took him needs him alive."

No one spoke for a moment, but the thought hung in the air like a cloud of lethal gas. *Was* Evan still alive?

Fortunately Deirdre knocked at that moment and came in with a tray of tea and snacks. The sight of food made me feel slightly ill. But when Deirdre put a warm cup of Earl Grey tea in my hand, the scent revived me somewhat.

Deirdre finished serving and then stood respectfully, hovering about, which meant she had something to ask.

"Yes, Deirdre?" I invited her to ask it.

"Miss Sabrina would like to know if you will be joining her for dinner."

I sighed, exhausted: the little darling. "She wants to know what's going on, doesn't she?"

"I gather that is part of the reason for her request," Deirdre answered.

"What's the other part?" Ginny wanted to know.

"I would speculate that Miss Sabrina would very much like to be of service to her sister."

Ginny looked at me. "She's feeling left out," she said. I nodded; I hadn't given Sabrina a second thought, but now I realized that it was probably killing her to be sitting around exiled from helping. It would have driven me to distraction.

Turning back to Deirdre, I said, "Tell her I will join her for dinner, but let's eat in the kitchen. It's more comforting." The thought of food turned my stomach again, so I added, "Something very bland, please." Deirdre nodded but still didn't leave, her eyes finally cutting to Curtis.

I took the cue. "Would you like to stay, Curtis?" I prayed he would say no. What if I got a message from the kidnappers while he was there? Ginny's eyes cut away and she did not add the weight of a request onto mine.

He looked surprised; I seemed to have plucked him out of deep thought. "Uh, no. Thank you, though. The whole precinct is working on this, and I'm coordinating, so I need to be there, but first I want to ask you one other thing."

Deirdre immediately made her departure. "I spent some time looking through Evan's emails after you left today," Curtis said, shifting uncomfortably and looking away long enough for Ginny and me to exchange a glance. "Do you, by any chance, know someone that he was dealing with who had the initial *B*?"

It took all my poker face skills not to react. *Were there more? What did they say?* "Not that I can think of offhand," I replied as I pretended to consider it. "Isn't your lieutenant named Bickson, or something?"

Curtis shook his head. "No, that's not it."

Ginny's eyes had ignited. I wanted to warn her that she looked too interested, but her leg was too out in the open for me to get a kick in. She leaned forward and asked, "Can't you trace the email address?"

Good question. I hoped I didn't look as eager as she did as I waited for the answer.

"I'm not sure if it's relevant or not," Curtis responded. "But"—he slapped his thighs as he stood up—"it's worth a shot. I better go get started."

"I'll walk you out," Ginny said, and as they crossed the room, Curtis put his arm around her. She nestled her head into his shoulder and clung to him more than was necessary. I empathized completely.

The door opened again almost immediately after Ginny and Curtis had exited, and Carmen, my housekeeper, came into the room. She was carrying a vase filled with so many red roses that I had to peer through them to see her slightly puzzled and apprehensive face.

"Miss Wilde?" she began, looking very out of sorts to be interrupting me when I was in such a bad situation. But Carmen had been with my father before me, and I considered her a friend as well as an employee. I wanted to put her at ease, though I didn't have much confidence to spare.

"Yes, Carmen?"

She extended the flowers out toward me and, looking confused, she said, "A man, outside, he give me this and say I should give it to you. Only you."

"What? What man?" I crossed to her in a few urgent strides,

and my heart froze when I saw what was nestled among the bloodred blossoms.

It was a white, card-sized envelope that bulged slightly, with the word *Baby* written on it.

Taking the envelope, I asked, "How did this man get through the gate?"

"No. No. A man on the street, when I was waiting for the gate to open he came up in a car and give to me. It's okay?"

"What did he look like?" I asked. Ginny reentered the room and stopped when she saw my face.

"He look normal," Carmen said, shrugging. "He ask me very nice, in Spanish."

"Could you recognize him if you saw him?" I asked her, though I knew chances were good this was just a delivery guy and we would never see him again.

"Maybe," Carmen mused. "I think so." She ended more firmly and smiled, eager to be helpful, as always.

"Okay. Thanks." She turned to leave, and Ginny was next to me in a moment.

"Carmen," I called out before she got to the door. "Could you please take those flowers out?"

She looked at the magnificent bouquet curiously. Even for my level of luxury they were impressive. "You may have them," I said. She looked delighted, but she tried to hide it. "Just take them out of the house, please."

Inside the envelope was another postcard, one of those old-fashioned ones, black and white tinted with pastel color. Ignoring the image, I flipped it over with a hand that could barely feel. It read, "Three million in unmarked bills by Thursday, noon." The only other thing on it was an address. I recognized the street as an expensive address high in the Hollywood Hills.

"What the fuck?" Ginny muttered. "Is that where you're supposed to take the money?" I turned the card over to see if there was a clue in the picture.

The image was of a forties pinup girl posed in front of the Hollywood sign. Other than the fact that the address was probably in that vicinity, we couldn't find anything relevant in the image of the model. She was an attractive, shapely blonde, who reminded me a little of Sabrina.

"What else is in there?" Ginny asked, reaching out to feel the envelope that I still held in my shaking hand.

I looked up at her, my heart beating hard and fast. "I'm afraid," I whispered.

Ginny's head moved in a barely perceptible nod. She held out her hand.

I turned the envelope upside down and a piece of fabric, torn from a shirt, slid into Ginny's palm.

It had a piece of the collar attached, and in tiny stitching that had once been as white as the fine cotton were the initials *E.P.*

It was stained a dark, deep red.

Blood red.

Chapter
5

Another knock on the door startled me so badly that it produced a muffled yell from me, which Deirdre misinterpreted as an invitation to enter. I barely had time to put the offensive shred of fabric in the top drawer of my desk before she'd entered the room, trailing a tall, thin youth with lanky blond hair.

"Mr. Wayne Sebert," Deirdre announced, and then she shimmered off. I had told her I was expecting him.

Wayne looked nervous. Then again, he always looked nervous. He shuffled his feet and rubbed one thumb against the palm of the other hand so hard that it looked like he was trying to make a pinch bowl out of clay. He let go of the pottery project long enough to make a small, anxious wave. "Hi, Cally," he mumbled.

Wayne had set up the computer and phone systems at both my home and my office, so he'd spent quite a bit of time working for me.

I always tried to greet him warmly in an effort to put him at ease. It never worked, but I did it anyway. Now I was so shaken that I fell on the luke side of warm as I extended my hand to him. "Hello, Wayne, thank you so much for coming on such short notice. You remember my friend, Virginia."

Wayne's eyes flicked uncomfortably to Ginny's face to register acknowledgment and then dropped again. Ginny said, "What's up, Wayne?" and the less-than-perfect union of souls was over.

I offered Wayne tea, soda, coffee, snacks—all of which he declined, as always—and then sat him down to explain the situation. It was a little tricky when I got to the "we can't tell anybody about this" part. The thought came to me that he was used to setting up computer systems for secured companies and identity-theft paranoid individuals on a daily basis, so our little task would probably seem minor league to him.

After I skirted around the issue uncomfortably for a while, Ginny got impatient. "Look, Wayne, what Goody Two-shoes here is trying to say is, we want you to find out who sent these emails, and we don't care if it's legal or not. Are you in?"

I turned to her with my mouth open, but before I could veto any further incriminating outbursts, Wayne responded with a "Yeah, sure. No problem."

"Well, okay," I said. I went to my desk and pulled up both emails on the screen. Wayne, as always, had been drawn into the vortex when the artificial light from the screen hit his face, and he started right in, punching at intricate combinations of keys, complex commands known only to the exalted few. I knew from experience that he wouldn't speak again until he surfaced with some pertinent information. I gestured Ginny out of the room.

We crossed the entrance hall quickly and headed up the wide staircase toward my master suite. Ginny still had the postcard with the address on it in her hand. She held it up and pointed to the hills featured behind the shapely model. "Get dressed," she said. "I think we need to go do a drive-by."

Wincing at the violent reference, I detoured briefly to Sabrina's room, which was the fourth bedroom down the opposite hallway. She had one of the five upstairs suites. It used to be called the yellow suite, but she had redecorated since she'd moved in and I recoiled at the floral curtains and the mountainous pile of stuffed animals on her bed.

"Sabrina?" The only answer was a soft snore, and I recognized her form in a plush light pink sweat suit, sandwiched in among some of the larger pastel-colored stuffies. She seemed to have fallen asleep hugging a chenille teddy bear with a lime-colored bow on its head. I stood for a moment watching her while a deep tenderness washed over me. Distrusting the sensation, I closed the door softly and joined Ginny.

To get to the address on the postcard, we took one of my cars, the Porsche SUV, and Ginny drove. She almost always did because I trusted her more than myself, in spite of the frequent thrills involved with being the passenger of a stunt driver.

The tension in the car was thicker than the traffic on Sunset Boulevard. I clenched my hands into fists in an attempt to make the trembling stop. Fear for Curtis and Evan might have made us reckless, but we both knew what we were doing was dangerous. We had no idea what we were looking for or what we would find at this address. I had a vaguely formed plan that we would cruise past it, and then figure out what to do next. We were both desperate to know what was going on. My stomach burned, and I continually struggled to take a deep enough breath. From the way she kept smiling at me reassuringly, I knew Ginny was scared too.

Eventually, we got across Sunset and turned up into the hills. We kept going up, and up, until the street had narrowed to almost a single lane and twisted like the spine of a writhing snake. We found the address on the back of the Hollywood postcard, but the only thing visible from the street was a high wooden fence and gate that bordered the thin strip of sidewalk.

The numbers themselves, fashioned out of thick, artsy, metallic glass, were mounted on the fence.

Ginny pulled up to the curb a little ways down the street, where we could see the entrance.

"Now what?" I asked, but even as I spoke the gate began to move. It opened a couple of feet and then stopped. Two figures emerged, both wearing motorcycle helmets with tinted visors and leather outfits. As they climbed onto a Ducati, the smaller of the pair put something into his left jacket pocket, then they took off. The numbers on the license plate were too small and distant for me to make out.

Ginny looked at me. The gate still stood partially open. We both nodded, and I unzipped my Prada purse to take out the precautions I had stashed there.

Evan's gun, the larger, heavier one, I gave to Ginny. Unlike me, she yanked the clip back and checked the chamber with an effortless, professional precision. Pulling up her shirt, she stuck the gun in the front of her Armani pants. I pulled out my own handgun, a smaller, somewhat more ladylike nine-millimeter, and nestled it in the pocket of my linen jacket.

We made our way to the opening in the gate and peeked inside. A path led to a doorway of what looked like a small, one-level home. On either side of the home, however, the ground dropped away, and, based on the view of the city far below, my guess was that this house was one of those deceivingly giant hillside homes built onto an impossible lot with engineering that was either a brilliant feat or a rash gamble. Which of those it would turn out to be depended on three things: your point of view, the accuracy of your geological surveys, and the mercurial whims of Mother Nature.

Seeing nothing, we eased our way toward the front door, and I shrugged my shoulders at Ginny. "What now?" I asked for the second time in three minutes.

"We didn't come all the way up here for nothing." Ginny had

a glint in her eye that I recognized as the danger zone. It was equal parts outrage and restlessness.

"I know. Maybe we could go around the side, peek in a window."

"Fuck that! They took Evan, they threatened Curtis, and they sent us this address. I'm not waiting." Somewhere, deeply embedded in Ginny's DNA, was an action-hero gene.

Before I could stop her, she jabbed the bell with a long, rapierlike finger. I could hear the deep, resonant tones echo through a large space; I stepped to one side of the door and put my hand on the hilt of the gun in my pocket, but the chimes brought no response.

Ginny's keenness was contagious. With a growing craving to stop floundering, to gain some kind of advantage, I tried the doorknob; it turned. I pushed the door with my foot and was surprised when it swung easily open.

We entered cautiously onto an upper landing with a stairway that led down to a living room that must have been thirty feet high and fifty feet long. The view through the wall of glass, framing all of downtown L.A., gave me a sense of vertigo as we started down the stairway, clutching at the wrought-iron railing.

The artwork too showed a sense of money and style. Whoever lived here had put this place together with a great deal of expense, and it looked to me like they had purchased everything, from the carpets to the knickknacks, all at once. Growing up with money had given me an eye for the nouveaux riches, even when they had taste.

Neither of us spoke, but Ginny arched her eyebrows at me to say "Not bad." I had to agree with her there—it was all very well done. We moved off to the room on the right, which turned out to be the kitchen, not unexpectedly accessorized in Viking appliances and Malibu tile.

Everything in the house was beautifully put together.

Even the dead girl on the floor.

Chapter 6

oly shit," said Ginny. I could have said it twice, since this was my second dead body today, which was a lot, even for me. I'd had some bad luck with this kind of thing in the past, but two in one day was an all-time high.

"I *really* wish I could call Curtis now," I said instead, as I checked for a pulse. Doing so was more a matter of form than anything else. She was obviously inanimate, and there was a dark hole in her left temple and a pool of blood under her head. She was, however, still warm.

Ginny dragged her eyes off the mesmerizing pull of death and looked sharply around, then whispered, "What if whoever killed her is still here?"

I shook my head but answered in a like voice, "I'm guessing those two in the motorcycle helmets we saw hustling out of here are responsible for this. Besides, would you kill somebody and then hang around? But look." I pointed to a gun that was lying loosely in the woman's hand. "It's supposed to look like a suicide."

Ginny glared at me with disdain. "Please," she said. "Did they really expect anyone to believe she blow-dried her hair and put on lip gloss before she shot herself?" She shook her head. "Fucking men."

I knew what she meant, but I said, "She's only been dead a few minutes." Thinking of how close we'd come to running directly into the killers made me dizzy. "Why are we here? Is this where we're supposed to deliver the money?"

For the first time, I noticed something in the woman's limp left hand; it was a curled piece of paper. Knowing that it was probably the wrong thing to do, I reached over and slid it out of her manicured fingers.

"What if they come back?" Ginny wanted to know.

"Would you?" I asked her, but before she had time to answer, we heard a sound coming from the living room.

Ginny's forefinger flew to her lips in a completely unnecessary directive of silence. My eyes scanned around the kitchen, looking for a place to hide as I slipped the paper into my pocket. To my right, a door led out to the patio that ran the length of the house. Other than what appeared to be a small pantry, which would be the first place someone would look, no other exit or possibility presented itself.

Moving to the kitchen door, I cracked it, looking out into the living room, then returned to Ginny. "It's the guy in the houndstooth jacket, the same man I saw at Evan's!" I hissed. "He's gone into the bedrooms on the other side."

At Evan's house, I had wondered why he didn't shoot me, and I'd landed at the shaky assumption that maybe he wouldn't kill a woman. Now I understood that if it *wasn't* the two Ducati riders but Houndstooth who was responsible for killing the lady of the house, that assumption was as dead wrong as the fresh corpse on the floor.

Ginny pushed me hard toward the exit to the patio, whispering in my ear. "Hurry." Once outside, I realized anyone in either the entrance hall or the kitchen would have an unobstructed view of our presence through the wall of glass. I couldn't see anywhere to hide, and I wondered what the hell Ginny was up to. She had Evan's gun in her hand, though I hadn't even seen her draw it.

But now, she tucked it quickly into her pants again and unbuckled her thick leather belt, which hung loosely at her hips. She threw it around me, pulling it up under my arms and fastening the buckle on the last hole, leaving about six inches of slack.

"What the fuck?" I breathed, but she shushed me and dragged me to the edge of the patio. I looked over the low stucco wall that served as a railing, and my head swam. Sixty feet below me, the foundation of the house hit a steep rocky hillside at just enough of an angle to break your fall before you continued to bounce down another thirty feet to the back of the neighbor's backyard wall. I looked up at Ginny; what was she thinking? Every couple of feet along the low wall, there were short polished log accents that ran all the way through the stucco and protruded out about twelve inches on both sides, adobe style. She was testing her weight on one of the pieces of wood that stuck out over the stomach-churning height. "You are not," was all I could manage to say.

Her response was a grim smile.

"You're out of your mind, I am not going over . . ."

But just at that moment, a door on the far side of the patio began to open and we both scrambled up onto the foot-wide lip of the wall, the ground wavering sickeningly far below. Ginny slipped her arm up to the elbow through the slack of the belt she'd fastened around me and pushed me off over the dizzying height.

The world swung as I started to fall, a liquid scream turned to frozen ice that crystallized and dissolved to dust in my throat without any utterance. I saw the distant rocky slope below, then the sky above me, and then, with a jerk, my downward free fall was arrested. I swung back and forth like a pendulum, the leather that was keeping me alive cutting cruelly into the skin under my arms. Terrified to look down, I looked up. Ginny had hooked her other arm around the jutting wooden accent and had linked her wrists. I could see from the strain on her face how much effort it was taking to hold my weight along with her own. It didn't take a stunt coordinator to see that she couldn't last long.

We hung there forever, listening to the footsteps of the man as he walked the length of the patio, hearing the sound of the kitchen door opening and closing. A second eternity passed as we gave the killer time to climb the stairs and, please God, exit the house.

Finally Ginny, through gritted teeth, said to me, "I'm going to swing you back up. Kick off the side."

I felt incapable of moving, paralyzed and mute.

"Do it now!" Ginny gasped.

So I did it. Forcing life into my frozen limbs, I kicked at the sheer face of the wall and started a swing. With two swinging pulls from Ginny, my feet hit the ledge and I scrabbled to get on top of it, holding on to Ginny's arm for all I was worth. Yanking her up and over the side, I collapsed with her onto the slate. I had just enough wits to look through the glass into the living room.

Houndstooth was standing on the top of the landing, looking right down at me through the glass. My arms shaking with a massive overdose of adrenaline, I retrieved the gun from my pocket and moved in front of Ginny, who, because she was lying facedown and breathing hard, had not seen him.

I tried to steady myself, to hold the gun so that the point of it was honed in on him. My vision was clouded by sweat and the tint of the glass. I squeezed my eyes shut for a second to try to clear them. Somewhere, distantly, I heard the sound of sirens.

Blinking furiously to clear the fog from my vision, I searched for Houndstooth down the wavering sights, trying to get a bead on him.

But apparently he had heard the sirens as well, because all I caught was a flash of houndstooth check as he disappeared out the door.

Chapter

7

Exhausted, I had just let my arm drop to the ground and flopped limply down on my back next to Ginny when I heard sirens draw up in front of the house.

Before we'd even had time to sufficiently catch our breath, the front door to the house burst open again, and this time it was Curtis I saw through the glass.

Ginny sat up roughly and said to me, "What now?"

"It's okay," I assured her as I patted her arm, which was still trembling. "It's your boyfriend."

"Oh," said Ginny. "Good." She slipped back down again and lay there like she didn't have any intention of altering that position for a good long while.

I, on the other hand, put some effort into standing to try to greet Curtis with a semblance of respect—which I felt he deserved, given my covert behavior without a suitable explanation. My brain seemed to remain flat on its back, though; I couldn't make it sit up straight and pay attention, sort out what the hell Curtis was doing there. Not that I wasn't happy to see him. I figured it wouldn't be too wild a stab to assume he wouldn't be overly delighted with me or Ginny, and I was surprised to find that I was only right on one count.

Ginny raised her head as he came through the door; he'd merely glanced at the body in the kitchen on his way to us. "You're late," she said to him.

"Obviously," was his curt reply. "You two okay?"

"Fine," Ginny said, but the arm she waved as she said it was rubbed raw on the inside, the skin scratched and bleeding from her bicep to her wrist.

"What the . . . ?" Squatting down next to us, Curtis reached out and took Ginny's wrist gently, examining the damage on the inside of her arm.

"We needed a place to hide," Ginny said, as though that explained everything.

I told Curtis quickly how we had hidden from the man in the living room by dangling off the equivalent of a six-story drop. He stood and leaned out over the edge, gazing down at the fatal distance. "And that was your best option?" he asked wryly, but he looked at Ginny, impressed.

"Best I could do with two seconds' notice," she said, as though if she'd had three, she could have done something much more remarkable.

Curtis helped her up. "I will give you a ten for style. But a little advice?"

"Very generous of you," Ginny responded. "I'm all ears."

"Next time pick the gun over gravity; shooters sometimes miss, the ground never does."

The casualness of their tone and demeanor would have led any bystander to think they were talking about an afternoon at the botanical gardens, but that's how they were. I gave them both a ten in cool.

Two uniformed officers had followed Curtis in and stopped

by the body in the kitchen; one of them now called from the doorway, "Everything all right out there?"

Curtis shifted his attention easily. "Yeah, call for forensics and get me an ambulance."

Ginny protested, but Curtis insisted that they at least look at her arm. Both of them agreed, very nonchalantly as usual, that the EMTs would wrap her arm but then she would go home instead of to the hospital. As relieved as I was to see Curtis, the thought that Evan wasn't free to come to my rescue felt like my own fresh abrasion.

"I don't understand, how did you know we were here?" I asked Curtis.

He turned his gaze to me, and the warmth that was in it for Ginny died away when he regarded me. He didn't have to say a word, but I knew that he was thinking that I had endangered Ginny's life as well as my own. It was a little unfair, but I made no comment.

"Because," he said harshly, "I put a man outside your house and he followed you here, and then he called me. If *you* had called me first, maybe I could have gotten here in time to do something about that." He jerked his head in the direction of the rapidly cooling body on the kitchen floor. His eyes sparked with anger. "I knew you had some kind of information you weren't telling me this morning, so I asked Ginny to keep me updated. Which," he added with a reproachful look at her, "she seems to have ignored." I opened my mouth to protest, but he pressed on. "Now, I'm gonna go clean up this mess. You two are going to wait for the ambulance in the driveway and then go home, and you're going to wait there until I join you. Why don't you spend your time remembering every single detail of what's gone on and be ready to tell me everything *without leaving anything out* when I get there." Ginny and I exchanged a look; "everything" included his own death threat. His voice was contained, but the anger underneath the words was powerful and frightening. "And just maybe, I can save *my* best friend's life." He turned his back on me and walked briskly away.

I was aware that Ginny was staring at Curtis through the glass as he stooped over the body of the girl. She looked up at me, obviously torn. "I guess it's only fair; he should know."

Of course, she was right. We'd tell him. But was it right for me to ask her to jeopardize his life to try to get Evan back? The reality of my selfishness of involving either of them made me feel harshly uncomfortable. I shoved my hands into my pockets sulkily, and my fingers touched the piece of paper I'd taken from the dead woman's hand.

Slowly, I pulled it out and unrolled it.

It read, "Look familiar?"

Chapter 8

When he saw the image of himself as a target displayed on my computer screen, Curtis's face hardened and some of his ruddy color drained away, as though he'd been suddenly frozen and covered with frost. But he showed very little emotion other than the fact that his attitude toward me softened considerably.

"So," Ginny said, the lightness of her touch on his arm betraying the firmness in her voice, "you'll let somebody else work on this, right?"

The thought of not having Curtis's help opened a trapdoor in me, and all my courage dumped out. I couldn't stop myself from exclaiming, "Oh, Curtis, please, you can't leave Evan out there! You're the only one he trusts!"

"How can you be so selfish?" Ginny spun on me, and I reeled back from the strength and the truth of her accusation. "You want him to walk right in front of a bullet? What good will that do Evan?"

"Shhh." Curtis quieted her softly, then looked down at the

bloodstained swatch of fabric in his hand, which I'd placed in a plastic bag, the way I'd seen forensics do it.

"No. I won't stop trying to find these bastards." When Ginny began to object, he went on determinedly. "As his partner, and his friend, it wouldn't be realistic or possible for me not to be looking for him. But it might be smart if it didn't seem that I was getting any help from you."

I avoided Ginny's glare and asked, "What about you showing up at the Hollywood house? Do you think they'll assume I told you?"

Curtis crinkled the plastic in his fingers. "I would."

Ginny shifted uncomfortably, her arms crossed over her chest. I could tell from her tone that she was trying to be helpful in spite of her indignant fury. "Well, maybe they don't know you were there."

Curtis made no response to that. Instead he said, "Now, I've got some information for you about the two murders." He closed the offensive email and we all sat down, Ginny moving deliberately away from me. My heart sank.

"First off, the Russian turned out to be a guy named Manouk Kavukchyan. Seems to be his first foray into kidnapping, but he did time for embezzling and money laundering. Not a major player, but connected to some very badly wanted ringleaders. We're checking ballistics to see if the gun we found, which *is* Evan's, killed him. Next, the girl. Her name was Josie Banks. She looks clean. She recently inherited a big chunk of money from a remote relative and quit her job. The gun that killed her had no serial number."

"How much money?" I asked, but I knew from the house that it must be in the millions.

"Looks like several million."

Ginny whistled. "Thank you, third cousin Fred, twice removed. The house must have cost her at least two."

I did the math quickly in my head. "If she got three to four million and she invested intelligently, she could live off the balance pretty sweetly, especially if she paid for the house outright."

Curtis looked impatient, so I quickly made my point. "I mean, it seems strange that she would inherit all that money, start a new life, and *then* kill herself. Doesn't it?"

But Curtis didn't seem to care. "Fascinating as I'm sure her financial situation is, her murder falls under the Hollywood division; it's *technically* not my case. So what I'm interested in is this—why the fuck did someone send *you* there?"

"Maybe," Ginny suggested, "to lure Callaway there and kill her."

"What for?" Curtis asked tartly, his curtness directed not so much at Ginny as at his own frustration. "They let her know they want three million dollars, and they haven't gotten it yet. What good is Callaway to them if she's dead?"

"Ah, yes. There is that," she concurred, sounding slightly put out that her suggestion wasn't a valid one. "But what about the note that she was holding? Did they mean for Callaway to get that?"

"And it was definitely Houndstooth I saw there," I told them. "You don't forget a face behind a gun. And he could have killed me earlier in the day," I reminded them both. The vicious visual of his gun point blank in my face superimposed itself over my current vision. I shook it off, remembering that Evan's gun in my hand had been equally in *his* face with my finger a hair's breath away from firing. "Or, at least," I added grimly, "he could have tried."

Looking down into my tea, I watched the fragments of loose leaves that had escaped the strainer swirl as though I could see not the future but the present in the dregs of my cup. "Isn't it obvious why they sent me there?" I asked.

Curtis squinted his gray eyes at me and waited.

"The note said it. 'Look familiar?' I don't know why they

would have killed *her*, or what her involvement is, if any. But did you notice how she looked?"

"Dead?" asked Ginny, whose sense of humor sometimes had the gentleness of acetone nail-polish remover.

"Blond," I answered. "Pretty, obviously moneyed." I stopped listing similarities out of a false sense of humility, but my reasoning was understood.

Curtis concurred. "I spotted the similarities too. But I didn't think of it that way." He stood and walked to the French doors and back. Realizing he was troubled, I stayed silent.

Ginny, of course, had no such restraint. She fixed me with a doubting gaze, in which I thought I saw the beginnings of a peaceful settlement, and said, "So you're saying that they killed this poor Josie chick because she was *similar* to you?"

"First of all," Curtis interrupted, "we haven't ruled out suicide."

"Yeah," Ginny said. "First thing I do when I'm so depressed I'm contemplating suicide is make absolutely sure my hair looks perfect."

"It's my job to consider it," Curtis said with a warning note.

"I know," Ginny cajoled. "But then, what's with the note? What kind of suicide note would that be?"

"Suicidal people aren't thinking rationally," Curtis pointed out.

Ginny snorted lightly and went on. "Let's assume that the people who have Evan *did* kill this Josie to prove they would kill Callaway." She turned to me. "That's what you're saying, right?"

"And to scare me into doing whatever they want. Does that seem crazy?" I asked her.

"Fuck no," she said. "In fact, it's standard plot development in any big Hollywood script. The bad guy has to kill someone similar to the heroine to make it clear to the audience that he can *and will* do it, proving that she's in legitimate danger." She mused for a moment. "Of course, in that case, the heroine doesn't have to know. It's more for the benefit and knowledge of the audience."

Curtis nodded thoughtfully.

"And if it *isn't* suicide," Ginny said with a sarcastic lilt, "was it the guy in the houndstooth jacket who killed her, or the two guys on the motorcycle?"

"Did you find anything else at the house?" I asked.

Curtis shook his head. "Nothing. The place was sparkling clean, even the trash cans were empty. We found a wrapper from a mini-digital videotape in one, and that's about it. So unless somebody was planning on videotaping . . ." Curtis's voice trailed off, and his eyes went distant. He looked at Ginny. "Script, heroine," he muttered, as though he was replaying what she had said.

We waited, and then Curtis asked me, "You said that one of the two motorcycle riders was carrying something in his hand, and that he put it in his pocket when they got on the bike, right?"

"Yeah."

"How big?"

"Uhm," I muttered as I looked at Ginny. "I couldn't see very well, they weren't close, but it fit in one hand, fairly small. We thought it must have been a gun, right?" As soon as I made the suggestion I realized that the gun that had killed Josie Banks had been left in her hand.

Curtis leaned forward and pinned me to the sofa with his eyes. "Think—could it have been a digital video camera? One of the little ones?"

I saw it again, the swiping movement from thigh to jacket pocket. "Yes. It could have, but I can't be sure."

"All right. It makes sense that they killed the woman and then sent Callaway there as a warning to make sure that she does whatever they ask her to do, but there's another level to this, another possibility. Which means . . ."

He rose. After kissing Ginny in a sexy, openmouthed, but preoccupied way, he said, "I'd better get out of here. I need to go to work." There was a light in his eye that hadn't been there a moment before.

"Which means *what*?" asked Ginny.

He looked at us curiously, as though hesitant to share his theory. "Maybe nothing," he said slowly. "But if you wanted to force someone to do something for you, what better way to blackmail them into doing it than having a video of them committing another crime?"

Ginny and I exchanged looks; she appeared to be as confused as I felt. "But who else would they want to involve in this?" she asked. "And why?"

Curtis's eyes swiveled to me, and his expression was deep and unreadable. "That's what I need to find out," he said tensely.

"What about the money?" I asked. "Should I put it together?"

Curtis looked thoughtful. "It's only fifty-fifty you'll get him back if you pay it," he said factually, as though staying businesslike would keep us both from going insane.

I tried to smile. "Two to one, not bad odds at the track."

"Then get it ready. You might be asked to show it at some point, and it would be best to have it ready."

"I'll call Kelly, but I'm going to have to let her in on this and have an armored truck company transport the money. The bank's not going to just let me stuff it in a duffel bag like in the movies."

Curtis nodded again. "I'm guessing you'll get the next directive very soon.

"Jesus God, I hope so," I murmured, desperate for it.

"But it won't come when I'm here," Curtis said. "So keep your email on, and let me know—from you"—he reprimanded us, pointing a finger at Ginny—"when it happens. We'll figure out where to go from there."

"I'll walk you out," I said to him, and the three of us rose and walked quietly to the entrance hall.

I opened the front door, thanked Curtis, and hung back to give him a moment with Ginny, but I couldn't resist watching them hug tightly and move into a kiss. It made me ache for Evan, the Evan I thought I had had.

As I watched them, they pulled apart, and Ginny smiled sweetly at Curtis, then put her head on his shoulder in a hug.

Suddenly, she twisted her body and shoved Curtis to the ground, landing hard on top of him. A shard of marble in the archway around the door chipped off and flew toward me, stinging my cheek.

"What the fuck?" Curtis wheezed, the breath knocked out of him.

"Sniper, on the wall!" Ginny shouted. And in unison, both of them rolled into the safety of the house, Ginny reaching up to yank me back by the arm out of the line of fire.

In a single second, Curtis's gun was drawn and he was on one knee leaning to see around the doorway. He had his cell phone in the other hand, and he was calling for a black and white.

You never know where a cop is when you need one. I flew across the open doorway and hit the panic button on my alarm panel. The private security company guards were always in the neighborhood, quick to respond, and heavily armed.

"Get down!" Curtis snapped at me. I got behind the heavy oak door and pushed it closed. There were no more shots.

Ginny had crept to the window and was peeking cautiously over the ledge. "He's gone," she said. "And he'll be long gone before the cops get here." She forced a wink at Curtis. "Any *other* cops, I mean."

"Well, I think we can assume one thing," Curtis said, his breath coming heavily and, I noticed with concern, one hand on his chest, as though it pained him. "They know you talked to me." He looked at Ginny and smiled. "Nice move. Thanks, baby."

She answered flippantly, but the look in her eyes said that she felt the possibility of losing him as deeply as I felt the possibility of losing Evan. "Nothing you wouldn't do for me."

Curtis's face went dead serious, and he reached out a hand to take hers. "I hope to hell I never have to."

Chapter
9

Neither the police reinforcements nor the security company found anything except a few scuff marks on a ficus tree the sniper had climbed and used for cover.

"Well," Curtis said before he left, "these guys sure know how to make a dramatic point."

We'd decided it would be best if he stayed away, for his good as well as ours. Ginny would talk to him at regular intervals, keeping him updated on any new emails or communications. He had arranged to have my security company leave an armed guard in the driveway, but he'd also said he didn't think that there would be any more shooters in the neighborhood, something I thought he might have added to comfort himself as much as to reassure us.

The evening came on, and despite my extreme yearning for a missive or instructions from the kidnappers, none materialized. I felt suffocated by so many people hovering over me with concerned faces. Sabrina's would-be beau, Darrien, had reappeared, and she left him every five minutes to ask me if I needed something. Ginny knew enough to leave me alone, but even she found excuses to come into any room I was in, and her eyes would cut to me, filled with concern.

I'm not used to being around people all the time. As much as I appreciated everyone's concern, thirty-five years of practiced solitude made it very hard for me to play well with others.

And the more time that went by without details about the ransom demand, the further I felt Evan slipping away from me, and the antsier I got.

The combination of hovering and the crackling tension in my nervous system was making me squeamish. I needed to be alone and think about Evan, and even my roomy house made me feel claustrophobic. The nagging, brutal possibility that Evan wasn't what I thought forced me up and out into the garden, where I could breathe, think.

The moon was so bright I could see my shadow on the lower lawn, and I felt exposed as I moved through it to the tall sycamores at the edge of the property, which was surrounded by a ten-foot wall. I came to the orangery and opened the glass-and-wrought-iron door.

Inside the whimsical atrium, the tart smell of citrus fruit mingled with the rich, humid smell of earth. Fifty miniature lemon, orange, lime, and kumquat trees in giant red clay pots were positioned in groups and rows. Among them were white wrought-iron benches. I stopped and breathed in the scent of fertile things. This favorite place had a personality all its own, lush and earthy, but at the same time tart and alert.

The moonlight, strained by the branches of the sycamores and softened by the beveled-glass ceiling, was more comforting here. I walked to one of the benches, listening to the soft crunch of fine gravel beneath my feet, then settled into the plush cushions.

It was funny, I thought to myself, I almost never came down here. It seemed so far from the house, which of course it wasn't. I wondered what I was so busy doing that kept me from what I loved.

A sparkle on the edge of my vision caught my eye. I moved my left hand slowly, watching the yellow, heart-shaped diamond engagement ring that Evan had given me. The moonlight gave it a golden hue, as liquid as honey.

Why would he ask me to marry him if he was seeing someone else? It just didn't fit. *Who is B.?* For that matter, who was Evan? Did I really know? I'd fallen in love with him so quickly. High above my head, on the roof of the glass house, the delicate spray of the irrigation came on, and the moonlight streaming through the clear ceiling turned to effervescent beams of silver. Though it was usually balmy inside the elegant greenhouse, the mist felt reviving and cool. I shivered as the spray, fine as dust in the night air, touched my bare shoulders. Looking up into the gauzy, dancing moisture, I realized that I had to know for sure, one way or the other. Except for my father, I'd felt alone most of my life, and when he'd left me, I'd resigned myself to being all right with that, whether I really was or not.

Evan had changed that. The cool sting of mist on my skin drew me into a memory, a time when, with our bodies locked together, I had felt connected to him. We had gone for a midnight swim and I'd climbed out to sit at the water's edge. The night air had had just enough of a chill to be invigorating. I'd wrapped myself in a thick robe and admired Evan's strong body slicing through the water as he swam the length of the pool toward me. The underwater lights had played impressionistic tricks with his beauty, and I'd lain back on the slate at the edge of the pool and closed my eyes.

A trickle of water on my foot had alerted me to his hand hovering above it. I'd smiled as his fingers trailed across the top of my shin, up my thigh, slowly parting the plush terry-cloth robe I'd worn. Each new section of my skin had felt the rush of chill air and the exploration of his skillful hands. I had reveled in the slow progress, shivering slightly until finally I'd worn nothing but the cool night air. Still I'd kept my eyes closed, my breath coming in excited little gasps with each touch.

Then I had heard him pull his body out of the water and felt the warmth of it, mixed with the contrast of the cold water dripping from him as he'd lowered himself against me, into me, and I'd pressed back up against him. We had moved, with the heat increasing, until I'd been lost in him. And then he had spoken. "Open your eyes," he had whispered huskily. "Look at me."

And I had, I had looked into his eyes and seen lust and love and a man who hid nothing from me. I had come looking into those eyes, orgasmed with my eyes open, seeing exactly what I had always wanted.

A man who hid nothing from me, that's what I'd thought.

Without looking down, I slipped the ring off my finger and put it in my pocket. When I was sure, I'd put it on again, or— the thought chilled me—I'd give it back.

The soft hiss of the misters and the luminous, eerie glow of the moonlight on the veil of water suited my mood so well that I sat perfectly still and alone, feeling that I would stay, wallowing in a bittersweet melancholy, forever.

And then, without warning or overture, the moment was shattered by a thunderous crash.

Chapter

10

One of the eight-foot panels of beveled glass that made up the roof of the orangery had shattered. Shards, some as big and deadly as the jagged weapons of mythical giants, lay broken on the white gravel.

The dangerous implosion had occurred at the far end of the glass house, but I sat upright, rigid, wondering what the hell had happened. If it was an earthquake, this was the very last place I wanted to be.

But the earth did not, as they say, move. The mist that had gathered on my skin, as thin as the lightest sheen of sweat, seemed to have turned to ice. I was sure it would crack and cut me if I moved. I strained to listen, trying to discern any disturbance that would have caused the glass to splinter and disintegrate like that. But all I could hear was the light wind in the sycamore branches above the new opening in the roof, and the more distant sound of the cascading fountain on the upper lawn.

Then another sound came to my pounding ears. Voices were calling out desperately. I stood and moved to the door. As I stepped out onto the lawn I was almost run down by a man moving so fast toward me that I only saw him as a dark shadow. I stifled a scream as he caught me by the shoulders, gripping hard.

"It's okay, Callaway, it's me." Darrien's voice washed over me and I sank down onto the soft grass below the trees. "Are you all right? What was that crash?" he asked. Beyond him I could see a second figure in the moonlight, coming down the expanse of marble stairs from the upper lawn and heading toward us in a full-out run.

"Callaway!" came the drawn-out wailing of my sister, Sabrina. She cleared the last forty yards separating the base of the stairs from the orangery in impressive time, considering she was no athlete.

"Oh my God, Cally. What happened?" She threw herself down next to me and nearly knocked what little wind I had left out of me.

"One of the panels broke, smashed. I don't know why." I looked up at Darrien, instinctively trusting him to investigate the mysterious situation. I couldn't make out his expression in the shadows of the trees, but I saw his head nod. Pulling out a gun that I had no idea he carried in his perfectly fitted, slim suit, he opened the door and went in, disappearing among the deep black-green of the citrus trees at night.

"Darrien and I were on my balcony, and we saw you walking across the yard. He thought we should give you your privacy but keep an ear out. So we came outside and sat by the fountain and we were just, uh, sitting there, uh, talking, when we heard the crash." I couldn't see her, but I would have bet a million bucks that she was blushing; "just talking," my ass. Before I could call her on it, she said, all in a rush, "Oh my God! I was so scared I just about jumped right out of my bloomers!"

I gave her a stern look, lost in the shadowy gloom, of course. "Where do you get these expressions from?" I asked her. "You sound like a bumpkin."

"That's because I *am* a bumpkin," she retorted hotly. "You keep on acting like that's a bad thing, but with all the trouble you and your city friends get into, I'm not so sure."

"Point taken," I said. Sabrina opened her mouth to begin a new onslaught of concern calicoed, no doubt, with country expletives, but I cut her off. Darrien was coming back toward us, the gravel crunching only slightly beneath his light footfall. *He moves almost as gracefully as Korosu*, I thought to myself, but when I thought of Korosu, I thought of one hundred percent man, the only one I had ever met besides Evan, and Darrien was still too young to hold that percentage.

The door opened and he came quickly to us.

In his hand was a brick, and tied onto the brick with what looked like kitchen twine was, I desperately hoped, the instructions to switch Evan for the money that I'd been waiting for.

By the time we got back up to the upper lawn, Ginny was outside looking for me. I spotted Joseph, the under-butler, who was headed to his apartment above the garages. I told him to let the gardeners know that the orangery was missing part of its roof. Ginny wanted to call Curtis and have him send a car to look for whoever it was who'd thrown the brick, but I shook my head.

"Pointless," I told her, and Darrien nodded in agreement as we passed through the door into the breakfast room. The windows facing the back garden were vintage Tiffany's in a wisteria garden theme, and I was grateful that the brick hadn't destroyed one of those irreplaceable panels.

"First of all, everything we've gotten, including a bullet meant for Curtis, has been untraceable, and second, nobody was going to heave a brick from my neighbor's yard and then sit down in one of their lounge chairs and wait for me to come over and ask them why."

"At least you could call them and ask if they saw anything," Sabrina suggested impatiently, like I should hurry up and do it.

I looked at her; she was about to score another point off me in the city-versus-country competition open to all half sisters whose date of original acquaintance had not yet passed its second anniversary. "I don't exactly know their number," I said.

"Well, look it up!" she insisted. "I'll get your phone book."

"That might be tough," I said, "seeing how I don't know their name."

She stared at me. "They are your neighbors," she enunciated as well as her two-syllables-to-every-one drawl would allow. Her voice rose to a squeal during the next question. "And you don't even know *their name*?"

Shrugging, I offered, "I think I saw a woman drive out of the gate once. That's about as close as anyone comes to a block party in this neighborhood."

"Unbelievable." Sabrina shook her head, disgusted. "In Louisiana, when somebody new moved into the house next door, you fixed them up a basket with some flowers and a loaf of something you just baked, took it over, and said, 'Hey neighbor!' And if they didn't stop what they were doing, cut you a slice, and brew up some coffee right then and there, you *knew*."

I took the bait. "Knew what?"

"That they were from out of state!"

Ginny was watching her, a pained expression on her face. "You, on the other hand, are not *just* from out of state," she said to Sabrina, "you dropped out of a time warp." She looked at me. "Loaf of something you just baked? In Los Angeles?" Ginny shook her head again. "Could be laced with anything. I wouldn't eat it, would you?"

"Probably not," I said, and then tried to get us back on track. "But the point is that whoever threw this brick is long gone." It felt like a bomb in my hand, yet I was anxious to see what message it sent.

We had passed into the kitchen again, and I drew a long, sharp knife out of the rack and impatiently sliced the kitchen string off the brick, freeing the paper around it.

It was a brochure, and across the top was printed "Fabulous Del Mar Racetrack." It folded out to show a large photo with racing horses in the foreground and the entire grandstand behind.

I flipped it. On the back was the race schedule. One of the dates was circled. Handwritten in pen were the words "Red hair, green dress."

"You don't think . . ." I let my voice trail off, remembering the lovely girl dead on her beautiful ceramic tile kitchen floor, her light blond hair stained with her own blood. I tried, mentally, to swipe the image away, but the picture was like a permanent stain; all I managed to do was smear the bloody image. "Why are they doing this? They need to tell me what they want me to do to make the damn switch! What's the point of killing someone else to make me do it if I don't fucking know what *it* is!" I was pissed. Nothing makes me as furious as feeling helpless and ineffectual. I threw the brochure onto the kitchen table as though it were a week-old fish, slimy to the touch.

"No," Ginny said, as if saying it could make another woman safe from any such fate. "If you're right, and that dead girl Josie *was* a warning, what would be the point of making the point twice?"

Darrien asked, "May I see the writing?"

I nodded, and he picked up the brochure and studied it, then turned it over again and held the pamphlet closer to his face, leaning under the lights suspended over the counter. "There's a little hand-drawn arrow here, on the picture side." He pointed to what looked like an exclusive area down front in the grandstand.

"Where?" I asked.

"It's one of the owners' boxes," he said as he gave the card back. "It's a restricted area. Nobody gets in but the owners."

"What's the date that's circled?" Ginny asked.

He repeated it, and while Ginny looked like she was sorting it out, Sabrina said, "That's tomorrow."

"Yes. Tomorrow," I spat out. "How am I going to get into the owners' boxes by tomorrow? You have to a) buy a horse, and b) buy a box for the entire season. This is midseason; they must all be taken by now. What am I supposed to do, get myself a donkey and then ask somebody to skooch over?" I was so angry at myself for not being able to effectively deal with the situation that I wanted to lash out, to hit something so hard it hurt me. Evan was in danger, and the more time that went by, the more unlikely it would be that we'd get him back unharmed.

Darrien smiled understandingly at me. "It would hardly be realistic to think that even if you could buy a horse that quickly, you could get it into one of the races taking place tomorrow night. I'm guessing that whoever sent you this assumes that with your money and business connections you will know someone who has access to the owners' boxes."

I wracked my brain. I must know someone! But no one came to mind. I socialized with people who golfed and played tennis. In the back of my mind, I had the nagging sense that someone I knew had mentioned going there, but I couldn't pull up a name.

"I don't know of anyone offhand," I groaned, frustrated.

"Yes, you do," Darrien said softly.

Ginny gave him her look that was usually reserved for people who dared to sass her or talk down to her. "Since when did you get a hold of her personal address book?"

"Not only do you know someone who has a horse," he continued with a small bow in Ginny's direction to acknowledge her far more intimate connection to me, "but that horse is racing tomorrow night." Darrien waited for it to dawn on me.

"Of course," I said, realizing whom he was talking about. "It makes perfect sense." And it did; owning a horse was just the sort of classy, expensive, and very entertaining thing he would do for his many international business associates. He did much more to entertain those ultrawealthy connections in traditional Japanese style at his perfect little boutique hotel downtown in Little Tokyo, but right now I didn't care about that.

"Can you call him, please?" I asked politely. "I don't think I kept his number." Throwing away his personal phone numbers had been a precaution I had taken when I'd committed to marrying Evan. The man was a serious temptation and I had an addictive personality, drugs and passion being on the top of my abusive-substances-of-choice list. I was prone to succumb to those and I knew it, and Ginny knew it too.

She narrowed her eyes at me. "Call whom?" she asked in a growl.

I looked into Darrien's eyes to avoid Ginny's. "Korosu, of course."

Chapter
11

It hadn't been easy to pretend to someone as smart and savvy as Korosu that I just needed an escort to the racetrack when I called to ask him to take me.

We had decided to tell anyone who asked that Evan was out of town for an indefinite number of days working on a case. Curtis sent a message via Ginny: "I'll be visibly busy elsewhere, but there will be an undercover officer keeping an eye out at the track. Good luck, keep your eyes peeled, and don't leave Korosu or his bodyguard for a minute."

I had studied the brochure and its tiny arrow late into the night, passing out around 3:00 a.m. with it still in my hand. What was I supposed to do? Go to that box? Meet someone there?

I had kept my cell phone with me, hoping desperately that Evan would call me. When I finally fell asleep I dreamed that he did call to tell me that he'd just been busy with work, that he'd be home soon, then he was there in the room with me, kissing my brow and telling me it was all right, but a woman standing behind him kept calling his name, and he turned around to smile at her, while pretending to me that she wasn't there.

But when Deirdre came and pulled the curtains back to let in the daylight in the middle of the morning, the phone still hadn't rung.

The day dragged interminably on. Darrien was to pick me up around four and take me to meet Korosu. Darrien had promised not to tell Korosu anything about Evan's disappearance and the resulting riptide, and it was reassuring for me to have Darrien both in the know and with me. About lunchtime, I found myself looking through my extensive closet wondering what outfit would be appropriate to wear to a racetrack when I was going with a man I was wildly attracted to but was diligently resisting, who was unwittingly trying to help me get my fiancé back from kidnappers, when Deirdre came into the room.

"Mr. Wayne Sebert is waiting for you in the library," she informed me.

That pepped things up a bit. "Did he look hopeful?" I asked her as I tossed a slinky red silk dress I'd been holding onto the bed and started for the door.

She picked up the Valentino cocktail dress and hung it carefully on a hook on the back of the closet door, smoothing out an imaginary offensive wrinkle. In the two years after my father's death and before I'd met Evan, she had stood by and guided me, without criticism, as I had struggled, trying to fill the loss of my father with man after inappropriate man. Every so often a raised eyebrow or a pointed look had steered me away from turning to my drug addiction, wallowing in self-pity, or committing an inappropriate fashion offense. She began to select a few other items, some slim black pants and a beaded sweater. "I believe this might be better for an outing to the racetrack with a friend; it could be cool in the evening." Her face revealed only a flicker of disapproval as she put away the inappropriately sexy selection.

Only then did she answer my query. "Mr. Sebert seems to be in a similar emotional state to that on each of his previous visits."

"Nervous to the point of collapse?" I asked her.

"Not an imprecise description," she said. "Although perhaps I would have chosen to define it as awkwardly self-conscious."

I hit the doorway and turned back. "Deirdre," I called out. She turned. "Yes, ma'am?"

"Thanks for taking care of . . ." I paused, for I had intended to say *me*, but it was too intimate. ". . . of everything for me."

"I'm glad to help," she responded with a sad smile. And then she added, "I'm sure Detective Paley will be back safely, very soon. He has the greatest confidence in Detective Curtis." She dropped her voice and added, "And so do I."

With a nod of thanks, I flew down the stairs before I succumbed to the tears that were threatening to fall.

Wayne was standing awkwardly in the middle of the library, though there were certainly ample places to sit. He looked out of place among the books, and I wondered fleetingly if this man who could track a single faulty piece of software would be at a loss if I asked him to find me a book using the Dewey decimal system.

"Good morning, Wayne. Have you found out anything?"

He pulled a crumpled piece of paper from his pocket and smoothed it out self-consciously before holding it out to me. He made eye contact only in a passing flicker, but in that transitory glimpse, I saw pride.

"I got the send locations from both B. and the other one, based on the email addresses. I also looked them up for you on MapQuest. The one from B. was sent from a Kinko's in an office building downtown, near Seventh and Figueroa."

"Oh," I responded. Not much help there. That address was the busiest business section of downtown. Both my corporate lawyers and my estate attorneys had offices on Seventh. So did two of my investment offices.

"But the second one is on Abbott Road, in Venice Beach." There was a map with printed directions beneath it. I looked up to Wayne, whose eyes kept on flicking past mine in that nervous-to-land-on-anything way, and I read the eagerness there. "It's a condo," he added.

"Wayne," I said with a broad smile and a hint of what he could interpret as attraction to his superior intellect, "you rock."

Beneath his fidgeting and twitching, he looked at first deeply pleased, then quickly mortified. "It's actually a condo *complex*. Twelve units."

"Well," I said, scraping my hopes up off the floor, "it might help."

I found Sabrina by the pool; she was wearing the two-piece bathing suit I'd talked her into buying, and I wondered, as I always did when I saw her naked or partially so, how any woman could have been so well endowed and not looked fat. She defied every high-fashion image of a skinny sexy woman by looking like a real one. God bless her.

When she saw me, she jumped up and blurted out, "What? Have you heard anything?"

I shook my head and sat down on the foot of her chaise, indicating that she should get comfortable. "No, nothing more from Evan or his . . . whoever took him." My panic took on a distinct demonic form and began to expand in my chest. With the greatest of effort I forced it back down to a manageable size. "But I need a favor."

"Anything, absolutely anything. I've just got to do something to help or I'll just die."

I smiled at her. "Don't do that," I said. "But listen, Wayne found out the address where the kidnappers' email was sent from. I know they have my email address, and they could be monitoring my messages. And Curtis told me not to call him. I need you to go to that internet café in the Village and forward this information to Curtis. Can you do that?"

She was looking at the paper. "I can do better than that," she said, looking up, and I was surprised that her eyes, such a cool blue color, could flash so hotly. "I can go to this place and ask them if they know who sent it!"

"No, ma'am," I said, snatching the paper back. Sabrina had a little history of "helping" me too much. Her efforts had caused trouble, including revealing a witness's whereabouts—just because she'd missed her and had wanted to visit. That kind of assistance could be fatal now. "You have to promise me, Sabrina"—I fixed her with my green eyes, a far more suitable color for flashing anger—"that you won't do anything more than what I ask you to do. Evan's life, and maybe other people's too, is at stake here. This is no time for amateurs." Even as I said it, my face flushed with the embarrassing memory of my sojourn in the Hollywood Hills.

"Okay." She backed off. "I promise."

"Good. Thank you. I need you to bring me any reply you get from Curtis, which might take a little while. Can you do that?"

She rolled her eyes. "Uh, duh."

I shook my head. "I forget how young you are."

"I'm nineteen! I've got friends my age who are married with kids back in Louisiana!"

"Probably some with grandchildren," I couldn't stop myself from saying.

It was Sabrina who passed the judgment. "I think they're crazy, of course, I can't imagine having a kid. 'Course when I lived there, getting married and having a nice little house seemed like the biggest thing you could do." She looked out over the pool and then back at me, the light off the water playing in her magnificent eyes. "But all that's different now that I've seen a little bit of the world. I want more." She mused for a minute, and I thought that she was referring to my money and success. But as always, she surprised and delighted me and, it must be admitted, made me look hard at myself. "There's so many people who need help, and I want to find a way to make a difference . . . to . . ." I watched her search for the phrase, one I'm sure she'd heard recently. "To 'be of service.'" She looked proud.

I nodded. "You will," I said, and I'd never spoken two words with so much confidence.

"But right now," Sabrina said, standing and grabbing her light robe with determination, "I've got something else to do."

"You go girl," I told her, offering the printout once again. "I'm counting on you."

And it was funny; for the first time since she'd been with me, I knew I could. I hadn't known Sabrina as a child, but she'd been so childlike when I'd met her at eighteen that I'd learned to treat her as the innocent she was. But now, with a swimming twinge in my stomach, I realized my baby sister was growing up. The proprietary sense of pride was accompanied with some other, less likable, feeling.

I loved her, and that made me vulnerable.

"Well," came Ginny's voice behind me, "are we going, or what?" I turned in surprise and saw her and Wayne standing behind me. His eyes bobbed over Sabrina's body like a rubber duck in a wave pool.

"Going where?" I asked.

She sighed and gestured to Wayne. "To find the SOB that sent the email, of course."

Sabrina pitched in. "I told her we should!"

"No!" I insisted, fighting back my own personal Rambo impulses. "I'm giving the address to Curtis, and he can check it out *discreetly*. I'm not putting you all in danger. Besides, I've got to be here to be picked up by Darrien at four; it's almost two now, and this complex is all the way down in Venice Beach. I just don't think we could make it in time."

My stuntwoman of a best friend made a sniffing sound and smiled wickedly at me.

Oh yeah, we could make it.

"But they know me," I protested lamely. I was being over-powered by the desire to take action, to do something; I was weakening.

"That's why I have to go!" Sabrina insisted.

"I can help too," Wayne said quickly. When we all looked at him, he dropped his eyes and muttered, "I mean, you might have technical questions, or I could, I don't know, something." His glance again went to Sabrina, who beamed at him. Great, now we'd never get rid of the poor guy.

But I tried one more time. "What are you going to do, Sabrina, go ring the bell and ask somebody, 'Hi, are you a kid-napper?' "

"Some *people*, plural," Wayne corrected. "Everyone in the complex basically has the same address." He kept his head down and watched his sneaker intently as he traced the toe of it along the grout around the slate.

"Of course not!" Sabrina said as contemptuously as her ea-gerness would allow, surprising the hell out of me. "My friend Bethy and I used to do this all the time when we went into Shreveport. We'd dare each other to go ring people's doorbells and tell some crazy story, like we used to live in this house, or that we lost our cat and someone said they had it. Crazy stuff like that."

"Cool." From the drugged look on Wayne's face, I'm not sure he'd heard a word she'd said, but he seemed immersed in the pleasure of just listening to her.

"Are you sure you're my sister?" I asked Sabrina. But the sug-gestion wasn't a bad one and better her than me, as the kidnap-pers obviously knew who both Ginny and I were since our visit to Hollywood Hills. "Okay," I finally consented.

"Let's go," barked Ginny, who was already headed back to the house. "Get some clothes on," she threw over her shoulder to Sabrina, "or computer boy won't be able to focus."

The four of us piled into my SUV and headed south toward Venice Beach. Traffic was heavy, but with Ginny at the wheel, we arrived in front of the complex within half an hour. It was a U-shaped affair, with a narrow garden walk down the middle.

"This is it," Wayne said from the backseat.

Sabrina nodded, a glint of daring in her eye. As she climbed out of the car, Ginny asked her, "What color is your cat?"

Sabrina turned without missing a beat, and her face went all sad and hopeful. "She's the most darling little tabby with white mittens, and she loves to play with balled-up paper. Her name is Miss Kitty, and I miss her so much." By the end of it I could swear I saw tears in her eyes. Then she smiled suddenly and asked, "How's that?"

"Really good," I said, impressed. "But how are you going to ask whether they sent me an email?"

"Just watch me."

So we watched as she made her way to the first door on the right. She rang the bell and waited. A heavyset woman in a bathrobe answered with her arms crossed belligerently in front of her.

From across the sidewalk and over the small, rectangular lawn, only the tones of Sabrina's voice carried, not the whole words. But within seconds the woman had uncrossed her arms and seemed to be comforting Sabrina. Finally, she shook her head with a sympathetic smile as Sabrina turned away and headed back to the car.

Sabrina climbed into the backseat and sat looking thoughtfully out at the apartment complex.

"Well, what did you say? What did she say?" I asked.

Sabrina sighed, then said, "She didn't send it. I told her that I got an email from my brother's girlfriend—who I never met—and that she was worried because she hadn't heard from him in weeks. I told her he left to go overseas and is under orders not to communicate his whereabouts with anyone and I was trying to locate his girlfriend to tell her why she wasn't hearing from him."

Sabrina stopped long enough to grab a tissue and blow her nose, draining the last effects of her dramatic interpretation from her nasal passages. "She told me that it *was* her email address, but when I told her your email address, she looked all glazed and told me she never sent anything there. And believe me. She was telling the truth."

From the seat next to her came a short, resigned sigh. "That's what I thought," said Wayne. "Wireless access cards." He nodded as though that explained everything.

Ginny's fingers went pale where she was gripping the wheel. "Let's pretend," she said with forced calm, "that I'm an idiot. What does that mean?"

"It means," Wayne began, "that that woman has an unsecured wireless network connection. And all someone had to do was pull up to the curb, the way we are right now, turn on their wireless computer, and search for a signal from someone else's wireless access card in the vicinity. Then, they just connect to it, and press send." He looked at each of us in turn. "I knew that was a possibility, but I was hoping maybe I was wrong."

"So what you're saying is"—I tried to stay calm—"whoever really sent it is completely untraceable."

Wayne looked a little sweaty and he was fidgeting. "Pretty much."

"Great," I said, suddenly too weary to sit up straight. "Let's go home."

As Ginny pulled the SUV out onto the street, I stared out the window, unable to muster the strength to face any of them. And then a thought came to me. Was it probable that whoever had sent the emails had driven to another part of town to send something anonymously? No, it was far more likely that they were nearby, and that was why they had connected from this particular location.

That meant that Evan could be here, somewhere close.

I sat up and looked around, my senses alerted to search for any signs that might point to him. But I wasn't particularly encouraged by what I saw: streets leading off into block after block of overbuilt neighborhoods with dozens of expensive houses on tiny plots of land. Property this close to the beach was outrageously valuable. Halfway down the block we passed a small side street, and the signs on both sides of it caught my eye. I read them with a sense of frustration and rage.

Dead End.

Chapter

12

I had assumed, mistakenly as so often happens, that we would be picking up Korosu downtown at his offices near Seventh and Figueroa, and then start the two-hour drive to Del Mar. But the driver turned south on the 405, bypassing downtown.

"Where is he?" I asked from the backseat. Darrien sat next to the driver in the front of the Mercedes limousine.

"Korosu-san is meeting a shipment at the pier. He asked us to join him there. From San Pedro it's not far to Del Mar."

Nodding, I settled back. It was a hot afternoon, and I had expected a long ride to Del Mar, which was just above San Diego, but I had thought Korosu would be with me. I felt grateful for the reprieve. It wouldn't have been easy to act as though everything was perfectly fine. I flipped on the TV. Nothing could hold my nervous attention, so I contented myself with looking out the window, wondering what I would feel when I saw the man again.

• • •

It was muggy on the pier, and the late afternoon sunlight shone thickly through the pungent air, which smelled of asphalt, shellfish, and diesel fuel in equal parts.

We pulled right through security and up to the unloading area of a gigantic freighter. Surreptitiously, I watched for Korosu, conscious of my appearance, my racing heart, my uncharacteristic lack of confidence, but I didn't see him anywhere. Darrien made a quick call on his cell phone and spoke a few words in Japanese before turning to me.

"He'll be right down," he said to me. "He is very sorry to keep you waiting."

"Oh, that's okay," I responded lamely, then wondered what he meant by "He'll be right down."

"Would you like to get out of the car?"

"That'd be great." I reached for the handle of the door, but before I could pull it, the driver had leaped out and performed the simple service for me. He stood respectfully while I emerged, blinking into the light unfiltered by the dark tint of the car windows.

Darrien had donned sunglasses, and I fished mine out of my bag and put them on, relieving my aching irises. But when I followed his gaze to the top of the freighter that towered above us, the sun was so bright behind it that I still had to shade my eyes with my hand.

On the deck, a huge crate was being unloaded. One of the giant sliding cranes was hooking its claw onto the top of it, and it was lifted up and then swung out over the side of the ship. Next to it stood several figures. It was easy to distinguish Korosu among the stocky, hardhat-clad dockworkers.

He was watching me. I felt it almost before I spotted him. Even from that distance, I could feel the intensity of his eyes and the power of his presence.

The crane began lowering the container, and as it came level with the ship, Korosu disappeared from my view, backing away from the edge.

Then, suddenly, his figure, in one long, seemingly easy stride, passed through eight feet of open air and landed with a light thud on the top of the container. My gasp drowned out some of the shouts of reprimand from the dockworkers. Obviously this move was not OSHA sanctioned.

The container continued down, dangling on a steel thread. When it made contact with the dock I walked over to it and looked up at him.

He spoke. "Hello, thank you for waiting."

I had thought I might have exaggerated how handsome he was in the few months since I'd seen him, but no. The face that gazed down at mine was sharply cut, and the black eyes, as almond as my own, smiled a secret at me.

He descended the built-in metal ladder on the back of the container and bowed to me. Then he pulled a handkerchief from his breast pocket and wiped his hands before taking one of mine.

"Callaway," he said, and it sounded like a compliment. "I was so pleased to get your call. I am, as always, at your service." He bowed again, briefly, over my hand, which he had not yet released.

"Thank you, Korosu-san." I bowed back, remembering not to bow more deeply than he had. I knew he would not have liked that.

He watched me silently for a moment before turning and gesturing to a worker on the dock. "Open it," he said, with a wave at the container.

The seal was cut and the metal doors swung open to reveal crate after crate, carefully stacked and marked Extremely Fragile. The worker referred first to a clipboard, then to tags on the boxes, until he found what he wanted—a smallish pine crate, which he brought out and placed on a waiting cart. Darrien stepped in and picked up a crowbar. He pried off the top of the crate with two deft motions, rummaged through the packing, and produced its contents. Two more minutes of carefully removing the wrapping unveiled a vase, which Darrien handed to Korosu as though it were made of priceless diamonds.

Korosu examined the vase with a covetous glint. Then he gestured me toward the car, and in a moment I found myself seated in the much cooler interior of the limo next to the second most attractive man in the world.

I cleared my throat and steeled myself to look at him in a friendly way, to resist his magnetism, to fight off any advances.

I should have known not to worry. One of the most attractive things about Korosu was his class. His manner toward me was one of absolute respect for the boundaries created by my relationship with Evan.

When I did look at him he was smiling softly and sympathetically at me, while holding the vase confidently in his hands. It was Ming dynasty; even I could see that.

"It's magnificent," I told him, and I meant it.

"I'm glad you like it," he said, and turned it slowly in his hands so that I could see all of the intricately painted decorations on its sumptuous surface. "It's for you." He held it out.

"What?" I sputtered. "This is priceless! Korosu, I can't accept such a gift." I fixed him with a meaningful look. "Especially from you, to whom I owe so much."

His face had a pleased, mischievous look. "I might not have made myself clear," he said. "This gift is for you *and* Detective Paley. I believe it is customary to give your friends a wedding present." He offered the vase again, and this time I took it gingerly, feeling the ancient weight of it as I cradled it in my lap. "And if it comes to the matter of debts, I am far more deeply in yours," he added.

"But how did you know we were engaged? We haven't made it . . . Oh"—the answer came to me—"Sabrina." He nodded, looking amused.

Overwhelmed by his grand gesture and grateful for his present help—not to mention feeling filleted when I thought about the fact that even if Evan did come back, there might not be a wedding—I was incapable of uttering even a banal response, much less an appropriate one.

He mistook my silence. "I hope you do not feel that the gift is inappropriate." But when I looked at him, I wondered if he wasn't deceived. He seemed to sense that so much more was wrong, and yet I knew that his sense of honor and respect for my privacy would never allow him to ask more than I was willing to tell.

I felt a sense of warmth and protection wash over me. Looking up into the face that somehow knew me so well, I said, "I think we can call any debt you mistakenly think you owe us even."

He laughed his rich, quiet laugh. "Now. I'll have Darrien put this away and we'll discuss this evening." He took the vase back and gave it to Darrien, who nestled it back into its crate and placed it in the trunk, before taking his place next to the driver.

As we pulled away from the dock I sighed and looked out the window, watching the small swatches of water between the giant ships and cranes as we drove past them. I slipped my hands under my thighs to stop the shaking. "I was thinking of investing in a horse," I began. "I have a new business connection who has gotten me very excited about the prospect. I'm grateful to you for letting me tag along this evening." I smiled at him; that last part, at least, was true.

"I'm just pleased to see you," Korosu said thoughtfully, making any further explanations unnecessary. "It's nice to see you without anyone being in imminent danger." He grinned.

Not sure how to respond to that, I shrugged and said innocently, "Whatever would make you say that?"

He looked at me knowingly. "If I recall correctly," he said as he sat back and straightened his impeccably hand-tailored suit, "when first we met, you were protecting someone, someone I care very much about, from a man with a gun."

I grimaced. "True," I yielded. "But I'm not sure Aya would thank me for it now. How is she?"

"Very well, considering." He glanced away, and I could see sadness wash over him.

Aya was one of the most beautiful women I had ever encountered. Stunning, sensuous, intelligent, everything a man would want, and Korosu cared for her very much. "She's a remarkable young lady," I commented.

His eyes sparked darkly at that. "And you are, as I have said before, an amazing woman."

I remembered when he had said those same words before, in a very intimate moment, when we'd been in close proximity. I had had to fight the effect the low rumble in his voice and the scent of him had had on me then, and I fought them again now. I muttered a "Thank you" and looked away, biting my tongue to keep from telling him everything. The kidnapping, the secretive phone call, the emails from the mystery person.

Once again, he seemed to misread my reaction. "Callaway, there is nothing I won't do for you." The memory of him facing down a Colombian drug lord flashed through my mind, and I knew that, because of his honor and his courage, anything Korosu said was true. "I am very happy for you," he added softly. I felt his hand on my arm as he pulled my hand from beneath my thigh and kissed it softly.

Turning, I met his eyes across the brush of lips on my skin, and I thought to myself that if anyone could get my lover back, it would be Korosu.

How ironic.

Chapter
13

Excitement was a palatable flavor at the racetrack. There was a tang of it in the air; you could feel it tingle on your skin, arousing and slightly desperate. The overall feel was crowded and noisy even though we were dropped off at a separate, private club entrance. The plush bar was filled with gigantic screens showing the action on the track. A large electronic readout over the bar listed the horses and their odds for each upcoming race.

It was with relief that I entered Korosu's private box. Though still surrounded by the noise of the crowd, I felt at least protected from the crush of bodies. I was introduced to the four other men who were there and three beautiful young Japanese women, each of them graceful, classy, and intent on pleasing. A waitress took our drink order, and I pulled out a pair of stabilizer binoculars. Korosu offered me his more powerful set, but I shook my head. I would be scanning the boxes nearby, not the more distant action on the field.

One of the young women brought Korosu a clear drink; she kept her eyes lowered as she offered it to him. She was exceptionally lovely, but he barely glanced at her. I could feel the brush of his silk-and-wool suit on my bare arm as he raised his drink to his lips.

The friction sparked heat in me and, distracted as I was, I took a deep breath of the scent of him, expensive, manly, tempting.

Raising a hand, he brushed a renegade wave of my hair back and let his fingers linger with just enough pressure to make me long for more.

"Are you happy?" he asked, so softly that I was unsure whether he wanted a positive answer or not.

I looked into his onyx eyes and felt a catch in my breath that wasn't all for Evan. "Mostly," I whispered back.

He smiled and inclined his head. "For us," he said, looking out over the racetrack, "perhaps that is the most honest answer we can give."

I bit my lip to keep from pursuing the subject, but I let myself lean against him slightly, imperceptible to anyone but us.

Darrien had stayed with the car, and without him I felt disarmed. Korosu's attention was soon required by one of his friends and I raised the glasses to my eyes, searching the grandstand. I had noted the box numbers on the way in, and I tried to make out which one was indicated on the brochure. After about three minutes of confused searching by counting rows and sections, I located it.

It was large, the kind most often owned by a company or organization, and it was filled with men in a varied collection of Tommy Bahama silk shirts—the sort of thing wealthy executives at a complete loss for fashion options beyond a business suit resort to for nice casual wear. I could only make out one woman in the area, and when I found her in my glasses, my breath froze in my body.

She was an attractive redhead, and she was wearing a pale green dress. I lowered the glasses and scanned for the best route to the box, which was on the same level as Korosu's. I was counting how many boxes were between us when I spotted something that sent the hair on my arms into full salute.

Raising my glasses deliberately so as not to lose the figure in the crowd, I peered through them and cursed under my breath.

It was a man, and he was looking through his binoculars at the same box I had been watching. As I tried to steady my hand to keep the image in focus, he lowered his binoculars and turned directly toward me. Once you've seen a face across the barrel of a lethal weapon, you don't soon forget it. It was Houndstooth.

Korosu had seen me stiffen, because I heard him ask if I was all right. "I'm fine," I told him, but my voice shook slightly. "I just saw someone I don't care to run into." The man on his left spoke, and Korosu turned to respond. Looking back through the glasses, I searched in vain for the redhead. She'd disappeared, and, when I looked again, so had the man.

"Excuse me," I interrupted Korosu, "I'm just going to the ladies' room." He nodded and stood while I exited the box.

Out in the crush, I started to make my way toward the other box. I gathered from the multitude of monitors and the increased excitement that a race was about to begin. People were rushing everywhere, to their seats, to the betting windows, to the concession stands; I remembered Evan always applying his practiced calm, and I tried not to rush, to keep both my head and my cool and move steadily toward my goal. Of course, I had absolutely no idea what my goal was or what I was going to do when I got there.

"Callaway?" a woman's voice called out from the crowd. I turned, confused, and recognized the smallish, pretty woman who had addressed me.

"Isabelle!" I tried to smile. I needed to keep moving; it wasn't a time to stop and socialize with the daughter of one of my father's cronies. "Hi, how are you?" My eyes shot nervously around.

"I'm great. I didn't know you were into horse racing."

That one I could answer honestly. "I'm not, as a rule. I'm here with a friend."

She smiled knowingly and raised her eyebrows once or twice in a comic manner. "Is it that handsome detective I met at the City of Hope benefit?"

Let the lying begin. "No, he's out of town, on a case. I'm here with a business associate, really. And I'm so sorry, but I've got to get back. How's your dad?" I remembered to ask at the last minute.

"Oh, he's busy as always. He's not here tonight; not that he'd be with me anyway." She sounded petulant. "He's usually up with the big boys in the owners' box. I'm down with the penny tickets."

"Tell him I said hello." I smiled and started away, but she glommed onto me. She had always been one of those women whose calls I couldn't return unless I had at least twenty minutes to chitchat. I liked Isabelle Ferris, but she was time consuming.

"Oh, now, wait just a second, I haven't seen you in months. Did you know I was gone almost a year setting up offices overseas?"

"So, you're moving up in the company?" I asked, distracted. "That's great, I can't wait to hear all about it when we—"

"Well, not *up* exactly." She cut off my cutoff. "More like sideways. It's such a boys' club." Her pretty face looked sour. "I know you want to go, but before I let you get away from me, I have a favor to ask you."

While she attached herself to my arm and started prattling about a charity event she was hosting and wanted me to attend, I kept watching the hallway behind her. For a flash, I saw the woman; she was watching me and Isabelle. When we made eye contact she shifted behind a group of people and remained half-hidden, but present. I realized that Isabelle was still speaking and tried to tune in and get it over with.

". . . it'll be up in Santa Ynez at the Rosens' ranch. He's the

CEO of my company, and I'm really close with his wife, Susan," she said smugly, the statement of friendship sounding like a brag. "She and I cochaired the event—so much work, but worth it— and if you could be one of the sponsors, it would just give us so much more clout." She dropped her voice and leaned in, stroking my arm. "I know you haven't been out much since your mom passed away, but it's such a good cause."

"Sure," I said hastily. "I'd love to. Call Kelly tomorrow, and she'll set it up." I detached her fingers from my arm by sweeping her into a quick hug while I checked for the redhead. She was there, but beginning to move away. "Great to see you! Gotta go." I turned away without waiting for a response, half running toward the disappearing figure.

For a full minute I saw nothing but a blur of faces and bodies, a smiling, scowling, hunching, hurrying, strutting, laughing mass of humanity.

Then I spotted her. She was going into the ladies' room. Breathing a temporary sigh of relief, I followed. I was still completely uncertain of what I could do, but at least, I felt, there was some certainty that Houndstooth would not be there.

The room was long, with stalls on either side. Hugging the stall doors on the right, I started to walk slowly along, looking at the feet underneath the stalls on the left, watching for shoes that would match the pale green dress. I was halfway down when a stall door behind me opened, and before I could turn or move away, a strong hand caught my arm and yanked me inside.

Chapter
14

A hand over my mouth kept me from screaming, but the cry that had been poised to leap from my vocal cords died when I saw that it was the redhead who had drawn me so forcefully into the stall. When she seemed reassured that I wouldn't call out, she closed and locked the metal door, leaning against it with obvious nervous exhaustion. She looked terrified, unsuited to this kind of cloak-and-dagger situation. As I opened my mouth to speak, she shook her head firmly and put a finger to her lips. Then she took my hand in hers and pressed it against her body, just below her breast.

Thinking, *Well, this is certainly not what I expected,* I remained silent and waited to see what would happen next. She moved my hand, pressing it harder against her body, and I felt it. She was wired for sound.

I nodded, and mouthed, "Thank you."

Her frightened eyes acknowledged me. Then she spoke, her voice shaky. "Are you Callaway Wilde?"

I nodded at her, but she gestured with fingers moving in front of her mouth that I should speak out loud, and so I answered.

"Yes, I am." I tried to think of what else I would say if a strange woman asked me that and I didn't know she was wired for sound, but no brilliant ad-libs flashed to mind.

She spared me the attempt by saying, "I have something for you." She reached into her purse and pulled out a cell phone, holding it out to me.

I took it and looked at it like an idiot who had forgotten how to use a phone. Then I looked at her.

She said, "There's someone who wants to speak to you."

"Oh." I continued the well-below-average-IQ stuff, but I was cognizant enough to put the phone to my ear. "Yes?"

"Cally? Is that you?" The voice was anxious and dry, as though unused for several days, but I would have known it anywhere. An acid wash flushed through my whole body, and though my throat constricted, I forced myself to speak.

"Evan? Oh, God, Evan. Are you all right?"

"I'm okay, *mon coeur.* I'm okay. Listen, I don't have much time. The people who . . ." I heard the grumbling sounds of indeterminate male voices, a thick smacking sound, and then Evan, breathing hard, spoke with apparent effort. ". . . my *hosts* have something they would like you to do. I want you to do it."

"What is it?"

"You need to make a deal with someone. Offer them money to keep her quiet." Evan's voice became stressed. "You need to get her to accept these terms."

"Why me?" I was amazed at how calm I was able to keep my voice even though I felt like screaming.

Evan's voice dropped into the affectionate pride I so often heard from him. "Nobody makes a deal better than you."

In spite of all my fear for him, a slight ripple of anger at the thought of his being involved with someone else found its way, like a sliver, into my mind. He had said "her." "Why *you*?" I asked.

He didn't respond immediately, but then he said, "Because I'm connected to both of you." The sliver slipped through my veins and stabbed my heart.

I heard the offstage voices again and struggled to make them out, while I forced myself to focus, to perform. "When do I do this?"

"Soon, *mon coeur,* soon." He was calling me "my heart" in French—something he hadn't done since I had told him he sounded like Maurice Chevalier. The endearment ripped at me. Was I his heart? Should I believe him?

"And then they'll release you?"

There was a long pause. I sensed a struggle going on in Evan; he wanted desperately to let me know something he couldn't say. There was a sudden smacking sound and the distorted male voices again.

When Evan spoke again it was with grim seriousness, like a soldier's good-bye. "It's her only chance, *chérie.*"

Then came another muffled sound, like a fist making contact with flesh, a scuffling, and several voices shouting angrily in a coarse language I couldn't distinguish. Then one of those male voices, harsh with a thick accent, came clearly through the air and into my ear. "If you want to see him again, just do what you're told."

Rage consumed me, and I felt as if I'd been standing in the very center of a detonated bomb and the flame and heat of it had liberated every cell in my body. "Who is this?"

With a phlegmy laugh, the voice said, "You can just call me Russian."

"If you hurt him," I said to the faceless, hated voice, "I will spend the rest of my life and every cent I have hunting you down."

As I said those words, I became aware of the redhead again. She had been standing not two feet in front of me with her back to the door watching me the whole time, but I had been so

utterly intent on the words and activities going on in some un-
known other place that I had forgotten her.

She had drawn in a quick breath and was looking at me with
surprise and something almost like admiration. As the line went
dead, I heard another noise, a click.

Before I could put together the fact that Red had unlocked
the stall door, she'd opened it and bolted out of the ladies' room
into a crowd of twenty thousand. With a jolt, I realized that the
solitary connection I had to finding Evan was about to vanish.

Chapter

15

Not knowing which way Red had gone, I desperately scanned the crowd. I only just caught a glimpse of her when I exited back into the crowded throughway, and then only by the merest chance. Struggling to keep up, I wound through the huge arena until I lost her from view behind a kiosk with multiple lines of bodies queued up for beer. I panicked and hurried through the thirsty customers, muttering insincere apologies as I trampled them along the way.

She was gone. She must have doubled back. And then I saw a double door, in the wall behind the kiosk. It registered in a vague way to me that there was a uniform sitting on a stool next to the door and as I started to press my weight against the door, the uniform became human.

"Hey," it said. "Hold on there. This is a restricted entry area."

Annoyed at being foiled, I spun to face the man with my brain whirling with excuses, arguments, and explanations. But the man's eyes had dropped to the badge swinging from a thick ribbon around my neck.

"Oh, okay. Go ahead." He smiled and nodded a little sheepishly. "Sorry, I didn't see your pass."

I glanced down at my forgotten Owners' Circle pass, mumbled, "It's okay," and blasted on through.

The door opened onto a wide stairwell that seemed to continue down for quite a long way. I could hear the sound of a large door swinging open several levels below me. I started to descend cautiously; three levels down I met more unmarked doors and a gate that blocked further descent. A sign on the bars read, Do Not Enter, Emergency Exit Only, Alarm Will Sound. Since I'd heard nothing more alarming than my own footsteps echoing on my way down, I chose the unmarked door and cracked it open.

About halfway down the hallway ahead of me, two very large archways led off to either side, and I was just in time to see a female figure turn the corner into the one on the right.

As I started forward, the smell of horses and a thousand questions were competing for attention in my brain. Who was this woman? Was she in danger? Was *I*? Where was Evan? Could he be *here*?

"For God's sake," I found myself saying under my breath as I started jogging as quickly and quietly as my Givenchy pumps would allow down the long, wide hallway, "I would have just given them the money if they'd asked for it. All this cloak-and-cell-phone business is just pissing me off." Not that anger was a bad thing; it kept the terror at bay.

The arched openings on either side, when I reached them, turned out to be stables—long, perfectly kept aisles smelling sharply of clean cedar shavings and hay, with the sweet mix of oats and horses hovering in the distinctive perfume.

Red had turned right, so I did too. There were at least twenty stalls on both sides, and I came to the conclusion that Red could not have disappeared all the way through the far end. So, slowly, I started down the aisle, checking in each stall on the right side.

This was easy when they were empty, not so easy when they

weren't. When I tried to approach, the gigantic, powerful animals tossed their aristocratic heads challengingly while their powerful legs slammed against the sides of the thick wooden stalls.

After only one attempt to stick my head around one of these massive, hopped-up creatures, during which only a sudden leap backward had kept me from being pounded against the support beam, I decided that it was unlikely she would be hiding in one of the occupied stalls. So, I checked the unoccupied ones; nothing.

Then I came to a small, partially opened door. It was dim inside, but the smell of leather was strong and I recognized it, even with my limited experience, as a tack room. There were high racks of saddles and rows of bridles against the back wall and, most important as far as I was concerned, lots of good hiding places.

With a deep breath and a heaping portion of something raw that could easily be identified as either courage or stupidity—depending on how things turned out—I entered the room.

The stupidity factor leaped into the number one position as a hand, a man's hand, clapped over my mouth and a meaty arm pinned my own to my sides, snatching me out of the open doorway and dragging me unceremoniously into the shadows.

It wasn't just the man's arms I could feel holding me roughly; there was the sharp bite of something metal in his hand that was digging into my lower ribs.

A gun.

Chapter 16

A voice spoke, very quietly but with great authority, into my ear. "Do not scream, or I'll kill her." Then he pointed his gun across the room and directly at a rack of blankets, which were almost, but not quite, covering a pair of shoes that matched the pale green dress.

He must have realized from the tick in my body that I had spotted her, because, still with his large hand firmly over my mouth, he turned me to face him.

It was Houndstooth. I nodded as best I could, and he removed the paw from my face, bringing one thick finger up to his lips in a warning. The gun was still pointing at the blankets and the girl who hid behind them.

Then I heard the voices. From our place in the shadows we could see two men coming toward us through the half-open door, a security guard and a civilian. The civilian came to the tack room door and my captor pulled me back hard against the wall, in a small space between some lockers, his gun never wavering from its target. The man in the doorway glanced in and called out, "Anyone in here?"

It killed me to stay silent. I wondered—hoped—that the "civilian" was the undercover cop that Curtis had assigned to watch over me. The urge to scream out, to call for help, was almost overwhelming, but I kept my eyes on the girl's department store shoes and pressed my lips together between my teeth until I could taste blood.

Then the men moved on, their footsteps fading away.

Houndstooth pressed me against the wall, and his eyes slid down my body quickly—it seemed more involuntary than lascivious—before he moved his mouth next to my ear. I realized that he didn't want the girl to hear him or think we knew she was there.

I don't know what I was expecting, but his first comment took me completely by surprise. He said, in a polite, husky whisper, "Nice outfit."

"Uh, thanks," I whispered back automatically. But it threw me off my guard.

His mouth went to my ear again. "What are you doing here?"

What kind of game was this? *What does he think I'm doing here?*

"Don't you know?" I asked, pleased to hear a certain amount of disdain in the delivery.

But what pleased me pissed him off. He placed his forearm across my chest and leaned his weight hard against it. I struggled to breathe against the pressure. "Don't play games with me, I haven't got the time or the patience."

I was incapable of responding, both from lack of breath and lack of brain function. He eased up a little and waited. I tried to come up with something. "I was . . . invited," I sputtered.

His eyes narrowed, and I was surprised to see that my explanation sounded as inane to him as it did to me. I could also see that he couldn't decide whether to believe me or not.

"By whom?" he asked.

It crossed my mind that his English was excellent for a thug.

"It wasn't you?" My confusion was so complete that he almost bought it.

Wrong answer. He brought the gun up and pointed it at the blankets again, drawing me away from the wall into the middle of the tack room. Still speaking quietly, he said, "I think it's time to ask our friend some questions."

He turned his head and looked down the barrel of his gun, aiming it at a point just above the satin shoes.

"No!" I shouted. "Don't!" I lunged for his arm, but he tightened his grip on my wrist and yanked me backward with a snap.

Which was a really good thing. Because just at that moment, something heavy hit Houndstooth's extended gun arm. I heard a crack and he let go of my arm, sending me crashing back into the lockers. The back of my head slammed into the metal; I squeezed my eyes shut and cursed as I took the blow, sinking down onto the cold concrete. I heard more struggling, a gun went off, and there was a rustle of movement; through eyes squinting with pain, I saw Red emerge and bolt out the door in the confusion.

A gun scuttled across the floor and stopped spinning near my left foot. I snatched it up and fumbled to choose a target, but all I could see from the floor was the new arrival's back in silhouette; he had moved in front of me protectively.

Houndstooth was watching him warily, holding his right arm tight against his body. He glanced at the blankets and the empty space beneath them, cursed, and disappeared out the door.

The man in front of me turned and came down on one knee. It wasn't the undercover officer, it was Korosu—he had obviously followed me. "Are you all right?"

"I'm fine. But that woman who was here, I think he might kill her, we've got to help her!" I tried to get up quickly, but the sudden movement sent a shooting pain down my neck.

Placing his hands on both of my shoulders, Korosu said, "Careful, don't move suddenly. Just sit still for a moment." He took the forty-five from my hand and stuck it into the waistband of his pants, under his jacket.

"But—"

"I don't think he'll be going after anyone tonight; that man's arm is broken. Do you have any idea how to find her?"

I remembered the sound of the bone crack and winced. "No," I muttered, then thought better of it. "Well, I know which box she was in. Could you find out who owns it?"

"Callaway," he said, shaking his head but unable to keep the humorous note out of his voice, "you are the most exciting woman I ever met, and as entrancing as that is, you have some explaining to do."

"All right," I said, and a huge weight lifted from my heart. "But it's going to take a few minutes."

Leaving no space for discussion, he said, "We'll go to my house. We can talk securely and you can spend the night there." He placed one hand firmly on my arm and pulled me gently toward the door.

"Your house?" I asked, hesitating.

He turned back, and the mischievous glint in his eye set off a fluttering in my chest. He said, "You can trust me."

I nodded and followed after him, thinking that it wasn't him I didn't trust—it was me.

Chapter 17

Korosu's house was a jewel case made of glass, rare wood, and molded concrete. It was smooth, calming, powerful, and striking all at once, very much like him.

Nestled inside the L-shaped patio of the glass house was a pool, long and languid, with an infinity edge that gave the appearance that the water was running off over the lip of the world. Far beyond and below that curtain of flowing liquid were the brilliant lights of downtown, and far beyond that, the darkness of the sea at night.

This perch, on an impressively sized, terraced property, truly gave you the sense of being king of all you surveyed. I thought, as I stood looking out through the panes of glass, that Korosu and I were two people who could take at least part of that saying seriously. From here, I was sure I could make out the buildings that one or the other of us owned.

A soft touch on the bare skin of my arm and the slight tinkle of ice in crystal brought my awareness back to a much more intimate proximity, and I became acutely aware that Korosu was in it.

I brushed his eyes with mine when I took the glass and muttered my thanks. To stand near him was to feel the heat of possibility. I retreated a couple of steps away and sank into the double chill of a leather chair and the task before me.

He sat across from me and said, "Now, tell me."

Not sure where to begin, I sipped my scotch; it was excellent, smoky, and warming. Korosu pulled a cigarette from a silver box on the coffee table and held it up. "Do you mind?"

"Not at all. In fact, I'll join you."

He offered the box and I slid one out.

Crossing one leg over the other, he rested his extended arm across the back of his chair. The smoke rose from his hand in a sleek white stream that flickered into horizontal lines as it reached some hidden current and disappeared. He sat completely still, relaxed and composed, with utterly no indication that he had broken a man's arm an hour before.

Drawing the sexy white smoke deeply into my lungs and feeling the calming effect of the nicotine on a nonsmoker, I said to him, "I didn't know you smoked."

"I don't." He smiled slyly and took a deliberate draw on the cigarette. "But, unlike the addling effects of certain other substances, I find I still like the effect of tobacco every now and then."

My sentiments precisely. He understood. I only smoked a solitary cigarette on rare occasions and never in front of Evan, not that I had ever wanted to, but I wasn't sure he would sympathize with the dynamics of addiction. Korosu, it seemed, did.

"Where is Detective Paley?" Korosu asked me softly.

My eyes dropped down to my drink as I took a long, slow sip. When I had mustered the strength to voice it, I said, "Kidnapped."

Only a sudden wrinkle in the perfect line of rising smoke showed that the news had affected Korosu enough to cause a tiny, involuntary jerk.

He said nothing, and that allowed me to tell him what I knew. It came out faltering and confused at first, but encouraged by his attentive silence, I gained both confidence and lucidity as I told him about the abduction, the attempt on Curtis's life, and the brief, painful cell phone conversation I had had with my fiancé earlier in the eventful evening.

I was starting to think, to process. This was my forum: overview. Look at a company, a situation, a problem, lay out the facts, sum them up, and arrive at a conclusive game plan. Buy. Sell. Trade. Retool. Take action.

It was Korosu's forte as well, and his concentration was like a spotlight on me. The cigarette burned down in his fingers, forgotten.

"And so tonight," I concluded, "I've got to find out who that woman was and what her part was in it. The box, where I first saw her, was indicated on the brochure, so it, or whoever owns it, must have some connection with Evan."

Korosu's eyes gleamed as he leaned forward and looked out at the night. "Maybe it does, but it seems to me that these people have been exceedingly careful, and that would be careless. I'm afraid it's more likely to be a place chosen for its randomness."

What he said was so logical that my hopes drooped. "Either way, I'll know who owns it by the morning," he said reassuringly.

The morning. It seemed so remote. Time seemed to be hovering for me; there wasn't any earlier or later, no place beyond this. Exhaustion was pressing down on me. I shook my head once to try to clear it. I had told Korosu everything.

Almost.

I'd left out my suspicions about the phone call and the emails from B.

"So," he said in that rumbling, even, soft-as-chamois-leather voice, "that's all then."

"No." I looked at him. "There's something else." It may have been the scotch and the nicotine, or the palliative effect of Korosu and his environment, but I felt detached enough to confess the whole truth. "Right before he disappeared he got a phone call. I'm certain it was a woman, from the tone of Evan's voice. He tried to hide it from me. When I asked him about it, I believed he was lying to me, covering something up. And there was an email referring to the call, a fairly intimate one, from someone who only signed B. It was obvious from the familiarity he had a history—and maybe a present—with the sender. We fought just before they took him, and I honestly don't know where I stand with him when he comes back." I stubbed out the now distasteful cigarette and tried to wash the staleness away with the last of the scotch before I let Korosu have a long look through my transparent armor. "Now," I said to him, "you know all of it."

Korosu rose, very slowly, and came to stand near me. I was afraid, terrified that he would touch me, that I would show weakness, or lose control.

But he did not touch me. Instead, he spoke. "I do not believe," he added with a slight change in his tone, "that he can be tempted by any other woman."

Looking up at him, I asked, "And why do you think that?"

He surprised me with a definite answer. "Because Aya tried to seduce him, and he refused her."

Aya. One of the sexiest and most feminine women I had ever met, one to whom discretion would have been a point of honor. If it had happened, I would never have found out, and Evan must have known that.

"Oh," I said. "How do you know?"

"She told me. She told me how happy it made her that you were with such a man, that you deserved him."

Shaking the uncomfortable image from my mind, I stood up next to him, so that, even though he was taller, I could speak to him on his level. "But what if there *is* someone else?"

For a moment the possibility we had never spoken of shimmered so furiously between us that I could almost hear it expanding with a shudder.

Behind Korosu a man appeared, and waited with his eyes averted for Korosu and me to finish our conversation.

"Cory, please take Ms. Wilde to the guest room, and make sure she has everything she needs."

"Of course, sir," Cory said with a quick nod of the head, then he waited for me to cross the room to him.

"Try to sleep," Korosu said. "I'm going to contact Detective Curtis and have the gun we recovered taken over to him."

Surprised, I turned back to him. "Aren't you going to sleep?"

The black eyes flashed again, but I couldn't read what sparked them this time. "I don't sleep very much. Pleasant dreams." He turned and went out another door.

The guest room was a sumptuous silken affair all done in natural textures and tones with accents of deep red. As I suspected I would, I found everything I needed and more in the bathroom cabinets, and when I came back from a quick shower I found a light cotton kimono and slippers in a neat package on the bed. I set them aside and climbed into the Egyptian cotton sheets naked, feeling the relief of sinking into the safety and comfort that they offered.

But sleep wouldn't come. I lay wondering where Evan was sleeping, if he'd been harmed, if he was afraid. There was a certain unquestioning faith in him that kept me from losing hope. Evan was everything. He was brave and tough and realistic. He was the smartest, most intuitive man I had ever met. No one had ever read me as thoroughly as he had.

Turning onto my side, I sighed out my need for him. It couldn't be true that he was involved with someone else. He had always been so brutally honest with me. Except about his past. No, I thought, even about his past. He'd been honest about the fact that he couldn't tell me everything; that it wouldn't be safe for me to know. Now, of course, it had turned out to be dangerous for both of us.

There was a soft knock on my door and I sat up, reaching for the robe, wondering what I would do if it were Korosu.

"Yes?"

But the face that appeared in the crack belonged to Cory. "There is a phone call for you, a Detective Curtis."

I leaped out of bed and met the butler halfway across the room, snatching the phone from his hand. "Curtis?"

"You all right?" Curtis's voice was tired.

"I'm okay. Did you hear what happened?"

"Not all of it. They lost you in the stable access area, but they saw you leave with Korosu, who filled me in on most of the other action. You staying there?"

"Uh, yeah, in the guest room." I sounded guilty.

But Curtis made no comment, and it was clear that there was something else on his mind. "Listen, the detective on the Josie Banks case came up with something. Found it in her jewelry box."

"What?"

"A man's watch, a Hamilton, antique."

"Uh-huh." My throat had constricted, making it hard to breathe. Swallowing with difficulty since my mouth was so dry, I asked, "Was it inscribed on the back?"

There was a scratchy silence, then Curtis said, " 'Merry Christmas, love Callaway.' "

I wanted to ask him what it meant, why it was there, how the fuck this could all be going on, but the shock had left me speechless. I was thinking, *Josie Banks, B., Banks.*

"Cally?" I made the sound of a small hum to let him know I was still there, and he went on, speaking as though to convince himself as well as me. "All this proves is that Josie Banks was somehow connected to the kidnappers. But I do have a question for you."

"Hmm?" It was all I could manage.

"Was Evan wearing the watch when they took him?"

I tried to think, tried to help, to be competent, human, but I was nothing more than a swirling mass of stunned emotions. "Um, I don't know. He was wearing a towel when I went into the shower, but he must have gotten dressed before he went downstairs. Just a second." I lowered the phone and slapped myself hard across the face, to make myself feel something, to stun the stupidity out of me. It didn't really help. I put the phone back up to my ear and said, "I talked to him tonight."

"What did he say?" I could hear the relief in Curtis's voice, and I knew that he had also doubted that Evan was still alive.

"That I had to offer someone else money to make them go away."

"Did he say how?"

"No, but . . ." My voice sounded like someone else's. Someone much older.

"What?"

"But I could hear them hitting him."

There was an extended sigh, then Curtis said, "Can you use Korosu's computer and send me an email with everything you remember to the precinct?"

"I'm sure I can."

"And you've heard nothing further from them?"

"No. Sabrina has been watching my email, and Deirdre is at the house; if anything came, from either source, they would call me immediately."

"All right. As soon as you can get me the info, then." He said good-bye and left me standing in the middle of an unfamiliar bedroom in a world I no longer recognized.

I pressed the bell for Cory, and he brought me a laptop. I wrote as much as I could bear, sent it to Curtis, then tried to go back to bed.

I tossed again, but it was no use; I couldn't sleep. Who was the redhead and why had she warned me about the wire? Why had Houndstooth seemed not to know why I was there? And why was he after Red? Did he suspect she had tipped me off to the wire? I got up and put on the kimono and the slippers. Maybe tea would help. I wondered if I should call Cory, but I felt guilty about waking him again, and I wanted to be alone.

I opened the door to the hallway and listened, but I could hear nothing from that direction except the coursing hum of electricity that lived in all modern houses. My footfalls in the soft-soled slippers were practically silent as I trailed down the thickly carpeted hall, coming to the doorway I knew to be the living room.

All of the interior lights were out, and the large aquarium of a room was saturated with the underwater light from the pool outside, blue waves of dancing reflections that were eerily beautiful. As I stepped forward I heard something, a soft moaning sound; I advanced into the room, searching around for the source.

And then I found it.

She was stunning. It was the young Asian woman who had served our drinks at the racetrack. Her black hair had been artfully piled on her head earlier, but now it reached all the way down her back. Naked and absolutely perfect, she was standing on the edge of the deck, and her lovely shape was outlined by the distant lights behind her, lit only by the tentative blue wash from the pool, which ran its fingers of light over her with seemingly eager delight.

She was not alone; Korosu was standing next to her, wearing a black robe. He was touching her, holding her firmly with one hand on the back of her neck while he stroked the other hand over her body, slowly and deliberately. Starting at her graceful neck and moving down across one breast, over her waist, down her hip, across, pausing, and back up to start again. She stood with her legs slightly parted and her eyes closed, moaning softly as his hands controlled her body.

I knew I should turn away, but I was riveted to the spot. Still in the shadow of the doorway, it would have been almost impossible for them to see me.

Unable and unwilling to deprive myself of this pleasure, I leaned against the wall and feasted my eyes. My curiosity, as well as my sense of desire, needed to be sated. I had been told, by Aya, that Korosu was a connoisseur of many things, meaning sex, and it had piqued my interest in him before we'd ever met, an interest that had grown since then. From the look of pleasure and the sweet sounds coming from the woman he was entertaining now, I could well believe it.

As I watched, he turned the flawless woman to face out over the city and traced the outline of her back with both his hands. Starting at her shoulders, he moved his hands down to her tiny waist and then around her hips. Slowly, he went down on his knees, and what he did next made my breath come quickly. The woman grasped at the railing and her body swayed with pleasure, something I would have thought difficult in her five-inch heels. Just when it seemed she might explode with pleasure, he pulled away and rose to his feet.

Opening his robe, he let it fall to the deck and I was surprised to hear a moan nearby, before I realized it was my own voice that trembled in the air.

Korosu's body was sleek and strong, muscular but lean, and his skin seemed almost to glow in that watery light.

He came up behind her and pressed himself into her. She moved with rhythmic, sinuous motions that quickened until she was gasping and crying out with pleasure and release, and he followed closely after, throwing his head back and letting the orgasm pulse through his whole body, another visual I knew I would recall many times. Then they slowed, embraced, and finally moved apart. Korosu picked up a kimono from the deck and wrapped her gently in it before donning his own and leading her to a deck chair the size of a double bed. He kissed her lightly on both eyes and then each hand and foot before reclining next to her.

"Could I get you something?" The voice spoke just behind me, and I jumped so violently as I spun around that it felt like I left my skin behind.

It was Cory, the butler, still dressed in his suit and obviously very much awake.

"Oh, uhm." It was impossible to hope that he hadn't noticed that I had been watching the couple outside. "I wanted some tea, I couldn't sleep," I started explaining ineptly. "I didn't want to wake you, so I was looking for the kitchen."

Cory smiled at me, and his eyes flicked to the deck and then back. "I don't sleep when I'm working. Would you care to have your tea in the kitchen or in your bedroom?" He smiled, and I followed him, grateful for his tact and discretion. Based on what I'd witnessed, discretion would be an important part of his job description.

"I'll have it in my bedroom, thanks."

He nodded. "That's what I would do," he said with the vaguest upward flicker of his eyebrows, and before I could feel shocked he asked, "Chamomile?"

"That would be lovely," I muttered, and slunk off down the hallway.

When I'd finished the tea, I slid back under the sheets and lay thinking.

Sighing repeatedly, I rolled impatiently from one side to the other. The sensuous picture of Korosu in the throes of pleasure kept rerunning through my mind, with the constant interruptions of images of Evan in danger, and then the stinging jealousy of imagining Evan with another woman.

A thought started to form in my mind, a sort of weapon that I was building to fend off a possible attack.

I wanted Evan back safely, that was the most important thing. But once he came back, if things weren't right . . .

The image of Korosu caressing the woman's body floated through my mind, and I felt a covetous sense of desire.

I would do whatever it took—pay the money, play the game, anything. I would not fail Evan.

And then, if, once he was safe, my suspicions of another woman were confirmed, I would go to Korosu.

Strangely quieted, I fell into an uneasy sleep.

Chapter

18

The smell of strong coffee and the sun streaming through the silk curtains woke me the next morning.

I'd barely had time to register where I was, and why I was naked and wrapped around a pillow like it was a cherished possession, when a voice spoke from the doorway.

"Good morning."

I sat up, pulling the sheer sheet up across my chest as I did. It was a silly reaction, like something out of a B movie, but it was instinctive.

Korosu moved through the brightness and held out a large china mug, over the top of which I could see a white dome of pearly froth.

"Cappuccino?" he asked. "I hope you don't mind my waking you." He sat nonchalantly on the edge of the bed, as though my nakedness, while pleasant, was nothing to comment on.

Remembering my new objectives from last night, I adjusted a pillow, leaned against the backboard with the sheet draped casually over me leaving one leg exposed, and accepted the perfect brew. Taking a sip, I realized it was sweetened with natural honey, exactly the way I liked it, and I wondered how he'd known that.

"Delicious, thank you." I hid a yawn behind my hand and added, "Good morning."

"Good morning. Sleep well?" he asked, and I thought I detected a hint of irony in the inquiry.

Feeling the impact of Curtis's news all over again, and wondering if he knew that I had witnessed his midnight performance, I only said, "I had some trouble getting to sleep, but when I finally did, I slept very well, thank you." I picked up my cell phone from beside the bed; it still had power. There were no messages, which meant no further word from the kidnappers. Frowning, I tossed it aside.

Korosu smiled briefly, then his face sobered. "I found out who owns the box at Del Mar."

Sitting up so quickly that the sheet fell down to my waist, I asked, "Who?"

Korosu's eyes didn't even flick downward from my face, and I restored my modesty, such as it was, as carelessly as I could manage.

"Three men own it together. They are all executives at a company called Webtech. Does that ring any bells?"

It did, in fact. They were a gigantic software-internet company, mostly financial and corporate programs. It was hard to read the business section and not know of Webtech. I had a vice president at one of my companies whom I had hired away from there. I'd never done business with them but my father had, so I'd known lots of people who had worked for or with them over the years.

"Well," I began, "I know who they are, of course." Korosu nodded; he would know of them as well. "My father was close to one of the VPs there, so I know people who work for them, quite a few actually. What are the names of the men?"

"Ted Issacs, Fred Rosen, and Kevin Cott."

"Don't know them. The VP my father knew was a man named Jim Ferris. They spent so much time together that I called him Uncle Jim. He had a daughter my age, so we did a lot of stuff together. I ran into her at the track last night." Korosu looked up curiously, so I answered his telepathic question. "No, he wasn't there with her."

I thought for a moment. "What could that redhead have to do with three guys from Webtech? Maybe she knows one of them and that was the most public place she, or Evan's kidnappers, could think of to meet with me? Maybe these men don't have any idea that they were being used?"

Korosu nodded his head thoughtfully. "Most likely they do not. Webtech is a highly respected financial institution run by very smart people. It seems improbable that they would be involved; it would certainly be a dead giveaway to have you meet a messenger anywhere that could connect back to them. That in itself seems to tell us that they are *not* involved. So it's far more likely that who-ever *is* responsible used the event as a meeting place."

My head was racing. Had Red, like me, asked someone who owned a box to include her in order to gain access? How could I find out who she was?

Korosu must have been thinking along the same lines, because he asked, "Would any of your connections at the company know who the redheaded woman was?"

"Maybe. Jim Ferris might know of her. Isabelle told me last night that he's usually invited to sit in the owners' box."

"But she wasn't?"

"No, I remember that because she seemed pissed off about it."

"So maybe Jim Ferris could find out?" Korosu suggested.

My heart fell a little. "But how can I ask? I mean, what do I say in *that* phone call? 'Hi, Uncle Jim. I know I haven't spoken to you since my father's funeral, but by the way, who was that red-head who passed me a cell phone so I could talk to my kid-napped fiancé?' "

Korosu looked sympathetic but not pitying. "Oh," he said, drawing the syllable out, "I'm sure you will think of something. His daughter might know who she is, and if you're friends with her, maybe you can coerce her into sharing a little gossip."

Laughing dryly, I asked, *"Coerce?* Isabelle's penchant for, and my distaste of, talking about other people is the reason I don't spend much time with her these days. As far as Isabelle Ferris is concerned, gossip is a competitive sport and *everybody's* on her team."

"What else did Isabelle say to you?"

"The usual, 'Call me, let's have lunch.' " I looked at Korosu, who was nodding.

"You call her," he dictated. "I'll have Wyatt book you a table at the Peninsula."

"And Wyatt is?"

Korosu rose and crossed the room, opening the door and creating a draft that sent the curtains swirling into the room, an eddy of swimming silk. "My day butler," he said, trying to hide a smile. "Also, very discreet."

And then he left me.

Chapter

19

Ginny met me in my entrance hall with arms crossed over her chest and eyes flashing.

"Imagine my surprise," she started in before even asking if I was okay, "when I got here early this morning and found that I had arrived home before you." Her eyebrows did a graceful pas de deux, and she shifted her weight accusingly onto one hip.

"I spent the night at Korosu's," I said defensively, then realized that it didn't sound like much of an excuse. "Lighten up," I told her. "Nobody had sex." A gorgeous image trilled through my body like a warble from a songbird, and on second thought I amended my statement. "Well, I didn't, anyway."

Sabrina came into the room in time to hear our confrontation. "Leave her alone, Ginny. How can you even suspect something like that when she's so worried about Evan?"

"Thank you," I said with a nod to Sabrina, though not without a rustle of guilt. "Now come on upstairs while I change, and I'll tell you what happened."

"And anyway," Sabrina continued as we climbed the stairway,

which was more than wide enough for the three of us to walk abreast, "Korosu called Deirdre and told him you were with him and that you just needed to sleep and everything was fine and so I wasn't worried."

That solved the mystery of the perfect cappuccino. Deirdre had told him exactly what to give me when I woke up in the morning. I'd never met a person who could anticipate my wants and needs more completely. Not for the first time, I thought that if Deirdre were a man, I'd marry him. Her. Whichever.

"Come on, you two," I said as I beckoned for them to follow as I started toward my suite. "I'm a little overdressed for breakfast."

As I took off the satin pants and beaded cashmere top I had redonned this morning and changed into jeans and one of Evan's button-down shirts, I recounted what had happened the night before at the racetrack. Sabrina gasped audibly several times and tried to break in with questions, but Ginny, who was sitting next to her on the bed, kept hitting her in the face with a pillow to silence her, so I got through the whole story without interruption.

"So," I concluded, "I'm having lunch with Isabelle Ferris."

Ginny, who had reclined on my bed in a posture of ownership, reached out a graceful, determined finger and punched a button on the phone. The intercom lit up and Deirdre's voice responded almost immediately.

"Yes, ma'am?"

"At ease, Deedee, it's just me."

"Yes, Miss Virginia?" Deirdre changed gears seamlessly. She always used Ginny's full name when Ginny shortened hers.

"Can you meet us in the library, please? And ask Sophie to whip up a pot of coffee and some toast or something." Ginny looked up to me questioningly, and I waved my okay. I still didn't have much of an appetite, but my stomach was churning and I knew I should put something solid in it.

"Of course. Mr. Sebert called and said he needed to come by to 'make an adjustment.' " Deirdre rang off.

As we traipsed back downstairs, the searing burn in the core of my body grew. I felt scorched, inside and out. As I entered the library, I glanced at a photo of my father and me on the desk, and I heard his voice whisper softly, *"You can do it, nothing to it."* A stab of pain cut through me. I had lost my father; would I lose Evan too? Yet at the same time, I felt the rip in my heart fill with a strange sense of strength. My father was with me still. He had taught me well. I would not lie down and be anybody's victim.

Deirdre entered right behind us, bearing a tray with coffee and toast. Joseph followed her, holding a metal briefcase. I eyed it.

"Morning, Deirdre," I said, pleased that my voice sounded alert and professional. "Is that the package I was expecting?"

"Yes, ma'am."

I took the case and felt its considerable weight. I realized that for all my money, I'd never held three million in cash in my hand before. Sliding it under the desk, I asked, "When did Wayne call?"

"Thirty minutes ago," she said as she passed over two message slips. "And Detective Curtis as well."

Ginny and I both looked up, surprised. "Here?" Ginny asked.

Deirdre shook her head. "No. He called on my cell phone and asked for you to return his call on that line." She had the phone ready in her hand, Curtis's number displayed on the screen as she handed it to me. I had already spoken to him this morning, on Korosu's line, giving him the names of the men at Webtech who owned the box.

The doorbell sounded, distant in the entrance hall, and Deirdre left us.

"Okay." I steeled myself. "Before I call Curtis, there's something else I haven't told you." I tried to fill my lungs but could only manage a shallow breath. "I think I know who B. was."

"*Was?*" Ginny asked. I nodded. She looked thoughtful, and then her eyes widened as the reason I was using past tense occurred to her. "Banks? Are you saying it was that girl Josie *Banks?*"

Sabrina looked horrified. "You mean that's who Evan was trying to protect? Oh no!"

"I don't know for sure," I told them hesitantly, "but Curtis called me last night." I told them about the watch.

"Could have been planted!" Ginny interjected.

"I know that, and so does Curtis, but it seems very coincidental. I've been thinking about it, and it seems to fit into the whole 'Look familiar?' idea. I mean, it's possible . . ." My voice broke and I trailed off, fighting back tears as I thought of the beautiful girl, so like me. I couldn't finish the thought; I couldn't say out loud that one more similarity might have been that he had felt protective of, and maybe even loved, both of us.

"You think Evan was involved with her?" Ginny asked, looking dubious. All I could manage was a weak shrug.

Sabrina took the coffee cup from my hand and wrapped her arms around me. "It's gonna be okay," she said, rocking me gently. "You'll see, he loves you, and it's gonna be okay."

"Josie Banks. Bullshit," Ginny muttered under her breath, and I felt Sabrina glaring at her.

"I need to call Curtis back," I said, extricating myself and pressing send on the phone. He answered immediately, and I told him about lunch with Isabelle Ferris, as well as the names of the box owners.

"Just be careful what you say to anyone," he warned. "I found out something about the Josie Banks murder—we've definitely ruled out suicide."

Placing the tip of one finger over the tiny receiver, I whispered to Ginny and Sabrina, "Josie Banks, he says it's definitely murder, not suicide."

Ginny threw her hands in the air and made an indignant huffing noise.

"Get this, the company she left a few months ago was Webtech."

"You're kidding," I voiced, chilled.

"Not about this. Other than that, all I've found out is that she took the chunk of change she inherited from a rich uncle and quit to pursue her previously neglected career in art and that she spent a lot of money at exclusive spas."

"What did she do for Webtech?" I asked, feeling that this was the salient point, as anyone could be excused for spending a lot of money at exclusive spas. Personally, I thought that was a particularly good way to spend a lot of money.

"She was an assistant to one of the big honchos."

"Which one?"

"A guy named Ted Issacs."

My brain flipped through the conversation with Korosu that morning, like a series of three-by-five-inch index cards. Ted Issacs was one of the owners of the Webtech box. I reminded Curtis as much.

"Exactly. Something's up," Curtis said. "There's definitely a connection between Webtech and Evan, and I'm going to figure out what. Have you heard anything else?"

"Not yet this morning," I admitted reluctantly, feeling the pull on my already overextended nerves. "Isn't that odd?" I could easily have substituted a few other words for "odd," like "horrifying" and "cruel." However, I resisted the urge to indulge in my emotions for the simple reason that if I started screaming and couldn't stop, I wasn't likely to be very productive.

So I forced on my chairman-of-the-board attitude and asked, "What about Houndstooth's gun, anything?"

At the precise moment that I began the question, Deirdre reentered the room with Wayne close behind her.

Before Curtis had a chance to respond, Wayne crossed to me, took the cell phone from my hand, said into it, "She'll need to call you right back," and flipped it closed.

"What the fuck?" I was so shocked that I found I was still holding my phoneless hand out in midair.

"Sorry," Wayne mumbled, "not safe." Then he grimaced and raised a hand to press it against the side of his mouth.

For the first time I noticed that his lip looked split and one eye was reddened and starting to swell.

"Are you all right? What happened?"

"Well, I—" he began, but Sabrina cut him off.

"You're hurt! Deirdre, can you get us an ice pack?" My butler was out of the room before Sabrina had completed the request.

Wayne beamed at Sabrina gratefully. I had to prod him to continue. "You what?"

"Oh." He came back to earth. "I noticed a van parked on the service road that runs between the houses on your street and it just didn't seem right to me; I thought about the wireless hookup, and I realized what they could be doing."

"What?" asked Ginny.

"Well, you know," Wayne said, as though it were obvious.

"No, I don't," Ginny informed him. "So can you tell me?"

"Sure." Deirdre came back in with a flexible ice pack and a first-aid kit. Sabrina took it and steered Wayne into a chair, leaning over him to gently press the pack against his eye. His remaining eye fixed on her breasts, nine inches from his face, and we suffered another delay until I could summon him back from nirvana.

"You were saying?"

"Uh, yeah. What I told you about hooking into a wireless modem? You can do the same thing with cell phones, or even a remote phone in a house. With a receiver, they can find the frequency and listen in. Heck, they can see picture from a video camera, like a security camera."

I thought about what Curtis and I had been discussing and the fact that it had been him on the phone. "Wow," I said to Wayne. "Nice timing." But now how would I let him know that

I was all right? He must be alarmed at the manner in which he'd been cut off.

Deirdre had been standing respectfully next to Sabrina. She said, "I think it might be wise to send Joseph to a pay phone to explain to Detective Curtis what happened. Otherwise, he might be overly concerned." Barely waiting for my nod, she headed off.

Ginny was shaking her head affectionately. She said, "If that woman ever leaves you, you're gonna have to pay her alimony."

"I know. I'm planning on marrying her if things don't work out with Evan," I replied, making lighter than I felt of the possibility.

Sabrina looked shocked. "You can't do that!"

I shot her a look that I hoped would pass as infinite patience. "I'm just kidding, Sabrina. But for your information, people of the same sex do get married. Some of them much more successfully than their heterosexual counterparts."

My sister looked almost as flustered as Wayne. "I know that. It's just, well . . ."

"Not in Louisiana?" I asked.

"Can we deal with your Deep South homophobia later, if you don't mind?" Ginny cut in. She looked away from Sabrina—who was mouthing the word "homophobia" as though she wanted to look it up before she made any response—and eagerly asked Wayne, "Okay, what's up with your face?"

He lowered the ice pack and explained. "I figured I'd better take a look, so I circled the block, got out my map to the stars' homes, that, uh, I use sometimes as a cover." His face reddened, but Sabrina's lit up. She'd wanted to buy one and I'd strictly forbidden it. "And I went up and knocked on the window. The guy rolled it down, and I pretended that I didn't speak English, but he didn't seem to either, and I kept trying to stick my head in the window and see something, and finally, well, he hit me."

Sabrina *tsk-tsk*ed and Ginny observed, "He hit you more than once."

"Yeah." Wayne's good eye flicked up to Sabrina, checking for approval. "I still hadn't seen anything, and I got a little mad, so I reached through the window and got a hold of his hair."

Ginny shook her head as though she'd heard the whole sad story before. "And that's when the other guys got out of the back and pummeled you?"

Wayne's good eye looked surprised. "How did you know?"

"Educated guess." She grinned. "Did it work?"

"Yeah. I mean, I couldn't see much, what with closing my eyes and curling up into a ball, but I got a glance into the back of the van. It was pretty advanced stuff."

I sank down into a chair and groaned. "Great."

Sabrina leaned down and looked into Wayne's face. With one hand holding the ice pack and the other pressed gently against his cheek, she said encouragingly, "You were so brave. Did you get the license plate number?"

For a moment I thought Wayne had gone catatonic, for he seemed to have lost the ability to speak or hear, but he finally answered, as though he were speaking only to the angel that had appeared before him.

"Some of it, and one other thing."

"What would that be?" Ginny asked loudly, to remind him that she and I were both there.

He turned his dreamlike eyes to us and said, "The placard around the license plate. It said, 'Venice Beach, California.' "

Chapter
20

Isabelle Ferris was wearing a silly hat. The fuchsia concoction made her look as if an especially flamboyant flamingo had picked the top of her head as a nesting site. But then, that was Isabelle, always an original, and I had to give her credit for that.

I had to say something about the opening act or I would have been insulting by omission. "Where," I started, hoping I sounded like I actually wanted to know, "did you get that hat?"

"Isn't it something?" she gushed, and I made a sound that meant it was definitely *something*. She went on. "It's from the Prada spring collection. The saleswoman talked me into it."

The image of Isabelle smiling coyly at herself in a full-length mirror as one of those professional sales nazis who worked on commission told her how fabulous she looked came easily to my mind.

"At first I wasn't sure," Isabelle said as she leaned in to kiss my cheek; I had to duck under the protruding feathers frozen like a pink fireworks explosion just over her head. "But now," Isabelle was rolling on, "*everyone* comments on it."

"How could they not?" I said. "It's absolutely breathtaking." It wasn't a lie, but I quickly shifted from fashion to family. "So, how is your mom?"

It was the wrong question. I could see that from her face. "Oh, I guess she's doing fine. We don't really talk much." She smiled thinly.

Struggling to remember what the drama was, I came up with nothing. All I could recall about Cindy Ferris was that she was the first woman I'd ever known who had a tennis necklace to match the bracelet, which she referred to as her "day diamonds." The few times I'd seen her at night, she had resembled a chandelier more than anything else. I decided the best defense for my insensitive ignorance was to lay it out on the beautifully set table.

"I'm sorry, Isabelle. Did you tell me that something happened with your mom and I've forgotten? The last couple of years have been a little stressful for me, and I'm sorry if I've been so caught up in my losses and melodramas that I've not paid enough attention to yours." The confession was laced with honest regret. I knew I wasn't very good at being a friend. I used to think people just didn't like me and that was their problem, but as I got older I realized that a lot of people didn't like me because I hadn't been very nice to them. Not that I'd been rotten to them exactly, I just hadn't noticed them very much. Isabelle had always been kind to me, and I had basically ignored her in the last few years. Looking at her now, I felt terrible. "I'm really sorry," I said.

Her face softened immediately. "Oh my goodness, I don't blame you. For heaven's sake, you lost your daddy, went through that whole terrible mess about your inheritance, and then your mom died. I'm so sorry you had to go through all that." She shook her head, squeezed my hand supportively, and looked pityingly at me.

That didn't happen very often. Most people who heard that my dad died seemed to think that it had been a stroke of massive good luck for me, seeing how I'd inherited his multimillions. It was sweet to have someone empathize instead.

"Thank you, Isabelle." Maybe I should have had lunch with her more often. "So, forgive me, but what happened to, or with, your mom?"

Shaking her head and looking disgusted, Isabelle said, "She left my dad and ran off with this young guy. I mean, *twenty years* younger than her."

If I hadn't always liked Isabelle's dad so much, and if I hadn't always thought that Isabelle's mom was a money-grubbing flake, I would have said, *"Good for her."* As it was, I stayed quiet and tried to let her tell it her way.

"And of course, he took her for just about everything she got from my dad."

"Oh no, poor Cindy."

Isabelle's head jerked with a snort that sent the little pink fireworks bobbing and wheeling around her. "Poor Cindy, my patootie!" Before I could stop her, she took a deep breath and was off. "Let me tell you about this gem she paired up with. See, she went skiing in Switzerland with my ex-friend Suzanne Everett— you know her; she owns the travel agency on Beverly. She's always had a bit of a problem with alcohol, and I should have known she'd be trouble."

That began a ten-minute string of six degrees stuff, which included dubious character sketches about several people I knew vaguely, all of whom she seemed to hold loosely responsible for Gerard, the French ski instructor who had swept Cindy off her feet and away to the Alps. When Isabelle paused for breath, I knew a great deal more about the whole incestuous gaggle of them than I had ever wanted to know. I was also growing more impatient by the moment.

"And now that 'Monsieur Gerard' has bought his place in Les Deux Alps with my mom's money, she's coming after my dad for more!"

"Poor Uncle Jim," I amended, and much to my surprise I heard his voice right behind me.

"We must be talking about Cindy."

I turned and smiled up at him. I hadn't seen Jim Ferris since my father's funeral, and he had aged considerably, though I suppose at around sixty men start to show their age more and more quickly.

"Jim," I said, and stood up to give him a hug. "I didn't know you were joining us."

Isabelle explained that when she had told him that she was having lunch with me he had insisted on stopping by to say hello.

"But I won't stay long," he said pointedly to his daughter. "I have no intention of interrupting your girl talk."

"Stay as long as you like," I told him, thinking I could hope for nothing better.

So we spoke for a while of my father, and a new home that Jim was buying in Thousand Oaks, and then, when my macaroni and cheese with truffles—a Peninsula specialty whose comfort quota I seriously craved—arrived, I managed to turn the talk to business.

"So, how are things at Webtech?"

Isabelle shrugged, but I thought I saw a shadow flicker across Jim's face. Was I misreading his expression? Was something amiss at his company?

"Fine," was Jim's verbal response, and even my paranoia couldn't detect a trace of trouble in his delivery. "Isabelle's moved up, did she tell you?" He looked proudly at his daughter.

"Oh, Daddy," Isabelle said with a smile. "It was just a little promotion."

"Honey, it's a big deal. She took over a division." He was beaming. "Fred Rosen, the CEO, noticed her work and took a personal interest."

My ears perked up at the name Rosen. "Really? Are you

the company golden girl?" Now I saw a shadow pass over Isabelle's face, as though something about the situation was distasteful.

"I wish I was, but I think it's more because I'm friends with Susan, his wife. I helped her put together this event for her pet charity, you know, the one I told you about." I vaguely recalled her mentioning something the night before.

"That's my little girl. She was always good at math, spelling, and corporate strategy."

"Dad, that's enough," Isabelle said, sounding slightly embarrassed. "I have two, count them, *two* people under me. I'm not exactly being offered a vice presidency."

"She's heading up international accounting and finance. For six months now."

Isabelle seemed to feel that enough had been said on the subject. She shushed him. "It's more sideways than up, Daddy," she said, but she looked very pleased that he was proud of her.

"Oh yeah? What about that new house at the beach?" he said teasingly.

"Okay, I did get a small raise," Isabelle consented, sounding as though the subject embarrassed her.

"I wonder if you'll get to sit in the owners' box at Del Mar soon," I suggested, thinking it was a very clever transition.

"Oh, let's not get carried away," she said sourly. "That's a pretty tight boys' club."

"Really?" I asked innocently. "Didn't I see a redheaded woman up there last night?"

Isabelle told her dad, who was looking lost, that she had run into me the night before. Neither one seemed inclined to comment on the presence of the mystery woman. So I had to do it. "That woman I saw was very striking. Does she work at Webtech too?"

They both looked blankly at me, as though it were unimportant. "I don't know," said Isabelle. "I couldn't tell you because I was sitting with the bourgeoisie." She sounded pouty, and her father gave her a warning look.

"Isabelle. For goodness sake, when you own a horse, you can get a box. It's not that big of a deal to sit up there. Let it go."

Trying to spark the gossip queen, I pretended to take her side in the eternal battle of girls versus boys. Winking at her, I crossed my arms and leaned near her to show solidarity. "I wonder how *that woman* got to sit up there then? Does *she* own a horse?"

"Yeah, who was *she*?" Isabelle leaned toward me, and we both faced off with Jim.

He sighed and looked put upon. "Someone's guest, I'm sure. One reason those three guys bought the box was to invite people to the races. I can't invite you because I don't own the box." Then he laughed a little and looked at me. "Isabelle's always been horse crazy, ever since she was little."

Isabelle looked defiantly at her dad. "Maybe I *will* buy a horse."

He laughed affectionately. "Hell, why not? You just bought a house that's bigger than mine. And—not that I don't want you to do well—but if I find out your salary is bigger than mine, I'm going to be a little put out." ·

His daughter's eyes cut to me self-consciously, and I hoped she hadn't gotten herself into something she couldn't afford. She said reproachfully, "I don't have to pay your alimony."

That sobered Jim; he shook his head. "Touché."

Thinking of the sign on the street in Venice, I thought, *Dead end*. But there was still Josie Banks. I threw out, "I read something in the paper about a woman who used to work with you being murdered. Is that true?"

Jim and Isabelle exchanged a sad look. "Unfortunately, yes." Jim sighed. "I knew her, she worked really closely with one of my good friends there." He shook his head. "It's so shocking. I mean, Josie left the company and was starting out on a new life, and now this." His head still waved mournfully from side to side. "It really makes you think."

Isabelle nodded. "I didn't really know her personally. I mean, I knew who she was, by sight. It was hard to miss her, she was so pretty, and so . . ." She looked as though she was searching for the right word, the way people do when they don't want to say something mean about a dead person. ". . . ambitious."

"Yes," Jim agreed. "She was doing really well. It was a surprise when she left the company."

I mentioned that she had inherited a big pile of cash, and Jim acknowledged that fact. "I heard that too," he agreed, "but I was still surprised she gave up the company and the position. She seemed to thrive on the competition and the energy. I've seen people like that before; we have quite a few at Webtech. They love the challenge, and yes, the money too. Josie just didn't seem to me like the kind of person who would be happy out of the game."

I understood what he meant. I could have chosen to never work again, but I couldn't imagine making that choice.

"So, you don't know why she left?" I asked.

Jim looked at me a little strangely. "Why are you so interested? You didn't know Josie, did you?"

"No," I said, trying to not look flustered and come up with a valid reason at the same time. "My fiancé is a detective, and I heard him mention it."

"Fiancé?" screamed Isabelle, so loudly that most of the other diners in the restaurant stopped eating and looked at her as though she had made an even worse faux pas than choosing that hat. "Oh my God! Congratulations. I can't believe it." She was beaming; she'd hit the big news jackpot.

"Well," I said, trying to slough it off as no big deal, "we haven't set a date or anything. In fact we haven't formally announced the engagement yet. We were kind of hoping to avoid the press circus, maybe even elope quietly. He *is* a detective, and we were just thinking that social announcements in *Vanity Fair* might not be good for his undercover work. Not that *VF*'s readership is really his usual clientele." With a sinking feeling I realized that by telling Isabelle, I had just told the world as surely as if I had taken out a page ad in the *L.A. Times*.

Jim gave me a congratulatory hug. Then, with an apology and an appointment as an excuse, he made his exit as Isabelle settled in to hear all the gory details of my engagement and imagined wedding. That was painful.

It was another fifteen minutes until I could extract myself, pay the bill, and say good-bye. To my annoyance, she walked out with me.

"Oh, you got me so excited, I almost forgot." Isabelle reached into her purse as we stood waiting for the valet to bring up our cars and extracted an envelope. I recognized it right away as an invitation to an expensive charity event. They always had the same sleek, exclusive look about them. Raised letterpress snuggled into a vellum envelope. Suggesting that only you were good enough to give them a very large sum of money.

"This is going to be such a terrific affair. I know that you already have your pet charities, but you can just come to this one for fun."

Glancing quickly at the reply card in the unsealed envelope, I saw that a table for four cost five thousand dollars. Fun.

"It's going to be this Friday evening at a fabulous ranch up in Santa Ynez. It's about an hour and a half drive from here, lots of people are going to stay overnight, so let me know if you want me to make arrangements for you."

"I'll try to make it," I said, noticing that she hadn't mentioned what the charity was for, which was typical of so many socialites who helped put on these stunning displays of opulent waste. I preferred my money to go to the charity and not the party, but I said nothing. She meant well.

We waited quietly for a moment, and then, just as my car was pulling up, she sighed and said, "What a shame."

"What is?" I asked curiously.

"Well, it's just sad, about Josie, I mean. And kind of weird." She turned and looked at me, her hat painfully vibrant in the hot summer sunshine.

I put on my sunglasses as I responded. "What's weird?"

"I had a friend, Molly, who worked at Webtech, and she was kind of like Josie. I mean, not exactly, but both Molly and Josie were really attractive, blond, terrific bodies. The kind of women everybody wants to hate because they are all that and smart too. Kind of like you." She gazed out at the street dumbly for a few seconds before spinning back and grasping at my arm. "Not that I hate you, not at all, that's not what I meant. I think you're *terrific!*"

She was so mortified that her apology would have been amusing if I had been capable of feeling anything but impatience. I cleared my throat and ignored the valet who had brought my car and was standing with the door open, waiting for me. "So, did Molly leave the company too?"

"She died," Isabelle said, and the two words shot through me like a harsh, bitter taste.

"Murdered?" I gasped.

"No! Accident. She was in a car crash. She and Josie were both so pretty. Men just fell all over themselves for them. They were both moving up in the company." She shook her head sadly. "Isn't it *weird* that they would both die within a couple of months of each other?"

It was my turn to look out over the street dumbly. I could almost hear Evan's voice in my ear, repeating one of his favorite dictums. *There is no such thing as a coincidence.*

Chapter
21

Deirdre met me on the way in, handing me a single piece of paper and saying, "From Detective Curtis." I read it as I headed across the hallway:

"Callaway, I was right about the spare gun at Evan's house, it was his. But the gun you collected from Houndstooth, as you refer to him, is the one that killed the man. The strange thing is, I can't get a registration on it. It's as though the gun never existed. I'm still working on it. I'm also trying to sort out the plates on the van, but I'm not expecting it to be a valid license plate. *Be careful!*"

I stood looking at the note for a moment without really understanding. Then I went straight to my computer, but it held no cryptic messages.

Suddenly, through the open French doors, I heard a woman cry out. Hesitating just long enough to pull my gun from the lockbox in the desk drawer and jam in the clip, I raced back out onto the patio and stood listening with all my might.

"Ahh!" This time the yell was followed by what sounded

like a body hitting the ground hard. Someone was being as-saulted just around the corner, and that someone sounded like my sister.

Sabrina, hold on, I'm coming.

The bushes were thick, but I pushed through them as quietly as my urgency would allow, and then, through a lace of green vegetation, I saw her.

She was in a defensive stance, panting, eyes wide. Her hair was a wild, messy mop, and her arms were raised in front of her like a bizarre parody of some kung fu movie. She was fac-ing a man with his back to me, and even as I spotted him, he went at her.

But as I raised my gun, I watched in amazement as Sabrina twisted sharply, thrusting one foot out and pushing hard with her arms, toppling the man to the ground.

I leaped forward and, holding the gun tightly in both hands, pointed it at the man's back.

Something hit me hard from the side, and I found my own face pressed into the moist grass. Winded, I rolled over, squinting up into the hot, glaring sun.

Sabrina stood over me, and she was inexplicably furious. "Put that stupid thing away! You're gonna kill somebody." Then she bent down and held out her hand to her attacker. "Are you okay, honey?" Her voice was sweeter than the endearment.

It was Darrien. I groaned and rolled back onto my stomach, wanting to sink into the ground.

"Nice reflexes," he was saying to Sabrina. "The throw was ex-cellent, but you probably shouldn't have used excessive force on your sister."

"Well," Sabrina said sulkily, "I thought she was going to shoot you."

"She might have if the gun had misfired when you tackled her," he said. "Are you all right, Callaway?"

I flopped back over and looked up at him, mortified at the

thought of what I'd almost done. I said, "No permanent damage." Though my arm hurt like hell.

He helped me to my feet.

"Darrien's teaching me some self-defense moves." Sabrina was as proud and excited as a kid who'd just learned to jump rope.

"No shit," I said, rubbing my solar plexus, trying to get the air to flow back into my lungs. "He seems to have covered a few *offensive* moves as well," I said, referring to how hard she'd hit me. "I think I'd like to sit down."

Sabrina's expressions changed as instantly as her thought processes. "So, what happened? Did you find out anything at your lunch? And we've got something to tell you."

"Yeah," I told them as we started the walk back to the house. "I found out that another woman who worked at Webtech turned up dead a couple of months ago, supposedly a car accident. What about you?"

"Well, Wayne and I went web surfing," she said, and I couldn't help smiling at her newfound computer lingo. "We found a bunch of newspaper articles about Webtech. Apparently, they're being investigated for missing funds. And there was some kind of scandal with a female employee who claimed sexual harassment, but it was settled out of court."

I nodded, thinking about Josie Banks and hearing Isabelle's words, *"They were both so pretty."* "Let's keep it in mind," I replied.

We'd reached my library, and Sabrina showed me the articles she and Wayne had printed out. The information was pretty general; the board had been questioned about misappropriation of funds, but the investigation didn't seem to have gone anywhere. The articles were all from three to four months earlier.

"So, we've got missing money, allegations of sexual misconduct, and somehow those things must be connected to Evan's disappearance," I said, trying to make it fall into some kind of recognizable pattern.

Darrien was nodding. "If we could find out who's specifically being investigated, it might help."

Then I told them what Isabelle had said about a woman named Molly dying, and we did a web search to see what we could find to match that name, a recent death, and Webtech.

There was a small article in the local paper, detailing the death of one Molly Anne Simpson, a six-figure salary holder at Webtech International; she'd apparently been out on a Saturday drive on the twisting road that climbed from Santa Barbara to Santa Ynez when she had met with a fatal accident. The article said that she had been alone, and sober.

There was a knock at the door and Deirdre came into the room without waiting for my reply. She never did that, and, alarmed, I rose quickly to meet her.

When I saw what was in her hand, all the blood seemed to leave my limbs, and the room swam.

Without apology or explanation, she held it out to me. My heart seized up painfully.

She was holding an envelope, addressed to me. With a shaking hand, I opened it and pulled out two things. The first was a postcard, and I shuffled it quickly behind the second item, which was a Polaroid. It was a picture of Evan taken against a blank cement wall. His face was bruised, but he looked alive, and, I was proud to note, defiant.

But right through the middle of the photo, where his heart would be, was a gaping bullet hole.

Chapter
22

The postcard was a shot of downtown L.A. on one of those once-in-a-decade days, when high winds follow a hard rain and wash away all of the smudging and filth left by the haze and the Hummers.

The glass monoliths of downtown L.A. were in the foreground, then the gentler hills of Hollywood and Beverly. Far beyond that, across the valley, the San Gabriel Mountains rose to snow-covered peaks.

There was, on closer inspection, a small pencil mark of an arrow pointing at the window of one building, and on the back, the words, "Find her. You have two days left."

Sabrina and Darrien came and peered over my shoulder. I felt frozen inside and sweaty outside, like an ice sculpture perspiring as it started to melt.

Dimly I became aware of them speaking and then moving around me.

"I'll pull up MapQuest," Sabrina was saying. Darrien had taken my arm and was pulling me to a chair.

Their words came slowly into my brain. "Okay, good," he was saying. "We have something to go on. Let's get to work."

Work. Yes, good, I could do that. Snapping out of it, I sat down next to Sabrina. She centered in on a map of downtown; by working from landmark buildings we could easily identify and assign a street number to, we figured out the address of the one marked with the pencil arrow.

When we had the address, a bell rang in my head and I snatched up the postcard from the desktop. "I know this building!" I said. "This is where the law firm that handles my estate planning is."

"Oh, right." Sabrina looked excited. "That's where we went to sign all the paperwork when you adopted me." She was being facetious. I hadn't adopted her, of course, but I was writing her into my will and making her the recipient of a portion of my estate. "That's that lady lawyer, Dana, right? The really pretty one."

"What floor is this?" I asked, holding out the postcard and pointing to the arrow.

Darrien and I both counted, and then double counted, the rows of windows up to the floor indicated on the postcard. Eighteen. "That's their floor!" I exclaimed.

Darrien looked at me. "Do they have the whole floor?"

"No," I answered. "There are definitely other offices on the same floor. I'd say they have, maybe"—I shrugged—"a quarter of the floor?"

"So, you could get in there," Darrien said.

"I suppose so." The thought of facing another situation like last night alone made me feel as spineless as a Slinky. "Where's Ginny?" I asked, my voice sounding childlike.

Sabrina told me that she had gone out to meet Curtis and that she'd promised to be back before two. I looked at my watch: 2:05. Punching a single digit on speed dial on my office phone, I waited, but it went straight to a recording. Her cell phone was off. Then, glancing at the perforated photo of Evan, I brought my spiral Slinky spine upright.

"Let's go." I stood. "But listen, I think when we get there, I should go in alone."

"Why?" Sabrina asked, looking affronted.

"Because it would be better for you two to stay outside and keep an eye out. Someone is definitely watching us, and maybe you can spot who."

Darrien was nodding. "It's a good idea. But we'll go up with you and wait in the hallway. All right?" Relieved to have his reassuring presence, I agreed.

While they drove me downtown to the building, Sabrina programmed Darrien's cell phone number into mine and made sure it was displayed.

"Now, all you have to do is push send. So just keep your finger on it. We'll be right outside, and we know where *you'll* be, so we can get to you in about one second."

Something felt odd. I looked at Sabrina and realized what it was. "Are you taking care of me?" I asked her.

She looked happy. "And I always will."

I nodded and turned away before the moment got uncomfortable and gushed the pink sticky sap of embarrassment all over us. I might have opened up in the last year, but I hadn't gone Hallmark.

We parked in front of the office building and walked past the busy street-level stores—a Rite-Aid pharmacy, a McDonald's, a Kinko's, a Taco Bell. I had called and said I needed to drop off some papers, so it wasn't a lie when I said we were expected at Scheiner, Meyers, and Alexander.

Once on the correct floor, we got our bearings and determined that the window we were looking for was definitely on the side of the building where my estate attorneys had their offices, possibly in their quarter of the building.

Okay, good start.

I left Darrien and Sabrina by the elevator and proceeded alone through the large heavy doors of the accounting firm.

The receptionist told me that Ms. Scheiner was expecting me. Did I know the way to her office?

Now I lied and said yes. I needed to count the windows. According to the postcard, the marked window was the eighth one from the south side of the building. If I could go through the door, all the way down the hall to the right, and then start counting on my way back, I should be able to figure it out.

"Ms. Scheiner's office is to the left," the helpful receptionist said.

I thanked him out loud and added a silent nod of gratitude to the architect who had designed the space so that reception did not overlook the rest of the offices. Ignoring the curious glances from the secretaries who sat at their posts across from the doors to their bosses' offices, I walked all the way to the right, pretended to have made a wrong turn, and started counting as I made my way back. Most of the office doors were open, and each seemed to have one large window. Hoping that the closed doors held no surprises, I counted off. When I had reached five, I passed the door to reception again, and when I came to eight, I stopped and stared at the nameplate beside the door with growing confusion.

It read: DANA SCHEINER.

What the fuck? I spotted her through the open door, and all that came to me was the thought that the kidnappers were going to try to kill my estate attorney.

She was sitting at her desk, looking out the window distractedly at the other scattered high-rises and the haze beyond them.

"Dana?" I asked as I knocked softly, thinking to myself, *Oh God, please don't go after someone I know.* But I tried to keep the fear off my face until I could learn something more.

"Callaway!" She looked surprised and stood up as I came in.

"Hi, I'm sorry, I was just thinking about this living trust." She put a hand flat on the thick stack of legal paperwork in front of her. It looked imposing.

"Did they tell you I was coming by?" I asked.

"Yes. Do you have something for me?" She seemed distracted, busy.

Although I'd had no idea that it was *her* office I was looking for, I had brought some paperwork as an explanation for my presence on her floor.

"Um, not exactly, but I wanted to make a couple of changes in the will for my half sister."

"Oh." She looked a little surprised, and I knew why; normally I would phone in the changes, or make an appointment, not just drop by. "Okay. Have a seat." Her phone buzzed and she said, "Excuse me, I'm so sorry, but I *have* to answer this."

As she took the call, I had a chance to study her. She was very beautiful and expensively dressed. I caught myself comparing her to me, and I remembered again being jealous of her because Evan had recommended her to me when I'd first met him. I recalled the way I'd questioned him about her.

We'd been driving, trying to get to the bottom of a very different situation, and I'd asked him, "So, is your relationship with Dana strictly professional?"

He had laughed and fixed his steely blue eyes, glittering with humor, on me. "You mean," he had asked, "like my 'professional' relationship with you?" My fiercely jealous side had let it rest at that. Later I'd found out he had his own millions and she handled *his* estate.

I sighed, the thought of his eyes and his smile warming me from the inside out. I wanted him back. Two days, I told myself. *Two days and whatever it takes.*

Dana was wrapping up the call when someone came in and dropped a delivery on her desk. She picked it up and opened it distractedly, ripping the top off and turning the padded envelope upside down.

A cell phone slid into her hand. Looking confused, Dana peered into the envelope.

The phone rang.

Dana's eyes went wide, and she looked up at me.

My heart was beating wildly, but I tried to stay calm. "Answer it."

Dana flipped the phone open and said, "Hello?" I watched her for any clue to what she might be hearing and tried to calm my wildly speculating mind. Dana's face went from white to gray as she listened, and then she began to stutter.

"No, please. I don't . . . why are you doing this? Who are you?" Her voice had a hysterical edge, and it was rising.

Reaching over the desk, I took the phone away from her.

"Who is this?" I asked.

It was Russian's voice that answered, thick with an eastern European accent and the rasp of a four-pack-a-day smoker. "Good for you, you found her."

"Yes," was all I would say.

"Now. You have two choices. Get her to take our offer—your three million and she leaves the country for good by Saturday at noon."

I fought to stay cool, to not show my panic on my face, but I turned deliberately away from Dana, who was watching me intently. "And if she refuses?" I asked.

"You kill her."

The room in front of me wavered for a second as I absorbed the impact of his words. "And if I won't?"

"I kill boyfriend. It's him or it's her."

Before I could respond, there was a shuffling, and then another voice and my heart leaped. "I'm sorry about this, *mon choux*," he said softly. It might have been my imagination, but he sounded weak.

"Are you all right?" I asked, close to collapsing from relief that he was still alive, and fury and frustration that I couldn't get to him.

"I'm fine. Don't worry about me. Listen, you have to get her to take the money."

"I don't understand, what should I do?"

There was another rustling noise, and the first voice came back on. "Just make sure you have the money. You'll get your instructions soon. And if you don't do exactly what I say . . ."

"What? You'll do what?" I pushed. "If you harm him, you won't get anything."

"Remember that snapshot I sent you?" There was a rustling, and then the sound of a gunshot retorted so loudly that I pulled the phone away from my ear.

The line went dead.

"Damn it!" I punched at the phone commands, trying to get the call number on the screen, but nothing came up.

I turned to Dana, who was standing with both hands up to her mouth and tears forming in her eyes.

"What did he say to you?" I asked. She shook her head. "Dana, tell me!"

"He said . . ." Her voice quavered. "He said that if I didn't do what he said, I'd end up like Josie Banks."

"Did you know her?" I asked, surprised.

Dana nodded. "She was a client."

Josie Banks, her inheritance, Dana. Click. Evan's watch. Had he recommended Dana to that beautiful corpse as well?

I forced myself back into the moment. The cell phone had arrived with me. Who knew I was here? Who had seen me walk in? There must be an informant in the office, or worse. "Come on," I said, grabbing her purse off the back of her chair. "We've got to get out of here, now!"

"Shouldn't we call the police or something?" Dana was looking at me with frightened eyes.

"Not yet. Come on." I grabbed her arm, and we started back out into the hall.

We managed to get into the hallway without exciting much more than a few curious looks. Sabrina and Darrien looked up at us in confusion as I corralled them toward the elevator.

"I'll explain later," I told them with a pointed glance at Dana's shocked face. We waited for the lift nervously.

When the doors slid open, I found myself face-to-face with the last person I wanted to see.

Houndstooth looked from Dana to me, and a smile spread across his face.

Chapter

23

Honing in on Dana, he reached inside his jacket. I backed away, pulling both Sabrina and Dana with me.

"Darrien, that's him!" I shouted, unsure of what he was supposed to do.

Darrien, however, was completely sure of what to do. Before Houndstooth could draw out his gun, Darrien had pinned him against the back of the elevator, trapping his arm inside his jacket. With one hand, Darrien punched the gray-haired man hard in the solar plexus, knocking the wind from him. Then he pressed a button on the panel and backed out of the elevator. As the doors slid closed again, Houndstooth recovered and lunged toward us.

Too late. The doors had closed and he was on his way to the lobby. I looked around. "Where are the stairs? We've got to get out!"

The exit sign was down the hall, and we all went for it. But once inside the landing, Darrien blocked me from heading downstairs.

"Go up!" he ordered, and when I looked at him, confused, he explained, "He'll be expecting us to take the stairs down; he'll be coming up. We'll go up two floors and then take the elevator down to the garage. Go!"

It was good thinking; it must be the kind of thing they teach you in bodyguard school.

We made it down to the lobby and out to the car without seeing a single gray hair. Thank God.

Darrien took the driver's seat and asked where we were going. Somehow I didn't think that either my home or Dana's was a good idea. "Just head toward Santa Monica," I told him. Turning to face the distraught woman next to me as we hit Century Boulevard, I said, "I think it might be a good idea if you didn't go in to work for a few days."

Her face, as she looked at me, was ashen. "Who was that man?" she asked.

"I don't know," I said honestly. "But I do know he's involved in something dangerous." Having no idea where to start, I decided to let her do it. "Tell me what's going on with you."

She broke down, but only for a second; her face dissolved and she covered it with her hands, rubbing hard to compose herself. When she had regained control she said, "It has something to do with Josie Banks."

Sabrina and I looked at each other; she opened her mouth, but I shook my head slightly to let her know not to speak.

"You were handling her estate?" I prompted, not letting on that I knew anything about the woman.

Dana took a deep breath and pressed her fingers to her temples. "A few months ago, maybe five or six months, I was contacted by a man, a lawyer from Santa Fe. He told me that a client of his had died and left a considerable sum of money to a relation in Los Angeles. He wanted me to get in touch with her and take care of the transfer of the will." She paused a moment and looked out the window. "Where are we going?" she asked.

"To a friend's house where I think we can talk safely," I said. "Go on."

She nodded. "Okay, yes. So, I executed the will and oversaw the transfer of the money to Josie Banks. It should have been standard stuff, but something just struck me as strange about the whole business."

"What?" I asked.

"Well, it's hard to say, but mostly, her." She looked at me as though she was hopeful I would understand, but I requested clarity.

"Her behavior?"

"Yes, she just seemed so, I don't know, *resentful*. I mean, most people don't behave that way when they come into millions of dollars."

Sabrina was nodding, and I remembered that she had had a similar experience. A lawyer had contacted her in the midst of her small-town life and told her she was the natural daughter of a multimillionaire. Surprise! Talk about a gamut of emotions. Before my severe look could stop her, Sabrina said, "You just don't know how you'll act before something like that happens to you. You assume it's like a gift from God to get a whole lot of money, but it makes people act more like the devil."

Dana tore her eyes off the Kewpie doll I call a sister and tried to focus on the subject at hand. "Not right away, but later, yes. The accounts that the money came from were numbered off-shore accounts. More like money that had been hidden than money someone had accrued and was leaving a relative. And though she seemed to know nothing about this man, she was the only one named in the will. And one more thing." Dana sat up, her dark eyes coming alive. "There was no property." She shook her head as though that just wasn't right. "This guy lived and died, and had no house? No car? No belongings of any kind? I just kept thinking how odd that was."

"Did you ask about it?"

"Of course. But neither Josie nor the lawyer in Santa Fe seemed inclined to give me an answer; they both just said that the man was eccentric and this was how he had left everything." She gave me a shared, sideways look as though only a simpleton would have accepted that bogus response.

"That doesn't sound quite right."

Dana almost snorted. "It has illegal money transfer written all over it. I didn't like it. I could have been held accountable, so I started looking into it." She looked past me out the window, and her expression clouded again. "And that was a big mistake."

Gently, so as to draw her back but not upset her, I asked in a soft, businesslike voice, "What happened next?"

"I went to speak to Josie. I had a feeling she was being used in some way. She was a bright girl, but not overly so, and I warned her that if she was involved in something illegal she could go to prison for life. She got very agitated and told me for my own good to just stay out of it." Dana took a deep breath and then continued. "That's when the threatening phone calls began. They told me not to go to the police, but I was so frightened. I called Evan Paley." She paused, and I shot a "Don't speak" look at Sabrina but she was pressing her lips together.

What Dana said next made me feel hollow. "You know, the detective who worked on your case? I know he recommended you to me, and I think I told you he was a client too, but I'm not sure you knew he and I were very much in love at one time, and we've stayed 'friends.' "

I wasn't sure which revelation was making the world outside spin around—the fact that Evan had been in love with this woman sitting next to me, or the fact that Evan had obviously not told her about us. *"The detective who worked on your case?"* I was reeling. Was it possible that Evan had kept me, and our relationship, a secret from Dana? Was this the real reason he hadn't wanted to announce our engagement?

She smiled softly as though recalling a bittersweet memory and said to me, "He used to call me Busenka, his little charm."

Busenka

B.

Bastard.

Chapter

24

Ginny's place, I decided, was the best choice for Dana to decompress until I could speak to Curtis.

After I arranged things with Ginny on the phone, she met us at her condo. It was a beautiful old home that had been turned into four exclusive addresses. I asked Darrien and Sabrina to wait in the car while I got Dana settled in.

We settled on the sofa. Struggling to find a voice and words that would not betray me, I asked, "So, what did Detective Paley say when you called him?"

"He said he would help me. I knew he would." She toyed with a chain bracelet on her wrist for a moment, and I was treated to a look of affectionate remembrance in her eyes. "He's always been there for me. It didn't work out the last time, but we've stayed close, and I've always felt that we'd get back together when the time was right." She seemed to draw herself back from the past reluctantly. "So anyway," she continued, "he started to look into the situation, trying to find out who was behind the phone calls. And then, one night, when he met me so that I could give him copies of the files . . ." She paused, as though the memory was stinging her, and then she collected herself and went on. "He met me at a restaurant downtown, and when we went to the carpark, a man was waiting for me. Evan . . ." She dropped off and looked down at her hands in her lap, which were now twisted into a knot any sailor would have been proud of. "He handled it."

I remembered a time when Evan had told me he'd "handled" things, and the blood on his shirt that had kept me from asking him any questions. The thought that he could be just as protective of another woman hurt me in a primitive way.

"Did he kill him?" My voice sounded flat, dead.

Dana looked up warily. "No. But I don't think I should tell you any more."

I nodded, feeling vaguely surprised that I could move at all. "And when was that?"

"A couple of weeks ago. And then I heard that Josie was dead, murdered." She choked on the word, and then, with a continually threatening note of panic in her voice, she went on. "And I tried to contact Evan, but I haven't been able to reach him. He's ignoring me, or, or—"

"Or what?" I asked. I needed to know.

"Or something's happened to him." She began to cry again. "What if I've lost him?"

In spite of the shocked numbness in my body, I felt a sensation of warmth on my knee. Looking down, I saw that Ginny had placed a firm hand there. I met her eyes dumbly, but all I could think was the same thing as Dana.

What if I've lost him?

Ginny took control of the situation and showed Dana to her guest room, where she could lie down for a little while.

Then Ginny came back, put an arm around me, and said, "Okay, we don't know anything for sure except that he owes you one *really good* explanation."

I was infinitely relieved; she had recognized my desperate hope that there was a simple, reasonable explanation. She was also the one person in the world, besides me, who could hear all of this about Evan and still be confident that there *could* be a viable explanation. "So let's hear his side first. And then we can beat him up or ditch him." I had to smile. "Have you still got the cell phone?" she asked.

"Yeah." I fished it out of my purse. "Here."

While she was checking it over, I said, "So we should be able to trace the number to somebody, right? I mean, someone gets a bill."

She looked at me in a pitying way. "Girl, you and your money are so out of touch. First of all, it could easily be stolen. But I think it's more likely that it's one of those phones you buy with a prepaid number of minutes on it. It's basically a disposable phone."

She was right; I was out of touch and I hated dealing with electronics. Kelly kept me in the latest cell phones, setting them up for me and then explaining any functions I would want to use. I had no idea you could buy a phone that was the portable equivalent of a phone card.

"You can do that?" I asked.

"And you can do it with cash. Untraceable," she explained. "But it's still live, so it could ring again."

I nodded; the same thought had occurred to me. "I'll keep it with me."

Ginny went and fumbled in a drawer. I could see from across the room that it was filled with a jumble of cords and cables. "Here!" she said victoriously as she extracted a black tangle. "This charger should work."

"Thanks," I said as I put the phone and its life force back into my bag.

"Now, what do I do with the big D.?" she asked me. I hesitated; I would have liked her to drop off the planet, yet that was exactly what I was going to try to prevent.

"Just keep her safe until Curtis lets us know what to do next. I suppose I'd better get back and wait for my next instructions. Am I supposed to give Dana the three million to shut her up, you think?"

"Looks that way."

"Will she take it? And anyway, what kind of guarantee would that be?"

Ginny shook her head. "I don't know."

I stood up and gathered my bag. "And, uh, let me know if she tells you anything else?" Ginny nodded. "You'll call Curtis?"

"He's already on it. He'll be here after you leave; he wants to put some space between my social visits."

"Thank you, Ginny." I started for the door.

"Hey," she called after me, and I stopped and turned back. Her eyes were shining strength at me. "It's gonna be all right. No matter what. It's gonna be all right."

"But what if he doesn't come back?" I choked on the rawness of my finally spoken fear.

"He will."

I nodded, letting the horror go, but a second force went through me, producing a thin sluice of tears.

"What if he does?" I whispered; it was all the voice I had.

She smiled as though I were a child and said, "Then, no matter what happens with this chick, you've got the strength to handle it with class. You've come a long way, and you are who you are with *or without* a man." She shrugged as though it was a done deal. "And, you'll have me."

"As long as I have you," I said with a smile, and she walked me out to the car, where Darrien and Sabrina were waiting.

After a silent ride through L.A. traffic, they dropped me back off at home. Sabrina wanted to commiserate, but after thanking her for the sentiment, I informed her that I didn't have time for it.

What I did have to do was get a look at any other communications between Evan and Dana. It only took me fifteen minutes to drive to Evan's house, where I used my key to let myself in. Going straight to his computer, I sat down and opened up his email.

A sound in the hallway alerted me to the fact that I was not alone. Footsteps were coming toward the office door. Retrieving my gun from my bag, I moved quickly to the wall beside the door and waited.

The footsteps stopped just outside, and there was a pause; whoever it was was standing still, listening. The light from the computer screen flickered through the darkened room, and I realized, too late, that the door was open a crack and the light could easily be detected.

I tensed as the door began, very slowly, to creak open. I counted to three, exhaled, and swung around, bringing my gun up in front of me.

A scream met me, and Evan's housekeeper stumbled backward, cowering, against the hallway wall.

"Maria! Christ, I'm sorry! I forgot you'd be here." I let my gun fall to my side, then went quickly to comfort her.

She was taking huge gulps of air. "I thought it was Detective Paley, I thought maybe he was back. I was hoping."

"No, I'm sorry. It's just me. I'm looking for something that might help him," I lied.

It took me a few minutes to get her calmed down, and then, when she'd gone to revive herself with a little nip of something, I got back to work.

Quickly, I reviewed his old emails, and there were a few from B., which I now knew to be Dana. Most of them were pleas asking for his help getting these people off her back, often punctuated with hints of continued feeling and connection. But no "I love yous," I noted. Quite a few of them had bounced back and forth, so I could see how Evan had responded. His notes back were always simple, reassuring, affectionate even, but not overtly so. To comfort myself I fabricated elaborate theories of a woman who couldn't let go of her feelings, who fantasized about a man still being in love with her.

But it just didn't seem to mesh with Dana Scheiner's formidable personality. And why had he not told her about us? What was the point of keeping me a secret? I knew that he had misgivings about me being a target if anyone wanted to come after him, but weren't we getting married? It wasn't like he would be able to keep me secret after that.

And then I found one email that I just couldn't explain away. It read: **Remember last night and how I feel about you.** He had signed it: **Your Evan.**

Confused, bruised, and barely able to think of what to do, I gathered up the fragments of my broken heart and walked out of the house. I needed to go somewhere safe, to talk to someone who could help me sort out the facts from the emotions.

And I could only think of one place. One person.

Chapter

25

Korosu's corporate office was on the top floor of a building on Figueroa. The double doors into his office opened onto a space with windows that overlooked most of the city. The floors were a polished black, and the furniture was tastefully minimal, a large desk, a few ultramodern chairs, and a built-in window seat that ran the length of the room, upholstered in a discreet black textile.

Nice.

When his secretary had shown me in, he'd come to the door to meet me, then he'd led me to the window seat.

"Tell me," he said as he offered me ice water from a silver pitcher. I accepted both invitations.

I told him about the most recent postcard and the photo of Evan sporting a bullet hole, finding out that the office was Dana's, the cell phone's arrival, and even the fact that Dana had been involved with Evan, that she had been B., though I tried to make it sound like their involvement was more of a possible clue than a crushing threat to me. He listened, intent. When I concluded with a lame "And I don't know what to do now," he leaned back against one of the frames separating the giant glass panes and looked thoughtfully at nothing in particular.

"You were in her office for how long when the phone came in?" he asked me.

"Not even a couple of minutes."

"And it rang right when she opened the package?"

"So it must be someone in her office, I know, I thought of that," I replied. "But the only people who could have seen me go in were the secretaries, who sit in a row down the inside wall. There are no partitions between them, and you can see all the way down the hallway. I checked, but nobody seemed to be paying the slightest attention to me being there."

"Could anyone see into the office?"

I laughed mirthlessly. "Not unless they had a crystal ball."

Korosu set down his glass. "But the caller seemed to know exactly when she opened the envelope. How could someone, even someone who knew the envelope was delivered, know when she would have the phone in her hand?" His eyes sparkled intelligently. He took my hand and pulled me to my feet, turning me to face the city. "Look," he said.

"What?" But almost immediately I understood. Though we were a good distance away from, and above, the nearest building across the street, I could clearly make out people working in their offices. "Holy shit," I breathed. "I can't believe I didn't think of that."

He came behind me and placed his hands on my shoulders. "Can you see her building from here?"

I looked around, got my bearings, and pointed. "There!"

"Okay, good. Now, can you tell which side her office window is on?"

That was easy, as I had spent so much time figuring that out earlier in the day. Her office looked toward the ocean. It was on the west side. Once we had established that, we found two buildings that would have a view into her office. Korosu crossed to his desk and pressed a button. Within seconds, his sharply dressed assistant came in, followed by an equally stylish young man.

"Get me the addresses and lists of tenants in both of those buildings." Korosu pointed them out. Neither of his employees showed any signs of this being an unusual request. "Do it now."

Both of them nodded and retreated with, I noticed, a sense of importance rather than servility.

"Now we wait," he said. We both sat down again, keeping a respectful distance between us. "Are you hungry? Would you like something to eat?" he asked solicitously.

The little I'd managed to eat at lunch was sitting uncomfortably in my stomach, so I thanked him but refused the offer.

I looked out at the city; the sun was low in the sky and that magical light that gilded everything, including the summer smog, was warming the room and our faces with a crimson wash. Somewhere out in that deceptively glowing city was Evan. I was sure of it. I needed him desperately, needed his safety and his reassurance.

Korosu was thoughtfully not watching me. But I couldn't stand it anymore; girlfriends and sisters were all very well, but there were times in my life when I needed to talk to a man. Suddenly, with everything I knew flying away from me, it was very important to me to have someone understand my feelings, to feel the pull of gravity again.

"Evan keeps certain things from me, to *protect* me, he says, but it's always made me feel . . ." I searched for the right words. ". . . shut out. You said you didn't think that there was any other woman. But today I found out that Dana and he were lovers, something he neglected to tell me. I even asked him once, and he made a joke of it. And now I find out that he'd also hidden our relationship from her.

"I don't know if he loves her still, or if there's anything sexual between them, I'm not sure. There is affection, certainly, that much I can read in the emails, and she loves him, she made that clear." Finally I turned and looked at Korosu. He met my eyes and waited. "I don't know if he's deceiving me."

He watched me without a flicker of assessment, and then he asked, very softly, "What do you feel?"

"Wounded," I whispered. "I feel like I'm bleeding. Vulnerable, and that's something that I've never allowed myself to be before."

And then I saw it, just for a second—the deep longing in the depths of his eyes. But it was gone so quickly that I could almost think I imagined it. "I believe that Detective Paley is both an honorable and an intelligent man. There are many women"—his voice dropped to a husky whisper, and I could hear the sincerity in his words—"but not any like you."

I felt the tears sting my eyes; loneliness and need swelled up and overtook me. I leaned forward and, parting my lips slightly, I kissed him. I wanted desperately to feel his strong arms around me, to be coveted, to be safe.

He put his arms around me, but, though his lips quivered slightly against mine, he did not return my kiss. Yet, for all his self-control, his voice shook as he whispered to me, "No, not like this." He pressed me to him, but it seemed only to stop himself from making a much more passionate move, from giving in. He pulled away and looked at me. "Callaway Wilde. I would not share you. Not you. I can wait." Then he took my face in his hands and kissed my mouth once, so lightly that I barely felt the brush of lips, and then he released me and got up from the window seat. I could see the effort that it cost him to walk away.

But when he spoke again, he said, "I have the greatest respect for and faith in Detective Paley. I not only believe that he loves you but that he will be safely back with you soon."

His personal feeling about what that meant to him was betrayed only by the faintest trace of sorrow in his eyes.

Somewhere a cell phone rang. The sound was muffled and

distant. Jumping up, I snatched my bag from the desk chair where I'd left it and fumbled inside until I came up with the phone that was ringing. It was my personal line; the readout said it was Kelly.

"Yes?" I answered, somewhat annoyed; I had asked her to hold my business calls.

"Callaway, hi. You got a call from an old friend of yours who used to have a house on the same lake as your family. He asked if you could call him as soon as it's convenient."

"What are you talking about?" I asked. But even as the question escaped me, I put it together. My mother had had a small cabin in a place called Curtis Lake. "Oh, never mind. Okay, thanks."

I hung up and turned to Korosu. "Can I use your phone?" I asked. "The office line?" He nodded and gestured me over to his desk.

Curtis picked up immediately. "Cally?"

"Yes. Any news?"

"Yeah. I found the report on the Molly Simpson accident. She seemed to run her car off the road for absolutely no apparent reason."

"I knew that from the newspaper article."

"What you don't know," Curtis went on impatiently, "is that she was coming from visiting the weekend home of the CEO of Webtech. When her family was questioned, it came out that they suspected she was having an affair with him. There were tire marks on the road near the turn where she went off. Multiple ones. The family demanded an inquiry."

"So she was having an affair with Fred Rosen and it wasn't an accident."

"The inquiry turned up nothing. Rosen's wife, one Susan Montgomery Rosen, gave him an alibi for that day, and the tire marks didn't prove anything other than the fact that she probably wasn't the only one who took that particular curve too fast."

"Oh."

"There's something else." Curtis sounded pained.

"What?" My heart felt as though it might leap out through my chest.

"When I looked it up on the computer, certain things seemed to be missing, deleted. So I went to pull the hard-copy file, but it was checked out . . . to Evan. And the parts that were deleted had been circled on the hard copy."

"Oh," I repeated. I didn't know what else to say. Korosu had walked discreetly away, but the sound of that syllable made him turn and look at me questioningly.

"I don't know how to say this to you, Cally, but it looks like Evan was pretty deeply involved in this."

The next word stuck in the back of my throat and came out hoarsely. "Illegally?"

There was a pause, then Curtis said, "I don't want to think so, but . . ." His voice dropped away, and I heard him clear his throat. "I'm on my way to meet with this Dana Scheiner. We'll see what she has to say about it. You go home, let me know if you hear anything."

I put the phone back on its base and stayed looking down at it for a moment.

Across the room Korosu remained motionless. I stirred myself from my thoughts and smiled sadly up at him.

"You," I said to him, "might be the only one left who trusts Evan."

Korosu sighed. "No," he said, "not the only one." He raised a finger to illustrate the single number and then tilted it slowly down until it was pointed at me.

I tried to smile. I wasn't even sure I trusted myself.

Chapter
26

When I got home, I was surprised to find Ginny in Sabrina's room, but before I could even question her presence she said, "Curtis," and I knew that he was with Dana at Ginny's condo.

Sabrina was perched on the end of her bed, and I had obviously caught them in mid-discussion.

"He told you about the Molly Simpson woman," Ginny began.

"All about it," I cut her off, wondering if she knew the whole story.

"Keep your shirt on," she said somewhat impatiently. "You haven't seen this." She pulled out a manila envelope and slid out a photograph. It was one of those corporate photos, but instead of the usual ugly mug, this woman could easily have been on the cover of *Cosmopolitan*.

"Is that her?" I asked, chilled to think of that smile extinguished.

"None other." Ginny took the photo back and said dryly, "Not too big a stretch to think *she* might be boffing the boss."

"That's not fair!" Sabrina cut in.

Ginny ignored her. "Apparently Fred Rosen's got a pretty sweet ranch spread up in Santa Ynez. And you know the 154. It's a scary, steep highway."

I remembered. Ginny had taken me for a little joy ride up that way once in my dad's vintage Ferrari, and the memory of it still gave me butterflies in my stomach. From the glint in Ginny's eye I could see that she also recalled the drive, more fondly than I did.

Something else came back to me. Isabelle's charity event. Sponsored by Fred and Susan Rosen at their Santa Ynez ranch.

My brain was ticking, and every click sounded like *Webtech, Webtech, Webtech.*

There had to be something going on there that would lead us to Evan.

If only Evan were here, he would know what to do. He always did. I felt overwhelmed by the injustice that the one person who probably could have gotten him back was himself.

What would he have done? I sank onto an ottoman upholstered in pink chenille, knocking aside a few of Sabrina's stuffies to make room for myself. I picked one up absently and punched its soft face before hugging it to me. It helped.

Evan would put someone inside Webtech. Of course! My eyes flicked around the room as I went over everyone I knew. Who would they hire without suspicion? Wayne? Maybe, but Webtech would have computer experts of their own. Darrien? As what? I was pretty sure most of the executives drove themselves, and we needed someone in the office. Kelly? No, too obvious as my personal assistant, and suspiciously overqualified to take a quick position. What we needed was something in the form of an intern. Someone who could look totally *un*suspicious, yet be capable of playing the part. Someone who could catch Fred Rosen's eye, as the other women had. I looked from the photo of the voluptuous blond Molly Simpson up at my sister. Someone like . . .

Sabrina.

Chapter
- - - - - - - - - - - -
27

Considering the possibility of putting Sabrina in danger sent a wave of nausea through me.

Motioning to Ginny to stay, I said, "Sabrina, would you check my emails for me?"

She jumped up, eager to help. "I've been checking them all afternoon, nothing," she said with a frown.

"Just to be sure," I told her.

I'd actually checked five minutes before, when I'd first gotten home, but I needed to run my idea by Ginny.

She was dead set against it.

"Are you crazy?" she said so loudly that it must have carried out into the hallway and I had to shush her. "You know how she is! She always makes a mess of things."

"True," I allowed, "but that was pretty much always when we didn't give her a specific job to do. She can't stand not being helpful. And," I paused, "she's changed, Ginny. She's gotten more mature."

Ginny shook her head and exhaled audibly. "Mature! Cally, she's got the body of a Vargas Girl and last Tuesday, when every man we passed was watching her ass walking down the street, she asked me if she had something stuck on the back of her skirt! Hello!"

"I know." I had no illusions about Sabrina's level of innocence in that department. "But remember how convincing she was with the woman at the condo complex? It's exactly her innocence that would make her believable. Even someone who knew that she was my half sister wouldn't think she was capable of being anything but sincere."

Ginny looked at me. "You know this could be dangerous."

"I know." I ran my fingertips along the thick pile of the chenille and tried to work out *how* dangerous. "On the other hand, if I can get Isabelle to set her up with a summer job, an apprenticeship, it's very likely that she'd just end up filing things in a back office."

"What good is that?"

"That's where the coffeemaker is!" I told her. Ginny looked at me like I was insane.

"Office gossip," I filled in. "If you knew something interesting, possibly illegal, was going on, and your life was corporate, wouldn't you want to spread the excitement? And," I added, "if you were going to tell anyone, it wouldn't be in your cubicle, it would be while you were on a break, chatting over your coffee. Also, it's likely that a male executive past his prime might want to try to impress Sabrina. Obviously, both Molly Simpson and Josie Banks attracted someone's attention."

"Which would be my point." Ginny put both hands flat on the bed next to her and leaned toward me. "You can't play with her life."

A guilty shudder went through me. "I know." I bowed my head, defeated. "I want Evan back, but I can't ask Sabrina."

"Ask me what?" Sabrina had appeared in the open doorway. Glancing at her bare feet, I realized why we hadn't heard her coming.

"Nothing," Ginny said warningly.

"Nuh-uh!" Sabrina insisted. "You better tell me right now." Her words had the same sound as *You're not the boss of me*.

Almost against my better judgment I told her, insisting that it had been a crazy idea.

Sabrina loved it. "I can do it!" she said enthusiastically. "You know I can. And I can tell them that Darrien's my boyfriend." She blushed slightly. "And he can come pick me up and drop me off and have lunch with me every day, so you know I'd be safe! I wouldn't go anywhere without him."

Glancing at Ginny, I saw that this had put a crack in the protective shielding device she had thrown up around Sabrina. Darrien's presence was a convincing argument in favor of the scheme.

Ginny looked from Sabrina's eager face to my torn expression and then back again. "I swear to God, if you get yourself killed," she said, raising her palm and waving it in a threatening manner, "I'm gonna murder you."

Isabelle was so eager to help that she sounded like she was willing to fire someone to make a space for Sabrina. She put me on hold while she called personnel and set up an early morning appointment for Sabrina the next morning.

Ginny went back to Dana, and I stayed up late with Sabrina briefing her on how to look interested in a career in internet finance, and how to stay out of trouble.

"I just have one question," Sabrina said at about midnight, after listening to me for the last two hours. "What am I trying to find out?"

It was an excellent question. "I wish I knew, exactly," I told her. "What I'm thinking is that there's something connected to Evan there, something to do with one of the three men who own the box at Del Mar, because I think one of them must have invited Red. Fred Rosen seems to be the most likely candidate, but Josie Banks worked for Ted Issacs, so it could be him too. Would they have a reason to kill these women to keep them quiet?" As I asked the question, I thought about Dana, and whether she was next on the list. And what was Evan's life worth once I'd done what they wanted?

I remembered my phone conversation with Russian in Dana's office. The man had said, "It's him or it's her." Sabrina knew nothing about my "options." I had to be smart, sharper than I'd ever been, to save Dana, Evan, and maybe myself. It was a twisted love/death triangle.

"Listen, Sabrina." I took her hand and felt the heaviness of it in mine as she trusted her weight to me completely. "If there's any sense of danger, or if anyone propositions you, you have to get out, right away. You're only there to see if you can find us some hint of who's got Evan or where he might be. Remember Dana's name might come up too."

"What are they going to do to Dana?" Sabrina asked tremulously.

"*They're* not going to do anything." I sighed. "They want me to do something."

"What does that mean?"

I looked at her. Russian had clearly laid out my choices. Him or her.

"It means," I said slowly, "that to get Evan back, I have to get Dana to take the bribe and disappear, or . . ." I paused and looked down at her smooth palm before I finished the thought. I thought of Josie's blond hair spread across the tile, stained with her still-warm blood.

"Or what?" Sabrina asked, her voice shaking slightly.

"Or I have to kill her."

Chapter

28

The next morning dawned hot and dry. I was woken by Deirdre, who drew the curtains to reveal the sweltering day before she handed me a note from Curtis:

"Fred Rosen was charged with sexual harassment two months ago, by a woman named Michelle Keyhe, who seems to have disappeared; no record of foul play, no record of anything. The case was settled out of court very quickly, but one of the women who was subpoenaed was your friend Isabelle Ferris. Can you find out what happened from her?"

I got up and dressed quickly, the word "disappeared" ricocheting around in my head.

"Deirdre? Where's Sabrina?" I asked, as she was handing me my coffee.

"She's gone to her job interview. She left twenty minutes ago."

Three women who worked at Webtech—disappeared, dead, and dead, but not necessarily in that order—and I'd sent Sabrina to apply for a job there. Suddenly the heat of the summer sun in the room, which moments before had been reassuring and warming, was now pressing down on me like a bulky coat in a sauna. The stifling clamminess that engulfed me was sickening.

Without speaking another word, I put down the coffee cup and walked rapidly through the house and out the back doors of the living room onto the lawn. The touch of the hot July sun set my skin on fire. Feeling as though I would swoon from the intense heat both in and around me, I walked down the cypress path to the pool. Setting the cell phone from Dana's package carefully on a table, I dove in fully dressed.

The cold water seemed to hiss as it hit my skin and kept me from bursting into flame. Floating on my back with my hair and my clothes hovering around me, I tried to think.

Evan. I wondered if he had gotten himself involved in something that would bring us all down, if his disregard for either me or the law was going to cost me more than the three million in my office safe.

Dana. I wanted her out of the picture, but if she refused the money and it meant that Evan would die, could I kill her to save him? I created a scenario in my mind where I was faced with Dana and Evan, a single bullet, and only one could live. The coldest, hardest part of me considered the option, and it shocked me to realize that if I knew Evan's life would end, I probably *could* choose to save the life I loved. I would have to. It was a conundrum both perverse and complicated, because I would find it near impossible to live with myself, either way.

And the plot laid by Russian and his cronies made sense in a sick, twisted way. If I killed Dana—and they could prove it— then I could never go back and turn on them. Evan would be forced to stay silent as well, or suffer letting me face life in prison.

I remembered Curtis's suggestion that they might have videotaped Josie's death. But who, besides Josie, starred in that direct-to-video release?

With everything but my nose and eyes submerged, I looked

up into the sky. It glared down at me, a ruthless blue, tinged with heat haze. I hated these days in L.A., when the Santa Ana winds blew, changing the direction of the wind from the cooling sea breezes from the west to the hot dry desert wind from the east. Every year they brought fires and destruction. This year they had brought me a kind of devastation as well.

My hearing was dulled as I glared back at the harsh summer sky, but from somewhere came an unfamiliar, muted sound. I turned my head to expose one ear; though it was still full of water, the sound was an iota more distinct. It sounded like . . . a cell phone ringing.

I was out of the water and grasping at the phone in two seconds flat.

"Yes! Hello?" I breathed into the phone.

That same hated voice, thick with cigarettes and the grinding-of-metal-gears accent of its native tongue, came across the line. "Did you get the money?"

"Yes," I said. "I got it."

"Good. Do you understand what you need to do?"

"Why don't you spell it out for me." I wasn't in the mood to be mistaken.

"It's very simple. Either you persuade her to take the money and leave the country permanently, or you kill her. Then you get lover-boy back."

Something in me swelled up. I couldn't help myself. I don't know if it was exhaustion, or insanity, or heat stroke, but I laughed.

"What the fuck is so funny?" He sounded disgusted.

"I was just wondering," I said. "What's to keep you from just killing me next? I mean, I kill Dana for you, why not have someone else kill me? Kind of a round robin."

Now he laughed, an ugly, gurgling sound. "We won't have to. Because you're going to give us a videotape of you doing it, and we're going to keep it as insurance."

That stopped any amusement, however misplaced, that I had found in the situation. "Oh," I said, "I see."

"I thought you might. Today is Thursday; it's ten a.m. She leaves the country with the money by noon Saturday or she's dead. You have fifty hours to produce results, or boyfriend bites it Saturday at 12:01 p.m. Understand?"

My panic expanded again, and I pressed back down hard, trying to keep it contained. "I understand." But what I was thinking was, *None of our lives is worth a damn cent.*

"Good. Here's another little reminder."

Rustling noises, and then Evan's voice. "Hey, baby." He sounded horrible, as though he had almost no life left in his body.

My doubts melted away. I tried to stay calm, to sound reassuring. "Hi there, I was just chatting with your keeper. We're working out a few details so you can come on home."

"That'd be nice," he said, his voice trailing off a bit at the end. "I know you'll get her to do what they want. I have absolute faith in you." He sounded so drained.

"Tell you what," I said, trying to hold back my tears, trying to comfort him. "How about if I take you away on a nice romantic trip when this is over?" I hardly knew what I was saying, I just wanted to keep him on the line, to distract us both. He didn't respond, so I babbled on. "How about the coast of Spain?"

I heard a soft moan, as though he was trying to cover pain, then he said, "I was definitely thinking France."

There was a loud smacking sound, and I heard something fall heavily, and then the phone went dead.

I stood with the useless cell phone in my hand as the hot wind blew right through me. Though the line was disconnected, the message came through clearly. These people were without mercy.

Even if I did what they asked, Evan was a dead man.

Chapter
29

In twenty minutes I was knocking on Ginny's door. She opened it immediately and cocked her head in the direction of the sofa. Dana was sitting there, having been alerted to the fact that I was on my way over to talk to her. She looked nervous.

"I got another call," I told her, setting the shiny aluminum briefcase down carefully on the coffee table. The confusion in her eyes lasted half a second before she put together whom the call had come from.

"And?" she asked, her fingernails digging into the sofa fabric.

"They want me to offer you money to keep you quiet about the whole Josie Banks affair." I didn't tell her it was my money.

"What?" She looked outraged. "Who are these people?"

I didn't have time to moralize. "Listen. There's more. They want you to take three million dollars and leave the country. For good." I held my breath and became slowly aware that I was praying she would take it and get out of my life. "By Saturday at noon."

She sputtered like a badly tuned sports car engine. "What?

That's absurd. Just give up my life and family and disappear? *In two days?* What they're doing is illegal. They're the ones who should pay for this, not me!"

"So your answer is no?" I spoke clearly; we had to get past all the *should haves* and *that's not fairs.*

"Definitely no." She puffed up a bit, like any movie-brainwashed American who believes that in this country, right is on their side and the bad guy always blows up in the exciting conclusion.

I came and sat on the coffee table in front of her, next to the briefcase. I couldn't tell her about the offer to kill her, of course, but I could tell her that someone else might die if she refused.

"Dana." I took one of her icy hands in mine. "There's something else. I know where Evan Paley is." The pupils of her eyes widened and a little fearful gasp escaped her, but she didn't speak. Detaching myself from my involvement as best I could, I said simply, "They have him."

"No!" She pulled her hand away and covered her face.

"Yes. I spoke to him. They're saying if you don't take this deal, they're going to kill him."

She pulled her hands down and looked at me. "Why didn't you tell me this before?"

"Because Detective Curtis didn't think that anyone should know, and I didn't see how it could help you up until now. And honestly, I didn't know until they asked me to make this deal with you how it was connected."

"But why you?" she asked. It was a good question, and I could only think of one answer quickly, the one Evan had supplied me with.

"Because I'm connected to you and I'm a deal-maker, that's what I do." To punctuate the point and distract her usually whip-smart mind, I snapped open the latches on the briefcase and opened it.

It was impressive. "Three million dollars," I said as I watched her eyes widen. "The offer is—you take it, disappear, and Evan Paley goes free."

She stared at the neat stacks of cash, disbelieving. Then slowly she looked up at me. "Disappear *where?*" she asked.

"Wherever you want. With power of attorney, I could see to it that any assets you have here are transferred to a numbered account in, say, the Cayman Islands and you could have access to that as well.

She sank back onto the sofa, looking bewildered, but I could still see her sharp mind working. "Even if I did take this money, I'd never be safe. I'd spend my life being afraid and running, wouldn't I?"

There was no denying it. "Probably, yes."

She nodded. Ginny was standing in the doorway watching us. We exchanged glances.

"And I would never see Evan again." She stared at the open briefcase, then sat up abruptly and shut it. She placed both hands on top of it for a moment, then pulled them away and sank her nails into the fabric of the sofa, saying softly, "He's the only man I've ever really loved."

Before I could stop her, Ginny entered the fray. "What happened with you two?"

Dana looked up at her. "It was my fault," she said in a whisper. "He wanted a relationship, but he had this part of him that he couldn't share, and I said I wouldn't accept that."

She was looking down at the marks her fingernails were leaving in the pile of the sofa fabric, long, clawlike scratches that she would etch and then wipe smooth again with her palm, which gave me a chance to exchange another glance with Ginny. The scenario sounded eerily familiar.

She looked up at us now, smiled very sadly, and whispered, "I made a mistake. And then, in the last few weeks, we've gotten closer again. I really felt like he was coming back to me." A melancholy laugh gave way to tears of exhaustion. "Oh my God. What should I do? I'm so tired, I can't think. I haven't slept in days."

Turning to Ginny, I said, "You got any Ambien?"

"Sure, it's the only way I can sleep days when I'm on night shoots." She kept her voice casual, but her expression, unseen by Dana, was intensely alarmed. "I'll get her one."

Diverting Dana's hands from the sofa into mine, I looked her in the eye. "Listen, we don't have to decide this right this moment. I think you should get some sleep so that you can make a more coherent decision tomorrow. But Dana," I said as I leaned forward and spoke very clearly, *"it has to be tomorrow."* She nodded.

"And we have to be very careful. Do you understand?" I squeezed her hands tightly to make sure she was paying attention. "They told me if we give any of this information to the police, they'd kill Evan. I know you've talked to Curtis and you know that he and the rest of the police force are working on this publicly, and with our information *secretly*. But according to Detective Curtis, they have no solid leads, so to save Evan you might have no choice but to take the money and run." I stated the option as though it were the only conclusion, an old deal-closer I had learned from my father.

"Okay, yes. I understand."

Ginny reappeared with the pill and a glass of water. Dana downed it gratefully and went off to lie down.

Ginny put her arms around me.

I leaned into her and said quietly, "It's not looking good, is it?"

"Wait until you hear his side," she said.

A fuse had been lit in the base of my brain. "You know," I said, pulling away and starting to pace, "when I spoke to Evan, twice he used *French* endearments, something he's only ever done as a joke, even though he speaks French fluently."

Ginny said nothing, just watched me. "And then," I continued, "when I told him this last time that I'd take him to Spain when this was all over, he said, 'France.' And then it sounded like"—I broke off, pained, then went on—"someone hit him."

A hissed breath of anger came from Ginny, but all she said was, "And you think that means something?"

"Definitely. Look, Evan is as smart a detective as there is, it's his job, and his passion, to figure things out from clues that aren't always obvious. Why wouldn't he try to make use of that? Don't you think he would take any opportunity to pass clues on to me?"

Her eyes lit up. "Absolutely," she said.

The little sparkling flare was traveling along the string of fuse faster now. Somewhere in my brain was the answer, and if I could just keep that fuse lit, the spark would reach it and blow all the confusion and stupidity out of my brain.

"Okay," I muttered. "So, let's think." I screwed up my face with the effort to remember Evan's exact words. "One time he called me *chérie*, which means 'dear.' Another it was *mon coeur*, which is 'my heart.'" I paused and tried to remember the last French term he had used; it had been an odd choice. "Last, he called me *mon choux*."

"Which means?" Ginny prompted.

"It's hard to translate, it's kind of like calling someone 'muffin' or 'cupcake.'" I shook my head; it had seemed strange because neither of us was given to cutesy nicknames. I continued, "Okay, then he said we should go to France, and somebody didn't like him saying that, which is what leads me to think it's a clue."

"Or he might have been trying to get you to translate the words," Ginny said excitedly. "Which would be 'dear heart cupcake.' And since he might be trying to give you a clue about where he is, maybe it's the name of a street?"

I shot her a look. "Dear Heart Cupcake Street? This is L.A., not Candyland."

She shrugged her shoulders apologetically and shifted gears. "Something with 'deer,' the animal, in it?"

"Yes, that's possible," I said. "But I think there's something else. I think the fact that it's French comes into it somehow. I mean, he could have just called me 'dear,' which he never does either, and that could have been just as obvious. I'll stick Sabrina on the web, but," I said as I looked at her, feeling frustrated, "it's not much to go on. There must be thousands of matches to those words."

Ginny said, "It's a start, girl."

The minute I got home, I put the briefcase in the small office safe built into the bookshelves under a long marble table, and then I put Sabrina to work. She'd gone to her meeting at Webtech and was brimming with the news that she would start the next day, as an assistant to one of the executives' undersecretaries. You would have thought she'd been elected president, she was so proud.

Then I went upstairs to my bedroom and out onto the balcony. The warm wind was so dense that it seemed to hold me up for a moment, and then like an iron weight thrown into a murky lake, I sank down onto the floor, curling into a wounded bundle of nervous exhaustion. Then I just lay there, no more capable of movement or action than a rock sunk in thick mud.

I heard a soft knock at my bedroom door and tried to rally, but after a supreme effort only produced a one-inch elevation of my head, I gave up.

Deirdre appeared in the balcony doorway. "Are you all right?" she asked. I found I could move, but only laterally, so I rolled over onto my back, looking up at the high beams of the covered terrace, painted in the decorative style of a Tuscan villa.

"Sure. I'm fine," I told her, with all the intonation of a bottom feeder. Somehow I raised my right hand enough to wave it vaguely. "What's up?" I asked.

"Mr. Korosu is here to see you." She waited while I sighed, then she said, "Would you like me to help you up?"

"That would be nice." I looked up into her face, calm but clearly concerned, and accepted her outstretched hand.

I was still trying to revive myself when Deirdre showed Korosu out onto the balcony. "Am I intruding?" he asked.

Shaking my head, I tried to smile, failed, and dropped my face into my hands. He came to me and put his strong hands on my shoulders, pressing his skillful fingers into the wads of tension that had bubbled up there.

He smelled so good, like a man. I reveled in the comfort he offered for as long as I could allow, and then pulled away and told him about the last painful phone call and my French theory. He looked thoughtful, asked me to repeat the words. He mouthed them. *"Chérie, coeur,* and *choux."*

"I have the list of the businesses with offices that could see into Dana Scheiner's office," he said as he pulled out a spotlessly white, single sheet of paper that had been folded at exact thirds so that it fit neatly into his breast pocket. He unfolded it and slid it across the table to me.

And there it was. Only one company occupied every office from the fourteenth to the eighteenth floors in the building facing Dana's office.

Webtech.

"And I'll tell you something else." Korosu leaned in toward me. "There's a little bakery right around the corner that made excellent pastries before the family that ran it sold it. But before it changed hands a few months ago, I would sometimes have trays of pastries brought in with coffee for meetings. It's in a very old, freestanding three-story building."

"Really?" I asked, bewildered and somewhat annoyed at the digression. What the hell did éclairs and architecture have to do with anything?

But I should have known better; this was Korosu.

"What do you say," he suggested, "to you and me going for a drive downtown? I think you might be interested in this particular patisserie."

My brain was misty and my spirits were drained. "Why?" I

asked, the sheerness of my impatience making me ask the question perhaps not as politely as I should have.

"Because it is, rather *was*, a *French* bakery," he said liltingly, and then cocked his head to one side, which leveled out his one-sided smile. "Recently taken over by a Russian family."

I stared at him during that fraction of a second when the sparkling fuse made contact with the barrel of gunpowder, and I waited for the explosion.

"The new owners kept the old name," he said, leaning in even closer toward me. "It's called Choux de Coeur."

Chapter

30

Now I was sitting bolt upright next to Korosu in the passenger seat of his sedan, which he was driving himself; I was flooded with so much energy that a small neighborhood could have used me for a night-light.

Through his secretary, Korosu had been in touch with Curtis who had agreed we could check it out, but he was adamant that we confine our activity to a drive-by and a report back to him. Under no condition were we to allow ourselves to be seen.

The bakery, as Korosu had said, was about a block and a half away from the main doors of the building housing Webtech's offices. It was old, made of red brick, with the telltale iron crosses of earthquake retrofitting slapped up at seemingly random spots on the façade. The name, Choux de Coeur—Pastries and Chocolates, was painted on a red, white, and blue sign over the door, but posters in what I took to be Russian littered the front windows. Korosu slowed down as we went past, but he didn't stop. Instead, he made a right turn into an alley that ran beside it and once again drove slowly on by. On the alley side there were a few windows up on the second and third floors. You couldn't see through them from the street level, but at a glance—and based on the laundry hanging on the fire escape—I would have said that the second floor was living space. Quite a few of the windows on the third level had been broken out and repaired only with plywood, leading us to conclude that it was used primarily as warehouse storage space, and the best bet for hiding a hostage.

We circled only once more, so as not to draw attention, and then Korosu parked down the alleyway, close enough for us to see the back corner of the building and the fire escape, but not close enough for anyone to think we were interested in the bakery.

Korosu unlocked his briefcase, pulled out a sleek silver automatic, took a clip of bullets from the glove box, and loaded the gun, kicking a round neatly into the chamber.

"You don't keep it loaded?" I asked him.

"That wouldn't be legal," he said, and handed it to me, along with the car keys. "Stay here. Once I get out, move into the driver's seat and leave the car running."

"Where are you going?" I was suddenly panicked that he was going to leave me there.

"I'm just going to take a look."

"Here." I offered him the gun. "Take this, you might need it."

He smiled at me again, opening his jacket, and I saw the handsome weapon he wore nestled against his body in a holder so discreet that it was invisible, even under his perfectly tailored suit.

"Apparently your definition of legal is a little bit different from mine," I said as he opened the door, but then, we'd always known that.

I watched him cross the alley, looking as cool and unconcerned as James Bond on a Sunday outing. He walked along until he was under the fire escape, then he climbed easily onto a van that was parked underneath, grabbed the railing, and flipped himself up onto the metal grating of the first landing as sweetly as an Olympic gymnast.

As I watched, I was grateful for the blackout windows on his Mercedes. No one could see me, not even from the windows on the back of the bakery. Korosu went up the fire escape until he was on the third-story landing next to a patched window. With his back against the brick, he leaned around and looked in through one of the few remaining panes of glass.

Then I saw him reach into his jacket, and something flashed silver in sunlight. I stiffened. He moved quickly, leaning around again, now with his hand out in front of him. I picked up the gun he'd left with me and put the car into drive, ready to pull up under the fire escape if I was needed. Was he going to try to go in there alone? Should I follow?

But before I could make a decision, Korosu was climbing quickly down the stairs, avoiding the window on the second landing, dropping first onto the roof of the van, then to the street like a cat, and coming at a casual, unconcerned walk toward me. He came to the passenger door and got in.

"Let's go. Back up and turn around."

I obeyed his directives, and when we were out of view I looked at him questioningly.

Grimly, he said, "He's there."

I caught my breath in sharply. *Yes!* He was alive, and we'd found him in time.

"I saw him, and he saw me," Korosu continued.

"Does he look okay?" I asked anxiously.

Korosu smiled reassuringly. "He's as sharp as ever but perhaps not as well groomed as he might like."

"Why did you take your gun out?"

He looked at me, then said, "I didn't. It was my lighter. Evan was lying on a cot; he's handcuffed to it. I used the silver surface to reflect some light into his eyes to get his attention. Once I did, and he recognized me, he gave me a little information."

"He spoke to you?" I asked eagerly.

"No." Korosu looked thoughtful and impressed. "He's too smart for that. I could only see him through some stacked boxes. I couldn't see the whole room. He gestured with his free hand, down on one side of the cot, and I got the idea that he was letting me know that there was one person in the room with him, somewhere off by the foot of his cot, and three more in a room outside. I could see a door, but not where it led. I also take it, from the way he pointed to the cuffs and then to the door, that whoever is in that other room has the keys."

Once again too many emotions were competing for my attention. Impatience to get to Evan and anxiety for his current situation were chief among them, but gratitude and relief were running a close third and fourth.

When I stopped at a light on Seventh Avenue, I turned to Korosu. "Thank you," I said to him.

We regarded each other, as well as all the imminent looming possibilities, for a few eternal seconds, then he said simply, "Don't thank me yet."

I thought about the four probably armed and ruthless men who were watching Evan; I thought about Dana and what she meant to Evan; and I thought about Curtis's suspicions that Evan was illegally involved in this whole scenario.

"Okay," I said, "I won't."

Chapter
31

I was dialing Curtis's number to tell him we'd found Evan when my cell phone rang.

"Girl, it's me, Ginny." She spoke urgently, as though under stress, and in a hurry to transfer the information.

So, wasting no time on small talk, I asked, "What's going on?"

"Somebody's watching my place. I can see him right now. He's sitting in a car across the street."

My blood got an ice bath. "What does he look like?"

Korosu, who was now driving again, looked at me, concerned. I held up a finger, eager to pass on info, but I wanted to get it just right.

"I'm pretty sure it's your guy. Older, I'd say about fifty, gray hair, square-ish face."

"Oh shit."

"What do you want me to do?"

"We know where Evan is, but we need a little time. If we arrest Houndstooth right now, they might move him, or . . .

worse." I heard Ginny's relieved exclamation, which echoed my own, but now I was equally alarmed for her and Dana.

"I'm with Korosu, we can come right over."

"No!" Ginny exclaimed. "That would give everything away for sure. I'll call the cops and tell them some freakazoid's been following me and have them check him out. Any woman would do that, right? That should send him off for a little while."

I considered. I knew the gray-haired man was dangerous, but if he hadn't made a move yet, her plan might work. And Ginny was not an easy woman to take unawares.

"All right," I told her. "But call them *now*."

"I'm so on it." She hung up.

Curtis was just as on it as his lady. He made sure that a patrol car was already at Ginny's and then agreed to meet us at Korosu's office.

I was ready to round up a posse and ride into the Choux de Coeur ranch, guns blazing, but I could tell from the look of caution on Curtis's face that that wasn't going to happen.

"Callaway," Curtis said, sitting me down in a chair across from Korosu's desk, "listen to me. This is going to take a little bit of planning, and I need you to do something for me."

"If you tell me to sit and wait at home, I swear to God I'll pop you," I told him.

"No. I need our rescue to be a surprise. That means I need a diversion. Obviously they're watching you, that *was* making me nervous, but now it's going to give me the opening I need to get in there and get Evan. So it's very important that you are *not* with us, but preferably somewhere else that will throw them off."

"Uhm, I guess I could go to Webtech itself. That should get their attention."

"Cally, I need to handle this quietly; it's going to take some time to get the right guys on this. At least until tomorrow night. So, unless the Webtech offices are open on Friday night, we need another plan."

"Friday night." I was remembering something, something related. Reaching into my purse, I pulled out the sleek vellum envelope that Isabelle had given me and slid out the card.

Curtis was still speaking. "So, let's try to come up with some other plan for you before then."

Holding the letterpress violet card up in front of me, I said, "This will do."

He took it from me, and his eyebrows rose as he read the location of the soiree—the home of Fredrick and Susan Rosen—then the address in Santa Ynez, and scowled. He didn't seem to think it was as good an idea as I did.

"What's wrong?" Korosu asked him.

"It's a charity event at the primary suspect's home," Curtis said, frowning. "It would be perfect, except that I don't like the idea of taking one hostage back and handing them another, and I have a hard time thinking that Evan would be okay with putting you in danger either."

"Then I guess I shouldn't tell you that Sabrina starts work at Webtech tomorrow?" I said hesitantly.

Curtis shot up out of his chair. "What? Whose idea was that?"

"Well, mine, actually. She's just got a filing job, through my friend Isabelle. It's a long shot, I know, but we thought maybe she might overhear something, or find some connection between Rosen and either of the two women who died, or"—my voice dropped and I glanced at Korosu—"or between Evan and what's been going on."

Curtis visibly checked himself from letting me have it by spinning away from me. He walked across the room and back. I wondered what he was thinking, if he was weighing his need to find out if Evan was involved against any danger to Sabrina.

Surprising me, Korosu took up my side. "I have discussed this with Darrien, and he will drive her, and she is to check in with him every hour."

I hadn't known that Darrien had told him about Sabrina's job and his promise to protect her. Korosu smiled at me. "Did you expect that he would just not show up to work for me?"

"No, of course not. Well, actually I didn't think of that. I've been a little self-involved," I mumbled, looking nervously back up to Curtis, who was shifting his gaze from Korosu to me, deep in thought.

With a deep sigh, he said, "I suppose it would be all right for her to go there tomorrow. But I want hourly reports from your man." Curtis pointed a determined finger at Korosu, who nodded his head.

"Done."

"And as for sending you into the lion's den," Curtis said with a hard look.

Korosu came around from behind his desk to stand near me, and I wondered if he was even conscious of the protective move. "I could go with her."

"No!" I cried. We had already established that in order to keep Evan's rescue quiet, a small trusted group of "civilians" would make up the recovery team. Korosu, and three of his security men, one of whom was Darrien, along with two trusted cop friends of Evan's and Curtis's, would be the ones to go in with Curtis and get Evan back. The three detectives would be the ones who actually moved in; Korosu and his guys would be there in case of emergencies and to cover exits. Curtis felt sure that if he involved the force our opponents would find out, and, though this remained unspoken, I sensed that he also thought Evan might land in serious trouble for his "off-duty" involvement with Dana and whatever else he'd gotten himself into.

"You need to stay with Curtis; he needs you more than I do. Ginny can go with me," I said, volunteering her as I always did. Taking for granted that she would go, because she always did. "I can go with Ginny, and you can call me when you get Evan out and we'll leave right away."

Too late, I realized that I was suggesting possibly sacrificing the woman Curtis cared about. How very reassuring of me.

Curtis was shaking his head. "No way. There's a million reasons that could screw up. Your cell phone might not work in a remote area, for one. They, on the other hand, are sure to let the major players know by a regular phone line within seconds of Evan's release. That puts you in danger if Rosen and his crew are as deep into this as it looks. No."

Korosu was looking thoughtful. "What if she knew what was going on all the time? What if we could tell her, as the rescue was happening, when to get out?"

Curtis looked at him and then at me and narrowed his eyes. "A wireless?" he asked.

"Yes," said Korosu. "It would serve two purposes—keep her informed without her having to be on the scene and enable us to give her the message to get out before news of Evan's release reached the players."

Curtis looked like he was softening, so I threw in, "Curtis, you know that Webtech is involved but you don't know how or who. And you need proof to connect Fred Rosen or whoever it is at Webtech with the kidnappers. I *might* just find out something helpful. And it's possible that the redhead could show up. I mean, she was in the box at Del Mar, which means it's likely she's connected to one of the three men who owned it, and I'm *sure* all three will be at this shindig. I can talk to them."

Curtis made a clicking noise with his teeth that I had heard Evan make a hundred times when he was considering something; with a wrench in my heart I wondered if he had picked up the habit from Evan or if it was the other way around.

"I'm not gonna have time to be narrating this little adventure—"

"I can do it." Korosu cut him off, but politely. "I'm there to observe and support anyway."

"And you know"—I pushed a little harder—"that they won't

suspect anything if they think I'm snooping around the party, desperate for clues."

"Let me think about it," was all Curtis would say for now. Then the other two detectives arrived—Horace, a stocky, short man wearing a bad rug, and a woman, Bloom, who looked tougher than her partner but seemed to have her own hair intact. Throwing myself into my role as the decoy, I called Kelly, who told me that Isabelle had contacted her about the event, which I had told her to do, but that she'd put her off. Kelly was expert at that, having to do it at least three or four times a week, but this time I instructed my assistant to write the check and RSVP. At the very least, my name on the guest list would send out the message in advance that I would be there, whether I showed or not.

Darrien drove me home, but he wouldn't come in, insisting instead that he had to get back to Korosu's office.

Weary, yet strangely buoyant, I floated up the steps and let myself in. Deirdre met me at the door.

She was holding a postcard.

Chapter
32

I didn't even look at the picture. Flipping the card I read the words: "We know you've got her and the cops have talked to her. You have now forfeited the money option. The deal must be *terminated* and a how-to video given to us before Saturday at noon, or we will kill our end of the deal."

With a shaking hand, I turned the card over again and looked at the front, a cartoonish forties picture, meant to be an amusing statement of women's lib. A woman dressed in a conservative jacket and skirt tried to tug a briefcase away from a man in a flannel suit. This time, crudely drawn in pencil near the woman's throat, was a bloody knife.

Beyond the door, I heard the sound of Darrien's car pulling away. "Close the gates!" I shouted to Deirdre. Tearing the heavy front door open again, I ran after the car. He spotted me in the rearview mirror before he'd gone halfway down the drive and stopped. I ran up to his window, but he was already getting out, gun in hand.

"What's wrong?" he asked, even as he swept me around behind him.

"No, it's not me. Everything's okay here. But look." I showed him the card. "You've got to go get both Ginny and Dana and bring them back here. Please!"

Darrien nodded and got back in the car. "Go inside, call your security company, and have them leave a car in the driveway. Can you let Ginny know I'm on my way?"

"Done. Call Curtis and tell him, okay? Give me a minute to open the gates for you again."

He drove off as I went back inside.

When Ginny and Dana arrived, the former looked relieved to be off guard duty, and the latter looked slightly disoriented.

"What's going on? Why did Detective Curtis send us here?" Dana asked.

"This is my house," I told her. "There was someone watching Ginny's place. Detective Curtis thought this would be safer."

As I said it, I wondered if Russian also knew we had found Evan, if they would move him, if Curtis's efforts to rescue him would be in vain—and if I lost that window of opportunity, if I would seriously consider killing Dana to secure his release. I thought about the fact that if I *did* want to kill her, this would be the best place for me to get away with it. So maybe the word "safer" was a matter of perspective. I shook off the thought uncomfortably.

She took my upper arm in both of her hands and squeezed tightly. "Have you heard anything about Evan?"

I looked into her stunning brown eyes. Even sans makeup and ragged from lack of sleep, she was beautiful.

"He's still being held," I told her. "But his partner and the police are working on it. We just have to keep hoping."

She released me and swayed slightly, but she didn't fall or start to cry. Instead she took a deep breath and drew herself up with obvious effort. "Yes, we do." She looked at me and then at Ginny before saying, "I'd like to apologize. All of my whimpering hasn't been very helpful at all. If there's anything I can do, anything to help Evan or you, please let me know."

She was proud, she was formidable, she was nothing but class and beauty. At the very least Evan had loved her once and had hidden our engagement from her. Even in normal circumstances, my competitive nature would have felt deeply threatened.

And these circumstances were anything but normal.

Chapter
33

Sabrina had only been at Webtech for three hours when she called with info.

Everyone was nervous, rumors had been flying, and, as I had suspected, nobody could resist watching Sabrina's baby-blue eyes widen with stunned, innocent fascination as they filled in the new girl. There was talk of sexual harassment accusations high up and missing company funds. Most people seemed to think that Webtech was the object of an unofficial government investigation, but nobody knew anything for certain.

A good morning's work, I called it. It would have to be far more specific to convict anyone, but hell, the afternoon was ahead of us.

Because the kidnappers knew that Dana had been at Ginny's and had upped the ante with the demand for Dana's death, Curtis begrudgingly admitted that having Ginny and me attend the charity event could be the distraction we needed. I'd been fitted with all the appropriate hardware. This basically consisted of a tiny, skin-colored speaker that fit into my ear, which I would cover with my hair, a transmitter that snuggled nicely into one of my evening bags, and a power source placed in the trunk of my car—the two-seater German Mercedes, wider and lower than its American counterparts, perfect for the mountain roads. Since I had the handbag already chosen to fit the transmitter, I selected a gown to go with it—a pale gold, beaded Badgley Mischka, to which I added a simple gold chain rope necklace that dangled a pink diamond cut into a teardrop. Ginny went with a black Vera Wang, piling her thousand tiny braids up into an elegant knot and adding some showy emerald earrings I'd bought her from an estate sale in New York.

We had to leave early in the afternoon to beat the Friday traffic headed up to Santa Barbara. It was hard to enjoy the open view of the ocean when all I could think of was Evan handcuffed to a cot in a stifling warehouse. By the time we reached the turnoff and headed up into the mountains, it was going on five-thirty, and since the invitation had said cocktails at six, if we went slowly and carefully, we should arrive fifteen fashionable minutes late.

That meant I had to wait over an hour at the party before Evan's rescue attempt—plenty of time to scope out the major players and snoop around. We had decided that to save battery power, I would turn on the transmitter at a quarter after seven—fifteen minutes before Curtis and his team were scheduled to go in after Evan. By that time, Curtis would have had the bakery building cased by Bloom, who would be dressed as a civilian health inspector, and the downtown city streets would be mostly deserted after business hours, reducing the risk of a civilian injury.

My palms felt sweaty on the steering wheel. Though I usually let Ginny drive when we were together, I had taken the helm because I needed something to distract me.

As we pulled up to the hired valet, we got a look at the "ranch." It was a gigantic faux Mediterranean home on a sweeping property with vineyards and pastures inhabited by very happy—and very expensive—horses. When the young man opened my door, instead of handing over the keys, I slipped two crisp one-hundred-dollar bills into his hand.

"I'd really like to keep this right up front." I smiled at him in a way I knew men took to be sexy and moved up close to him. "You understand, if the party's not happening, I might want to make a quick getaway."

He looked me up and down, noting the slashed neckline of my Mischka, and then he checked out the car. His mouth was watering, but I couldn't tell if he found me or my wheels more tempting.

"Don't you worry," he said with an intimate wink. "I'll keep this baby right up here with me."

I handed over the keys and waited for him to park it a few feet away. Then I said to him, "And just in case you're busy, I'd like to keep the keys." I dropped my voice to a whisper and smiled suggestively. "But I hope that when we leave, you aren't too busy to say good-bye."

He caught a glimpse of the fabulous Ginny, who leaned on me seductively and fixed him with her gold-flecked eyes. He swallowed and croaked, "No problem." The keys dropped into my hand, and I let them fall into my bag.

"Thanks," I said over my shoulder, and we sashayed away.

We were gestured through the house and out into the back-yard, which had been covered with a tent big enough for a Russian circus. So big, in fact, that three full-size oak trees were included in the fabricated ballroom, and chandeliers hung everywhere. The effect was lovely.

It was Isabelle who greeted us at the door.

"Callaway!" she enthused. "Oh my God, you came! Thank you!" She said hello to Ginny but was glancing around behind me. She leaned in and asked conspiratorially, "Did you bring him?"

"No, I'm afraid he had to work." I tried to keep my voice only slightly disappointed. "But let me present my friend, Virginia Watson."

"I'm Isabelle Ferris," she said, taking one of Ginny's hands in both of hers as though Ginny were the pope. "I'm so glad you're both here. Oh, don't you look beautiful!"

Isabelle was wearing a pale green dress made of a spandex stocking, which hugged her too-thin body, swathed in mint green gauze. She looked like lime cotton candy.

"Do you like my dress?" she asked, eyes twinkling.

Ginny made an *mmmm* noise to avoid having to say anything else, and Isabelle was delighted.

"Thank you. I'm stuck at the door greeting for the next half hour, but after that I can't wait to introduce you around."

"I'd love to meet the men who own the box at Del Mar," I told her. "I'm really interested in racing now." My eyes were flicking around at the other guests. The place was about half full, and though, for the impact factor, I usually didn't like to make my entrance until everyone was there, this time it was better to blend away into a corner for a while and observe.

"Of course! They're all here. I'll be with you as soon as I can get away." Isabelle turned to greet the next arrivals, and we wandered away toward one of the bars, where I asked for club soda.

Ginny scoped the room from behind her Diet Coke and asked, "See anybody you recognize?"

"You mean anyone with gray or red hair?"

She nodded, and I responded with a negative.

Just then I spotted Jim Ferris, and he spotted me. Crossing the room with a giant smile, he kissed me on both cheeks and introduced himself gallantly to Ginny.

We stood and chatted for a few minutes as other guests joined the party. Ginny was drawn into conversation with a handsome man who was looking at her like she was the crown jewels. The subject of my father came up between Jim and me and we both fell silent for a moment. Having someone who understood the depth of my relationship with him and what his loss had meant to me made it much more difficult to close the lid on the box I'd constructed to hide my grief.

I felt Jim's hand fall across my shoulders. He gave me a gentle hug. "You know, Callaway," he said, gently but conversationally enough to keep me from bursting into tears, "if you ever need someone to talk to, or just listen, I'm here. I understand that everyone thinks you're tough and don't need any support, and I know what jealous bullshit that is. You inherited not only massive responsibility but also some huge shoes to fill, and at the same time you lost the one person who could help you through it. Don't be afraid to ask for help or support. We all need it. I know that no one can ever replace Frank for you, but I'd like you to know that I'm here for you."

Turning to look up at him, I saw the compassion in his eyes, and I thought how lucky Isabelle was to still have her father. "Thank you, Jim." I smiled. "That means a lot to me. I might just take you up on that."

"Any time."

Then Jim spotted someone. "Oh, there's our host." He dropped his voice to a sarcastic scowl. "I can't wait for him to meet you," he continued, but he avoided my look when I turned my raised eyebrows to him. I sensed competition between them. Men like Fred Rosen didn't get where they were without being competitive, ambitious, and sometimes ruthless. If he was the one behind Evan's kidnapping, ruthless would be putting it mildly.

I followed Jim's gaze to a striking man, about sixty, with silver hair.

Fredrick Rosen stood with a woman on his arm, whom I took to be his wife, Susan. Unlike him, she was remarkable mostly for her plainness next to her dashing husband. Although I was thinking for the thousandth time how unfair it was that men could hold their looks until sixty or later when their wives started to fade at forty-five, I couldn't help thinking that she had obviously never been as handsome as he was.

Leaning in toward Jim, I said what I was thinking, a bad habit that has often landed me a well-heeled foot in the mouth. "Let me guess, he married the boss's daughter."

Jim looked at me reproachfully, but with a sly smile. "Now Callaway, be nice."

Feeling guilty, I admonished myself. Looks weren't everything. I told myself sharply that I needed to curb my harsh assumptions. Begging Ginny's forgiveness, Jim took my arm and started to lead me forward.

"Of course," he said into my ear, "you're absolutely right. *She* was the one with the money."

So much for curb service.

Fred Rosen's eyes took me in like the featured selection on a gourmet buffet. His wife watched him watch me and then surveyed me with a look that said it all. To me it was apparent that she knew her husband had what she would call "indiscretions" and that she expected it, but that *she* was "the Wife."

I watched for signs of recognition or defensiveness in Fredrick Rosen, but unless I was very much mistaken, I saw none of either until Jim mentioned my name. Then there was a distinct change. His eyes flickered with uncertainty and guarded curiosity as they met mine.

"Callaway Wilde." Fred Rosen tested the name as he shook my hand and recovered with strong eye contact. "I knew your father. I was very sorry to hear about his passing."

"Thank you," I told him, and then to escape the questioning gaze, I turned to his wife. "What a delightful home you have, Susan. It was very gracious of you to lend it for . . . such a worthy cause." The hesitation in my voice was a result of still not knowing what the "worthy cause" was.

Her look had changed also. She regarded me now as an equal,

someone of her social class, and probably way out of her husband's league in the liaison department. She looked pleased as she latched onto my arm.

"I'm so delighted that you could come," she said warmly. Her voice was cultured, almost European in accent. "I'm sure you gentlemen have something to discuss, and I would like to introduce Ms. Wilde to a few of the important doctors from Children's Hospital," she said to Jim and her husband as she drew me away.

Oh, Children's Hospital. Good. Got it. I was relieved to have the time to collect myself. I didn't want to get into a tête-à-tête with Rosen just yet. Glancing back, I saw that Ginny's young man was obviously hitting on her. She had also watched the whole exchange, making note of the key player. She glanced at Rosen and nodded at me, to let me know she had marked him.

"So," Susan was saying as she led me along, "you're friends with Isabelle."

"Yes. Our fathers were friends, and so we were allowed to drive the golf cart."

She laughed. "I like her very much. I've been helping her decorate her new beach house."

"Oh, are you a decorator?" I inquired.

She smiled demurely. "I dabble. Have you been to her house?" I had to admit that I hadn't. "You should, it has the most amazing view and a lovely garden. Which is very unusual for a home on the boardwalk. Ah, I'd like you to meet Ted Issacs, he's president of Webtech and my husband's right-hand man."

I turned to face the shorter, pleasant-looking man I had seen only through my opera glasses in the Webtech box at Del Mar. Susan was called away by the caterer, and I was left to pursue my line of questioning.

"Isabelle pointed your box out to me when I was at the track."

"Isabelle?" He seemed embarrassed not to recognize the name.

"Isabelle Ferris, Jim's daughter." The light of partial recognition came to his eyes, and he nodded. "I don't see your girlfriend here tonight," I said smilingly. Now he looked confused. "Maybe I'm wrong"—I plowed ahead—"but weren't you with a very attractive redhead at Del Mar?"

"Oh, no, she was a guest of the company. I don't recall her name, she didn't stay long. She had something to do with the Moscow office, and so Fredrick invited her." A smile passed across his face. "Fredrick has a tendency to be charitable to nice-looking ladies." He looked more amused at his friend's behavior than scandalized.

Glancing at my watch, I noted the time: seven-fifteen. "I see, well, it was lovely talking to you."

Leaving Ted Issacs abruptly, I hurried away. Safely in the elegant bathroom with the door locked, I opened my bag and switched on the transmitter.

There was a tiny mike on it, and, holding it near my mouth, I breathed, "Hello? Can you hear me?"

There was a moment of static, then Korosu's voice, faint in volume yet reassuringly strong in tone and presence, sounded in my ear. "I'm here. We are in the cars now, in position."

My heart thumped loudly as someone knocked at the door. I called out, "Just a moment."

I heard Ginny say, "It's me, girl, let me in."

At the same time Korosu's voice came clearly into my right ear. "Are you hearing me all right?"

"Okay," I said to Ginny and into the mike, "Yes, I can hear you just fine."

This was mind-boggling. Hearing two conversations at once and trying to reply to them both would take some getting used to. I reminded myself firmly to only respond to what I heard in my left ear but to keep my focus on what was coming in the right. Yeow.

"Is it working?" Ginny was asking me as Korosu was saying, "I'm going to fill you in every minute or so, to make sure we have contact. Remember what Curtis told you; if for any reason you lose me, get out of there, right away. Understand?"

"Yes," I said to both of them, then shook my head at Ginny. "This is weird," I told her.

"Yeah, it gets weirder," she said grimly. "Guess who's here?"

"The redhead?"

"No, Houndstooth."

"No way," I breathed. "Where is he?"

"Lurking around by the catering station, staying in the shadows, but I spotted him. That guy is like a fungus, you just can't get him off of you," she said.

"Well, the best thing for a fungus is to expose him to light. Let's stay out in the open. Don't leave the crowd, and watch your back!"

Ginny checked her watch. "We have twelve minutes until seven-thirty; we should be able to handle twelve minutes in the spotlight at a major social event. I think I saw some photographers, they have really bright flashes."

Me and my money were always good for a shot in the social pages, and I *was* in this season's couture. "Good plan, let's go."

She opened the door, looked out, gave me the okay, and we rejoined the throng. I was constantly on the lookout for the gray-haired man, my eyes darting into every dark corner.

Isabelle, who had left her welcome post, was delighted to join us for the photos. Every sixty seconds or so, I would jump when Korosu's voice came through the ear piece. I prayed that no one noticed how my conversation faltered and my attention lapsed.

Isabelle certainly didn't notice; she was off and running. "So, you didn't bring the fiancé? I can't believe he would turn you loose at a social event looking absolutely fabulous." She glanced around theatrically and then whispered, "Look out for Fred

Rosen, he's quite the ladies' man." In my ear I heard Korosu speak. "Okay, this is it, we're moving in."

My heart somersaulted, but I smiled wanly at Isabelle and remembered that she'd been named a witness in the sexual misconduct suit against him. "You sound like you're speaking from experience," I prompted. My heartbeat sounded like several horses trotting along a wooden bridge, almost drowning out all else.

She grimaced a little but sidestepped the question. "It's obvious Susan knows, everybody does, maybe she doesn't think she can keep him unless he's on a long leash. Anyway"—she drew breath and launched in—"*she* was the one with the money, Susan Montgomery of the railroad Montgomerys. Her father was the son of William Montgomery, and you know who he is. When the railroads started to be replaced by trucking, he went into communications, starting with overseas telecommunications. Next thing you know he's conglomerated it all into a little information company called Webtech, and a young rising executive had his eye on . . ."

Isabelle trailed off and looked up at me questioningly as I jabbed her in the ribs; the subject of our gossip himself was coming straight toward us. Korosu's voice said, "I'm standing by the car. Darrien and Detective Bloom have gone up the fire escape. Curtis and Detective Horace cut the alarm system and are making their way through the building."

My heart beat wildly and I tried, without success, to fill my lungs with air. Before I could turn away and pretend I didn't see him, Rosen was on me.

Korosu was still speaking, his voice steady and unhurried. "They've given the signal, Bloom is breaking out the window, they're in."

Fred Rosen was standing in front of me, and through my haze of frozen fear I saw his mouth move and I forced myself to focus on what he was saying.

I heard Korosu say in my right ear, "Damn it!" just as, with my left ear, I heard Rosen ask me, "May I have the honor of a dance?"

I looked up and smiled in what I hoped was a charmingly polite way, as, from the tiny speaker nestled next to my inner ear, I heard something that doused me in ice water. Like little pops in the distance on the Fourth of July, I heard the unmistakable retorts of gunfire as I placed my hand in Rosen's.

Chapter
3 4

I found myself swept out onto the dance floor, heard myself mutter something about what a pleasant party this was, as every nerve fiber in my body strained to hear anything from Korosu.

Rosen was speaking to me, and I had no choice but to listen and respond.

"I've been an admirer of yours from afar for quite some time. You could say I've been intrigued."

"Are you interested in intrigue?" I asked, trying to be vague, yet elicit some kind of telling response. Except for a quick report that everything was still quiet, Korosu was not speaking.

"Very," Rosen said, and the suggestive tone was unmistakable. "I find life very boring without it. Don't you?"

He was watching me, reading my responses as much as I was his. I tried to keep the wrenching panic and terror off my face as I smiled and glanced away from him. "Oh, I don't know. I could do with a great deal less of it, to tell you the truth."

He laughed and moved his face close into my right ear just as Korosu said, "Darrien and I are going in. I have to be silent now."

I turned my face quickly to Rosen, afraid that he would hear the tiny voice in my ear. To cover the move, I asked the first thing that came into my mind. "So, I understand there's some trouble at Webtech?"

Not exactly the most tactful of questions, but since it was in my head and I needed a diversion, it had leaped out on its own. I tried to look like it was casual conversation.

He regarded me with some surprise and open curiosity, but his hands, one on my back and the other holding mine, tightened their grip. "Where did you hear that?"

"Just rumors, you know, office stuff. I might have read it somewhere."

His eyes glinted a bit as he spun me with a flourish. "You have to be so careful interpreting what you read, or hear," he said. "Rumors can cause an undue amount of alarm. I should know, I've had to put out quite a few fires about myself. Office scandal is a waste of time and money."

"So, what would you advise?" I asked him. "If I had that kind of trouble?"

In his smile I saw the bitter steel that had facilitated this man's rise to great wealth and power. It chilled me; he brought his mouth to my left ear and whispered, "Kill it as quickly as possible."

My face would certainly have given me away if I hadn't turned to scan the crowd for Ginny.

I caught sight of her, and then directly behind her I spotted Houndstooth working his way through the crowd, his eyes fixed on my beautiful friend.

"Who is that man?" I released Rosen's hand for a moment and pointed. "With the gray hair, over by the bar?"

Rosen followed my look and then glanced back at me, once again seeming to question my motive for asking. Was he wondering, like I was, if we were having one conversation or another? "A temporary inconvenience is what I would call him. But for the sake of niceties we'll say that he's here to make sure everything runs smoothly."

"For whom?" I asked, but he merely gave a tiny shrug. I strained to catch Ginny's eye, to warn her.

Korosu was still silent. *What is happening? Who fired the shots and was anyone hit?*

Rosen turned me so that I was facing away from Ginny. I told myself that she was safe, there were too many people here for Houndstooth to try anything. He spoke again. "You and I should get together and talk privately."

That was the last thing I wanted. He smiled that dangerous smile again, then continued in a breezily unconcerned way. "You should come up to my office. On a clear day, you can see all the way to the ocean."

"That's impressive, but I can see the ocean from my bedroom, thank you." Too late I realized the sexual implication of what I'd said.

"That would work nicely as well."

I tried to steer the conversation another way. "You think we have something to talk about?"

"Oh, I'm quite sure of it."

Before I could ask what, Korosu's voice fairly exploded in my ear.

"We've got him! We're out!"

I gasped audibly and went rigid. Rosen looked at me questioningly, and then asked, very coolly, "My dear, are you quite all right?"

"I'm fine," I said, fighting for composure. "I'm just a little light-headed, too much champagne, no doubt."

Rosen grinned at the shallow excuse. "No doubt."

I was desperate to get away, to get to Ginny. The song ended and I moved to break away, but Rosen took my arm firmly and led me from the dance floor. "Let's get you some air."

"No!" I said hastily, pulling back. "I'm fine, really. I just need to go to the ladies' room."

But Rosen would not relinquish my arm. "I think I'd better keep an eye on you. I'll show you inside to the private bath."

He pulled firmly, and I shot Ginny a panicked look; without any hesitation she started toward me. I was just about to twist my arm away violently when a butler approached us. "I'm very sorry to interrupt, sir, but you are wanted on the telephone."

This was it, the call. In a moment he would know.

Rosen looked angry, but before he could dismiss the butler, the man added, "It seems to be a matter of extreme importance."

Korosu's voice sounded in my head again with a message that hardly needed repeating. "Callaway, get out of there. We've got him, he's in the car with Curtis. Leave now!"

Reluctantly, Rosen released my arm and said, "If you'll excuse me."

He hurried away and I spun around, Ginny was halfway across the crowded dance floor. Houndstooth had made his way through the tight crowd and was now right behind her. I held up one finger and made a spinning motion.

Without hesitation, Ginny turned, spotted the man, and the next thing I knew he was down, crashing into several other guests. With everyone distracted and craning to see what the excitement was, she had no trouble getting to me, and we rushed as inconspicuously as possible for the door.

"They got him. He's okay," I told her, realizing as I said it that Korosu hadn't said he was okay, only that he was out.

When we reached the car, I had my keys in my hand. I started to hand them to Ginny, but she was already moving for the portable valet station, and I saw why. My car was blocked in, by a Bentley. "Get in and get the motor running!" she yelled. Then she yanked open the metal box that held the car keys and within seconds had the only Bentley key in her hand.

One of the valets came running up and shouted, "Hey! Can I help you? You can't do that—"

"Just did!" Ginny cut him off, flashing a brilliant smile that served to disarm him and bring him to a halt. She got into the pale yellow car, and with two smooth moves that looked impossible in the congested driveway, she cleared a space for me to get out. She exited the Bentley, threw the keys to the affronted valet so hard that he ducked, and jumped into my passenger seat.

"Go!" she shouted.

I wasted no time on that one. The sports car moved forward so quickly that it pressed us back into our seats and took the first few curves of the driveway like it was glued to the road.

Ginny's the better driver, I admit it, but I don't exactly drive like a girl. We were on the main highway before we saw lights behind us.

Ginny turned around and watched them.

"Are they following us?" I asked.

"Don't know," she responded flatly. It would have taken Rosen at least a minute or two to find out that Evan had gotten away, and that should give us a lead on them. "Just keep driving. If it looks safe later, we'll switch."

Korosu's voice sounded in my ear again. "Callaway? Can you hear me? Are you somewhere you can speak to me? Let me know that you're out."

"Give me my bag," I said to Ginny. She found it on the floor by her feet where I'd thrown it, and I pulled out the transmitter. "I'm here. Is everyone all right?"

"Yes, are you?"

"We're fine."

There was a short silence filled with mutual relief, and then Korosu's voice, sounding distinctly happier, asked, "How was the party?"

"Oh, you know." I was smiling, though there were tears in my eyes. "The usual. The canapés were soggy, the champagne was domestic, and the guests were heavily armed."

"Oh, you didn't tell me the party was in South Central Santa Ynez," he quipped.

"Can I speak to Evan?" I asked him.

"He's in the car ahead of me, but hold on, they're pulling over," Korosu said.

I listened for possibly forty seconds. And then . . .

"Hey, baby." His voice was melted Scharffen Berger chocolate; it dribbled into my ear, down through the lump in my throat, and soaked into my heart.

"Hi." I was too overwhelmed to say more. He was safe, he was alive.

"Are you okay?"

"Sure," I lied. "Did you get the bad guys?"

Evan's voice crackled with bitterness. "One of them. The others, including the man who calls himself Russian, got away."

"Oh," I said flatly. I wanted to care, but right now I didn't.

"How long until you get home?" Evan asked.

"About two hours." Unable to stop myself, I begged, "Tell me you'll be there." Tears flowed so rapidly to my eyes that the road in front of me blurred and I had to blink furiously to clear my vision.

"Wild horses couldn't drag me away."

Suddenly, I thought of Dana, of the fact that she was at my house and would see him first. A blade of hot red light seemed to stab through me. Frustrated and foiled, I fumed at myself. I had set this up! Fool! I wanted to see him first, to confront him. And I had to admit, I was afraid that she would get the advantage.

A coldness crept over me. "I'll see you then."

He was quiet. "Is everything all right?" he asked.

"Sure." Defensive detaching came so easily when you'd spent a lifetime learning how to do it. "Everything's fine." My voice sounded frozen and flippant in equal parts.

Buy it, he did not. "We'll talk when you get back."

"Great. Okay, I'll see you then."

"Callaway." He wasn't going to let me off that way.

"Yeah? Still here."

"I love you."

The part of me that was connected to him, invested in everything we had become, the part that would have believed anything he said, swelled up inside me and I choked.

I forced out my response through a thick cloud of what I recognized as pure, pain-filled me.

No matter what else happened. No matter how much he might hurt me, or how badly he had betrayed me, it was true.

"I love you too."

Chapter

35

Ginny hadn't been able to hear Evan's part of my conversation and she didn't seem at all interested in hearing about it now. Instead she slumped slightly in her seat with her eyes targeted on the side mirror.

"Okay, now we concentrate on driving." She still didn't look at me.

"You want me to pull over and switch with you?" I asked, slightly miffed that she hadn't noticed my emotional seesaw act.

"Nope. I want you to turn off up here, on the canyon road that goes past the old stagecoach stop restaurant, just before the bridge."

I glanced nervously in the rearview mirror. There were headlights behind us, not too close, but getting closer. Glancing at the speedometer, I saw that I was doing an easy ninety-five.

"Oh boy." I exhaled. "I guess this means we can't stop for a beer."

"I'll split a keg with you when we get home," Ginny said dryly. "Now, here's what I want you to do. The turn's coming up fast. Whatever you do, *don't put on your signal.* When I tell you to, I want you to turn out your lights, drop out of gear, cut the engine, and make the turn."

"In the pitch black?" I didn't have to say I thought she was insane; the tone of my voice said it for me.

"Exactly. Now, remember that the power steering is gonna go out when you cut the car's engine, so the faster you go into the turn, the easier it'll be to control the steering wheel. I'll help you if you need it."

I took my eyes off the road long enough to stare daggers. Lost on her, of course, as she was completely concentrated on the gaining headlights in the mirror and the intersection a half mile ahead. "Is this the kind of thing they teach you in stunt driving school?"

With her eyes glued to the road ahead she said, "No, this is the kind of thing you learn from a couple years of running drugs."

We'd have to go into that later.

"Okay, get ready, it's coming up. Don't hit the brakes, but take your foot off the gas and gear down." She was sitting forward now, tense, with one hand raised to grab the wheel if I needed help and the other one holding the handgrip above her door.

I did everything she said. I couldn't see the turnoff yet, it being out of range of my lights, but I knew from the Bridge Ahead sign that it was coming up. The bridge was an impossible span of metal and concrete that bypassed a deeply rutted canyon. I tried not to think about what that fall would be like if we miscalculated the turn and went off-roading into the space between the bridge and the intersection. Keeping one eye on the road and the other on the speedometer, I watched it fall, wondering how fast even this car could take a right-angle curve without flipping. I dropped into third gear, eighty miles an hour, seventy, sixty, fifty, the car speeded briefly on from its own volition as I hit the clutch to shift down to second; the engine whined in protest, forty miles per hour, thirty, and then I finally saw the turn.

"Now!" Ginny yelled. I memorized the distance to the turn, then turned off the lights and then the car.

Blackness. Motion, wind, thrust, silence. And then, as my eyes adjusted enough to tell the difference between the blackness of the road and the grayness of the pastures on both sides, I started the turn. Wheels screamed as the racing tread rubber scrabbled to hold us to the road, the car suddenly transformed from a highly maneuverable machine to an awkward, dead weight.

Now, I pressed the brake, and it felt like a thick straw mat had been placed between it and the floorboard. I was pulling down on the steering wheel with all my might, and the car was turning slower, much slower than I had anticipated. Ginny's left hand closed over mine, and her grip was so tight that I almost cried out.

We made the turn, rolled on for a ways, and Ginny spun around to look behind us. She saw the car speed through the intersection. It was a Hummer.

"I *hate* those cars!" I said with a passion.

"Shut up," Ginny snapped. She had rolled down her window and stuck her head out. We both heard the screech as the heavy vehicle hit the brakes. It had been going so fast that it must have been in the middle of the bridge when it had finally come to a stop. Next came the sound of another car honking insanely, and squealing tires, and then the ugly crunch of metal.

"Go, go, go!" Ginny ordered.

Barely pausing to pray that the oncoming car had survived the crash—and stayed on the bridge—I fired up the engine and took off again.

This road was nothing but a narrow two-lane with hairpin curves, the old stagecoach route that had taken hours or days to traverse what the bridge now sent you flying over with nothing more than a dizzying glance at the drop below you. It would have been a simple thing to outrun the heavy Hummer on these tight curves—child's play—*if* we hadn't come up behind a rusty old rattletrap of an RV lugging itself up the steep hill within the first forty-five seconds. It was taking up both lanes on the curves, and it moved as though all the spunk had gone out of it after it had crossed the country for the seventeenth time back in ninety-two and didn't seem to think there was much point of going on with life.

Another quarter of a minute brought us the unhappy reflection of the Hummer's headlights again.

"Shit!" Ginny swore. There were no turnoffs, just the occasional isolated driveway that would have trapped us against the side of the mountain.

The monster truck came up close behind us, its highly placed halogen lights blinding us as it crept closer.

Because of the blinding headlights it was hard to make out anything more than the gray outlines of two bulky men in the truck. There was no license plate.

Near the top of the canyon, the RV finally put on its left blinker and, after an interminable interlude, scraped its way through the branches of some pine trees on both sides of a narrow dirt driveway. We took off with the Hummer's engine churning like an ocean liner just behind us. For the first two corkscrew turns, the more maneuverable, lighter Mercedes managed to pull well ahead, but as I took the last severe turn—cutting off a good section of it to keep up my speed—I almost ran head-on into a car minding its own business in its own lane, which I was occupying most of. I swerved, missed it narrowly, swallowed my heart again, and almost immediately came out on the crest of the canyon. A long, straight stretch of road lay ahead of us, then curved sharply off to the left. Dead ahead was a guardrail, beyond which I could see nothing but night sky.

"Jesus Christ, Ginny," I swore. "If I keep driving like this, I'm going to kill somebody."

"As long as it's not us," she answered dryly.

"It might very well be!"

"Okay, calm down, I've got another idea. Ease off on the gas."

Swearing again, I followed her advice, and the huge Hummer, with an engine the size of an eighteen-wheeler, came up close behind us and rode right on our tail.

One hundred yards from the curve, Ginny turned to me. I didn't look back at her, I couldn't, but I could feel her eyes on me.

"Do you trust me?" she asked.

"Usually," was the most affirmative answer I could give right at that moment.

"Then slow down."

"What?"

The mammoth was actually scraping my bumper.

"Just do it, now!"

Wondering if my life would flash before my eyes when the bastard pushed us over the cliff coming up fast—and hoping some parts would be edited if it did—I put my foot on the brake and pressed. Immediately, the sound of crunching metal told me that the Hummer was officially up our ass. I started to try to turn into the curve, but the larger car was forcing us forward. I pressed harder on the brake, futilely trying to hold back both vehicles from the fast-approaching metal railing. The brakes locked, the skid started, and we planed across rubber and asphalt. Out of control.

Five yards from the railing, Ginny's left leg came over the gearshift and kicked my right foot hard, knocking it off the brake as she stomped the accelerator to the floorboard. The burst of speed caused the wheels of the Mercedes to spin again, reinstating their traction, and I sensed the return of control as the tires grabbed the road. I yanked the steering wheel hard to the left, feeling the amazing centrifugal pull in the opposite direction as the low, wide car hugged the pavement and hurtled on through the turn—leaving the Hummer, too heavy and accelerating too fast to make the turn, on an unstoppable forward flight. The obscenely oversized passenger vehicle skated at an unnatural angle and hit the guardrail, which was far too low to do anything but flip the monstrosity up and over the railing and on into the open air. It was bizarrely graceful, in a disturbingly wrong way. Like a defensive lineman for the Chicago Bears being launched into a grand jeté, floating impossibly up and out, defying gravity, until gravity said fuck you and sent it spinning downward to its final resting place.

I slowed down, pulled over, and let my arms—vibrating with adrenaline—drop into my lap. The car, God bless it, sat humming in idle inertness. Turning, I looked at Ginny; even she looked more than a little shaken.

"Now *that,*" she said emphatically, "is what they teach you in stunt driving school."

Chapter

36

Ginny checked the back of the Mercedes. It was slightly dented and scratched, but amazingly intact. We headed back the way we'd come, my thoughts now on the crash we'd heard on the bridge. A state trooper was already on the scene. We slowed down and did a little rubbernecking, an activity I normally despise, but feeling somewhat responsible, I needed to know if anyone was hurt.

It looked good. The car, a small blue Honda Accord, had sideswiped the railing. The front of it was smashed, presumably where it had confronted the Hummer turning around on a two-lane bridge. The driver was out of the car and looked fine, though somewhat stunned.

"Get the license plate number," I said to Ginny. "I think that guy deserves a new car from an anonymous source."

Ginny got a pen out of the glove box. I asked, "Do you think we should say that we saw another 'accident'?"

"Do you want to be here all fucking night?" Ginny asked.

"But what if they're still alive?"

We looked at each other. A flash of blue light from the cop car illuminated Ginny's face as we passed by it, giving me a clear view of what she thought the odds were on that.

"Okay, they're dead," I said. "But we should notify somebody—"

"I'll call Curtis and let him deal with it."

"Don't." Suddenly I didn't want Curtis, or Evan, or anyone to take care of me right now. In the last few days, we'd been stalked, watched over, spied on, and we'd almost died more than once, and I was reveling in the feeling of driving through the night without anyone knowing where we were. The wind from the half-opened window pushed a few loose tendrils of hair against my face, and life felt precious, blissful. "Let's just take our time, get home, and then wallow out into the quagmire of shit again." I turned and looked at her, feeling blessed beyond belief at the grand experience of having her with me through everything. "Okay?"

She smiled, recognizing the depth of my request and understanding it as only she could. She nodded, placed a hand firmly on my shoulder for a moment, then rolled down her window, stuck her head all the way out, and whooped with every ounce of her very substantial lung power.

I knew just how she felt.

The rest of the drive we spent in our own reflective silences, until we pulled up at the gate in front of my house.

"Whatever happens," Ginny said smoothly, "it's going to be all right."

The tears I'd been denying crawled out from behind the curtains of my lids and showed themselves. "Promise?" I whispered.

"Promise. Now, wipe your face, get your shit together, and step up to the next plate."

I took a deep breath, and the fear morphed into a kind of resigned sadness. "Does it ever end?" I asked her, sighing mournfully.

Ginny laughed out loud, which surprised me, though I can't

say why, since it was exactly the sort of thing she would do. "You can't stop the waves, girl," she said, and looked at me with shining, brave eyes. She cocked her head to one side and poked me in the ribs. "But you can learn to surf."

Now, I laughed. And as the gate opened, I took us both up the long, curving drive.

Pulling up in front, I was disappointed that Evan wasn't there to greet me. As we got out of the car and started for the door, it flew open, and my heart fluttered faster than a hummingbird's wings. But it wasn't Evan waiting to welcome me. It was Sabrina, who threw herself into my arms with a joyous yelp.

"Thank Gawd!" she drawled. "Everybody's home safe. Are you okay? How was the drive home?"

Glancing at Ginny, I said, "Textbook." Unable to stop myself, I asked, "Where's Evan?"

"He was in the library with Curtis, they made me leave the room about an hour ago," she said, looking pouty. "I told them they can trust me, but they still made me leave."

She couldn't wait to pass on her information. "Evan looks okay. He had a shower and something to eat, and you won't believe this! Detective Bloom got shot!" Before I could recover, she rolled over me like she was a large piece of harvesting equipment and I was ripe wheat. "But she had on a vest and even though she got bruised, she's fine. Oh my God, can you imagine if it hadn't hit the vest? They won't tell me, but I think they shot one of the bad guys, and . . ."

We were in the door now, and still there was no sign of Evan. I was absolutely sure that Deirdre, at least, would have alerted him that I had come in the gate. The security system sounded a specific beep when the gate opened, and there was a video monitor in the kitchen.

Sabrina was still ranting enthusiastically, but I'd stopped listening to her. I started across the entrance hall toward the library. Deirdre met me halfway.

"Welcome home," she said, and subtly smiled her relief to have me there.

"Thank you, Deirdre. Where's Evan?" I asked her, my distress at his lack of attendance apparent in my voice. As much as I hated looking weak, I couldn't care enough to control it right now.

"He was with Detective Curtis in the library—"

Before she could finish I had swept around her and crossed to the library door; my palms were sweaty as I grasped the metal handle and twisted it open. With mingled apprehension, eagerness, and rising anger, I stepped into the room. And found it empty.

Deirdre was right behind me; she spoke quickly. "Detective Curtis is on the phone in the kitchen." Behind her, I saw Ginny turn purposefully in that direction, attaching herself to Sabrina's arm as she went. She seemed to be slightly miffed as well. "And Detective Paley is upstairs."

I started for the stairs. In spite of my heart rising at the thought of seeing Evan alone, I asked suspiciously, "Did you tell him I was here?"

She was following me. "I knocked on the door, but there was no answer."

When I reached the landing, I turned to the left to go to my bedroom, but before I'd taken two steps, Deirdre stopped me with two words, spoken respectfully, but I could tell she was conscious of my feelings.

"No, ma'am," she said quietly. "He's in the blue suite." She said nothing for a moment, then asked, "Shall I go and get him?"

"No," I told her. My body had gone all rubbery and cold.

The blue suite was where we had put Dana.

Chapter
37

It took every fraction of strength I had left, and some that I called up only by promising my soul to a darker place, to force my legs to walk to my bedroom door.

I couldn't see what was in front of me. Everything had gone colorless and flat. The fibers of my nerves pulsed horrifically and felt like they were a thousand tiny barbed wires that pierced my skin in as many places and were being drawn back and forth through me at a fantastic speed. They were screaming at me with a multitude of different voices, united as one incensed mob: "Go get him!" But I could not, would not, allow it.

He had chosen Dana over me.

Without turning on the light, I sank onto my bed and lay in the darkness. Oddly, I recognized this place of waiting. I wasn't waiting for Evan, or for redemption, or even calm. I was willing myself to get through the next few minutes, to contain the panic and the pain. To somehow reassure myself enough to know that the storm that raged in my heart and mind would lessen, that I would live, that this too would pass.

My mouth moved, and without sound I formed the words, "You can do it, nothing to it. You can do it, nothing to it," my father's constant mantra of confidence in me.

I struggled not to feel. But my protective shell was cracking, I was losing.

Goddamn it! Not me! I never lose!

The realization of loneliness was next, its arctic permafrost setting quickly over my entire skin. I cried more softly now.

I'm alone. I knew it. I'll always be alone.

And then something touched me. I turned my face into the pillow, not wanting anyone to see me, not able to connect to any other human.

The hand on the small of my back wrapped around me and I felt the body tuck in behind me. Like an overcoat, another arm snaked underneath me until I was enveloped, and still I sobbed, so grateful for the reminder that I was alive, but unable to escape the enclosure of isolation.

Then I felt, more than heard, words breathed on the back of my neck, low and reassuring, then a man's hand, large and strong, came up and brushed my hair, stuck to my face by my tears, back away from my skin. Very slowly, he turned me toward him in the dark and my face pressed into the wide chest as the arms pulled me in closer.

For the first time, I made out words spoken by the rich voice. "It's all right now, I'm here."

"Callaway?" a second male voice called from the doorway, and then a light was switched on. I found myself in an interesting tableau.

I was lying wrapped in Korosu's arms, and he had made no move to release me when Evan called out and turned on the light.

There was a long, surreal moment. And then Korosu sat up slowly, raising me with him. He pulled a silk handkerchief from his breast pocket and handed it to me.

"Are you all right now?" he asked.

I could have laughed if it hadn't been so tragic. How ironic. Evan runs off to Dana's arms and I get caught in Korosu's.

Unable to look at Evan, I covered my distraught face with my hands, and then looked through my fingers at Korosu.

"Oh, I'm fine," I told him, feeling slightly hysterical, shaken and stirred. "Never better."

"You can call me if you need me," he said. Then he rose and walked past Evan and out the door without a word. I noticed that Evan didn't look at him.

I was feeling too vulnerable sitting on the bed while Evan stood over me. Moving to the sitting area, I poured myself a cognac with shaking hands. As I did so, I remembered the first time Evan had been in this room. In reference to that I said, without looking at him, "Cognac? Why don't you just hold one so I don't feel like I'm drinking alone?"

I poured two in large heavy crystal snifters, took a burning gulp and a deep cooling breath, and turned a tepid face to him. What else was there to do?

He had the oddest expression on his face as he moved into the room and closed the door: guilty and pained at the same time.

"All right. I'll take one," he said, and our fingers brushed as he accepted the glass. I pulled my hand away as though I'd received an electric shock. "Callaway, what's going on?"

Now I did laugh. It was mirthless and cruel sounding, but I couldn't help it. "That's rich," I couldn't help saying. "You keep everything from me and then you want *me* to tell *you* what's going on."

Instead of responding to my accusation, he asked, "Why were you crying?"

My arm jerked so hard with the impulse to throw the glass at him that some of the liquor sloshed over the rim and left a machine-gun-fire stain of small dark spots across the carpet. I looked down at the damage. At least a dozen biting responses came to mind, but I forced myself to keep them back and said instead, "It's been a rough night."

"I'm sorry I didn't meet you when you came in. Is that what's bothering you?" He made it sound petty.

I smiled icily and shook my head. "No, I'm sure you were busy. Like I said, I had a tough night."

Evan sighed, took a swig of the liquor, and set his glass down. "Look, can we start over?" He came to me and held out his arms.

No matter what, I was glad he was alive and back safely. I allowed him to hug me.

It was impossible not to melt into his embrace. The smell of him, so longed for and so needed, infiltrated my defenses. In spite of myself, I found my resolve weakening, so far that I asked for an explanation, albeit in an accusing way.

"So, how's Dana?" My voice was cold enough for a far less astute man than Evan to decipher its meaning.

He pulled back and looked at me. "She's very upset. Let's not forget that these people still want her dead."

She wasn't the only one, I thought to myself, feeling the splintered remnants of terror in my bloodstream and hearing the ugly grate of metal on metal as the Hummer had pushed us, out of control, toward a gaping black death. "No, let's not forget that," I said.

"Callaway?" Evan took my shoulders firmly in his hands, and his face was as serious and open as I have ever seen it. But then, I'd trusted that face before. "Do you think that something is going on between Dana and me?"

"Isn't it?" I asked, and then, afraid of the answer, I went on before he could respond, "I do find it very interesting that you never told me you were involved with her before."

"It never came up," he said, honestly enough. "I never asked you about who you were involved with. I'm assuming there were men before me."

"Many," I said flippantly, hoping to suggest to him and myself that he was easily replaceable, which would be a blatant self-deception, even if it worked on him.

Evan let go of me and backed away. I could see him containing his anger. "I'm *not* involved with Dana Scheiner. She came to me because she didn't know where else to go when she got into trouble. I was trying to help her. It wasn't the kind of thing that was safe for me to talk about. That's the end of the story."

Now I was in an interesting predicament. Unless I wanted to tell him I had snooped through his emails, I couldn't let on that I knew anything more. Though at first it had been innocent enough, looking for clues, there was a nagging place in my gut that told me I had crossed the line into spying on him.

I wanted to believe him, but I had had too much time to think about it. If I had come home to his eager arms, and Dana had seemed less important to him than me, than *us,* then maybe I could have bought it all.

"So, you're just helping out a friend?" My voice was still soggy with sarcasm.

The anger flashed in his eyes again and I told myself I didn't care, that I was the wronged one.

"This is business," he spoke quietly. "We should talk about this after the crisis is over."

"Evan?" I smiled at him, but I couldn't stop the tears from growing like the crest of a wave in my eyes. "There's always a crisis."

Brushing past him, I went to the door, downing my drink as I went.

He caught my arm and pinned me against the bedroom wall. His mouth found mine, and he whispered, "Don't do this."

The pressure of his body against mine was like a comforter after an icy plunge on a cold, cold night. Still I fought it, struggling to hold on to my anger; he held my face tightly in his hands and looked into my eyes.

"Don't doubt me," he whispered fiercely.

And I couldn't. I couldn't fight his strength and the conviction in his voice. I couldn't deny the passion in his eyes. I kissed him hard, pulled him up against me, and let go of all my fear.

Crying and gasping, I wrapped my legs around him as he pressed me against the wall. He carried me back to the bed and enveloped me with his mouth, his hands, his words. I needed him with me, beside me, inside me.

Come what may.

Chapter
3 8

I woke the next morning to a sinking heavy feeling, which increased as I thought over the events of last night. We'd sat at the kitchen table and heard the news that the bodies in the Hummer had been found with no identification on them and the car itself had been stolen. Though I'd been able to feel Evan's intensity whenever his eyes had caught mine, I hadn't been able to entirely let go of feeling neglected. I had gone to bed late, and alone, leaving Evan and Curtis talking in the kitchen.

Glancing next to me, I could see that Evan hadn't come to bed, that was certain from the neatness of the sheets and the fullness of the pillow. My heart took on water and sank deeper, as I lay listlessly, riddled with doubts.

The door opened and Ginny came in. She stood for a moment regarding me. I felt like a rag doll. Boneless.

She had brought me a coffee, which she handed me; bless her. Then she ripped the curtains open, frying my eyes with the brilliant summer sun; curse her.

"Okay, genius, get up."

I turned and looked at her, shielding my eyes from the light. "I can't," I told her weakly, but with a Herculean effort I roused myself into a sitting position to receive the morning injection of caffeine and her "I told you so."

She handed the first one over and sat next to me to deliver the second. "Now, I'm sure that you were fair and open when you talked to Evan last night, right?" She was using her kindergarten teacher voice.

"Of course I was," I answered indignantly.

"And what did he say?" Ginny asked me.

I fidgeted a bit. "That he wasn't seeing Dana." Ginny held her hands palms up, but while she was saying "I knew it" I went on defensively, "But I had good reason to be suspicious, and you know it! He was *with* Dana when I came home, and when I asked why he never told me he dated her before we met he said, 'You never asked me.' Convenient, don't you think?"

She nodded sympathetically and draped an arm protectively around me. I was so pleased that she was going to take my side, defend my position. "Dirty bastard," she said, shaking her head and making a *tsk*ing noise.

"I mean, please, what a stupid thing to say, right?" I asked.

"Stupid," Ginny agreed. "Idiotic. How much of an imbecile can you be?" She shook her head. "What a pathetic excuse." Then she screwed up her face and asked, seemingly innocently, "Just out of curiosity, did you ever tell him about Joe?"

"I don't remember, I'm sure I must have," I lied blatantly, not liking the tack she was taking.

"Chase?"

"I forget."

"Vince?"

"I can't recall."

"Mm-hmm. Can I have a sip of that coffee?" I handed it over, and her arm moved from around my shoulders to the side of my head. She shoved, sending me off the bed onto the floor. Before I could recover, she was standing over me, looking like a magnificent, vengeful Amazon queen in Prada pants, which, I'm certain, is what any given Amazon queen defending justice would have chosen to wear if she'd been active in today's fashion scene.

"*Convenient.*" She snarled down at me. "You 'can't recall' whether or not you told Evan about any of the six dozen men you've fucked in the last three years, but you're ready to ditch the only man who ever loved you for who you are when you find out he wasn't a virgin before he met you."

I flashed on Korosu, who seemed to love me too, but all I said was, "Six dozen is a smidgen exaggerated, don't you think?"

She wasn't done. "Call it a baker's dozen then, I don't care. You think *maybe* you were looking for an excuse because you're scared to trust *anybody.*"

That pissed me off. She didn't know everything. How dare she call me scared. "Bullshit!" I said. "I had really good reasons to be suspicious."

"Like what?"

"Like the fact that Dana is still obviously in love with him. Like all his sweetie-pie emails to her, which you didn't see by the way," I lashed out.

She took a sip of my coffee and squinted at me. "He called her sweetie-pie?"

"Well, no, not exactly, but you know what I mean. He was meeting her!"

Ginny scowled. "And—based on the events of the last few days—do you think there might have been a legitimate reason for that?"

I bypassed the logic with my insecure fury. "It's hard to trust someone who won't tell you everything."

"Why should he?" she asked, and I sputtered.

"What? Because we're supposed to be getting married, we're supposed to *trust* each other."

"Girl." She shook her head, still towering over me. "What are you so afraid of? Trust doesn't mean knowing *everything*. Can't you see now why Evan wouldn't have wanted to involve you with these criminals?"

Once again the sensibility of what she was saying struck me like an Amazon warrior's spear through the gut; I didn't want to hear it, I fumbled for a shield. "I wasn't threatened by Evan having a *normal* work and social life!" But as I said it, I realized that I was. Though my jealousy over his leaping to Dana's defense might be reasonable, I had to admit that even the thought of him getting along fine in the world without me left me feeling irrationally deserted. It was insane; it was weak. I hated myself.

"No? You're not a little nervous that if he can exist without you, you might disappear?"

"Bullshit," I repeated, losing variety in my vocabulary in my defensiveness. "Playing poker with the boys isn't what we're talking about here, and you know it. I have a life outside of Evan's. I don't tell him everything I do when I spend the day at the office, he doesn't have a clue who I talk to or have meetings with. Hell, he doesn't even ask," I ended bitterly.

"Then why do you think he should tell you everything?"

"Because this is different! He *was* in love with her, and she's *still* in love with him."

She nodded and sat on the end of the bed again. "And why"—she fixed me with her golden eyes so exactly like a cat watching its prey that I swear, if she'd had a tail it would have swished sharply from side to side—"is he marrying you?"

My first response would have been a convenient and predictable "For my money," but seeing how Evan had his own, it didn't bear weight. "I don't know," I had to admit.

"Why can't you trust him? What are you afraid of?" she asked.

"I'm not afraid," I repeated, trying to make it true. "I'm cautious!"

She seemed to not hear that answer and instead offered up

one of her own. "Are you afraid that if you trust him and find out he lied, you'll look like a fool?"

"No! Well, okay, yes!" I struggled to free myself from the twisted tangle of sheets I had landed in on the floor.

"Girl, you don't need a man to look like a fool." She offered a hand, extracting me from the linen. "He's *Evan*, not a french-fryer at McDonald's. Things are bound to be a little exciting. What do you want, a guarantee? Buy something at Sears." She gave me back my coffee.

In spite of myself, I laughed, then changed the subject. "How'd it go with Curtis? You didn't look too happy that he wasn't at the door to meet you either."

"And so *I told him that.*" She enunciated the sentence very clearly, as though I were hard of hearing. "And he explained that he was on the phone with the morgue, getting the pertinent info about the men in the Hummer, and then," she went on at a nice clip, "we had fabulous sex." She smiled at me knowingly. "Real men are hard to find, and maybe scarier to get to know, because they're not going to follow us around like puppies. We've both been pet owners more than enough times."

"So many different breeds," I agreed.

"Evan is a real man. *Trust him,*" she urged. "Take a chance, what have you got to lose?"

Trust him. I was trying, but it was far easier said than done after a lifetime of learning to keep everyone a straight arm away from my heart. I smiled thinly and said nothing, but I thought to myself, *What have I got to lose?*

Everything.

Chapter
39

I slunk downstairs, ready to try and bond.

Evan wasn't there. He and Curtis had gone out, Deirdre didn't know where. Dana was in her room and hadn't come out yet today. I took my coffee into the living room to sulk.

My private line rang and I picked it up. It was Kelly.

"Ms. Wilde, I have Mr. Ferris on the line, would you like to speak to him?"

"Thank you, Kelly." I heard the muffled tone change of Kelly transferring the call and said, "Jim?"

"Callaway, you disappeared last night. Is everything okay?"

"Yes, actually. I'm sorry I had to leave suddenly. But I would love to see you, have a cup of coffee or something." I was thinking that I wanted to ask him about a few things. If he knew who Houndstooth was, and why and how Fredrick Rosen had settled his harassment charge out of court.

Jim picked it up beautifully. "Do you want to meet somewhere?"

"That would be great," I answered, flushed with embarrassment as I realized he probably assumed I wanted to get together to talk about the loss of my father. He was acting as though it were the most natural thing in the world for someone to call and just want to talk. I supposed—with a jolt of abrupt awakening—that to most people it was.

"I had to come into the office today. Would you mind meeting me downtown?"

"You're working on Saturday?"

"I have meetings, believe it or not. In fact, starting around lunchtime."

He asked if I'd mind meeting him at a café downstairs in his building, apologizing that it wasn't very fancy, but that suited me fine.

The café was more like a cafeteria, tucked into the back of the Webtech building. I took a small booth for two near the window and sat waiting for Jim.

A smart shock of red hair pulled up in a practical working style caught my eye at a corner booth. The woman had her back to me, but as I tensed and watched, she turned her head, just a profile, but it was enough to recognize her; it was Red. Cautiously, I rose and moved toward the woman, who was sitting alone. I wasn't going to risk her running away again, so, approaching from behind, I slid into the booth next to her, effectively blocking her exit.

She turned in startled surprise, her irises wide with honest fear, and then they darted around, looking for a way out.

"I just want to talk to you for a moment," I told her in a soothing, calming tone.

"I can't talk to you." She looked furtively around, seeking escape, or checking for enemies, I couldn't tell which. Maybe it was both.

"Are you afraid?"

She said nothing, but in her eyes was a combination of desperation and "No shit."

"Who made you be the go-between?" I asked her quietly.

"I can't say anything. Please let me go." Her hands fidgeted incessantly with a couple of white paper napkins that sat next to her plate.

Realizing that she would be terrified she was being watched, I said very quietly, "I can help you."

"Don't you understand?" Her voice was quiet but tremulous with angst. "No one can help me!" She was tapping her fingers furiously on the table, on top of the napkin, making her point.

With a sudden movement, she shoved me, sending me, and the contents of my opened purse, onto the checkered floor of the restaurant. With a movement as quick as a scurrying mouse, she was over me and out the door.

Heads turned, but they didn't seem to notice Red; they all focused on me in my inelegant position. I looked around, muttered something about being clumsy, and started gathering up my personal belongings. My Montblanc fountain pen had rolled back under the booth table, and I had no choice but to scramble after it on my hands and knees. It was while I was in this dignified pose that I heard Jim's voice.

"Callaway? Did you lose something?"

"Oh," I sighed as I backed out, butt first, from beneath the table. "Just my pride. And I'll be damned if I can find it." He helped me up, and we sat at the now empty booth.

He looked at the half-eaten sandwich on the plate in front of me. "Did you already eat?"

"No."

"Isabelle's upstairs," he confided, "and, of course, she wanted to come down and join us, but I said you wanted to discuss business. I knew you might not want to talk in front of her. I love my daughter more than anything, but I'm well aware she's not the most, shall we say, discreet of friends."

"Thank you," I said gratefully. "I really wanted to talk to you alone today." I looked at Jim for a moment, sizing him up. I had known him for a long time. "Jim, I want to ask you some things."

He nodded and smiled kindly. "Shoot," he said. I'm sure he thought I meant some personal things, but I needed to ask him about the company he worked for, about murder and deception. I hoped he would listen.

He waited and I cleared my throat, wondering where to dive in. I settled on the deep end. "You know"—I bent my knees and pushed off—"I find that I can't do that without telling you the whole story, which you might not like very much, or at all."

His brows went up a little, but he said nothing. I launched myself into the water, and once I was in, swimming was easier than I had expected. I told Jim about the murders, about our suspicions that someone at Webtech was behind them. I filled him in on Dana and her unwitting involvement and the fact that she was at my house, though I left out the part about the instructions for me to kill her. I gave a full description of the chase after the party. I choked a bit on the part about Evan's seeming involvement with Dana.

Through it all Jim's face was a reflection of my story. He looked alternately alarmed for my safety, concerned about my emotional dilemma, dubious yet deeply unhappy at the possible involvement of his company, and overwhelmed by the scope of my story. I finished with a brief description of my recent meeting with the redhead, and Jim shook his head in puzzlement.

"Well?" I asked. "Say something."

When he did, I was surprised at what he said. "Callaway, what have you gotten yourself into?"

Anger flashed across my heart; he sounded like Evan. *It's not my fault!* But the feeling faded as quickly as it came, and I could see what he meant. His brow furrowed, and he studied the wooden block tabletop. "I know that the company has attracted federal interest lately, but I'm equally sure that it will all turn out to be on the up and up. I can't believe it, Callaway. I just can't believe that anyone I work with, *who I have known for years,* is capable of kidnapping and murder!"

"I know," I sighed. "I really know what you mean." I fixed him with a steady look; he knew most of the details of the personal betrayals in my family. "It's not easy to accept that someone you trust could be completely untrustworthy. In fact, it's downright painful."

Jim smiled softly at me. "I forgot who I was talking to for a minute. Yes, you would know, wouldn't you?" He looked sympathetically at me and then he glanced away, as though he'd had a sudden thought.

"And on that theme," he murmured as he reached across the table and took my hand, proceeding with gentleness in his voice, "Callaway, what about your fiancé? I hate to have to bring this up, but he seems to be involved in a way that you don't really understand. Maybe"—he paused, as though he didn't want to hurt me—"maybe, he's in deeper than you know."

My first response was a knee-jerk reaction. I'd decided to trust him, hadn't I? "No way." I shook my head vehemently, but even before the words settled, I was remembering his watch at Josie Banks's, Molly Simpson's altered files that Curtis had found on his desk, the doubt in Curtis's voice. I had to admit it was possible.

My face must have shown that I was considering the possibility, because Jim stroked my hand to call me back. "Cally?"

"Yeah?" I answered, and looked up at him sadly.

"You haven't known him very long, have you?"

A year. Just over a year. His life before that, and even segments of it during that year, were a blank to me.

"Listen to me," he said. "I'm going to do whatever I can to find out what's going on here." When I started to object, he squeezed my fingers reassuringly. "I'll be very careful. First, I'm going to find out who the redhead is. In the meantime, don't tell anyone that you came and talked to me today, just in case."

I nodded; that was smart. If I told Evan, and he *was* involved—the thought made my stomach lurch like a sudden altitude drop in a plane—then it could be a fatal move for Jim.

"Now I have to go back to wondering whether to trust Evan or not." Tears started in my eyes.

Jim smiled again, in such a protective, fatherly way that it increased, rather than stemmed, the demonstrative flow. "I can't tell you that. Maybe it will all turn out to be someone who is trying to use Webtech as a decoy, and maybe your fiancé got involved innocently. I hope so." He gave my hand one more dose of loving pressure and released it. "But, in the meantime, be careful." He got up, looking grim and serious. "I'll call you as soon as I know anything. Are you going to be okay?"

"Oh, I guess so." I tried to give him a reassuring smile.

He put his hand on my head, as though I were a child, then left. Trying to pull myself together, I picked up the top napkin in the pile left on the table by Red and wiped my eyes.

Underneath it, something had been roughly drawn on the white surface of the next napkin. The water in my eyes blurred the image and the few scribbled words beneath it. Remembering now how she had tapped at the napkins in what I had assumed was agitation, I blinked my tears furiously away and focused on what I hoped was a message.

It was a simple doodle, crudely drawn: two circles, one inside the other, and an arrow inside the center. Around the outside of that was the rough shape of something that made my skin crawl: a police badge. The words were harder to make out, scratched hurriedly onto the flimsy surface, which had torn in several places from the contact with the writing implement. Three words.

Trust no one.

Chapter
40

As soon as I got home, I found Evan in the kitchen with Curtis. I showed them the note, making eye contact with Curtis when Evan looked away. Curtis looked disturbed, but a shake of his head warned me not to say anything. I told them about going to talk to Jim Ferris, though I made it sound like I'd gone to explain my sudden disappearance the night before.

Maybe it was paranoia that kept me cautious, and maybe it was intelligence. Cross me once, shame on you. Cross me twice, just go ahead and shoot me.

They speculated on the meaning of the doodle. The words themselves seemed to be clear enough, but whom did they refer to?

"Could it be the insignia of some other company?" I asked, looking at the circle within a circle within a badge and the crude arrow.

"Possible," Curtis mused. "Possible that she spotted you before you saw her, and wrote you a message, or the shapes could be something she was just doodling before she wrote the words that were meant for you. Did she have a pen?"

"Not that I saw, but she wasn't writing when I sat down. But what about the badge?" I said hesitantly.

Evan answered, almost too quickly, dispersing the innuendo by bringing it out in the open. "Could be trying to throw suspicion on me, or the police in general. Or even a security company . . ." His voice trailed off and he looked distracted. He sighed deeply and ran his hands through his thick black hair.

He turned to me and said, "So you asked Jim who this redhead is?" I nodded. "I'd certainly like to know what her connection is to all this," he went on. "Also this Houndstooth who keeps showing up at all the pertinent places. Although it's odd, your description of him doesn't fit any of the men who took or held me."

"But," I protested, "he was there when you were taken."

Evan nodded. "Right, so he could be the head guy who's keeping out of view."

"Not out of my view!" I said vehemently. "I've seen all too much of him, thank you."

"True." Evan tapped his fingertips on the tabletop and said with a wry smile, in which I was sure I detected a hint of jealousy, "And he's seen all too much of you."

I thought of standing naked on the stairs, my hair dripping wet as I pointed Evan's gun at the man. I didn't know whether to be pleased at Evan's comment or annoyed.

Evan said, "If he was at Rosen's party and Rosen acknowledged him, that's a definite giveaway that they're working together."

"But why," I asked, exasperated with the whole confusing subject, "didn't they just offer Dana the money themselves? Why in the hell did they need to involve me, you, and a plot line of *Murder, She Wrote?*"

Curtis was looking at me, surprised. "Didn't Sabrina tell you that Webtech was being investigated?"

So had Jim, so had the newspaper articles, but it still didn't mean anything to me. I hated to look stupid, so I said, "Of course."

Evan explained, "So that means it would be virtually impossible for the company or any of its major players to move a couple of million dollars without it being traced. So if someone did want to pay off Dana, they couldn't do it themselves. *And* they're getting someone else to commit the crime." He looked over at Curtis and shrugged.

"Quite brilliant really," Evan said.

"Wish I'd thought of it," Curtis agreed.

"By the way," Evan said to me, "where is the money?"

"It's in the small safe in my office," I told him, feeling oddly relieved that I was the only one who knew the combination.

He held out the napkin. "Put this in there as well, just in case."

I took it and put it in my pocket for now.

"One thing I'd like to make perfectly clear," Evan said. "Sabrina is not to go back there. It wasn't a smart idea."

I bristled, though I knew he was right. "Where is she, anyway?"

"She went to breakfast with Darrien," Curtis told me.

I jumped as the buzzer for the front gate sounded. Deirdre came into the kitchen and checked the monitor. She turned to us. "It's a delivery service."

I glanced up at the kitchen clock. Noon. Saturday. Curtis and Evan followed my eyes. For ten seconds no one spoke.

Evan crossed over, squinted at the screen, then pushed the audio button. "Can I help you?"

"Hi, Fast Delivery. I have a package for, uh"—they saw him hold the package up to read the name—"uh, E. Playly?" he read haltingly.

"Okay, bring it in please." Evan and Curtis both drew their guns. Evan went out the door leading to the entrance hall and Curtis remained in the kitchen, studying the surveillance screen until the gate had closed behind the young man. Then he followed Evan, with me at his heels.

Evan was standing in the open door with his gun behind his back as the young man drove up in a battered old Honda. We all watched as he exited the car, which, through the open door and windows, appeared to be empty except for him and a considerable amount of fast-food trash. He came smiling up the steps.

His smile died as Evan produced a badge, pushed him up against the side of the house, and patted him down. Curtis relieved him of the package, which turned out to contain an unmarked videotape. They questioned the man for five minutes, but it seemed clear that he'd been sent by the service he worked for to deliver this package, as well as several others, this afternoon. The only thing he could say about the sender was that the package was marked as a "walk in, paid cash," not a regular, billed client.

"Didn't really think the Russian Mafia would have opened an account," Curtis said wryly when the young man had gotten into his car and spun his tires on my driveway in his haste to get out of there.

"No. Let's go see what's on the tape," Evan said grimly. "Callaway, would you mind giving us a few moments?" He started to turn away.

"Yes."

"Excuse me?" Evan asked, turning back, surprised.

"Yes, I would mind. I want to see it." I straightened up and braced myself. I would tolerate no more secrets.

His eyes flashed, but he could see beyond my petulance, and so he nodded. "All right. But if it's not pretty—"

"She won't say you didn't warn her," Curtis finished for him impatiently. He regarded the black piece of plastic. "I hope it's something I haven't seen before," he said with a false eagerness in his voice, but I could see the trepidation in his eyes.

At first it looked like a still picture of a deserted parking garage, lit only by glaring fluorescents. A solitary car sat, parked in a corner made of concrete walls, and nothing moved for a few seconds. Then a male figure walked into the frame. The gait and the build were familiar, though the face was away from the camera.

A second male figure appeared from an opposite direction, a large, burly man with the look of an eastern European. There was no sound, but even from a distance you could see the tense body language and the friction of an altercation.

Then, very quickly, the bulkier man turned away and the other grabbed him from behind, twisting his arm up and forcing him down to the ground.

What followed wasn't a fair fight. The man on the ground was left lying, moaning in pain. It was obvious that one of his arms was broken, and his face was badly altered.

The attacker turned away from the injured man on the ground and approached the camera, eventually walking just underneath it. Any doubts I might have had fractured and dissipated, and the reason the man had seemed familiar became crystal clear. It was, without question, Evan.

The image went black, and then a note printed on a white sheet of paper lit our faces with a sudden brightness.

It read: "You have bought yourselves twenty-four hours. This will be released for public viewing at noon tomorrow, Sunday, unless we receive a video of Dana Scheiner's death to replace it."

I fast-forwarded for a bit, mostly to avoid looking at Evan or Curtis, but also to see if there was anything else on the tape.

When I did look up, Curtis had his head in his hands. His eyes were closed. Finally he took a deep breath and released it forcefully. "Well," he said, standing up. "I'm glad I never saw that." His voice was low and hard. "I'm sure you had a damn good reason to violate seventeen laws and jeopardize everything you've ever worked for."

Evan looked pale and grim, but not apologetic. "He was threatening Dana. I thought it was only him."

Just as I was about to give up looking for anything further, something else appeared on the screen. It took me a minute before I recognized it as coming from one of my own video monitors, the one on the parking area by my garage. I watched as Darrien pulled up and Dana and Ginny got out of the car. I recognized the scene as Dana's first arrival at the house.

"Oh, shit," Curtis swore under his breath.

Then another note: "Go look outside."

Pulling his gun, Evan snapped, "Stay behind me," as he followed Curtis out into the entrance hall. We made for the kitchen window, which had a view of the parking area we had seen on the video, though the scene before us was different. Darrien's car was gone, but Sabrina's Mustang sat, parked and empty, a few feet from the garage door. She was always too lazy to pull it in.

I leaned around Evan to try to get a wider view, but he pushed me back.

Without warning, the car exploded, rocking on its tires and bursting into flame.

The glass in the kitchen window shattered and fell onto the counters, into the sink, and onto us. "Christ! Get down!" Curtis shouted needlessly. I was already on the floor with Evan on top of me, shielding me with his body from the jagged rain.

Chapter
41

The fire department and the bomb squad had spent a little over two hours combing the place before announcing it bomb free. The charred frame of Sabrina's once cherry-red Mustang had been towed away, I had called to be sure she was safe, and the final analysis was that someone could have jumped the fence or that the bomb could have been an inside job.

An inside job.

Curtis, Evan, and I returned to the library and watched the video again, watched Evan brutally beat a man who was threatening Dana, looking for anything we might have missed, letting it run all the way to the end of the tape.

My hands were shaking as I took the video out of the machine; my thoughts were equally rattled. *So that was what it looked like, the darkness, a brutal act in a brightly lit parking garage.* All my thoughts of judgment or revulsion, my awe at his courage and daring, even a sense of primitive pride, were nothing compared to the single thought, singing like a high note over the underlying symphony beneath: *He did this for her.*

As I ejected the tape and laid it on the desk, I was vaguely aware of Evan moving to stand near me. I heard Curtis say, "I'll be in the kitchen."

Evan was so close behind me that I could feel his breath on my hair. Something was stirring in me, something that the image of Evan, so capable and fearless, aroused deep in me. On my most primal level, it turned me on.

"Callaway?" His voice was husky and insistent.

"Yes?"

"Look at me," he ordered.

I was afraid to. Not afraid of him, afraid of my need, my desire, my weakness, but there was no denying him. I turned and looked up into his eyes.

"What did you see on that tape?" It was a whisper, a command to speak my deepest thoughts.

My whole body was trembling; I felt like a wisp of smoke in a stiff breeze, unstable, sheer. I bypassed my brain and spoke from my fear. "You, doing something for Dana, something that I think you should only do for me."

There. It was out, the invisible barrier that stood between us materialized.

He breathed in, searched my eyes, and traced a finger along my lips. "These," he said with an ultimate softness in his tone, "can say nothing but the truth."

"It's knowing what the truth is that I find very difficult," I told him, watching his eyes adore my mouth, loving it in spite of myself.

"You can't even imagine how much *more* I would do for you," he said, and he kissed me so hard that my lips were crushed beneath his, and the pain was welcome. I grasped his body to mine, struggling to find his skin, to feel it burning against me. Pulling his head toward me, with both my arms wrapped around behind him, I attacked his mouth and then ripped at his shirt. His hands found my T-shirt and tore it away, his lips moved down my chest and showed the same eagerness for my breasts as they had for my lips. Hands fumbled, pants fell, my skirt was lifted, and then need met saturation as he picked me up, holding my thighs in his wonderful, strong, dangerous hands. I kept thinking of those hands and what they could do, and the heat grew unbearable. Turning me easily, he laid me down on the ottoman, where he could gain the traction he needed. My moans sounded as animal as the lust I felt, and I didn't care. He thrust hard and fast, and I pulled him deeper inside me. Wanting it all, needing more. We came together, both of us lost in the separate intensity of complete accord.

When we finally cooled and slowed, he stayed right where he was. His lips still brushing against mine, constantly exploring and keeping contact. I stroked the smooth skin on his back and thought to myself:

Mine.

Chapter 42

We sat down as a group to a tense dinner. Sophie's roast duck and fresh chicory salad were wasted on me; I didn't know if Evan, Curtis, and Ginny could taste them. Dana hadn't come down yet. Deirdre and Joseph were serving the meal in the dining room when we heard Sabrina calling out my name from the entrance hall.

"She's ba-ack," I said to Evan, as Deirdre set down the serving dish on the sideboard and went to get her.

"She's picking right up on the finer points of etiquette," he said dryly.

"Does she think she's calling in the hogs?" Ginny had put her fork down and was shaking her head. "Do they have obedience school for half-wit siblings raised in outhouses?"

"Trailer parks," I corrected.

"Single-family dwellings," Curtis contributed.

"Well so is this!" Ginny said, waving both her arms in a giant semicircle to indicate my home. "And as ostentatious as that may be, if she's going to live in *this* single-family dwelling, that girl has got to come up a few steps on the social registry."

We could hear her coming down the hall, still shouting, though obviously Deirdre had told her where we were.

"Calla-waay?" She drew out the call with an upward sustained tilt on the last syllable.

I waited until she was standing in the room. "Hello, Sabrina."

"Why didn't you answer me?" She looked indignant. "I was call'n you!" Darrien came into the room behind her looking extremely embarrassed.

"You were *shouting for* me," I said to her, trying to gently prod her memory. We'd talked about this before.

She looked exasperated. "Well, couldn't you hear me?"

Ginny stood up, came around behind her, and smacked her on the butt. "Sit down, and the next time you come in here screaming like a banshee and expecting us all to come running, I'm gonna send you out to the woodshed to cut a switch, that's something you might understand."

Sabrina looked hurt as she rubbed her backside and moved to the place that was set for her. "Well, what was I supposed to do?" she said, sulking.

"Use the intercom system or come looking for me." I turned to Darrien, who was lurking in the doorway. "Darrien, would you like to join us?"

"Thank you, no. I am needed at Korosu's."

"Thank *you*," I said sincerely. "Thank you for keeping her safe."

Sabrina looked at Darrien, even more hurt than before. "Can't you stay for a little while?" She pouted. He smiled and shook his head. "Well, okay then, I'll call you later." Her voice sounded like a child's, and when he departed, she blushed to see us all smiling at the obvious flirt. "What?" she asked, and, always the one with an appetite, started right in eating.

"Has he tried to get to second base yet?" Ginny teased.

"What happened to the kitchen window?" Sabrina asked as Deirdre put her napkin in her lap.

There was a brief, uncomfortable silence and then Ginny cleared her throat and said, "The same thing that happened to your car." She smiled at Sabrina and said cheerily, "It blew up."

Sabrina blinked twice, opened her mouth, closed it again, then turned slowly to me with her eyes narrowed. "My car," she said, "blew up?"

"I'm sorry," I told her.

"My red Mustang?" she asked. I nodded, affirming that it was indeed the red Mustang. "It exploded?" she rephrased the question. I nodded again. She looked about to explode herself as she asked, "Spontaneously? Or was there a reason?"

I turned to Evan. "You want to help me out here?"

"It was a warning," he said. "One we will pay attention to." Then before Sabrina could comment he went on placatingly, "Your sister already ordered you a new car."

Sabrina's emotional state hung on the answer to her next question. "Red?" she asked.

"Of course," I said.

That seemed to satisfy her and she dove into her dinner.

Evan moved on as well by saying, "I need to know if you found anything significant at Webtech."

Sabrina looked up with her mouth full and said, "I got into all free offishes."

Curtis translated without commenting on the manners violation of speaking with your mouth full. "All three offices? You mean of the three men who might know Red?"

She nodded briskly, swallowed, then added, "And let me tell you, that Fred Rosen guy, he's a real piece of work; he put his hand on my backside!"

"So did Ginny, just now," Curtis noted, and, tense as I was, I couldn't help laughing.

Deirdre had reentered the room. Looking at the empty place

at the table, I forced myself to ask, "Is Ms. Scheiner coming down?"

"I'll go and ask her." She glided out of the room.

Evan's hand went over my knee under the table. I turned to Sabrina. "Okay, so what did you find out?" I asked.

"Absolutely nothing." She brightened. "Except that all of them have the most amazing view of the ocean, especially Rosen, he's got the corner office. I mean, it was a little hazy, but wow!"

Sabrina filled her mouth with food again. It didn't surprise me that Rosen would have claimed the primo space for himself; it suited him. "So, he harassed you? That's interesting."

"I'm glad you think so," she sputtered.

I looked at Ginny. "That means the sexual harassment suit filed by that first girl, Michelle Key—something—the one who disappeared—was probably legit?"

"Like you didn't know that after he rubbed all over you at the children's charity ball," Ginny tattled.

After that comment I stayed turned away from Evan. But he didn't seem interested. "Did he catch you looking around in his office?" he asked Sabrina as Joseph was pouring Coca-Cola out of a can, just like she liked it, into a crystal water glass filled with crushed ice. She had originally wanted to drink from the can with a plastic straw at dinner, but I had nixed that early on. I imagined how the supersweet drink would negate the delicate flavor of the duck and sighed; at least she was willing to try the duck.

"No, I was supposed to deliver some papers there, and I had already snooped around when he came in. I was on my way out, but he checked me out like I was something you could buy at a dime store and asked me if I might like to come and work for him for a while."

Alarmed, I looked up at her. "And what did you say?"

"I said, 'Yes, provided you don't work with your hands'!"

Ginny laughed, and Curtis said, "How did he take that?"

"He laughed and said he'd get me transferred." She stabbed a piece of the frilly lettuce and looked at it distrustfully. "I still think you need to cook this stuff."

Ginny said, "It's *chicory,* not something that grows in the woods out back that you have to boil for three days with a hunk of fatback before you can eat it."

I turned to Evan. "Do you think he knows who she is?"

He was watching Sabrina. "You were using the name Valley, right?" When she responded positively, he looked at me. "Who knows she's your sister?"

"Just Isabelle Ferris."

"Does Isabelle have direct contact with Rosen?"

I thought. "No. I'm sure, from things she's said, that she's not in with the big boys. She gets most of her perks from being Jim's daughter, but there is a problem."

Evan's brow furrowed with concern. I explained, "Isabelle is probably the biggest gossip I've ever met in my life. She couldn't keep a secret if it was a matter of national security. If it's news, she'll tell it."

"But all she knows," Sabrina cut in, "is that I needed a summer job, and that's true. There's no reason for her to think anything more. And I didn't even work anywhere near her; the place has four floors! I never saw her!"

"You did well," Evan said. "But it's too dangerous now, you won't be going back to Webtech. Curtis and I will handle this."

"Just give me two more days! I'm safe! Darrien takes me and picks me up." Her baby-doll face went all serious and determined; it was like watching Darla from *The Little Rascals* deciding to shoplift an all-day sucker. "And that Rosen guy tried to hurt Callaway, and I want to help stop him."

Curtis cleared his throat and said pointedly, "We haven't convicted him yet."

"What are you waiting for?" I asked angrily. "The son of a bitch sent those bastards in the Hummer after Ginny and me, and they tried to kill us. And now they've blown up Sabrina's car in my driveway? What more do you need?"

Evan's eyes looked at me empathetically. I knew he could sense my outrage and I could sense that he shared it; the bond tightened.

"Proof," he said with soft strength. "We need proof."

There was the sound of someone coming down the hall, and Dana came into the room.

"I'm sorry, I didn't mean to keep you waiting."

Joseph pulled out her chair between Sabrina and Ginny, and she sat upright while she was served by Deirdre. Then she picked up her fork and pushed the food around on her plate.

"Evan, I just can't stop smiling when I think how happy I am that you're back safely." She beamed at him. I had to look away. "But," she began hesitantly, "I want to get back to my life."

Curtis and Evan glanced to each other, then Evan said, "You must know it's not safe yet. I've got to find out who's behind this."

She reached across Sabrina for his hand. He gave it, while Sabrina leaned back and looked suspiciously down at the clasped hands hovering over her salad. The sight of their hands linked together caused a shell of disdain to form around me like an icy crust. I removed Evan's hand from my leg beneath the table.

"What can I do to help?" Dana asked him.

Ginny said loudly, "Dana, could you pass me the salt?"

Dana looked surprised by Ginny's request, but she released Evan's hand to give Ginny the condiment.

Evan shot a look to me and then said to Dana, "I think it's time that you know what it is these people want. What Callaway has been asked to do and why."

I waited for him to tell her that we were engaged, that he'd been kidnapped so that I would use my money and influence to make her go away.

But no. Instead he said, "She offered you the option of the money and going away, so you know about that. But there was another option."

Dana looked curious, interest sparkling in her eyes.

"The second option," Evan continued, "was for her to kill you, and to give them a videotape of her doing it."

Dana gasped softly and Curtis spoke. "Who's behind this, we don't know. But the group headed by this guy Russian"—his voice went sour—"who got away when we retrieved Evan"—a deep breath restored his normal voice—"are obviously ruthless professionals and this is how they work. They get tape of someone committing a crime. Then, it seems, they use the tape to either blackmail that person into doing other dirty work, or as an insurance policy to keep that person silent." He stopped for a moment, waiting for everyone to catch up to his explanation.

Dana watched him, listening intently. Then, slowly, she turned to Evan. "Oh no," she said, her face pale. "They have a tape of you? . . ." He nodded. "But *how*?"

"Security monitors," Evan said grimly. "They can steal the video right out of the airwaves."

"But that would ruin you," she whispered. "I see." She cleared her throat and asked, "So, what do they want now?"

"The same thing," Evan said.

"I see." No one spoke for a few seconds, then Dana looked around the table. "And the explosion today was their way of saying that they'd kill someone else if you don't give them the video of my death, wasn't it?"

Curtis said, "Yes."

"You've all been so kind," Dana said to everyone. "I wish I could somehow make them believe I was dead, but I can't." Dana's handsome brown eyes filled with tears that she did not let fall, and her gaze landed on Evan. "I could go, I could just disappear. I don't need the money. But they'll still have the tape of you. You need to go too." She looked at him hopefully. "We could go together. That's the only thing that would make every-one else safe. That's the only answer."

No one spoke for a second. I was so shocked that I couldn't think of anything to say. Then the china on the table rattled, and everyone jerked back in their seats as Ginny smacked her hand down hard on the white linen.

"Got it!" she shouted.

For just a second, I thought she had killed a spider, but then I saw the way she was focused on Dana.

"Wha-what?" Dana asked, shaken.

Ginny said, "That's it. You disappear."

"No," I reminded them. "They said that option was closed, remember?" I was thinking of the three million in cash in my safe and thinking that I would gladly pay twice that if she *would* go away.

Grinning broadly, Ginny laid her long arm around Dana's shoulders and gripped her in a viselike hug. "Relax, girl. You look nervous."

"Should I be?" Dana asked suspiciously.

"Naw," Ginny said. "We're just gonna kill you a little bit."

Chapter
43

"N ick is one of the best in the business," Evan said as I was shaking hands with a well-groomed man wearing a denim work shirt and carrying a large bag and a toolbox. He could have been there to fix the plumbing, except that he had an air of detachment that I assumed came from working in his highly "specialized" field.

I was nervous. We all went down into the basement, passed through a large recreation room used by no one but the staff on occasion, and into a smaller, windowless space with concrete walls and a row of large-capacity water heaters.

Dana and Ginny were already there. Dana sat in a folding chair against the cement wall looking frightened, and Ginny was busying herself setting up a small digital video camera on a tripod. Nick asked us solemnly to leave him with Dana.

After we waited about an hour in the rec room, he reemerged, looking grim. "Okay, everything is ready," he informed us.

Evan came and took my shoulders. "We'll be out here. Remember to show the whole room, and don't forget to turn the camera off."

"Got it."

I went in. Dana was still sitting in the chair, but now her hands were tied behind her back. She looked up at me with eyes so frightened that I almost wanted to call the whole thing off.

No. Use it.

"Are you ready?" I asked her.

"I'm afraid," she said, her beautiful brown eyes haunted and rimmed with red. "I don't want to go without Evan, I don't want to be so alone."

So he still hadn't told her about us. A cold hand reached into my chest and grabbed hold of my lungs, squeezing the breath out of them. "Maybe you won't be. But this has to be done."

She shuddered, her whole body convulsing with the motion. I didn't move to comfort her. In fact, I watched distantly, as an interested but unfeeling observer.

I picked up the camera and turned it on, raising it to my eye. I scanned around the room to show that it was empty, that I was doing this alone, then set it back on the table, checking to see that Dana and the area around her were in view.

From my pocket, I took a handgun, just a small one, a hammerless, five-shot Smith and Wesson, something ladylike. I had chosen it because it seemed appropriate, and because you could see the bullets in the chamber. Holding the gun a foot or so in front of the camera, I hit the barrel release with my thumb and flipped it open to show that all the chambers were filled. Then, flipping it closed with a metallic click, I walked into the frame and pointed the gun at Dana.

Her eyes were wide with fear as she stared at the barrel of the weapon. Her mouth moved, but the only sound that came out was a choking, serrated gasp. I pulled a thick silk scarf, bloodred, from around my neck and tied it around her eyes.

"Get up." When she didn't move, I shoved her out of the

chair and ordered, "Stand up on the chair." She hesitated, and I shouted, "Get up on the chair!" She still didn't move, so, aiming carefully just past her head, I fired one shot, and a chunk of the cement wall disintegrated behind her. She whimpered and scrambled up onto the chair, swaying unsteadily without any visual reference points to keep her balance. Dragging over a second chair from the wall, I came up beside her and pulled down a rope that was coiled among the ducts above. One end of the rope was securely tied to a strong thick pipe, the other end was looped into a noose.

As I put the rope around Dana's neck, she uttered one sharp, broken cry, then went quiet and motionless, except for her lips, which were moving rapidly but soundlessly. I tightened the noose down around her neck, taking an extra second or two to make sure it was making contact in the back.

Then I stepped back down, turned until I was looking right into the camera, and kicked the chair out from underneath Dana Scheiner.

She dropped. And swung. Her feet kicked, and she struggled for longer than I would have thought possible, and then the kicks got weaker.

And then they stopped and she swung slightly, lifeless.

Chapter
44

I walked to the camera and hit the stop button, turning the power off for good measure.

Then yelling, "Help me!" I ran for Dana, throwing my arms around her waist and lifting her, trying to take the weight off her neck. The door flew open behind me and Nick was the first one in, moving quickly up onto a chair next to Dana. Evan was right behind him, and he took Dana's weight as Ginny shoved the second chair under her feet and we waited for Nick to unhook the rope.

"Okay, let her down."

Evan and I lowered her body carefully into the chair, and I got a good look at her pale face, mouth agape; ripping the scarf off revealed her eyes, which were still closed.

"Is she dead?" Ginny sounded unnerved.

All of us leaned over her inert form, Evan placing a hand on the side of her neck to check for a pulse. A long moment passed when I could hear only my own breathing.

Dana bolted upright with a jerk and a sharp, deep inhalation, sending us all scampering back a foot. "Get this thing off of me!" she screamed, tearing at her shirt. "It's cutting into me!" Nick helped her out of the long-sleeved blouse, revealing a body harness with a clasp at the back of her neck, which I had hooked to a safety clamp as I'd "tightened" the noose. Dana was crying. "That was horrible," she sobbed, "horrible."

I thought the next part was even more horrible. Evan took her into his arms and kissed the top of her head. "It's okay," he murmured, "it's all over now." He rocked her slowly back and forth. He looked at me over the top of her head, but I was incapable of offering my blessing. I turned and walked stiffly from the oppressive room.

Ginny left with Nick, making kissy faces, trying to give the appearance that he had come to take her out on a date, instead of to stage a murder in case anyone was watching.

Much later, Evan and I made a big show of smuggling out a black-plastic-wrapped "body" in full view of the video monitors. Dana herself left the next morning, in my housekeeper Carmen's car, wearing an outfit borrowed from one of the other housemaids. It was Sunday, and Carmen and the two other housekeepers always went to church on Sunday. With her dark hair, sunglasses, and clothes padded to make her look thirty pounds heavier than she was, Dana could easily have been mistaken for one of the staff.

Carmen drove Dana to a prearranged meeting place with Curtis, where he would put her in an apartment to wait until it was safe for her to return to her life.

I had watched her teary good-bye with Evan from an uncomfortable but jaded place, casting myself in the role of a vulturelike onlooker passing a wreck on the freeway: appalled, yet eager for the sight of blood.

She clung, she cried, he soothed. No words of love or promise were given in my earshot, only reassurances. But what else could he say with me standing in the doorway? Evan had promised her that if the official police investigation didn't turn anything up soon, he would go public with what he did know—a possibility that chilled me. She was still completely oblivious to the fact that Evan and I were a "couple."

I was not happy.

But there wasn't exactly time for a soul-searching talk over a glass of cabernet. Eager to prevent any more leaks of information, we'd recruited Wayne to check the phone lines and I was standing in the kitchen with Sabrina a few moments after Dana's departure when Wayne came into the kitchen holding one of those plug-in phones that the phone company repairmen use.

"Hi, Wayne!" Sabrina gushed.

"Hi," he muttered back, looking love-struck. There was a knock on the kitchen door and Darrien entered. He'd come to escort Sabrina to church. It was the only way Evan would allow her to go.

Wayne glanced at the tall, formidable bodyguard and seemed to wilt.

"I gotta go," Sabrina said to Wayne. "See you later, okay?"

"Anything?" I asked Wayne, trying to distract him.

"Uh, yeah." He drew himself back from watching my sister exit on Darrien's arm like a man who sees his destiny and it isn't good. "The hard-wired lines seem to be clean," he told me, "but don't use a remote handset, they can pick that up. I drove around your house on the way over, and I didn't see anything suspicious. No vans, nobody sitting in a car, nothing like that."

Evan had come into the kitchen behind me. "How close would someone have to be to pick up a cell or remote phone call?"

"Pretty close." Wayne shifted his eyes around, seeming uncomfortable addressing such a large crowd of two. "I mean, you couldn't be on the next street over, or even behind your house, the backyard is too big. The van that was out there before had fairly sophisticated hardware, from what I could see"—he brought his hand up to his partially healed lip and rubbed it without seeming to realize what he was doing—"which wasn't much, but you get more and more interference the farther away you are. There's just too much stuff in the air."

Evan narrowed his eyes. "So, in order to pick up the picture on a security monitor, for instance, you would have to be close to it."

Wayne tilted his head to one side and nodded diagonally. "Pretty close," he repeated.

"What about barriers? Walls, fences, electric lines?" Evan asked.

"Cement is bad," Wayne said. "The thicker, the harder to get through. Wood doesn't cause much trouble, or a normal house wall. No big deal. Electric lines"—he held out a hand and see-sawed it in the air—"depends."

"On what?" Evan wanted to know.

"How many, how high, how powerful."

"So normal 220-volt lines wouldn't—" Evan was cut off by the sound of the cell phone that had been sent to Dana's office ringing in the depths of my pocket. I snatched it out and flipped it open.

Russian's unpleasant voice asked simply, "You have the tape?"

"I have it," I replied, my voice adequately shaking with rage and helplessness. Wayne's eyes widened in fear, and he slipped away.

"Give me the boyfriend."

Evan was watching me intently. I handed over the phone. He put it to his ear and listened, gesturing for a pen and paper. I was already fumbling for them in a kitchen drawer; he took them, and I watched as he wrote down an address.

"Not that I have any reason to distrust you," Evan said dryly, "but I'd like to have my 'greatest hits' original back." He listened to Russian's response, his eyes flicking up to me fearfully for a moment, and then he said angrily, "No deal. Callaway is not coming near you. It's me or no one."

He was offering himself up instead of me; my heart felt lighter in spite of being pounded flat. I heard what sounded in tone like an onslaught of ugly cursing in a harsh language, but Evan held firm.

"You don't get her, she's done," he repeated, his jaw clenched so tightly that I could hear his teeth scrape while he was listening. He reached out one hand and brushed my cheek with the back of his curved fingers before clenching them into a fist on the counter and saying, "Noon. One hour."

He flipped the phone closed. I tried to get a look at the address he had written, but he folded the paper quickly and put it in his pocket.

"All right, it's set." I watched him take the small videotape from his pocket, as though checking that it was still there, and then replace it again.

"Why did they want me to bring it?"

"I don't know, maybe they think I'll try to pull something."

"Do you really think that they'll give you the other tape?"

He smiled sagely. "One of their many copies, I'm sure. This is their game, obviously; they get something on people and then they can play them like puppets. They're not likely to cut the strings on such a promising player as an LAPD detective. The best we can hope for is that they back off the detonations until I can nail the bastards to a tree."

"But, what if—"

"Videotapes aren't admissible in a trial." He lowered his voice and muttered, "Not a murder trial anyway." The second part of the statement negated the first as his tape did not show a murder, but neither of us commented on that fact. "It's too easy to alter videos these days." His smile was slightly bitter; we both knew what would happen if his superiors and/or the press got hold of his tape. Field day.

My own recent screen debut would be incidental after this was over. Not only was Dana still alive but also Nick would be around to explain how he had staged the whole thing, from the sound-activated charge in the hole he'd dug in the cement wall, to the special "hangman's" rigging and Ginny's coaching of Dana's death scene. But for now, nobody needed to know that but us.

Evan was staring out the window, and I watched his rugged, handsome face, tense with apprehension and preoccupation. I knew better than to intrude. He was thinking.

After a few moments, he moved and took a deep breath, signaling some conclusion to his musings. "What?" I asked him.

"It's too complicated," he muttered, still looking out the window.

"Try me," I suggested, insulted.

He turned now and looked at me. "No, I don't mean that it's too complicated for you to figure out." He smiled as though it amused him that I had taken it that way; I felt my face redden, but I pretended not to understand him. "I mean that the whole scheme . . . it's just too complicated. It's not good business. From what we know, Webtech is being investigated for financial wrongdoing. That means money disappeared. And if Fred Rosen was the one who took it, say to cover his indiscretions by paying off women, why has he brought in the Russian Front? Why would he pay off these women and *then* kill them?" He tapped his fingers on the counter, and his voice sounded angry as he said, "Somehow, I'm missing something."

I thought the something he was missing was not telling Dana about me, but I didn't think it was the moment to say so.

Then I remembered something else. "I don't know if this is connected or not, but I know Webtech has an office in Russia, or they did, anyway," I told him. "I remember Ted Issacs mentioning that the redhead had something to do with their Moscow office. Is that important, do you think?"

"Could be. From what I've heard, it's tough to do business in that country without dealing with a few 'unethical' connections.

So it wouldn't be too hard to hook up with someone who was willing to cross the line for a price."

He shifted gears and came to me now. "Got gun?" he asked, his eyes locked on mine. I couldn't read what was in them.

"Got gun," I said, producing the pistol that I'd used to take a chunk out of my rec room wall. I had replaced the blanks with real bullets.

"Good. Stay behind it, lock the door, and don't answer it unless you see me or Curtis on that video." He pointed to the gate monitor. A lump swelled up in my throat, and I couldn't speak; to cover my fear, I started to turn away.

Evan caught my arm and spun me back roughly to him, saying gutturally, "Don't you dare." He pulled me into his chest and cradled me as though he could pull me up inside him. I basked in the heat coming from him, knowing full well that he was risking his life for me. I accepted the gift like the dangerous double-edged sword that it was. I would stay, safe at home, and he would go.

The question was: *Would he be back?*

Chapter

45

Inactivity makes me feel like an army of ants is having a cha-cha fiesta and my skin is their dance floor. A great deal of this is because when I try to be still, I can hear my brain screaming. A thousand accusing voices, telling me I'll fail, I'll disappear if I'm not always achieving, succeeding, that I've never done enough.

So sitting in my bedroom on my ass while Evan, who had just returned from captivity, was possibly walking right back into the hands of a faceless enemy was agonizing.

Pacing and muttering, I crossed the room again and again, frantic for a way to be useful.

My personal line rang and I jumped. The caller ID said "Ferris, Jim." I snatched it up.

"Jim?"

"Callaway. I found out who our mystery redhead is." He sounded pleased with himself. "Her name is Patricia Adman. She worked in Rosen's office for short a time. Red hair, good-looking, not too tall but nice body. Does that sound right?"

"Yes, that sounds like her."

"She left about six months ago, but here's the thing." He cleared his throat and continued, "She's still on the payroll. She gets a nice fat 'consulting' fee every two months. The last check was mailed out three days ago."

"What did she do for Rosen?" I asked, wondering how the fee was justified.

"Translator. But she only worked for him a couple of months. After that she transferred to our international division."

An indicator light went on in my brain. "Do you know why?"

Jim sounded surprised. "I could try to find out. The other thing I want to find out is who's authorizing her checks. And get this, her checks go to a PO box at the main post office on Brand in Glendale, no other information on her, no phone, address, nothing on the company roster. Just a minute." He put me on hold, then came on the line again and said in a rush, "I've got to go, I'll call you back."

"Okay, thanks, Jim." I worried that maybe someone had caught him snooping.

I thought about Red, Patricia; she had looked so frightened at the racetrack, and then at the café, she had looked terrified, not like someone who threatened or kidnapped people on a weekly basis. Had she been drawn in the way I had?

As though my many ants all sunk their little claws into my skin and pulled simultaneously, I felt a surge go through me. I had to do something.

Her last check was mailed three days ago. There was a possibility that Patricia Adman would check her box to see if it had arrived. It was Sunday, but anyone who had a post office box had access to it twenty-four hours, seven days a week.

It couldn't hurt.

Knowing the response I'd get from Evan if I told him that I intended to stake out Red, I picked the phone up and punched in Curtis's number, not really expecting an answer because I knew he was busy relocating Dana and was therefore incommunicado. It went to his voice mail. Oddly relieved, I told him my plan and promised to stay out of trouble, adding that if he thought it was a good idea he could send someone to watch the post office for me.

I gathered my purse and put my gun in it, then stood for a moment trying to gather my courage as well. Going alone, anywhere, wasn't the brightest idea, and my daddy didn't raise a fool.

The kitchen door swung open and Wayne came in, trailing multicolored wires, and holding something that looked like a police scanner.

"Wayne," I said sweetly, "are you busy for the next couple of hours?"

He stopped abruptly at my tone and looked at me with serious distrust. "Why?" he asked.

"I thought you might like to go on a little reconnaissance mission with me."

"What are we 'reconnaissancing'?" he asked dubiously.

I raised my eyebrows and tried to look enthusiastic.

"Redheads."

Chapter
46

The post office was a big marble-fronted affair. We parked in the merciful shade of a jacaranda tree on the wide side street and rolled down the windows. Wayne started sweating the moment I turned off the car. His was a constitution made for refrigerated, recycled air.

"It's hot," he mumbled.

"Oh, it's not so bad," I lied, unsticking my white cotton shirt from my chest. "We won't be here that long, anyway." I checked the time on my cell phone: 11:22. Evan was scheduled to make the trade-off at noon. I tried to put it out of my mind, but it was as easy as turning my back on a charging tiger.

"How long?" Wayne was asking me as he turned on one of his little gadgets.

"Oh," I said, smiling tensely, "maybe an hour." I pretended not to hear his groan and watched the door of the post office.

It was surprisingly busy for a Sunday; there was a flow, not constant but steady, of people coming in and out. Every six or seven minutes the sun would flash on the glass door as it opened. Through it, I could see walls of post office boxes in varying sizes.

"What's that?" I asked Wayne when I got bored. He was holding the device that looked like a police scanner and twisting knobs; he had put a tiny earpiece in his ear and plugged the other end of the cord into the device. When I spoke, he unplugged it and I heard voices, fragments of conversations. He turned the knob, searching, and snatches of different voices came clearly into my car.

"Is that? . . ."

He nodded his head toward a woman walking down the sidewalk toward us with her cell phone pressed to her ear. "I think it's her."

I watched the woman's mouth move, and, with a half-a-second delay, I heard a voice say, ". . . so, tell him you can't go. You're too fucking nice, Chloe, you need to . . ." She paused as another higher voice, also a woman's, cut in. "But he gets so mad," the whining voice said, and I watched the woman on the sidewalk throw up one hand as though Chloe were standing in front of her and she was making her point. "He's insecure! You need to walk away . . ." She came level with us, and Wayne turned the volume off as she passed the open window.

"Wow," I said. "Wayne, this really puts you in a whole other light." I couldn't help smiling at the embarrassed pleasure on his face. "You're a Badboy!"

He looked shocked. "No! I mean, I don't, I mean, I do, but I never . . ."

I laughed. "It's okay. I'm glad you know about this stuff. You've helped me so much. Thanks."

I glanced back at the glass door and saw a flash of red hair disappearing inside.

"Oh shit, did you see that?" I asked.

"See what?" asked Wayne, looking up from his toy.

That answered my question. I waited tensely for several

minutes. Then she emerged, looked nervously in both directions, and hurried down the sidewalk on the other side of the street.

"That's her," I said, and started the car.

"Uh, what are you planning to do?" Wayne asked.

"I'm going to follow her, of course. I want to find out where she lives."

Wayne swallowed hard, but there was a light in his eyes that betrayed his excitement. "Okay."

We followed Red to a small house in a North Hollywood neighborhood where you didn't get much for your eight hundred thousand—a two-bedroom house surrounded by other similar houses with yards that were appropriately named, as they could be measured by three or four yards themselves. Every few minutes a plane took off from Burbank Airport, which was a half mile away, and passed almost directly over the house, obliterating any other sound.

I circled the block once and then pulled up down the street. Wayne was twisting buttons ferociously.

"Get anything?" I asked.

He nodded. "Way too much. These houses are so close together that it's almost impossible to tell what I'm picking up. Can you pull up closer?"

With my heartbeat throbbing in my throat, I pulled forward until I was just across the street from her house and kept the car running. Wayne twisted and adjusted the position of the device in his lap until suddenly he froze, and a slow satisfied look came over his face.

Pulling the plug from the earpiece, Wayne adjusted the volume until I could hear a male voice over the fan of the air-conditioning.

". . . and then you'll be finished."

I knew the voice. I knew the accent. It was Russian.

Then I heard Patricia Adman answering. "No, no more killing, please!" She sounded desperate.

A strange new feeling thrilled through me, and I recognized it almost instantly. I was spying on *them*. I had turned the tables.

"I can't," Patricia said, and her voice sounded weak, exhausted.

"Then die," Russian's hated voice said, and then there was nothing but static.

Wayne was watching me. "What are you going to do?" he asked. "Should we call somebody?"

"Who?" I asked. "Evan's in the middle of an evidence swap and Curtis is securing a woman who's supposed to be dead." Too late, I realized that Wayne had no idea what I was talking about. "It sounds like she wants out, doesn't it?" I glanced toward the door.

"No, Callaway. Please don't go in there." Wayne had read my mind.

I considered for a moment. Maybe I could get her to come with me, maybe she would trust me. She had drawn the shape of a badge above the words "Trust no one." Maybe she didn't trust the police. It seemed possible, likely even, that she was an unwilling participant. If I could offer her safety, a way out, she might have enough information to put a stop to this whole ugly affair.

"Okay," I said to Wayne. "I won't go in." He sighed with relief. "I'll stay outside, but I'm going to try to talk to her. Keep your head down out of sight, I don't want to scare her."

Wayne made a few sputtering noises but could manage nothing intelligible as he watched me pull my gun out of my purse, check the loads, and slip it into my pocket.

With one hand firmly on the hilt of my gun, I walked to the front door, my eyes darting from one darkened window to the other, watching for movement. I knocked, then stood just to the side, out of a direct line of fire, in case a bullet came through it.

The door opened and there stood Red; I looked quickly around behind her but saw no one else in the room. She gasped. "What are you doing here?"

"I followed you from the post office," I told her truthfully. "I want to talk to you. I think I can help you."

For half a minute neither of us spoke, and I watched a gamut of emotions cross her face. "Are you alone?" she asked.

"Yes," I lied, praying that Wayne had the sense to stay hidden.

"Come in," she said.

"I'd rather stay outside," I told her, "no offense."

She laughed a not-so-stable laugh and responded, "None taken, but . . ." She scanned the street behind me. "It's not safe in the open."

I had to admit that was probably true. Standing on her front steps I felt pretty much like a rabbit in a shooting gallery waiting for the *ping*.

"At least let's go to the side of the house, behind the gate," she suggested. She came out and quickly led me to a large gate crossing the driveway. I waved my free hand behind my back, hoping to reassure Wayne if he was watching, then followed Patricia through the gate. She turned to me just on the other side.

She wouldn't look directly at me. She looked haunted; her eyes had dark circles and her cheeks were gaunt.

"If I could guarantee that you'd be safe, would you go with me?" I prompted.

She smiled sadly. "You can't," she said.

A plane was taking off and coming near, flying low over the neighborhood, throttles fully opened as it fought the thin air to defy gravity and support its heavy metal body. "I can promise you that I'll do whatever I can to help you and protect you. That's more than you've got now," I urged.

She looked up toward the approaching jet and seemed to consider it, her face twisting with angst. "I've got something to show you," she said, loudly enough for me to make out the words. As she reached behind her, lifting her loose T-shirt to pull something from the small of her back, the whine of the jet rattled the windows of the house. Her eyes came up and focused directly on me for the first time, with a concentration that chilled me. I knew that look.

She was aiming.

I watched her pull her gun from her waistband and raise it toward me; I was trying to get my gun out of my pocket, but I knew it was hopeless, that she had every advantage.

What a fool I am!

In rage and fear I shouted, "No!" as though the word would stop her like a naughty child caught in the act. The syllable was lost in the rolling waves of sound that buffeted the earth as the jet passed directly overhead.

My gun cleared my pocket even as hers came level with my chest. *Shit, I'm going to die in Burbank and it's my own stupid fault!*

Her eyes narrowed and then suddenly opened wide, as though she were surprised. The very air around us seemed to pulse, roiling with the noise of the jet. I saw her mouth move, but it was a futile action, as any words only met with a solid, impenetrable wall of sound. She didn't fire. Just as I got my gun clear of my jacket and started to bring it up, she let hers drop to the pavement. She looked down.

On the front of her pale pink shirt a dark stain was growing around a tiny hole. She looked back up at me, tilting her head as though questioning how that little hole had gotten there. And then her hands went to her chest. She dropped first to her knees, then to the hot pavement. Even as I watched in awed disbelief, she looked up at me and smiled with what looked like relief before closing her eyes.

Gathering my wits, I spun around. One of the windows behind me was opened about six inches, and a curtain fluttered through it.

Get out of here! As fast as I could force myself to move, I unlatched the gate, but before I could start out, I found myself looking into the gaping hole of a gun. Houndstooth was standing right behind it.

Chapter
47

This felt familiar. We both held, looking down our guns at each other. In the relative quiet of the receding jet I said, "So now what?" Somebody had to say something. I wanted to shoot him, to get him first, but somehow, knowing that he had made the choice—twice now—to not shoot me, I stayed my trigger finger.

"We both put our guns down and we talk," he said, but he didn't move.

I couldn't help it; I smiled. "You first."

There was a pause while he watched my eyes and considered me. Then he said, "All right."

Slowly he pulled the gun back until it was facing the sky, both hands up. "Now, I'm going to get something out of my pocket, okay?"

"What?" I asked suspiciously. Contrary to his plan, I was still training my gun on him.

"ID," he said. Still with his gun in his right hand, which I watched without blinking, he reached his left hand into his breast pocket and produced a folding wallet. He flipped it open and . . .

"No way," I said briefly, "I'm not buying it."

What was dangling in front of me was an ID card that read, "Federal Bureau of Investigation, Special Agent Craig Gillespie."

"Call them," he said. "I'm putting my gun down," he added.

I hesitated, considered the fact that he could have shot me in the back as easily as he had shot the woman facing me, and nodded. He put the gun down, backed away a few steps, and said, "Do you need to borrow a phone?"

"No thanks, I've got two." Still keeping him in my sights, I fished out my phone by feel and flipped it open.

"I know the number," he offered helpfully.

"I'm sure you do. I prefer to get it from a neutral source." I heard the gate creak behind him and called out, "It's okay, Wayne. Come in slowly."

White-faced, shiny with sweat, and clutching a garden rake raised over his head, Wayne moved cautiously into view. "Could you pick up that gun and hold it on him?" I asked, gesturing with the cell phone at the alleged FBI agent.

Wayne's gigantic eyes went from me, to the burly man in a jacket on a sweltering day, to the large handgun on the ground. From there it was only a few feet to the body of Patricia Adman.

"Jesus Christ!" Wayne exclaimed, jumping backward and dropping the rake with a clatter.

Gillespie frowned at him and then me. "Nice backup."

"Thank you. Wayne, the gun, *please*." He picked it up and held it limply in one hand.

The information operator came on. "Federal Bureau of Investigation," I said, and was automatically connected. It took a few minutes to get someone on the line who could verify the name, badge number, and give me an adequate description of Gillespie. I thanked them, hung up, and kept my gun on him.

"Not good enough?" he asked.

"Can we call the police *now*?" Wayne asked, sweat dripping from his brow so fast that he had to keep wiping it away.

"Why did you act like you were going to kill Patricia at the racetrack when she was hiding in the tack room? This *is* Patricia, I suppose?" I gestured to the body at my feet without looking down at the sad sight.

He nodded. "Yes, I threatened to kill her because I needed information fast, and I thought it might encourage you to give me some."

"How's your arm?" I inquired, noticing for the first time that there was an elastic brace peeking out from his cuff.

"Recovering, thank you. Just a fracture."

"I came here to offer to help her. Why did she want to kill me?"

He sighed and looked down at her. "She didn't. But she wasn't given a choice in the matter. We should call an ambulance, she's still alive."

I didn't go for the trick. Most people would have looked down at the body, which would have given him an easy chance to disarm me. I didn't have much faith in Wayne's killer instinct. So instead, I kept my eyes and my gun on Gillespie and backed around the body on the ground until I could see both Patricia and him at the same time. She wasn't moving, but I could see her chest rising and falling ever so faintly.

"Do it," I said, tossing him the cell phone.

He reported a gunshot wound to the 911 operator, and I knew the police would be on their way. That made me feel a bit more confident, and I let my gun fall to my side but kept it in my hand. Then Gillespie moved to the woman on the ground to try to help her. The gun in Wayne's outstretched hand was shaking like a leaf.

"It's okay, Wayne. It's probably best if you don't point that at anyone." He looked relieved and let it fall to his side, massaging his upper arm. He looked green.

"I think I'm going to be sick," he said.

Gillespie looked up at me. "He can go in the house. There's nobody else in there."

I nodded to Wayne, indicating that the air-conditioning and the facilities were at his disposal. He disappeared gratefully around the back.

I took the opportunity to ask a few more questions while we were waiting for an ambulance. "What do you mean, she didn't have a choice?" I asked when he began to tell me why he'd been following Red.

"It's a long story. She got embroiled with some people who wouldn't take no for an answer. Next thing she knew she was helping someone at Webtech embezzle larger and larger sums of money and funnel it into private hands in Russia. She was the chief translator for the Webtech Moscow office. It wasn't that hard to change a few words or amounts here and there, next thing you knew, she was in deep with people who were far more barbaric than she imagined."

"How did you find this out?"

"We keep an eye on Russian/American business relations. There are certain personalities that trigger suspicion. I was assigned to investigate one of those, and it led me back here. I've been watching Webtech for the last few months."

"I heard about that."

He looked up sharply. "You heard about me?"

"No, but there are rumors that they're being investigated by the Feds."

"Well, that's true, but that's out in the open. I'm not. Someone at Webtech—maybe some few—are in this up to their eyeballs, and I've been trying to find out who.

"The trick is to see who's getting the kickback. But it's been hard to trace. Josie Banks was one of the recipients, but she was basically a mule, they were funneling money through her."

"I saw you at her house." I let it hang.

He sighed and went on applying pressure to Patricia Adman's wound. "Too late. I figured out that Patricia was going to the Banks house and guessed why, but by the time I got there, Josie Banks was dead."

"I thought you killed her."

"No." He looked down at the unconscious figure. "She did."

"Red killed Josie? No way! I saw the guys leave on a motorcycle!"

He glanced up sharply at me. "You saw someone leave? What did they look like?"

I thought about it. "I'm not sure. They were both wearing helmets and dressed in leathers."

"So it could have been a man and a woman."

I nodded. "Yes."

"And the man videotaped her doing it. That's how they work. Blackmail. Force someone to commit a crime, and keep a record of it. She had no choice but to do whatever they asked her to do next."

I knew that routine, but I revealed nothing. "Like killing me?" I asked. "Was she filming this?" I heard the siren of the ambulance as it turned onto the street and pulled up in front of the house.

"No, they already had a tape of her killing one person, they didn't need two. But they did want you dead."

"Why?" I asked, still rocking from the possibility of being dead.

The paramedics climbed out of the ambulance and another jet passed overhead, obliterating any possible reply.

Chapter
48

Much to my secret delight, Evan was beside himself when he found out where I'd gone. He gave me his curt opinion of my behavior in a few well-phrased sentences. Luckily, showing up with an FBI agent in tow spared me any further remonstrance.

I did, however, feel bad when I got to the part of my story where Patricia Adman drew her gun. Evan put his face in his hands and rubbed his eyes hard. He wouldn't look at me. Curtis had a gleam in his eye that told me he had a smart-ass comment to make, but he confined it to a slight lift in one eyebrow. Instead of revisiting my sense of stupidity at putting myself in that situation, I worked up some indignation and wrapped it protectively around myself.

Evan had gone to a crowded outdoor mall, where a ten-year-old child on a bicycle had met him for the videotape switch. When Evan had questioned him, he would only say that "some white guy" had given him ten bucks and the tape, pointed Evan out, and disappeared. As Evan searched the faces in the crowd, the boy had broken away and, jumping on his bike, had quickly outdistanced him. Without backup, Evan had reluctantly given up both his pursuit of the boy and his hope of spotting one of the men he could recognize. He finished his story with a keen note of self-disgust in his voice.

Then we listened to Gillespie's story as we sat in the living room. He'd been tracking this case for months. Patricia Adman had been connected to all the major players at Webtech at one time or another, and he was trying to find out which ones were involved with the illegal, and now fatal, dealings. When I made the point that Rosen knew about him, he told us that Rosen thought he was an independent auditor assigned by the government to review the company's books. This had given him access to the financial records and led him to Patricia.

At this point Evan interrupted to ask, "So, Patricia Adman didn't know you were an agent?"

"That's right," Gillespie answered. I thought about the crude drawing of the badge and wondered if it was true.

"How did you come to be at my house during the kidnapping?" Evan asked, his voice suspicious.

"After," Gillespie corrected, "just after. I was tracking Dana Scheiner, trying to trace the money transfers to Josie Banks, and you got involved. I had access to your emails and phone lines. I knew something was up, but I didn't know what."

He stopped and looked right at Evan. "I wasn't sure if you were involved, I did a little checking up on you, and though your record is clean, you have a reputation for doing things, shall we say, *your own way*."

Curtis finally spoke up; his comment was direct yet disarming as usual. "Whatever works," he said as though he were talking about using duct tape to fix a leaky sewage line. But he exchanged glances with me, and I got the message to say nothing.

Watching Evan, I thought of the note, "Trust no one." With a feeling like I'd eaten a live snake for breakfast and it was trying to climb out of my stomach, I waited for Evan's response.

"Did you find out anything interesting while you were digging around?" he asked, grimly amused. That was all I got. From Gillespie's glancing frown, I would say that the answer was yes but that he didn't necessarily think less of Evan for it.

"So," Gillespie went on without responding directly to Evan's question, "you got in deeper than you meant to, I'm sure. I went to your house the morning you were kidnapped because of something I heard about you on Josies Banks's phone tap."

"May I ask what?" Evan inquired.

Gillespie smiled but shook his head. "No," he said. "You can ask, but I can't tell you."

Evan sighed, as though he'd expected that. The serpent in my belly rolled. *Josie Banks knew about Evan. The watch might not have been planted.* Evan looked to me, and I saw the thought in his eyes. He knew I had reason to doubt him now, reason to think he was in deeper than he had admitted, ammo, proof.

He sighed again and said, "Okay, the sooner we solve this thing, the sooner we can get on with our usually mundane lives." He looked to me again with the sort of sadness you have when parting for a long voyage, then he returned his attention to the FBI agent. "So, what do we know?"

Gillespie took up the yarn and started knitting a theory. "Someone at Webtech is embezzling money, millions of dollars. Most of it is being funneled to a Russian crime syndicate, that's how I got involved. We don't know where it started, or where it ends, but we do know that two women have been killed." He grimaced, and I had the same thought. "Maybe three, if Patricia Adman doesn't pull through."

"How is she?" I asked, feeling a pang of sympathy in spite of knowing that without Gillespie I would have a bullet in *my* chest.

"Critical," he said grimly. His voice dropped to a clenched

murmur as he said, "And if she does die, that will make two women who lost their lives because of me."

I spoke up. "You saved my life."

He looked at me sadly, but sighed.

"You weren't responsible for Molly Simpson's death either, she died in a crash," Evan reminded him.

"Molly Simpson was feeding me information. She was my connection at the company before I went in undercover. I found her because she was ready to press a sexual harassment suit against Rosen and Webtech, and I knew she would be willing to dig up some dirt on anyone there." Gillespie's face went very hard for a moment.

I spoke up again. "So her death wasn't an accident."

"No." He looked at me and smiled sadly. "It was a mistake. Mine." He shook his head. "I've been one step behind everything these people have done, because I can't find the source."

"Who's had contact with the Russians?" Curtis asked.

"Quite a few people, their international division is gigantic. It starts with Rosen and the rest of the board officers and goes all the way down to runners, employees who just fly paperwork back and forth."

"I think Patricia was trying to give me a clue," I said suddenly. "She wrote something on a napkin, she must have meant it for me, because when I was talking to her, she kept pointing at the napkin. It looked like this." I picked up a pad and a pen and drew the shapes from memory, and then wrote the words "Trust no one" exactly as they had been written. "But I've been asking myself why she would have been there unless it was to meet with someone. Do you think she was trying to mislead us?"

Gillespie was looking at the paper. "I don't know. I listened to enough of her phone conversations with these people to know that she truly wanted out of this situation, that she was tortured by what she'd done."

"Do you know how she got involved?" Curtis asked.

"Yes. Patricia and her sister Jane both spoke perfect Russian because they were raised by a Russian grandmother who'd never learned to speak English. Both women worked as translators in Moscow. This group of organized criminals threatened to kill Jane if Patricia didn't work for them. Jane, who is definitely not involved, has since moved back to the States, but by then, Patricia was in too deep to get out."

"Why did she try to kill me today?" I asked.

"She was told that if she did, she would be free of them. I don't think she really believed it, but she was desperate."

"Why do they want me dead?" I forced myself to ask.

Everyone looked up at Gillespie. "Because, in the end, they don't leave loose ends."

Evan said nothing; my throat went dry.

"So they won't stop until Evan and I are both dead?" I asked as matter-of-factly as I could manage.

Gillespie's eyes were sharp and hard as he answered me without flinching. "No. Not unless we can stop them."

Evan had taken the paper from Gillespie's hand, and he stared down at it. His brow furrowed, then he looked up at us and shook his head.

"How obvious can it be?" he asked. We looked at him; me blankly, Gillespie with a sense of expectation, and Curtis with a cautious smile, as though watching a machine start up. Evan started his pacing.

Gillespie watched him with a slight irritation. "You want to sit down?" he asked.

But Curtis waved a hand at him, signifying "relax." "Just watch," he told the agent.

Evan's whole body was alert; he moved like a sprinter just before a race. "Of course. A circle within a circle. The inner circle. She's saying that we can't trust anyone in the inner circle at Webtech."

"Well, we knew that!" I dismissed. "And what about the badge?"

"She could have meant me, or you, Gillespie, if she knew more than you thought she did." Evan exchanged a look with Gillespie, who seemed to acknowledge the possibility.

Evan directed his gaze to me. "Who would know who's considered to be in the inner circle? Remember, it won't necessarily be the highest-ranking company officers."

"Jim would know."

"Can you call him?"

I was already on my way to my phone book. Since it was Sunday, I chose to try his cell phone.

"Hello?"

"Jim, hi, it's Cally. Listen, remember what we talked about at the café? I need a little help." I asked him to name whoever he considered to be in the inner circle.

"Well, let's see, besides Fred and Kevin and Ted, who share the box at Del Mar with him, I would say there's maybe three more, Maurice Weinstock, Edward Wager, and Ronald Cooper. But Callaway, none of them is a murderer," he said, sounding annoyed.

"Maybe not. But we do know that the investigation has something to do with Russia and your foreign office. Thanks anyway," I responded.

There was a silence, and then I heard, "Was the info . . . about the . . . head . . . useful?" he asked me.

"I'm sorry, Jim, you're breaking up."

"Sorry, I'm . . . up to the ranch . . . to work . . . Fred."

"You're going up to Santa Ynez?"

"Ye . . ."

"Jim, be careful," I said.

I thought I heard him laugh, and then the connection died.

Gillespie was watching me with narrowed eyes. "Why did you

tell him about the Russian connection? And what did you tell him before at the café?" Evan and Curtis said nothing, but they looked like they were wondering the same thing.

"I've known him my whole life. His daughter is a friend of mine. When I met him the other day to ask about the redhead, I warned him that something was going on in the company, that's all." I realized as the words left my mouth that maybe I should have kept it shut.

"Callaway," said Evan reproachfully, "that could have ruined all Agent Gillespie's work."

"Well, I didn't know Agent Gillespie was on our side," I defended myself. "And Jim found out who Patricia Adman was, and the fact that she was in the international division. That's more than you did," I snapped at him.

Gillespie intervened, "Okay, okay, it's done. And maybe his information will help us out. Let's go over those names."

Deliberately choosing Gillespie, I handed him the list.

Evan looked down at the names, and I could see his brain working.

"Are you familiar with all of these men?" Evan asked Gillespie.

"Very."

"Do you know where their offices are located, I mean, the layout of the building?"

Gillespie narrowed his eyes at Evan, as though trying to follow his thought pattern. "Yes," he said, "I've spent time in all of them." The corner of his mouth twitched. "Though not necessarily during business hours."

Evan flipped a page on the pad and handed it to Gillespie. "Can you draw me a diagram? Let me know the floors and just a rough north/south direction layout of the building."

"Oh, they're all on the same floor, the top floor. These guys are all in a row. Now that I think of it," he said while he started to draw a rough sketch, "it makes sense that Rosen would have given his buddies all the best views of the ocean."

Evan tensed and leaned in. "They *all* look out to the west? Are you sure?" he asked.

"Oh yeah."

"Damn it!" Evan got up and started pacing.

"What?" I asked.

"We know that someone could see into Dana's office from Webtech, and that's how it was possible for them to get the phone delivered while you were there. That means they had to be looking out toward the *east*."

Curtis looked mildly impressed.

"They could have been in a broom closet," I said.

But Gillespie brushed off my contribution. "Broom closets don't have views." He started drawing the diagram. "It's possible that they could have used someone else's office, though. Actually, let me see, about seven people that I can think of have views that face directly east. Quite a few face north." He started blocking off cubes and writing names in each one.

"How can you remember all of that?" I asked, impressed.

He gave me a quick smile. "It's all part of the company training."

When he was finished we looked over the double diagram. Four separate floors. Three of them were below Dana's floor. They were out of the running, as it would have been impossible to see anything except someone standing directly in the window, and we hadn't been.

That narrowed it down to the accounting department, and, in the coveted corner office, Jim Ferris.

Three sets of eyes, all belonging to professional lawmen, looked at me. "It's a coincidence," I said. "It doesn't mean anything."

If Evan had said the usual "There's no such thing as a coincidence," I swear I would have slapped him. What he did say was, "He was pretty adamant that none of his cronies could be involved with this, right?"

I nodded; what else could I do?

"And does he socialize with them quite a bit?" Curtis asked.

"I don't know, I would imagine so. I remember Isabelle being miffed because her dad got to sit in the owners' box when he went to the racetrack and she didn't."

"So, he could be one of the inner circle?" Gillespie asked.

"He's not on the list!" I insisted, a sort of unreal panic rising in me, a familiar sense of upheaval that I could think I knew someone so well, only to find that I was dead wrong.

"He *gave us* the list," Evan said gently but very firmly. He reached out to put his hand on my arm, but I snatched myself out of his reach.

"It might have been modesty that kept him from including himself," Curtis said without conviction.

"Isn't it possible that one of these other guys used his office when they knew he wasn't there to make the phone call?" I asked.

Maybe, yeah, that was probably it.

"Not likely," Gillespie said without Evan's empathetic consideration for my growing rage and distress. "Did you plan when you were going to Scheiner's office? Did you make a phone call or send an email to tell someone?"

I thought, casting back on the intense moments of those days. "I called to say I might be dropping off some papers, but I didn't say when," I finally answered weakly.

"So, whoever it was had to be in their office most of the day. It's unlikely that one of these other guys would have spent their whole day sitting in another man's office." Gillespie's shrewd eyes flashed ironically as he added, "Or in a broom closet."

"One of the Russian guys could have done it!" I grasped for some other explanation.

"Callaway." Evan's voice was calming and warning me to stay that way. "Wouldn't a Russian thug be a little conspicuous sitting in a busy office?"

I had to concede that this was true.

"Someone, in one of these offices," Evan concluded, pointing to the row of east-facing windows on the eighteenth-floor diagram, "was watching Dana's office, someone who could time the delivery of the package to coincide with your arrival." He turned to Gillespie. "We need to at least eliminate Ferris."

"Let's pick him up." Gillespie stood.

"What are you going to do?" I asked, afraid.

"Ask him some questions." It was Evan who answered me.

All three men were on their feet and—it would have been comical if it hadn't been so tragic—checking their weapons.

"Let's go," Gillespie said to Evan and Curtis. He nodded and I grabbed my bag, but Evan put his hand on my shaking arm.

"You're not going."

"Yes, I am!"

"Look at me, Callaway." I didn't want to, but I couldn't very well insist on going if I couldn't even look the man in the eye, so I did. "There is nothing you can do except split my focus, make me have to protect you, and be an emotional complication in this situation. You have to help us, and *stay here.*"

"I'm going!" I shouted, and I would have started screaming that I was perfectly calm if Ginny hadn't come into the room.

"Where is she not going?" Ginny asked, making the assumption—I noted with annoyance—that Evan would win out.

Evan turned and transferred his commands to her, and I knew as I watched her face that she was being sworn in as his deputy. I hated them both.

"Nowhere. We have to go talk to someone, and Callaway will explain everything to you when we're gone. Don't let her leave." He kissed my forehead before I could push him away.

They were at the door when Curtis stopped, came back, kissed Ginny hard on the mouth, and said, "And don't you leave either." Her eyes narrowed, and I was pleased to see that *she* didn't like being told what to do either; served her right.

And then they were gone. I stood there helpless with rage and frustration. A heaviness more debilitating than exhaustion forced me to sit down and stare at the floor.

"What's going on?" Ginny asked as she sat down in front of me.

"They think it's Jim," I muttered, unable to comprehend what was going on. How could Jim have been behind this? It didn't make any sense. I thought about Isabelle saying that his ex-wife, Cindy, wanted more money, about the fact that Jim had always been a vice president at Webtech, but that had never seemed to anger him. Was it possible that he was far more ambitious—or desperate—than I had ever imagined? I'd been misled so many times before, but this just felt wrong.

Ginny was waiting, watching me with a tense, forced patience. So I gathered the last resources of my energy and explained to her how the three lawmen had come to that conclusion.

"Jesus, it couldn't be Jim. I can't go through this again," I concluded, and let my body fall back against the cushions of the armchair.

"You can't trust everybody," Ginny said.

"Shit, I can't trust anybody except you," I said thickly, and I was grateful that Ginny didn't contradict me. Nor did she agree. That would have finished me off.

An hour went by, then two. Ginny and I passed the time discussing my suppositions and theories, dismissing and considering alternatives. I told her what Gillespie had said about Evan having a reputation for doing things his own way, and she told me that I had always known that, and liked it, which was true enough.

I heard voices in the entrance hall, and Sabrina came into the living room followed by Wayne. "Look who's here!" my sister said as though this would certainly cheer me up.

Somehow in all the confusion at Patricia Adman's house, Wayne had gotten lost in the shuffle, and I had frankly forgotten about him.

"Wayne! How did you get home? I'm sorry."

"Oh, it's okay, I had to go answer a bunch of questions at the precinct and then one of the officers dropped me off back here." He looked as though he was afraid he'd offended me. "My car is here."

"I know. I'm sorry."

"Oh, it's no big deal. I know you're busy, and all. But I wanted to tell you something." He had that glint in his eye that I'd seen there before, a kind of excitement.

"What?"

"Well." He shifted his body back and forth from one foot to the other and worked his thumb on his palm. "I, uh, remember when I went in the house, when you were, uh, outside?"

"At Patricia's?" I asked.

"Yeah. Well, I, uh . . ." His eyes cut to Sabrina self-consciously, and his face reddened. I recalled how green it had been and why he'd needed to go into the house. "I used the restroom, and then I noticed her computer in the bedroom, and I thought, maybe, while I was waiting . . ."

Sitting forward in my chair, I asked, "What did you find, Wayne?"

He pulled a pair of papers from his back pocket. "Well, there was nothing in her in or sent boxes. She'd deleted everything, and it took a little retrieval action to find anything and I didn't have time to print much, but I did notice there were quite a few emails from a certain condo complex in Venice Beach."

"Oh," I said, somewhat disappointed. "That would be from Russian; it makes sense that he would have sent her directions at the same time as he was sending them to me."

Wayne was sorting through the short stack of papers. "But it's funny, because there's something about a party in Santa Ynez, and they mention 'the girlfriend.' "

He handed over one of the sheets of paper. I read it out loud to include Ginny. "It was sent Friday morning, at 11:03. It says, 'The girlfriend will attend party, stand by to delete.' "

I looked up at him. "They knew I was going to the event in Santa Ynez?"

It was Ginny who answered. "Must have, that's how they knew to follow us. We thought it was Houndstooth, but seeing how he wasn't commingled with the dashboard of a Hummer, it obviously wasn't."

"They probably picked up the info from the waves," Wayne said, gesturing to the air above his head.

"Yeah, probably," I agreed.

"So I was looking for a reply, and I found this in her deleted sent mail." He held out the remaining paper to me and refused to meet my eye as I took it.

Looking at the printed message on top, I noticed the sent to address first. It was Evan's email address at the precinct.

Expecting it to be threats directed at stopping him, I read the single line below.

It said, "transaction complete, delete C." It was dated shortly after noon today. There was a link to a website, and it was CC'd to an address I didn't recognize, but which contained what was obviously a Russian name. She must have sent it moments before I appeared at her door.

I looked up at Ginny, who had read the remaining emails over my shoulder. She met my eyes slowly.

"Shit," she said, looking torn. "Here we go again."

"Wayne," I said, my voice shaking, "did you go to this link?" I held up the paper.

"Didn't have time," he said.

"Can you do it now, please?"

We all went to my library, and Wayne sat at my desk. With a few deft clicks he had an image on the screen.

"What is that?" Sabrina asked, leaning over.

"It looks like a webcam, something that stays on and you can log on and watch the image," Wayne explained. "But usually they're of a street, or a bar, or something. This is odd."

We all stared at the screen; it was a close-up of what seemed to be a dial of some kind.

"What the hell?" Ginny asked.

"It looks like the combination lock of a safe," I said. "Hell, it looks like the lock on my—" The words died, and I backed away from the desk. Spinning around, I crossed the room to a long table stacked with books near the base of the bookshelves. I got down on my hands and knees and crawled underneath. "Tell me if you see anything!" I called out as I stretched out my hand to touch the dial on the safe that was there.

"Yes!" shouted Ginny. "It's a hand."

I pulled my hand back as though I'd been stung. "Wayne!" I called out. He was next to me in a flash, and I backed out so that he could move in and search the underside of the wide marble table.

"Yep," he said, "there it is. Micro camera, remote."

"Don't take it yet," I told him. "First, turn the dial on the safe."

I watched the image on my computer screen as Wayne's hand came in and twisted. The tiny camera was perfectly positioned to demonstrate the safe's combination.

A Siberian chill ran down my spine. "Take the camera," I said, and even my voice sounded cold.

Wayne emerged from under the table holding the tiny camera. I took his spot and opened the safe with trembling fingers. When the tumblers slipped into place, I grasped the handle and pulled. Slowly, the heavy, small-refrigerator-sized door swung open.

The briefcase was gone.

Chapter
49

E van's the only one, besides Curtis, who knew that the safe
was even there!" I said through my tears. "Shit, oh shit." All
I could think were the words "inside job." Who else could have
put in a camera? Or a bomb.

"But"—Wayne looked so thoroughly discomfited that he had
broken a sweat—"the website was copied to this other address.
So someone else could have known the combination."

"No one else has been here today!" I shouted. "And he insisted on going to meet the connection himself. He could have
handed over the money to them then."

"He handed three million to a ten-year-old on a bicycle?"
Ginny asked incredulously.

"All we know about the exchange is *what Evan told us!* And he
didn't take any backup, so there are no witnesses!"

"But why would he do that?" Ginny asked.

"To save his own skin." They all looked doubtful. But then
they hadn't seen the videotape of Evan's brutal attack.

Sabrina was frowning at me. "So, you think that all this time,

Evan's been pretending about being kidnapped and helping Dana to get money from you?" She sounded as though the thought was painful and difficult.

"No, I'm saying that he got himself involved in this and now he's being used by them, at the very least," I finished feebly.

"Bullshit!" Sabrina said with the full force of her considerable lung power. "You know that's not right!"

I looked over at her and said, "I don't know what's right anymore, Sabrina, I just don't know what to think. I mean, what if he tries to pin this all on Jim? It'll be my fault."

The phone rang and I stared at it, afraid to pick it up; the name on the caller ID was unrecognizable, yet it struck a familiar chord. Hesitantly, I answered.

"Callaway?"

"Dana?" I was surprised that she would be calling, when we had taken such pains to make her disappear. Surprise was quickly replaced by annoyance. "Why are you calling me? This is not smart." I didn't want to say the phone had been tapped, but I supposed it was too late anyway.

"Where's Evan?" she asked, her voice quavering with emotion.

"He's not here, and you cannot call him. You know that." If anyone was listening, she had already given away everything.

There was quiet for a moment, and then I heard her whisper, "Help me."

"What? What's wrong?"

"Please, I don't have much time. They left the room for a few minutes and I don't think they thought I would find the phone." I had to strain to hear her words; Ginny opened her mouth to ask what was going on, but I silenced her with a hand and pressed the phone harder to my ear. "A man came and found me, he took me . . ." She cut off, then said, "They're coming. Please help me." She hung up.

I held the phone out and looked at it.

"What the fuck was that?" Ginny looked more annoyed than I felt.

"Dana, she says someone took her." My voice conveyed my confusion and fear.

"Who?" asked Sabrina.

"I don't know. She had to hang up."

Wayne grabbed the phone from me and punched a couple of buttons until he was into the redial directory. He held out the tiny screen for me to see. It read, "Montgomery, S." "Who is that?"

When I'd seen it, it had rung a bell because I'd known I'd heard it recently. Now, as I remembered where and made the connection, the bell turned into a train whistle. I guess if you have a name people associate with old money and big railroads, you keep it. Hell, I'd keep mine, and my money was only second generation.

"Susan Montgomery of the railroad Montgomerys," I muttered to myself. "Rosen," I told Ginny firmly, exhilarated by the fact that I hadn't been wrong about Jim. "Dana's been taken to his house."

Chapter
50

I knew from experience that most of the mountainous road on the way up to Santa Ynez was an out-of-service area, which is what the recording told us when we tried to call Curtis.

There wasn't much choice, Ginny and I told ourselves; we had to go. If Evan was involved, Dana, Jim, and even Curtis could be in danger, and if, by some miracle, Evan *wasn't* involved, then he and Curtis were headed right into a trap. Gillespie had been one step behind the game the whole way, and it looked like he was still dancing off the beat. With no way to contact the men and other police out of the loop, we climbed into the Porsche SUV and took off.

Ginny drove, of course, breaking her constant speed of one hundred and twenty miles an hour only when we hit an area likely to contain a state trooper. We met none, making the two-hour drive in just over an hour.

When we started up the 154 I saw that my phone too was now "searching for service." Tossing it into the space between the seats, I voiced something that had been bothering me. "What the hell is Jim doing up here if he isn't involved?"

"Don't kid yourself," she said as she accelerated neatly and passed a camper by using the rough shoulder of the road on the inside of a hairpin turn while I braced myself with hands against the door and the dashboard. She went on, speaking loudly over the drone of the camper's horn. "He's involved somehow. Maybe he's working with Rosen, maybe he doesn't realize what's really going on, and he still trusts his cronies."

"I told him what was going on!" I insisted.

"Well, you said he didn't want to believe you."

I fell silent again. As I felt the centrifugal force of another sharp turn tugging at me, its unseen hand trying to pluck me from my seat and slingshot me out over a frightening drop, I tried not to remember the Hummer's sudden descent after it cleared the guardrail. The roller-coaster thrills drove any further speculation from my mind, and faster than I could have believed, we pulled up on the street outside Rosen's ranch. The gate was closed, and down the long, tree-lined, sloping drive we could see the sprawling home.

"I think we walk from here," Ginny said.

"Good plan," I muttered. "Not that we have one," I amended.

"Sure we do." Ginny smiled at me and pulled my pistol out of a locked briefcase in the backseat before loading the chamber and handing the weapon to me. I pocketed it while she was stuffing a second gun into her jeans beneath her shirt. "We creep up to the house, keeping in that tree line," she explained as she pointed out what seemed to be the left edge of the property, where rows of grapevines gave way to a large, shady grove of oaks. "And we look around. If we see the men we tell Curtis what we know, but it might be best to avoid any males, regardless of their color, race, or political affiliation. The main object is to get Dana and get out."

"What if we don't find her?"

Ginny shrugged. "I got a funny premonition that it's not going to be a piña-coladas-by-the-pool kind of an afternoon." She looked at me, and, as always, I was reassured by her flippant bravado. I followed her to the end of the white-railed fence and we slipped through, into the woods.

We landed on the far side of the patio that had been tented the night of the party. Now it looked like a vast unprotected space that separated us from the crosshatched pane windows, which afforded us very little view into the home and absolutely no cover. I nudged Ginny and pointed up at a second-floor balcony. There was a man smoking a cigarette—a large, hard-looking man. As he threw the butt away from him, his jacket opened and the shoulder holster was easily visible. Under my breath I hissed, "Russian." Ginny held up a finger to her lips to silence me.

A man and a woman were talking near the pool house, and though it was apparent that they were trying to keep their voices down, the level of strain and intensity in the conversation was exceeding whispered levels with increasing regularity.

With a subtle yank on my arm Ginny pulled me back into the trees and we made a wide arc, coming back to the edge of the lush landscaping closer to the argument. Now we could hear bits of the conversation. The male voice was Jim's, and though I strained, I couldn't recognize the other voice—it was cultured and haughty, someone of social rank and breeding. It could be Susan Montgomery, but I'd been so wound up the night of the party that I couldn't recall her voice clearly.

"How could she let this happen?" Jim was clearly angry and distressed.

"You need to calm yourself." The woman's voice, it must be Susan's, was smooth as polished steel, and just as hard. "It wasn't a good idea to come here."

"What choice did I have?" Jim sounded bitter and desperate.

"How could she let this happen?" he repeated, his voice rising in distress.

"Stay calm. Now listen." Her voice dropped to nothing more than a murmur that blended into the rustling of the leaves in the hot wind.

Sweat was dripping down my chest, and several obnoxious insects had chosen me as their home planet; they kept trying to dock in my eyes and they buzzed in my ears, until I thought I would crack if I couldn't swat one. Taking a breath to try to calm myself, I sucked one into my lungs. Ginny heard the sputtering and spun around to clasp her hand over my mouth, but someone beat her to it.

Chapter
51

As I was yanked backward into the woods, I got just a momentary glance at Ginny's startled face before she too was gagged by an oven-mitt-sized paw. Though I shut my eyes to avoid the branches that I was being dragged through, I was aware of a dull thump and the sharp exhale of breath that told me Ginny had landed an elbow in the solar plexus of her attacker. I pushed back off my feet hard and sent myself, and the man who was holding me, sprawling backward. He cursed in Russian as I landed hard on top of him, and then I heard the sharp, sickening thud of metal on a skull and the man beneath me went limp.

Terrified, I glanced over to see Ginny tucking her gun back into her jeans. Two men lay on the thick compost of the manicured undergrowth; neither was moving, and it looked like they wouldn't be for a while.

"Reception committee," Ginny mouthed, and I smiled gratefully at her.

"Where're Evan and Curtis?" I mouthed back as we waited with bated breath to see if our brief confrontation would attract any more attention. She shrugged and after a couple of tense but mercifully quiet moments, we crept forward again.

We reached a place near the edge of a grass strip that led to the raised stone terrace where Jim had been arguing with Susan Montgomery. There was no sign of Evan, Curtis, or Gillespie. Through the thick leafy greens that shrouded us I could see Jim, facing a woman in a wide-brimmed hat, the kind you wear for gardening, with a white veil that came over the face and wrapped lightly around the neck to guard against the small black flies that hovered incessantly around us. I couldn't make out a face behind it from this distance. In her hand was a pair of expensive gardening shears. Her back was to us. She rose even as we tried to settle ourselves soundlessly. "You need to go now," she said to Jim, and moved toward the house. Jim grabbed at her arm, and for a brief second I saw the glint of a chain bracelet on her arm, and then the stainless steel blades of the shears as she stabbed them down into Jim's arm. He cried out in pain, and, from seemingly nowhere, two men appeared, large burly men with heavy brows and very small foreheads. They were both holding guns.

"Freeze, FBI!" came a shout from our left. The command was followed by the sound of crunching shrubbery as, I assumed, Gillespie clambered from the landscaping.

One of the hired hands raised his gun and fired in Gillespie's direction as Susan slipped behind the henchman and disappeared into the house. Ginny's weight knocked me to the ground, and gunfire retorted from seemingly every direction for a half a minute. It stopped as suddenly as it had begun, and I heard Evan's voice saying, "Stay down! Curtis, follow him!"

Ginny and I sat up and strained to see what was happening. There were two men bleeding on the slate patio. One was the henchman who had fired his weapon—he was facedown and didn't look like he'd be getting up again—and the other was Jim Ferris, who was on his knees, holding his punctured forearm and looking like that was the least of his concerns. Evan was standing over him, his gun drawn.

"You!" said Jim, and there was a strange, strangled quality to his voice.

"You know who I am, don't you?" Evan asked, his voice as smooth and even as poured molasses.

"I've got the tapes," said Jim. "If you do anything more, if you don't walk away from this, it goes to the press and to the department. You'll spend the next ten years in jail and you'll be ruined for life." My heart flung itself into the leaf litter around me and started to decompose. *It was Jim who had videotaped Evan. Jim who was behind it all!*

I couldn't see Evan, but his voice actually sounded amused as he said, "Oh, somehow I don't think so."

"It won't help to kill me, someone else is holding the tapes. And"—Jim's voice was venomous now, a rattler striking for the kill—"everyone will know what you've done, how you've deceived these women. *People have died because of you!*"

I felt filleted. My gasping heart seized up in pain, and I turned to look desperately at Ginny. She had hold of my arm, but I couldn't feel anything; she shook her head slowly, warning me not to make a move.

Far off to the right, around the side of the house, I heard a woman cry out. Into the dark of my betrayal came a bolt of thought that struck like lightning, rousing me to action. *Dana is in that house. She's been deceived just like me, and I will not let her die!* Turning back quickly, I saw that there was no sign of the second thug, Curtis, Gillespie, or the woman. Ginny and I looked at each other and mouthed at the same time, "Go." We both stood up and crashed through the remaining barrier of leafy perennials. Evan's gun swung efficiently toward us, and we both froze.

"Where the fuck did you come from?" he asked coldly.

I looked at him. He had swung the barrel of his gun back to

Jim, who crouched instinctively away from it, but he kept his eyes locked on mine. What would he do? Was he as trapped as Jim, as venomous as Jim?

It was time to find out; I wasn't going to leave Dana to the mercy of desperate criminals.

Looking up at Evan, I said slowly and deliberately, "What are you gonna do? Shoot me?" And I turned my back and ran across the lawn, toward the far side of the house.

"Callaway!" His call was followed by curses and then a single shot. I ducked my head instinctively but I didn't stop, I didn't even turn until I reached the side of the house, and then only to check on Ginny's progress.

She wasn't following me. Evan was clearing the low stone seat at the edge of the patio and starting toward me. I paused and searched for Ginny, but I spotted only the back of her head over the ledge; she had gone down on her knees on the patio, behind where Jim was crouching. *What is going on?* Had Evan shot her? He was almost halfway across the lawn, closing the distance between us, his face taught with determination and anger.

Torn between going back to help Ginny and forward to help Dana, I uttered a strangled, frustrated cry and made my decision; Ginny was already down and Evan was between us. I bolted the other way.

Just around the corner, I came to the kitchen door, and next to it, a concrete piece of Chinese garden statuary that must have weighed a good forty pounds.

I flung open the door, grabbed the ornament, threw it into the bushes on the far side of the patio, and ran into the kitchen. Through the window over a sink, I saw the top of Evan's head as he came up to the corner of the house. I opened a louvered door that revealed the long counter of a butler's pantry. That would do. I climbed on top of it and closed the doors behind me.

As I had suspected he would, Evan had followed the sound of the crash created by the midget stone Fu dog. Through the open door, I could hear him brushing aside limbs of undergrowth for a moment before giving that up and cautiously entering the kitchen.

The narrow slats of the plantation shutter doors tilted tightly down and afforded me only a very limited view of the floor and counter from my perch on the shelf. My knees were tucked up under my chin.

I heard nothing for a moment, then Evan called out softly, "Callaway?"

His loafers made only the softest sound on the tiles of the kitchen floor as he crossed it. I heard the slight creak of a swinging door open on the far side of the kitchen.

My heart was pounding in my ears, and each slamming beat resounded in my chest. *What happened to Ginny?* The question and the gunshot reverberated in my brain.

Remembering, for the first time, the pistol in my pocket, I reached for it as silently as possible. My hands were shaking and numb. I sensed more than felt the heavy hilt in my palm and started to extract it. What would I do? If it came to it, would I shoot Evan? Could I?

The sense of fear for my friend gave me my answer. Yes. I could shoot anyone who had hurt Ginny.

Ginny. I had to get back to her. If Evan would just go on through the kitchen, I could backtrack, get Ginny, try to find Gillespie, and save Dana . . .

The gun was almost clear when the sight on the barrel caught the fabric of my pocket and I lost my grip on it. It fell, clattering to the marble countertop. I snatched at it, coming up onto my knees and steadying the gun in front of me, just as the door was ripped open and I found myself looking down the barrel of Evan's gun and straight into his eyes.

Chapter

52

Somehow—I can't imagine how I was even capable of noticing the fact—he seemed handsomer than he had ever been, ultimately powerful, and as seriously potent as the weapon that gaped at me. I tightened my finger on the trigger, starting the squeeze, but held. His eyes connected with mine, and what I saw there opened my brain to another level of consciousness, ultimate pain and love.

All three of us froze; Evan, time, and me. The end of my gun shook almost imperceptibly as I tried to will myself to fire.

There was a long moment of silence, during which the water from the kitchen faucet dripped very slowly and splattered with a quiet booming sound, with vast spaces of nothing in between, once, twice, three times.

Something was happening in Evan's eyes; I realized, through the fog of heightened awareness that only comes in the seconds before you die, that they were filling with tears.

Very softly, he said, "What are you gonna do? Shoot me?"

Then slowly, with excruciating deliberation and surrender, he lowered his gun and set it on the counter at my knees.

A bead of sweat trickled down my forehead and stung my eyes, but still I kept my gun trained on Evan, on the man I thought I knew.

The noise of movement came from the open doorway. I saw Evan's eyes cut in that direction but I resisted the impulse, knowing that it would give him a chance to knock my gun away at this close range. I was praying it would be Gillespie or Curtis, that they would come in and end this nightmare for me.

"What do you want me to do with this guy? I'm not standing out there with the carnivorous gnats all day." The voice was Ginny's. I heard her stop. "What the fuck are you doing?" she asked me.

My head swiveled. "Ginny! You . . . you're all right!" She had entered the kitchen, pushing Jim Ferris, who was handcuffed, in ahead of her. She was watching me, my gun three feet from Evan's face.

"Hello?" Her eyes cut back and forth from me to Evan. She took in the whole situation and my volatile instability in a single, erratic glance. "Girl, you need to put down that gun. He's not the enemy."

I wasn't sure. The money was gone. Jim had said he was involved, but he hadn't hurt Ginny, and so far, he hadn't hurt me. I lowered the gun slowly but kept it in my hand. "Start explaining," I said to Evan.

His face hardened slightly. "I've got a few other things to do first." As I had done to him, he turned his back on me and my gun. He crossed over to the kitchen door; realizing that none of us had any idea what he'd meet on the other side of it, I called out, "Wait. We think Dana's here, she called and—"

He cut me off. "I know."

"I told him," Ginny snapped at me. "Go!" she told Evan.

Ginny asked incredulously.

"Wait," I said, "you'd better take this." Picking up his gun, I tossed it across the room to him.

He caught it deftly. That look of shared irony I had seen so many times before glinted in his eyes and flashed across his face.

"Nice catch," I told him.

"I wouldn't have known you were there if you hadn't dropped the gun."

"I meant to do that." I let a small smile flicker at him and got one back, and then he was gone.

Looking after him, I found myself wondering if I could overlook a few small details like kidnapping and corporate larceny.

Reluctantly, I turned my gaze to Jim. He wasn't looking at me, or at anything. I had a million questions that wouldn't quite formulate in my mind. The one that overrode all the others was, *How could you betray me?* Even with my current fragile hold on logic, I could see that that might not be the most pertinent question while Evan and Curtis were playing cat and mouse with armed criminals.

Ginny was, as usual, far more practical. She sat Jim in a chair in the corner, gave him a clean dishtowel to wrap his arm, told him not to move, then suggested that we each face one door.

Once settled, I looked over my shoulder at Ginny while I asked, "Want a piña colada?"

Ginny responded, "More than you know, but not just yet, thanks. What was that about?"

"I thought Evan shot you," I said defensively.

"No, he shot the guy who was aiming at my head."

"Oh." I leaned back in my chair to try to ease the strain in my shoulders.

There was a crunching noise from outside the kitchen door, and both Ginny and I swung our guns up in that direction. Curtis rolled into view with his gun extended, then immediately made a right angle of his arms, pointing the expressive end of his weapon up at the ceiling.

"Tea party?" he asked casually, his eyes watching Jim.

"Yes," I answered as I lowered my gun back to my lap and Ginny did the same. I asked, "Oolong or Earl Grey?"

"I think the caffeine might kill the adrenaline rush. Thanks, though."

"Some other time, then," Ginny said.

He looked from Jim to Ginny. "Got him?"

"Got him," she said. Curtis nodded, passed through the kitchen, and went out the swinging door.

Five minutes of strained silence passed, each of us jerking with every small noise, real or imagined. Finally we heard the definitive sound of footsteps in the room beyond, and Ginny and I rose to face off with the unseen intruders.

"Coming in!" It was Curtis's gruff voice that broke through our panic, and we relaxed as he entered, followed by Gillespie and Evan. Dana was not with them.

"Did you find—?" I began, but Evan cut me off immediately.

"The answer is that everyone is safe and I'll be asking the questions."

They all came in and settled themselves around the kitchen.

"Where're the . . . uh, others?" I couldn't stop myself from slipping in.

"Dead or gone." Gillespie scowled. "We saw one of the cars headed off down the driveway, and since ours is parked a quarter mile down the road, there wasn't much sense in following them."

"But," Evan said, looking pointedly at me, "as I said, *no one* is currently in danger, and we have *everyone* we need to talk to right here."

By his inflection I assumed he meant that Dana was safe, and that Ginny and I were not to mention her. She and I exchanged looks; she'd gotten the same message. But Jim must know that Dana was here if he was the one behind her abduction.

"All right," Evan announced, "everybody get comfortable. It's time to answer a few questions."

For the first time I looked directly at Jim. He was staring at the floor, his shoulders slumped forward, an infinite, defeated sorrow etched in his face.

I was thinking that no one but me, and possibly Ginny, had heard what Jim had said to Evan on the patio, and I was wondering how Evan would cover it up now. So it surprised me when he brought it up right away.

"Mr. Ferris?" Evan began. Jim's head lifted a fraction, but not enough for him to look at Evan. "You said outside that people had died because of me. Who would that be?"

Jim's voice was muffled and oddly distant, as though he was thinking about what he was going to say, but then detaching himself from it. "Two innocent women who trusted you."

Gillespie and Curtis seemed unmoved by the accusation. It seemed that they had decided before coming into the room to let Evan ask the questions. I sat rigid and alert. What would happen when Jim gave them some kind of proof? Would they turn on Evan? Arrest him? Should I tell them now about the briefcase?

"How long have you been involved in this?" Evan was asking Jim.

Jim sighed. "Since the beginning. I assigned the people who set up the offices in Moscow, and I met some people from there who were willing enough to help me skim money off the accounts. It doesn't matter now. Just arrest me, and be done with the damn thing."

"And what about the videotapes that are, I assume, in your possession?"

"Oh, you'll go down too, as well you should. The videotape will be released when you arrest me."

Evan crossed his arms and leaned comfortably against the kitchen counter. He was far from done with the damn thing. "Who was the woman you were talking to on the patio?"

Now Jim's eyes flicked around the room, to each face, as though ticking them off on a list. "I don't know," he muttered.

"It sounded like you knew." Evan rolled his head to one side and massaged the back of his neck with one hand. "Was it Susan Montgomery?"

Jim's eyes shot up involuntarily to Evan's face and then looked quickly away. "No."

"Mrs. Rosen is an old friend of yours, isn't she?"

Jim sighed but said nothing.

"She was probably very upset to learn that her husband was having an affair with someone at work, don't you think?"

"She didn't know any such thing," Jim said, but his eyes flicked away this time. He was lying.

"Did Susan Montgomery Rosen kill Molly Simpson?"

"No!" Jim was looking straight at Evan, sitting bolt upright. Then he seemed to remember himself and bowed again, his chest caving in. "I don't know anything about that."

"No," Evan said, catching Jim and certainly me off guard, "I don't suppose you would."

Jim narrowed his eyes and cocked his head to one side. "Maybe *you* do though, Detective?" he said hatefully to Evan.

Evan didn't bite; instead he leaned forward and said, "Why would you have me kidnapped?"

Jim shook his head for a minute, then sat up and laughed. "That's rich," he said. Then he looked at Gillespie. "Your buddy here faked that whole thing." He jerked his head in Evan's direction and then turned to face him. "Didn't you? That's how you threw the suspicion on somebody else and ran the show at the same time." He shook his head again, laughing mirthlessly, and turned to me. "You see? You don't know anything about him."

I rocked back in my chair, stunned. Could it be? Feeling Evan's gaze on me, I met his eyes and it seemed he could feel the question. But Evan's expression didn't change as he watched my face. Instead he turned back to Jim and said, "Who are your connections in Moscow?"

The oddest blank look came over Jim's face, as though he had forgotten everything up until this moment, and then it turned into a look of resentful challenge. "I'm not saying anything else. I want a lawyer."

Evan sighed and turned to Gillespie. "I think he's all yours now." Evan turned back to Jim and said, "When you release that videotape . . . of me . . ." He waited for Jim to raise his head and look at him, and then finished very deliberately, *". . . don't forget to add the production credits."*

Jim's head snapped back a few inches, and this time there was a new fear in his eyes. But Evan only watched him for a minute before he turned away, holding his hand out to me. "Let's get you home."

I looked at his offered hand, then shot a panicked look to Curtis, who said quickly, "I'll take them," and nodded reassuringly to me.

I had the nerve-wracking feeling that the showdown we'd just been through was nothing compared to the one that was about to happen at my house.

Chapter
53

Curtis escorted us to our car, but as we were getting in, Evan approached us.

"We've got to go by St. John's," he said to Curtis. "Patricia Adman is conscious."

Curtis's head snapped up at that and I punched Ginny's arm across the seat. She spoke up. "Just give me one minute with my man, okay, Evan?" she pleaded.

Evan's eyes bored into me, but just then two unmarked blue sedans pulled up and several other people in dark suits got out. Evan said nothing, only turned away and went to meet Gillespie and the other FBI agents.

Conscious of Ginny gritting her teeth next to me, I told Curtis, in an undertone, about the missing briefcase and the two emails that had been sent to the precinct, slipping him the copies Wayne had given me with a guilty glance back at Evan. He was watching us, but he turned away when he saw me looking.

"Be careful," I told Curtis as he surreptitiously pocketed the papers and promised to check it out. The agents had put Jim in the back of one of the sedans and my last view of him was a disturbing one.

Just as they passed us, he turned, and his destroyed expression was marked with streaks of tears. In spite of myself, the sight of him that way tore at me. I turned away with a jerk, hoping to leave the splinter in my heart behind with the raw image, but it wouldn't dislodge.

The afternoon sun was streaking diagonally through the trees when we pulled up in front of the house, though a breeze from the sea was nudging aside the stifling heat with gentle insistence. But the wafting gusts did nothing to cool the fever of fear and anxiety in me. I had to face Evan, had to determine what his involvement in this whole scam had been, and there was still the matter of Dana Scheiner and his involvement with her.

As I walked toward the house, I noticed a sleek black Mercedes sedan parked near the edge of the house. Korosu's car.

My heart lifted. Somehow I felt as though his presence would make me safe, give me the strength I needed to face whatever came next. Korosu was my backup. My secret promise that, though he wasn't Evan, there was life beyond this relationship. It both relieved and terrified me to think of the possibility.

Deirdre threw the door open, and the anxiety melting from her face was all the admonishment I needed for not calling. I'd been so lost in my own self-pity that it hadn't even occurred to me that we would be missed by anyone else.

"The Misters Darrien and Korosu are in the living room," Deirdre informed me as she ushered us down the hall.

Korosu's eyes sparked, and he stood when I entered the living room. Darrien's face was contained relief. Sabrina rushed to hug first me, and then Ginny. "I called them after you left, and they both came over to wait with me."

I smiled my thanks. Each glance at Korosu found him watching me intently, as though he could read the new doubts that were brewing in me, but he said nothing.

A few moments later, Curtis arrived, and, with a toxic mixture of relief and disappointment, I saw that Dana was with him. They joined us in the living room.

"Where's Evan?" I asked, almost afraid, as I dropped into one of the big armchairs. The gun that I'd stuck into the waistband of my jeans bit the tender skin of my stomach. I pulled it out and set it on the small side table.

"He's answering some questions for our federal friends," Curtis informed us all. "They'll drop him off soon."

"I'm here," came Evan's voice, tired but strangely charged as he came into the living room.

"Feds are fast," Curtis commented.

"Oh, I'm not done," Evan said, acknowledging Korosu with a respectful but wary nod of his head. "Another couple dozen hours of debriefing ought to do it, but I needed to be here right now." He looked at me, and the rest of the room faded away.

Dana moved quickly to his side, breaking the connection between us. She buried her face in Evan's chest. I turned away.

Evan eased Dana into a chair next to Ginny, who pulled a tissue from a ceramic holder on the coffee table and handed it to Dana.

Crossing to the other side of the room, Evan turned his gaze to Dana. He asked firmly but gently, "Who took you today?"

Dana looked up at him, her beautiful brown eyes swimming in piteous tears. She smiled bravely and said, "It was two men, Russians."

"And you took Russian in college, right?" Evan asked her. Then he said, very softly, "So you would be able to identify the language as Russian, not, say, Yugoslavian?"

"No, definitely Russian." Dana nodded, then shrugged and added with a small, self-deprecating laugh, "I don't remember much of what I learned in college, but I do recall enough words to identify the language."

"Good, thank you." He continued to speak gently, respectful

of her emotional state. She'd been through so much; I knew I shouldn't resent the softness in his tone, the gentle way he handled her, but I did.

"Remember?" She smiled at him, as though none of us was there, as though they were sharing a tender moment over a candlelit dinner. "We used to use Russian endearments for each other."

"I do remember, you taught them to me." He smiled, as though the memory was deliciously sweet. Then he told her, "You're being modest. You were excellent at languages, especially accents. Remember how you used to call me and pretend to be someone else? You'd fool me every time."

Dana blushed at the compliment. "You were excellent at pretty much everything else you did too." She beamed at the inference and the compliment. "And knowing you as intimately as I do, I can guess that you've only gotten better."

My stomach quickly followed my heart, plummeted at his words.

"I picked up a little more Russian myself from my visits there," Evan said. "You probably didn't know that my brother bought several business interests in Moscow a few years after we dated. He's quite fluent."

Dana looked confused, as though she didn't know what this had to do with anything. "No, I didn't know that."

"And," Evan continued, still in that intimate conversational tone, "Curtis will tell you, we've had quite an influx of immigrants that we deal with on a pretty regular basis now."

"Nice group," Curtis said flatly.

"So, knowing a few words and phrases is not only handy, it's also mandatory for those of us on the force who want to make it clear that . . . oh, I don't know . . ."

"We don't want to die today so don't make us kill you?" Curtis suggested.

"For example. Yes," Evan agreed without so much as a glance

at his partner. "The phrase 'I want a lawyer' comes up a lot as well." Still watching Dana with fond familiarity, he continued, "When I was handcuffed to that cot in the warehouse, I didn't have much to do but try to translate what the men guarding me were saying. They, of course, had no idea that I knew any Russian at all."

A sense of outrage was growing in me, a rising bitter resentment. Here I was, supposedly engaged to Evan, and I knew none of these things about him. In fact, it seemed that what I did *not* know was vastly outweighing what I did.

"Evan." A look of fear had appeared on Dana's face. "I know what you're saying. They'll kill you, and me, if they find out I'm alive. What about the videos? What about you? You have to go away, and I have to go away, they won't stop, these people, you'll never catch them all." She trembled, her lips quivering. "We can go together, we can be together again."

Evan was looking at Dana with a smile, and he was nodding. As though my heart had been made of saturated cardboard, it burst, and liquid sadness gushed all through my body.

"Yes," Evan agreed. "We could." As I watched in disbelief, he got up and crossed over to sit just in front of her, on the edge of the coffee table. She took his hands in hers and looked pleadingly up into his face. Evan said, "I thought you might think of that."

I wanted to close my eyes, to turn away. I was vaguely aware of everyone else in the room watching me with a kind of vacant horror on their faces, but I didn't care, I couldn't look away from the love scene in front of me, the tender climax starring my fiancé and a woman who was distinctly not me. The afternoon sun came through the window and glinted off the tears in Dana's eyes. The only thing lacking was the swell of the orchestra as she raised one hand to touch his face, the golden light of the late afternoon sparking off a single stone set in white gold dangling from Dana's wrist.

Somewhere in my piteous brain, I heard a knocking, soft and

distant. A thought was scratching at a back door, but my sense of loss overwhelmed me and I wasn't up to entertaining any thoughts.

"Evan." Dana's whisper was filled with hope.

"Dana." Evan reached up and grasped the wrist of the hand that stroked his face. "Who's in this with you?"

She froze, then tried to extricate her hand from his, but he held tightly to her wrist and lifted it, looking pointedly at the bracelet. "Where did you put the three million dollars? You would need a backup plan in case I said no, and that plan would be to make me look as though I'd taken the money and killed Callaway. I know you got the combination to the safe, and I know you tried to make it look like I took it. You sent that webcam site to me through Patricia Adman." I could see how tightly Evan was holding Dana's wrist; there was a fine white line around his fingers where he'd cut the blood flow.

And then I recognized it, a white stone dangling from a silver chain; I had seen the sun glint from the same bracelet as that hand had slashed down on Jim Ferris's arm with garden shears. Evan leaned even farther forward and said, "Patricia Adman pulled through. She confessed."

"What?" Dana twisted her arm free and looked shocked and horrified. "What are you saying? Are you insane? I'm a victim in all this, you know that!" She stood up and backed away, toward the doorway. Careful not to draw anyone's attention, and staying a few steps behind her, I rose from my chair and moved in the same direction. Korosu, I could see, was making the same move from the opposite side of the room.

Evan kept speaking in an even voice. "Callaway was the one who clued me in. She said you told her that you didn't know about our engagement and our involvement. You knew perfectly well about all of that. I was explicit about the fact that I was with Callaway now, and any help I gave you was out of friendship. So, when she made it clear that you hadn't told her you knew—"

"She's lying to you!" Dana screamed.

"No," Evan responded calmly. "She cannot lie to me."

My heart felt rubbery again, like one of those balls you buy for a quarter.

"I remember quite a few words of Russian, Dana," Evan went on. "Two of them are 'lady' and 'lawyer.' The men around me used those words a lot. They used them in combination with another word. It means 'boss.' I kept thinking, who could it be? At first, when Gillespie told me that Molly Simpson had been Fred Rosen's lover, I thought it might have been his wife, Susan. But then, it all came down to you. You were the one who drew me in, you were the one with access to the money. When the Russian syndicate got suspicious of your independant ambitions, you devised the kidnapping scam to execute your most brilliant move, a videotape featuring your own death. The tape would incriminate Callaway, who would be dead and unable to deny it. How perfect, you could take all the money and disappear. Even the Russians would think you were dead. How many of them were on your payroll? Was that where Callaway's three million went?"

"No!" shouted Dana, her eyes desperate. "No! It wasn't like that! I needed your help, I really did. They were going to kill me!"

"Oh, I believe that. Because they found out that you had shanghaied huge portions of the money you were supposed to be directing back to them. That's why you needed me to protect you. At first they thought it was Josie, and that's why she died, isn't it? Then you tried to move the suspicion to me by having my kidnappers plant my watch at Josie's house. And what about making the video of me?"

She was sputtering. "I did no such thing!"

"Dana, there was only one car in the underground parking lot, yours. The camera needed to be tapped into from a source that wouldn't go through cement. There was no other place the recording equipment could have been. You, and whoever you were in this with, needed leverage to put me out of commission, to discredit me, to silence me in case things went wrong and I found out too much."

"No!" she shouted. "The video of you wasn't to bring you down, it was so you would go with me! I did this for us! There are millions of dollars waiting for us in a bank account in Switzerland. It will be easy."

"It's been clear to me for some time that you had your hand in this," Evan went on, his voice even. "I needed to see who you would lead me to. Who is it, Dana? Somebody has been helping you. Who is it?"

Dana's face was changing, twisting into an ugly semblance of need and loss. "You loved me once," she pleaded, and I could tell she was near the end of her frayed rope, and the few strands remaining were thin and brittle.

"Yes, but I recognized something in you even then. An ambition and a disregard for what was right as long as you could get what you wanted: more power, more money. I've never seen anyone rise to senior partner in a major law firm as fast as you did. You were good; you were clever. I'll give you that. You were always good at whatever you did, but I was afraid of the choices you made." Evan sighed, and for a moment he looked genuinely sad. "I felt sorry for you," he whispered.

I could have told him that that was too far to push a cornered woman. Accusations and even scorn she could have justified, defended, fought, but not pity.

With the cry of a wounded predator launching in for the kill, she lunged forward, but not toward Evan. Instead she grabbed Sabrina by the hair with one hand while with the other she snatched up my gun off the side table. I cursed my own stupidity. Evan had started to move even as Dana had, but the gun was at Sabrina's head so fast that even he was thwarted.

Everyone was on their feet but rooted to their places. Sabrina whimpered once, but no one spoke.

"Get out from behind me, now!" Dana barked at Korosu and me. "Stay against the wall. Get over there with the others."

Korosu and I exchanged glances, but when Dana yanked hard on Sabrina's hair, eliciting a squeal of pain, and pulled her around behind the armchair, we both did as we were told.

I moved toward Evan, but Dana didn't like that. "Stay away from him!" she snarled. I moved past him and toward Korosu, who shifted his weight so that he was half blocking my body. Ginny was standing with her fists clenched.

Darrien was watching Dana with such intense concentration that I thought he might levitate and fly across the room at her. But we were all separated from Dana and her hostage by several yards and large pieces of furniture.

Watching Sabrina's face, I read the terror there, and something else, something remarkably like anger.

Evan took one small step forward but held up his hands palms out to say that he wouldn't go any further. "Okay, tell you what. I'll go with you. Just let go of Sabrina and I'll walk out of here with you."

"Too late," Dana snapped. "As I suspected, you don't have the balls to be my partner, and I don't want you for a hostage."

Curtis cleared his throat and said, "How about me? I've got balls." He stepped to the left, away from Ginny as he said it, and I realized that he was trying to draw her fire by angering her. A wave of love for him and awe for his courage washed over me. But Dana didn't take the bait.

In fact she ignored everyone except Evan, as though they were the only people in the room. "I'm leaving," she said. "And I'm taking Malibu Barbie here with me. If no one interferes, I'll turn her loose somewhere." She glanced at Sabrina and snickered. "How about back to her dream house?" She jerked her head in Darrien's direction. "Then Asian Ken here can pick her up in the pink convertible."

Sabrina's eyes flashed, and she stomped down on Dana's foot

at the exact same moment that she reached up and grabbed her gun hand, twisting down hard. *"I am not from California!"* she screamed in her deepest Southern drawl.

Everyone moved at once. Darrien got to Sabrina first and wrenched her away from Dana; Evan was over the sofa and almost to Dana when she recovered her stance and raised the gun at me. Evan's arm came down to knock the gun away from its trajectory, and Korosu blocked my view of her by moving in front of me. I could hear the shot, but I had no idea what happened to the round. Straining to see over Korosu's shoulder, I watched Evan's left hand crush Dana's, forcing her to release the gun, as his right fist connected with a punch that sent her sprawling to the floor. The gun dropped, but Curtis was the one who went for it; Evan was already headed for me.

Korosu fell heavily into a chair, clearing the way for Evan to get to me.

Evan folded me tightly into his arms, his face filled with anxiety and concern. "Are you all right, are you hurt?" He crushed me up against him.

"I'm fine, I'm fine." I looked up into his eyes, his love and attention mine, all mine. "I'm fine, I'm better than fine," I started to say, and then I realized what he'd put me through. "I'm great. You *son of a bitch!*" I vented, smacking both my fists hard against his chest. But then I was smiling, pulling him hard up against me.

"Way to go, Sabrina!" Ginny whooped, and smacked a still fuming Sabrina on the back. Then Ginny turned to me, her eyes glowing with pride. In an instant her look of elation dissolved into fear. "Oh, Jesus, no," she whispered, and in two giant strides she was kneeling next to Korosu.

Evan and I pulled apart, and I looked down at Korosu. A crescent of red was staining the front of his perfect white shirt. Before any of the rest of us could react, Darrien was in front of him, ripping his employer's shirt open and pressing his hands against the wound to stanch the bleeding.

Curtis had handcuffed an unconscious Dana, and he came quickly to help the rest of us.

"Get him on the ground, get his feet elevated," Evan ordered, and I snatched pillows from the sofa as the men lowered Korosu carefully to the carpet. As I placed the cushions under his legs, Evan was calling for an ambulance. I reached for Korosu's hand, and he opened his eyes and looked at me.

"What have you done?" I whispered, my eyes filling with tears.

He said nothing. I'm not sure he could speak; his breathing was ragged, his eyes sad and wise, but the edges of his mouth flickered, and then turned up in a smile.

I had only seen a smile that brave, knowing, and resigned once before.

On my father's face, just before he died.

Chapter
5 4

Evan and I stood at the top of the stairs, his arm tight around my shoulders as we listened to the wail of the ambulance die away.

Curtis had taken Dana into custody, and the others were following the ambulance to the hospital.

"Will he be all right, do you think?" I asked tentatively, searching Evan's face.

All I got was "I don't know" and a look from deep behind his eyes that said what he was really thinking: *It could have been you.*

He hugged me hard up against him. "We should go to the hospital," I mumbled into his chest.

"Not yet," Evan said, and I felt him stir with purpose. "We have somewhere else to go first."

I had thought it was over, that we'd gotten to the bottom of the mystery, but I could see from the look on his face that the bottom was still a long ways down. With a swaying sense of vertigo I got into his car next to him, put my hand on his leg, and waited, miles away from him, until he looked at me, closing the space between us. Then I asked, "Where are we going?"

"Her partner isn't Jim Ferris," he said.

I hadn't given myself the space of a breath to think about it, but, given the leisure of a few moments uncluttered by sheer panic and gunfire, it made sense. Jim had thought Evan was involved, but Evan was being used. That meant we weren't finished. We weren't safe.

"Dana was involved with *someone* at Webtech. I'm sure of that," Evan said. "But not Jim."

"How do you know for sure?"

Evan looked at me as he pulled out of the drive, and his eyes glinted with that familiar brilliance. "Because he really thought she was dead, and he didn't recognize her when she was pretending to be Susan Rosen for our benefit."

"So he thought she was Susan?"

"No way, he was too close and knew Susan too well. My guess is that he thought it was someone who worked for Susan. Remember, he kept asking, 'How could *she* let this happen?' "

"Then it must be her or Fred Rosen. It makes sense, Dana went to their house and tried to get me up there!"

"Where she would have had you killed and pinned it on me, according to Patricia Adman. But the Rosens are out of the country for two weeks," Evan said flatly. "Susan Montgomery is in this somehow, I know she knew Molly Simpson was having an affair with her husband until he dropped her for someone else. Susan might have found out when Molly threatened to file a sexual harassment suit, and done something to try to stop her. If Susan was in this with Dana, then it's possible that Dana had access to her house, but I think there was a link between Susan and Dana."

"How do you know Susan found out about Molly Simpson?"

"Gillespie. He was getting information from Simpson before her fatal accident. Whether or not Susan Montgomery was behind Molly's death, I don't know yet."

"Was the 'somebody else' that Fred dropped Molly for Josie Banks?"

"No, I don't think so. Josie was helping the Russian syndicate reroute the money. I don't know if she was forced into it or not, but Gillespie doesn't think so. It looks like she was a willing participant, and there weren't any personal links to Rosen that either of us could find."

A liquid-crystal-sharp picture of the beautiful dead girl on the floor of her kitchen flashed across my mental screen. She hadn't looked like a willing participant to me, but I said nothing.

"I'm sure that Jim thought Susan was involved, anyway," Evan continued.

"But then why didn't he tell us that? Why was he trying to protect her?"

"I think he was protecting someone else who was connected to Susan."

I thought of Jim insisting that no one at Webtech would be capable of committing these crimes, and how indignantly adamant he had been about it. I sighed. "Could be anyone."

Evan stopped at a light and turned to look at me. "Really? Do you think he would go to prison, take the blame for extortion, kidnapping, murder even, for just 'anyone'? "

"No." I realized that was a super-sized expectation, even from someone I had always thought was as decent as Jim.

"So, who would he go to that extreme for?"

"As far as I know, he's only got Isabelle that he really cares about, but maybe he *is* that kind of a friend." It sounded lame even as I suggested it.

"Who worked on the charity event you attended with Susan Montgomery? Who invited you? Who knew you were coming?"

"Well, Isabelle, but—"

"Who bumped into you at the racetrack, identifying you for Patricia Adman?"

"Isabelle, but . . ." I was dismissive; it couldn't be. The very thought was absurd. I thought about her gossiping inanely in the stupid pink hat.

"Who has an office facing Dana Scheiner's?"

"Lots of people! The entire accounting department."

Evan raised his brows and looked expectantly at me. I put it together. "And Isabelle is head of . . . holy shit . . . she's the head of *international* accounting."

"Ding, ding, ding, ding, ding." He made the sound of the bell that was going off in my head. I remembered him saying to Jim about the videotapes, "Don't forget to include the *production* credits."

"But, *Isabelle?*" I sputtered. "*Why?*"

"Love and money," he said as the light changed and we pulled away. "Love and money."

Chapter
55

Isabelle was staring out the window when we came into her office. I noticed how clearly you could see into the windows of the building across the street. She turned, and her eyes flashed a moment of panic when she saw me, but she recovered quickly.

"Callaway! What a surprise."

"I'll bet," I said, watching her in wonder. How could she be responsible for all the death and corruption? Simple little Isabelle. Yet the fear on her face when I'd entered had been apparent, and Evan's presence visibly increased her agitation.

"Isabelle Ferris?" Evan asked without waiting to be introduced. When she stammered a reply, he said to her, "You're under arrest." Then he touched my shoulder to break me from the disturbing visual of the stunned dead look on her face. "Cally, close the door."

Evan read Isabelle her rights, then said he'd like her to answer a few questions.

"I . . . what . . . Callaway, what is he talking about?" Isabelle's panic-stricken eyes went to me. The appeal for help in them was real.

"Tell me how you got involved with the Russians," Evan said calmly.

Isabelle's mouth fell open. "I want a lawyer, I don't have to tell you anything, I don't even know what you're talking about." Her eyes darted to the door, but there was no hope of escape there.

Evan looked at me and turned one hand up, moving it in Isabelle's general direction, inviting me to speak.

What did he want me to say? I didn't know half of what he did. What would make her talk to me?

Her father.

"Isabelle," I said, feeling such sadness as I gave her the news, "your father is in custody. He's confessed to all the crimes. The money laundering, the murder, all of it."

Her mouth stayed open, but her head moved in a slow circle, as though she was trying to find a pocket of air to breathe. I thought about my father, the fact that I would have traded my life for his, that I'd always had the security of knowing that my happiness and safety had been the most important things to him. I wondered if she and Jim were that close. I waited to see if they were, if the amount of love would overbalance the greed and the fear.

"It was me." Isabelle's voice was little more than a forced rasp. "He had nothing to do with it. He got suspicious, because of you." Her eyes bored into me, but there was no resentment there. "He found out that I authorized Patricia Adman's checks, and then he came in my office and found the tapes and confronted me. I told him that it was all handled, that he didn't need to worry about it . . ." She broke off in a sob. "The way he looked at me—"

"And then what happened?" Evan spoke in a neutral, dispassionate tone that helped put a distance between the emotion and the events.

"He got a phone call, and he left." She looked down at her desk, and then at her hands, clenched now on the arms of her chair. "I don't know how it got so far out of control," she said weakly. "We only meant to scare her."

"Scare who?" Evan asked, pulling her back, trying to keep her on track.

"Molly." Isabelle's gaze frosted over, fog on a dark highway, then she seemed to remember us. "Molly Simpson," she said more loudly, but still with an emptiness in her face. "She wouldn't let go of Fred, she was going to ruin him and his reputation. Susan and I were working together on the charity, we got to be friends, and she told me about all of it. It was ripping her apart.

"I'd met some people when my father sent me to set up the Moscow accounting office. They had approached me about altering the books, just a little, and it would be profitable for me, and I knew that they had connections here, people who would do almost anything for a price. They had bragged about that. So I told Susan that we could get these people to send Molly a message, they would make it clear that she needed to go away, but it went wrong." Isabelle folded forward, pulling her hands up to her face.

"What happened?" I asked quietly, fascinated by the woman unraveling before me.

"She . . . she died. They ran her off the road. It wasn't what was supposed to happen. But what Susan and I didn't know was that they had videotaped us asking them to take care of her and of money changing hands, and it looked like we were asking them to kill her, and after that I didn't have much choice but to do the other things they wanted."

"That's when the sizable embezzlement and laundering really began?" Evan asked her.

Isabelle looked up, as though she was ready to deny the charge, then she slumped again and laughed sadly. "Yes, it was just a small thing before that, little diversions of payments, it was so easy, and well"—she laughed again, mirthlessly, and looked up at me—"you know how hard it is to move up the other way. They just don't see you . . . the same." The frost dusted over her gaze again. It was like watching ice crystals distort clear glass. She repeated, more softly, "They just don't see you."

Evan leaned in, allowed her a moment to drift, and then, in a soft voice that only seemed to suggest rather than ask, he voiced, "Did Fred Rosen see you?"

On the other side of the ice, moisture formed, and large tears, as heavy as the salty water of the Dead Sea, started the slow slide down the contours of her face.

"I thought he did. I was wrong."

"Did Susan know about you and her husband?"

The voice had gone as heavy as the expression from which it emerged. "No, I was a nobody."

"So your father knew nothing about the crime syndicate and your involvement before today?" Evan asked.

A tiny flicker of need came into Isabelle's eyes, and she looked at Evan for the first time. "No, nothing. You've got to believe me."

"I do," Evan said. "He didn't know enough details for any charges to stick to him."

Isabelle looked bitterly at me. "So, you didn't need my confession to clear him."

"You didn't want him to go through more police questioning," I said, but she cut me off.

"It doesn't matter. I'm glad. It's a relief really. Justifying how I could afford the big house in Venice, hiding the money, being afraid, lying, I'm finished." The last two words were spoken with a detachment, a kind of paralysis.

"Is there anything else you want to tell us?" Evan asked her.

She looked at him and smiled faintly. "Yes, thank you. Thank you for ending it."

This wasn't the end, her life was about to become a living hell of shame and failure; soon enough, Isabelle would wake up, face the attorneys, the profound disappointment on the faces of her family and friends, and the stark, harsh reality of prison.

"Okay," Evan said, "thank you for making this easy on all of us. We have a confession from Dana Scheiner; it was you who brought her in, I assume?"

Isabelle shook her head, but not in denial. "Actually, yes. I had heard about her taking over Callaway's estate, and I thought she'd be the perfect 'reputable' person to handle the laundering through Josie. Big mistake," she said. "She was too clever, too ambitious. She figured out what was going on, and then connected with the minor players here. They started working with her. With her experience in handling multimillion-dollar living trusts and estates, she was able to handle and hide much greater sums of money, and so I got stuck getting those sums for her. Then the boys back in Moscow got wind of her taking over here and she wanted to disappear. I tried to talk her out of it, but she used you to protect her, and then came up with this scheme for kidnapping you and faking her own death by using Callaway, and using Callaway's money to pay off her 'employees' here. She knew that unless the syndicate thought she was dead, they'd hunt her down and kill her."

"Were all of the men who helped her in on the laundering scheme, or were they just paid hands?"

"I'm not sure. I think there was one guy who was the head of it, I know for sure he was the one who made poor Patricia do all those things, but I wasn't in on all that. Dana just told me what to do. It was all her idea, not that it matters. I was already in so deep that I was never getting out."

Evan said, "I can help you. If you give me the names of anyone else who's involved, especially your contacts in Russia, I think I can guarantee that the Bureau will make serious reductions in your charges."

She was still looking at him, but now it was as though she was watching him from the deck of the *Titanic* as it pulled away from the pier. "They'll kill me," she said, as simply as if that was neither here nor there.

"We can protect you," Evan said. Isabelle smiled at him sadly, as though he were a child who just didn't understand, then turned her eyes to look out the window. Evan said gently, "We're going to walk out of here now."

Isabelle nodded.

"I'm not going to handcuff you," Evan said kindly. "We're going to walk out calmly and quietly. Nobody here needs to know why, okay?"

"Yes, it doesn't matter though," Isabelle said. She stood up, swayed slightly, her knees seeming to buckle once or twice before she got them under control. She looked out the window and fixed her sights on a single open patch of blue sky. "Nothing matters."

"Let's go," Evan said, taking her arm.

She pulled her arm free, not defensively or quickly, but slowly and with an absentminded deliberateness. He allowed it. She took one hesitant step, then another, and then she reached out to me.

Instinctively, I took her hand to help her, to get her through the next few minutes. We went through the doorway together and past the watching, curious faces of the secretaries, through reception and into the hallway.

The elevator bell chimed, the doors slid open, and a man with a rolling cart stocked with what looked like food and drinks for a large lunch conference started to roll his wares out. Fifty or so glasses of water, each individually covered with clear plastic wrap, clinked invitingly as the cart rolled over the ridged bump of the elevator opening. Isabelle and I stepped to one side, Evan to the other.

With a display of strength and force that shocked me, Isabelle placed both hands on my back and shoved. I went flying into the three-level cart, knocking it sideways into and on top of

Evan, sending the water glasses crashing down between us. The icy chill and the edge of the cart knocked the wind from my lungs.

Before either of us could recover, Isabelle bolted for the fire exit. Evan struggled out and pulled me from the tangle while the food service man stood watching, apparently too stunned to help.

"Are you all right?" I asked Evan.

"I'm fine. Go, go!" He gestured to the door where Isabelle had disappeared.

We stopped just inside the stairway and listened. We could hear running footsteps headed up toward the roof one floor above.

"What the hell?" I muttered, but Evan had already gone on, taking the stairs two at a time.

The door to the roof was standing open, and Evan stopped just inside, drawing his gun. I caught up with him and stayed behind him. The bone of my hip and the undercarriage of my rib cage were still smarting from where they had connected hard with the cart, and I wasn't eager to add to my list of painful injuries.

Evan warned me with his eyes to be silent, and then he swung out quickly, turning his gun rapidly one direction and then another.

I followed him out into the heat blast of the tarred roof, which took the full brunt of unobstructed pounding sunlight all day. Coupled with the hot wind, it was like walking into a convection oven in mid-bake. I looked around, squinting at the white glare that blinded me after the dark stairwell, looking for another exit, another way down, expecting that Isabelle would know of one, would have found it. As the pain in my eyes subsided and they adjusted, I spotted her. She had found another way down.

She was standing on the ledge, looking not down but up, at the hot, brown-blue sky.

"Isabelle!" I called out, and started to rush toward her, but Evan caught me and held me back.

"Don't rush her," he said urgently. "Speak calmly, tell her there's hope."

I tried to swallow, but the air felt too hot to inhale, and the smell of tar gravel from the roof and the thought of the steaming pavement far below sickened me. Keeping my eyes fixed on the figure silhouetted against the haze, I nodded, and Evan released me.

I started forward, willing her to stay where she was, to stick to the spot. When I was ten feet away, I spoke, struggling to steady my voice. "Isabelle."

She didn't seem to hear me. But she wavered a bit and slowly turned her head to look over her shoulder. She had the strangest look on her face—it was distant but oddly blissful.

"It's okay," she said to me. "It's time."

"No, Isabelle, listen to me." I didn't know what to say, it was horrible, the sensation that only I tethered her to life, that the wrong word would cut the tie and send her on the flight through the last air that she would ever breathe.

"Listen, it doesn't have to be this way. Evan can help you. I know. He's done it before." My words sounded desperate, and I could see that they had no meaning to her. "We've known each other for a long time, Isabelle, you know I wouldn't lie to you. Please."

She turned away again and raised her arms as though embracing some great, invisible force. Evan was creeping, with impossible care and slowness, toward her. I knew I had to keep her from looking in his direction.

My heart pounded in my throat and my brain felt stupid and heavy. *Think, Cally!*

"Isabelle, I know that you don't want to face your father. I understand that, but for one minute, for one second, think about how much he loves you." Then I got it. "Try to imagine," I said to her insistently, willing her to hear me, to feel my words, "try to imagine your father at your funeral."

For a second I thought she'd been shot, though I had heard no sound. She jolted and clutched her chest. She sucked in a breath and then screamed, a long, wailing, horrible sound. Closing her eyes, she started to double over; Evan seized the opportunity, leaping forward and yanking her harshly off the ledge.

She started to sob, gasping in huge breaths of air, to try to facilitate speaking. When she finally could, it was to rage at me. "Damn you!" she cried. "Damn you."

But I felt nothing but relief and understanding. "Isabelle," I said over her sobs, "you couldn't let your father take the blame." I heard the metallic click of the handcuffs resound loudly against the background noise of the city, a lifetime below us.

"He'll never forgive me," she wailed.

I put a hand on her forehead and shaded her eyes from the brutal sun. "You're wrong," I said softly. "Jim loves you so much that there's only one thing he would never forgive you for."

She tried to look up at me, her body still racked with sobs, her eyes filled with fear. "Wha—what?"

I gazed down at her. "Leaving him."

Chapter 56

Asubdued group sat in the waiting room of Cedars-Sinai Hospital. Ginny, Sabrina, and Darrien were with me, but I was deeply lost in my own concern and thoughts.

It was dark outside the windows. I had joined the others there while Evan had taken Isabelle in to start the first step in a long performance of procedures and processing, a complicated line dance through the U.S. justice system.

Korosu had been in surgery for two hours when Evan came into the waiting room.

I was surprised to see him so soon. "What happened?"

"Gillespie is going to take over on this one. She's given them plenty of names. There'll be a sweep of arrests. I'm not sure if it'll extend to Moscow, but it will amputate this particular arm of the Russian syndicate's operations." He pulled my worried head up against his chest, *my chest,* and whispered to me, "Her father is with her."

I smiled up at him. "I'm glad," I whispered back.

He stroked my hair. "You did good."

"Nice catch," I responded. There was no doubt in my mind that Isabelle would have tumbled off the roof if he hadn't moved so quickly.

"We're a good team." He smiled with his eyes. Then, both of us realizing we'd left out the others for too long, he asked, "How is he?" directing the question to Darrien.

"No news," Ginny responded for him. Darrien's handsome face was pinched and pale.

He said, "I failed. It was my job to protect him, and I failed."

Evan released me and crossed over until he was standing right in front of the younger, slightly smaller man.

"No." He shook his head adamantly. "You did exactly what Korosu asked you to do. You protected Sabrina. I think we both know Korosu well enough to know that that would have been his wish."

Darrien looked at Evan, and I could see the weight of what Evan had said. I also knew that the same statement, however true, would have meant next to nothing to him coming from any of the rest of us. But coming from Evan, he could trust it as being more than comforting words. He could believe it was true.

Slowly, Darrien nodded and turned to look affectionately at Sabrina.

"You are right," he said softly. "Korosu could not have borne anything happening to Sabrina, and neither could I."

Evan nodded. "I know exactly how you feel," he said, but he was looking at me.

"Who is here for Mr. Korosu?" A surgeon was standing in the entrance to the room. He was a portly man with a face that would have looked right at home in an Irish pub—his nose slightly red, his field-green eyes set off by his graying red hair.

We all started to speak at once, but Evan took charge. He stepped forward, showed his badge, and said, "I'm the officer on the case, and these are all his friends."

The surgeon looked dubious. "No family?"

My heart was chilled by the morbid tone in his voice. Family? Did that mean Korosu was dead and he needed to notify the family first?

"Please," I spoke up, "please tell us how he is."

The surgeon didn't speak right away, his eyes instead scanning the faces that all watched him. Finally he sighed and said, "Well, the surgery went well, considering. We lost him . . ."

"No!" gasped Sabrina.

". . . but we were able to revive him," the surgeon hurried on. "It was less than two minutes. There was no serious loss of oxygen to the brain. The bullet entered his lung, causing it to collapse. It missed the left major pulmonary artery but we had to repair several intercostal arteries and muscle, reinflate the lung. He's lost a good deal of blood, but he's in critical, but stable, condition now."

I was nodding as though this was all making perfect sense to me, when the truth was it felt like the most freakish work of fiction I could contemplate.

Nobody spoke for a moment, then Darrien cleared his throat and said in a steady voice, "Will he live?"

I saw Sabrina put her hand on Darrien's arm and he covered her hand with his, each of them giving and drawing strength from the other.

"I think so." The doctor smiled for the first time. "He's a fighter, and in incredibly good shape. So, although I can't guarantee that there won't be complications, I'm giving him a ninety-five percent chance at a full recovery."

In unison, five bodies exhaled. Ginny said, "Hallelujah." Sabrina squealed and threw her arms around Darrien, who was visibly fighting back tears of relief. I laughed for the joy of it, and Evan held out his hand to the surgeon. "Thank you, Doctor, that's wonderful news."

The surgeon looked very pleased to have been able to give the wonderful news, but he contained his flushed grin and returned to business. "He's got to get through the next few hours, but his vitals are so strong that I feel pretty confident in giving you these odds now." He turned to Evan again. "I'll have one of the nurses bring you the bullet as soon as they're done with the post-op."

"Yes, please," Evan told him. The doctor received a round of thanks, handshakes, and a body-crushing hug from Sabrina.

"Although," mused Evan at our now beaming faces, "I don't suppose I'll need a bullet with six eye witnesses. Nice defensive tactic, by the way." Evan smiled at Sabrina.

"Yes, thank you, Darrien," I added, "for teaching her those self-defense moves."

Darrien smiled and said, "You'll have to thank Ginny. *That* was a move I've never seen before."

Ginny waved a hand regally through the air, dismissing the praise. "That was just a little thing I learned at Marshall High. Dirty, but very effective."

With Korosu apparently out of life-threatening danger, I turned my attention to Evan.

"What else did you find out?" I asked him. "What about Susan Montgomery?"

"She's in Switzerland with Fredrick. I guess when Sabrina turned him down, he remembered he had a wife," he joked. "She'll be arrested when she reenters the country, and she'll be charged with conspiring to commit a felony. Let's hope the possibility that his actions drove his wife to committing a serious crime will teach Fred Rosen a little lesson."

"It won't be his only class in women's rights," Sabrina said, a naughty smile on her face. We all looked at her. "I warned him not to put his hand on my backside"—she was shaking her head—"but he wouldn't listen. I was bringing him some coffee I just made, and it was really especially hot. He must have forgot about respecting my personal space, because he took a liberty and, well . . ." Her eyes lolled up to the ceiling and she sighed exaggeratedly. "I guess I just tripped a little over the corner of that rug, and that coffee just shot right out of my hand and right at his," she said, gesturing to her crotch, "you know." She pressed her lips together, trying not to laugh, and her eyes watered with the effort. "I said I was *so* sorry that I was *so* clumsy. It's a shame about his nice suit and how extra hot that coffee was, seeing how I had put it in the microwave until it boiled, but on a positive note, I do think it took his mind off my behind."

We all looked at her in delighted silence. Finally I said, "Who are you and what have you done with my sister?"

"Girl," Sabrina said, using Ginny's inflection on the word, "I left her in a trailer park in Louisiana."

Ginny leaned toward her and extended her hand. "Welcome to California."

We all laughed, and Darrien said that he would wait the long hours until he could see Korosu. Sabrina settled herself in to wait with him.

"I seem to be missing somebody," Ginny said pointedly to Evan.

"He's still processing Dana," Evan told her. "Sorry," he added.

"Has he had dinner?" she asked, sounding almost like a wife. I felt my eyes widen.

Evan said, "Nope."

"He's at the station?"

"Yep."

"I'll pick us up something from Jerry's and take it over to him. You might want to close your mouth, girl," she said to me. "You look like a Venus flytrap in a Mexican stable. People in relationships take care of each other. That's how it works."

Though she looked pointedly from me to Evan before she left, I was thinking that she and Curtis were a match for taking care of each other. I'm not sure anybody else could have done it.

Chapter

57

After extracting a promise from Darrien and Sabrina to call us as soon as Korosu was conscious, Evan and I strolled unhurriedly from the building. His car was on the roof level of the parking structure. You couldn't see many stars past the halogen lights, but the few that fought through seemed to belong to us.

Finally, we were alone, and I was feeling damned awkward. I still felt distant from Evan. There had been so much doubt and distrust and suspicion between us.

"I'm still overwhelmed by what Korosu did," I said, feeling incapable of choosing a more intimate topic of conversation.

Evan was quiet at first, and then he said, almost introspectively, "Well, it's fairly apparent that he's in love with you."

"Oh, please," I retorted, somewhat embarrassed, "let's not compare obsessions. I mean, sure, Korosu was ready to *take* a bullet for me, but Dana was ready to fire them into other people for *you*."

Evan stopped and turned me to him. "I'm not blaming you.

I'll be grateful to him all my life. But listen to me, because this is something *I know.* He stepped between you and a gun that was going to fire. That's not a small thing. That is not a frivolous act of chivalry; not something he would have, or even could have, done for anyone else. It takes overcoming every instinct you've got. And it is not something that every man could do even for someone they loved. He's a hell of a man." He paused for a moment, seeming reluctant to go on. Then he said, pointedly and firmly, as though he were opening a door, "And you could choose him if you wanted."

I said nothing. I thought about the fact that Evan had also moved to try to block the shot, though he'd only been able to reach Dana just as she'd fired.

Evan sighed, and there was such intensity in his manner; all of his forceful concentration was bent on me. He considered me with a quizzical gaze. I could feel how the emotions in both of us were swirling around, like two primary colors that couldn't quite blend into a new one. He asked, "How do you feel about me now?"

I considered the question. "Like there are too many secrets, too many things I don't know about you. I thought that we were closer than we are. It's funny, how you invent someone for the first few months of a relationship, make them who you want them to be, and then reality hits." I looked up at him, and I was not afraid. I knew I could lose him, but what he said was true; I couldn't lie to him, and this was the truth. I wasn't sure. "And our reality, mine *and* yours, is a pretty big bag of tricks."

"And how do you feel about him?"

I silenced the first flippant response that came to mind and took the time to let the feeling seep through me. *How do I feel about Korosu?* Only a fool could deny the attraction between us, and now he had shown that he would sacrifice himself for me. The bond between us was for life.

"How do I feel about Korosu?" I asked to buy time, asking

myself more than repeating Evan's query. "He is, as you say, a hell of a man."

Evan nodded and looked away, out over the moving colored lights of traffic on La Cienega Boulevard below us. The warm wind lifted his hair off his forehead, and I could see that it was creased with concern.

"But he isn't you," I said, reaching up and touching his lips with one finger. "There is only one you."

Evan smiled, but his eyes were guarded. "But you have feelings for him."

"Yes, that's true. *Untested*," I said, stressing the word, "but I won't deny it."

He drew me up against him, and, just as before, nothing rivaled the feeling that this was it, he was the one, yet . . .

"Do you still want to marry me?" he asked me, and there was neither fear nor cockiness in his voice.

Yes! I wanted to shout it, to be with him, to make him be mine, keep him there always. But I didn't want things to go back to the way they had been, didn't want to continue to feel unsure, suspicious, left out. I had far too many scars from that kind of wound that still burned at the hint of the knife.

"What I want," I said slowly, "is to *know* you, and for you to know me. I want to come to you and feel safe and understood so that when I go back out into the world I'm stronger and better." I felt as though I was fumbling, not saying it right. "You and I," I tried to explain, "we're huge people. We take up a lot of space, and that's important. It's important that we get to be ourselves, but I don't need to be with you, or with *anyone*, only to feel like I'm still alone. Can you understand what I'm trying to say, and failing at desperately?"

He nodded. "You're saying it rather well, actually. I understand completely."

"So, maybe"—fear was building now, my heart was beating fast, knocking against my chest as though it wanted to get out—

"what I think would be best, is for us to get to know each other. Take more time, come out of hiding." I prayed that he would not take it as a rejection. It wasn't that, it was an invitation to something more, something deeper than we had now. I didn't know if I was up to it, but then, you never know until you try. And knowing there was a whole other level of intimacy to reach, and *not* trying to reach it, was as impossible for me as touching the moon.

And, I hoped, impossible for him.

Evan's forefinger came up and traced a line from my forehead down the side of my face, over my cheekbone, under my chin, and hooked itself there, lifting my face to his, to a kiss so soft it felt like a whispered good-bye.

I sucked in, pulling the breath from his mouth, trying to hold him there with me, to make him understand what it was I wanted, hoping he could respond.

"I told you before," he said softly, "that I couldn't tell you everything, that I needed to keep things from you to keep you safe. But it didn't work. It put you in danger, and it made you lose faith in me, question my feelings. There are two things I could not live with. One is something happening to you." He pulled me hard against his chest again, and I caught the rippling movement there of a breath that suppressed a sob. He held me tightly for a long time.

Finally I asked, because I had to know. "And what is the second?"

"You doubting me." He put his hands on either side of my face and turned it up to him, his eyes glowing with hurt in a face of harsh strength. "I love you, and I'm afraid that could hurt you."

"I'm willing to take that chance." I pursed my lips and said, "I have a feeling getting closer to me won't exactly be an effortless flow of ecstasy and bliss, either."

"I'll chance it."

When we were finally able to unwind ourselves from our mutual bond of need, lust, and limbs, he said, "The wedding will have to wait. But can we still go on a honeymoon?"

"Like a rehearsal one?" I asked, pretending to consider the idea.

"Sure, like a rehearsal one. Practice makes perfect."

"I suppose so. As long as we leave sisters, partners, ex-lovers, and *work* behind. As long as it's just the two of us; you and me."

His eyes came back to mine and connected. At last I felt connected to him. He kissed me, softly, so softly, and made his point with a whispered smile.

"No, not 'you and me.' *Us.*"

It sounded good.

Possible.

Scary.

Us.

Up Close and Personal with the Author

THIS IS THE THIRD INSTALLMENT OF CALLAWAY AND EVAN'S ADVENTURES. DOES IT GET STALE?

No. There's always more for me to discover about my characters and what they might do or say. I'm often as surprised as the reader. Also, I love going further into the relationships between them, especially in this one where we are never quite sure about Evan's motives.

DID YOU ALWAYS KNOW EVAN HAD THIS DARK PAST?

Definitely. I had a very clear idea about who Evan was going into the first book, and I know from my acting experience that hidden layers can add so much interest to a character. Just like in real life. Someone who has been through a lot and made tough choices is almost always a more interesting—and less predictable—person than someone who has had smooth sailing.

YET YOU SAY THAT YOUR CHARACTERS SURPRISE YOU. HOW CAN THAT BE IF YOU'VE PLANNED THEM OUT?

It's like being a mom; you give birth to the characters, you add in values and stress beliefs and experiences, but in the end your children become individuals. At least they do if you've done it right.

WHO IS THE FIRST ONE TO READ YOUR BOOKS?

Usually my amazing man, Joseph, whom I often go to for "masculine" advice. In this case, though, I think it was my eleven-year-old, who I caught reading my first two novels though she'd been told they were not appropriate for her. After I took the third copy of *Loaded* away from her, she told me, "If you didn't want me to read it, you shouldn't have so many copies!" So I caved. She read both *Loaded* and *Lethal* in a couple of days and then sat next to me while I was working on *The Man She Thought She Knew,* asking, "Are you finished yet?" To which I responded, "I'll be done a lot quicker if you go away." The little darling. After that it's my agent and then my editor, Amy, who does the slash and burn . . . I mean, uh . . . makes suggestions.

YOU MEAN YOU MAKE CHANGES?

Uh, yeah. A couple.

IS IT HARD TO TAKE SOMEONE ELSE'S SUGGESTIONS?

Only when they're right.

HAVE YOU THOUGHT ABOUT DOING A SPIN-OFF WITH ANY OF THE OTHER CHARACTERS?

Yes. In fact, I've been asked often if Ginny could have her own book. She'd certainly like one! It would suit her, and using a movie set as a backdrop would be lots of fun. Some of the stunt people I've met over the years are amazing characters, they are the real stars on the set. When they come out, the "name" actors stand back and watch in awe. I'd also love to tell a story from Sabrina's point of view. Wouldn't it be fun to hear what she thinks of Callaway and her lifestyle?

WILL THERE BE A FOURTH CALLAWAY WILDE BOOK?

I can't imagine *not* going to the wedding. Can't you just picture the party favors? Manolo Blahnik evening bags, fourteen-karat cufflinks, and personalized sterling silver pistol clips, fully loaded.